Inviolate

Books by Karen Turner:

All That & Everything

Broughton Hall series:
Torn
Inviolate
Stormbird
Counterpoint

Inviolate

Karen Turner

Published in 2023 by Karen Turner

www.karenturner.com.au

First published 2014 by Palmer Higgs Pty Ltd

INVIOLATE

Designed and typeset by Look Up Media
Original design and typeset by Palmer Higgs Pty Ltd

Cover image by bigstock.com

ISBN: 978-0-6450002-6-9 (pbk)
        978-0-9924420-2-6 (ebk–ePub)

A catalogue record for this book is available from the National Library of Australia

To the good times and the freedom to fly.
071008301012

PROLOGUE

The baby stirred, and Anne closed her eyes and splayed her hands over her abdomen. Holding her breath, she acknowledged the odd shapes bulging and shifting, pushing into her palms and against her fingers beneath her nightgown.

As the child settled she opened her eyes and released her breath in a sigh that created a damp cloud before her face: the November night was cold and still. She shivered and belted her robe across her belly and continued along the path.

Her nightly wanderings were her own furtive sanctuary; she drew comfort from the silent park and found refuge within the walled gardens and gates of Broughton Hall, for in the progress of her pregnancy the oblivion of sleep was increasingly elusive.

Under the concealing blanket of the night, she was released from the rigid self-control she imposed on herself when in the company of others – the facade erected for the benefit of those who did not, or would not, understand.

This child, this perfect and natural result of an affair too briefly enjoyed, was Anne's burden to carry. Her dismissal by its father was her heartbreak.

He had rejected her, cast her off under a shower of harsh words.

Her beauty had not swayed him – nor had her threats and pleas.

Yet in the honesty of night, she relived those splendid moments spent in his arms. She saw his face, smelled the pomade he used in his hair and heard again his passionate declarations of love. And then … the reality of his deceit.

Anne gasped with remembered pain as he had thrust that white-hot blade of truth beneath her ribs, slicing upward, carving her heart clean from her breast.

He had killed her. His words had killed her as surely as would a knife because she had staggered from his sight that night as though she were dead.

She breathed deeply through her nose feeling the icy dampness burn her throat and lungs. She did not weep. She would never weep again.

Anne was leaning against the cold stone of the house as the moon appeared from behind threads of clouds. It was full and fat and cast intermittent light and shade across the kitchen garden. The path wending its way among cruciferous and root vegetables was slick and wet.

A soft thud among the leaves sounded unnaturally loud in the night – no doubt the rabbit that Cook had complained of. To hear her go on, one would be forgiven for thinking the creature had an appetite equal to a herd of elephants!

Anne smiled to herself and edged along the path, moving silently, hoping to spy the little creature in a moment of unbridled vandalism.

Wisps of clouds drifted across the moon again. Maeve used to call it a witch's moon and Anne gave a superstitious little shiver and paused, waiting for the clouds to clear.

She heard the thud again and a rustling among the cabbage leaves. She stood very still and held her breath, eyes fixed on the garden bed before her.

The clouds drifted slowly by, and at the same time, too quickly for Anne to register, the hairs on the back of her neck rose. Her heart began to pound as the creeping light of the moon gradually revealed the curved back of a crouching, elderly woman.

Anne watched in disbelief as the crone appeared to work, digging and cursing to herself, not more than five yards from where she stood.

A thief!

But who was she and where did she come from?

Suddenly Anne didn't care. The woman was no doubt some kind of vagabond, a gypsy, and she was trespassing! Anne drew herself up and noisily cleared her throat.

The woman, oblivious, continued her labours.

Taking a few tentative steps along the path, Anne drew closer. "You!" She announced imperiously. The figure should have started in surprise, but again there was no reaction.

"You there!" Anne said, adding disconcertedly, "What are you doing?"

The woman did not respond but now paused and sat back on her heels. Anne crept closer and squinted through the dark. She seemed to be holding a box, and as Anne watched, she caressed its lid and murmured something indiscernible. Then she proceeded to bury it.

Anne stood very still. She was growing confused. There was something familiar in this old crone. Familiar, yes, but carrying a whiff of the unnatural and impossible.

As the woman pushed herself to her feet, she slowly turned.

And the blood froze in Anne's veins; the old woman looked straight through her …

… and Anne knew her face.

CHAPTER 1

November 1813

Simon turned away from the counter and smiled. One side of his face was perfectly, devastatingly handsome; the other was cruelly disfigured. He held two keys, each with a wooden tag attached.

"Two rooms, side-by-side. Here …" he handed over one of the keys.

Adjusting to his disfigurement must have been terribly difficult. My brother's previously unearthly good looks had always drawn comment and attention. Now, the attention his face attracted was founded in curiosity, sometimes fear, and some treated him as repellent. As painful as it was to witness, I could not imagine what it was like for him, yet he remained his charming and cheerful self.

We had arrived in Leeds that morning and gone directly to a cafe for lunch. My brother and I were here to visit mother's seamstress, at her suggestion – the occasion of my impending wedding required more professional services than those offered by Mrs Gladstone in Wolstone.

Immediately after lunch, Simon had brought us to one of the better hotels and we agreed to pass the afternoon relaxing so that we could make an early start the following day.

It was Mother's plan that my wedding gown should make a clear statement of wealth and position to our social inferiors. And her faith in Madam Clary's ability to deliver such an exquisite creation required that I visit the seamstress as a matter of priority. Only once Madam Clary had determined design and fabric, and taken my measurements, would Simon and I be free to visit other shops and see some of the sights afforded by the large city.

My room was clean and nicely furnished with a settee, a table, a ruffled bed, and a small balcony overlooking the busy thoroughfare below. I leaned over the railing, despite the chill in the air, to experience the life and clatter of the street. Leeds, with its 30,000 residents, was in the grip of industrial change. New factories and businesses, and housing for those working in them, were springing up like mushrooms, and even now, with night falling fast, the traffic seemed relentless.

Horses bore men in business attire, carriages transported well-dressed merchants' wives, nurses pushed prams, and parents held their children's hands; all dodged and weaved, hurriedly completing the last of the day's affairs before returning to their homes.

I washed and changed into an evening gown, and met Simon downstairs before supper – our plan being to retire early so we could begin afresh the next morning.

Simon ordered a glass of sherry for each of us and we talked quietly of his plans for Broughton Hall and his hopes for children. By silent mutual consent, my marriage, the very reason we were in Leeds, was not mentioned. He spoke often of Maria and my gratitude to this lovely woman was immense, for without her love, my brother's horrific injuries would doubtless be even more burdensome to him. At length we were shown to the dining room where we enjoyed roasted pheasant with autumn vegetables.

Our meal having been completed, we had risen to leave when a very handsome lady entered the dining room and we gaped in shock as we recognised the gentleman whose arm she held.

"Your usual table, my Lord," the maître d' suggested. He received a distracted reply for Gerrard Washburn had seen us too, and we all three froze uncertainly. Flushing guiltily he indicated we remain at our table and obligingly, or curiously, we resumed our seats.

Settling his guest and making his apologies, he arrived at our table and immediately took a vacant seat.

Tugging at his earlobe, he said, "Hullo Simon, Alexandra. Visiting Leeds, er … of course you are, of course … your mother said … it er … slipped my mind."

"My wedding, Gerrard," I said.

"Er, yes, the wedding, of course, yes …" He was foundering, and his profound discomposure was painful to witness.

"Gerrard, *who exactly* is that woman?" Simon asked, a wry twist to his mouth.

"Oh … er … you mean Mrs Jamieson? She's … a business associate." He glanced to where Mrs Jamieson sat, eyeing us curiously, and offered her a mollifying smile.

Mrs Jamieson was a lovely-looking woman, around Mother's age and very expensively dressed in a blue velvet gown with a deeply scooped bodice. She wore cream lace gloves and as I watched she removed her gloves with an elegant action and placed them on the table beside her.

"And is Mother aware of this *business*?" Simon continued.

"Well, she is aware I have business in Leeds from time to time …"

"Just not this *type* of business."

"Very well, Simon, no – she is not aware of my business with Mrs Jamieson, and I would prefer it remain so, for it would serve no positive purpose to inform her."

Simon merely nodded and said quickly, "It's alright, Gerrard, we understand, more than you know. Your business arrangements are safe with us."

Gerrard let his breath out in a rush and clasped Simon's hand in both of his. I glanced at Mrs Jamieson who proffered a quick smile and I responded politely before turning to my brother. "Simon, we must go. We've an early start tomorrow."

∾

The next morning over breakfast a couple at the next table were staring at Simon, their heads bent together. To distract my brother, I said, "So, Gerrard's having an affair."

He smiled briefly before answering. "A saint would be hard-pressed remaining faithful to our Mother." He took a sip of coffee and looked at me assessingly. "Very well, you might as well know the truth."

And then he told me the tale of our mother – the courtesan who set her cap at the most wealthy men, married or no. The woman who knew better than to attempt to ensnare the mad but ever faithful King George, who instead embarked on a rather public, though embarrassingly brief, liaison with his son, the Prince of Wales.

Cast aside for a younger, prettier lady-in-waiting, and having failed to secure a pension or title for herself, Mother focused her attentions on the Earl of Thorncliffe.

The earl's son, newly arrived at court, refused to acknowledge a relationship between his father and the infamous widow. He made several attempts to convince his father to stay away – attracting Miriam Broughton's anger in the process – but Gerrard Washburn was easily infatuated with the beautiful woman and also rather gullible for their liaison continued and eventually resulted in a pregnancy that court rumourmongers whispered – with probable cause – was deliberate.

The public scandal that ensued became grist for the court gossip mill and the King, furious, ordered Mother to retire from court and demanded that the pair marry.

Unfortunately, this turn of events played directly into Mother's hands. Apparently, Gerrard had protested the marriage vehemently, claiming that since Mother regularly strolled in a field of thorns, how could she know which one had pricked her? Simon smiled at this. "Quite accurately describes our mother, I'm afraid."

"There's no doubting Meg's parentage. She's definitely Washburn," I said.

"True," Simon agreed. "But I think Gerrard was expecting a mistress he could dally with – he did not expect a wife. And this is where Patrick became involved again. Having been astute enough to gauge Mother's ambitions, he was not amused that his father had fallen victim to this predatory woman and was rather vocal in his outrage against the wedding. That's why he was unhappy about coming to Broughton Hall and why Mother was equally unenthusiastic."

The story was reasonably consistent with the one Patrick had told me and with nothing else to say on the matter, we completed our breakfast in ruminative silence.

∞

Evidently Simon had been advised to be patient for he made no comment as I spent several hours with Mother's pet seamstress. Madam Clary led me through a variety of designs and I eventually settled on one in the latest Empire style.

Moving on to fabrics, Madam Clary recommended a delicate shell-pink silk and told me that seed pearls would be sewn across the bodice, "To enhance the bosom," she explained, eyeing my boyish figure.

The skirt, she decided, would fall in folds from below the bodice, and a swathe of the most delicate sheer netting would be layered over the entire ensemble – as though I moved in a cloud of pink mist. A pearl headdress would complement the gown, and I would carry pink roses.

Finally, Madam Clary put away her measures and notebooks.

"I am done," she announced to Simon and he sighed with obvious relief.

The remainder of the day was spent making purchases from a lengthy list Maria and Mother had pressed upon us, before we returned to our hotel. There we found an invitation from Gerrard to join him for supper. Simon sent our acceptance and at the appointed hour, we took a horse-drawn cab.

Gerrard's nominated restaurant was very elegant, certainly the most well-to-do place I'd ever visited. The furnishings were sumptuous, the waiters respectful and the meal superb. As our plates were cleared away, a platter of chocolates was delivered and I indulged myself thoroughly.

No mention was made of our meeting on the previous evening and as Simon and I made ready to leave, Gerrard took my hand. "Lass, I understand he's not such a bad fellow, this betrothed of yours. If it is any consolation, I did suggest we discuss it with you, but your mother … her mind was made up. She accepted the suit immediately it was offered. It really is an excellent match, you know, and your acquiescence is agreeable – it is so much the better for everyone." Then he leaned closer and said, "We can't always marry where we would choose."

❧

Mother and Anne were very excited by the description of my wedding gown. Madam Clary had furnished me with copies of the sketches and samples of the fabric, and Mother was suitably impressed.

"Madam Clary will have completed it the week before the wedding," I told her.

She nodded. "I must tell you, Alexandra, I am most pleased that you see the logic in the arrangement of your marriage."

I gestured to show my helplessness. "It would not have been my choice, Mother, but since there's no alternative …"

"Particularly since you're no longer virgin – if that gets out …!" She made a grimace of dread. "In any case, you at least have something to look forward to."

"Thanks awfully, Mother," Anne said, grimly.

Mother smiled then, "Don't worry – we may have something for you. Your stepfather is negotiating with a fellow he knew at court. Will probably cost us a nice tract of land somewhere, but your child shall be delivered in wedlock."

Anne's face registered horror. "But what if I don't want to wed?"

"I'd hopes of marrying you and Patrick but it seems he had designs on you of a different nature. Even if we could locate him, it's doubtful he'd be submissive. In any case, you'll not visit disgrace upon this family, my girl, and if Gerrard's talks with George are not successful, we'll endeavour to find another match. Now, I'm due to visit the Fletchers over in Bolton so this conversation is closed."

We watched as she glided away. Anne glared after her, her hands on her swollen belly. "What shall I do, Alex?" she muttered despondently. "I can't marry some stranger – certainly not dregs scraped from the bottom of the wine barrel."

"But you must face the reality of it, Annie. What man will take another's bastard willingly? You –"

"What would *you* know about it?" I'd opened my mouth before thinking and now she rounded on me angrily and her pretty mouth twisted with ugly viciousness. "You think you know everything just because you had one night in Patrick's bed. But what have you experienced of life my *oh-so-wise-sister*? He played you for a fool, but at least *you* have Hamish. You've known Hamish for years and he's cultured and nice, and when it gets down to the bare bones of it, *you deceived him!*"

I stared aghast and defenceless in the face of the truths she threw at me. And she wasn't finished.

"You deceived your intended, but everyone is rallying around *you*, arranging the best wedding money can buy and pretending all's well. As for me … what a joke! I'm to be sold off to the first old fart desperate enough to accept damaged goods!"

"I'm sorry you feel that way," I said quietly.

She blew out her breath angrily but seemed to yield for her voice was gentler when she said, "Did you truly love Patrick?"

I felt the familiar burning sensation behind my eyes and nodded. "Did you?"

"Of course not, but I'd have willingly wed him. I knew Mother's plans to match us and I agreed to go to Devon with him – deep down I knew what he was after – we've always known what he's like. Even so, after those Italian men, Patrick was so unpretentious, so refreshing. I assumed that proving with child would merely serve to seal a match with him. I didn't expect he'd abscond as he did."

"He didn't abscond. He's a soldier – he went to war."

She shrugged off-handedly. "Abscond, go to war; result's the same for me."

I watched unhappily as she absently stroked the protruding curve of Patrick's child and wondered how I would withstand the pain should it resemble him.

"We've made such a mess of things, haven't we?" I whispered.

"Hmm," she responded grimly.

It wanted a week until my wedding. Hamish was due to arrive any day and I was miserable and fretful. I decided to ride over to visit Julia and sent a message to the stables to have one of the more sedate horses saddled for me. It had rained overnight, and the watery sunshine would not be enough to dry the wet garden, which would soon be blanketed with winter snow. By the spring thaw, I would have let for my new home in Scotland – I would have seen my last idle summer in my beautiful childhood home – a depressing thought that I pushed aside as I arrived at the Chapmans' country home and was shown to a neat little parlour.

"You look different," Julia said as we separated from our embrace. We sat on brocade chairs at either side of a table set with tea and sandwiches. "You're not happy."

My eyes wandered to the glowing fire in the grate and I lost myself momentarily in a small explosion that sent a spray of sparks up the chimney.

"You're still missing Patrick," she guessed. "And I can't believe you're really going to marry Hamish."

I drew my breath in through my nose and turned to her. "You must swear by all you hold dear never to repeat what I'm about to tell you."

"*Of course*," she responded emphatically.

"I really mean it, Jules. Mother will skin me alive if —"

"Then, don't tell me. Or trust me and stop going on about it."

She watched my face and we both knew I came here with the single purpose of confiding in her. "It's my sister, Anne. She's returned from Italy and … she's pregnant."

Julia looked unimpressed. "I'm not shocked by that, Alex. It does happen, you know."

"It's Patrick's child."

Her eyes widened and she sat back. "Now, I'm shocked."

"Please, *please* don't tell anyone," I implored, leaning towards her urgently.

She waved a dismissive hand. "Alex, I don't understand. Last time I saw you — you and Patrick … You were so … so *in love*. Then, I received the wedding invitation … Oh that's why you're marrying Hamish! What on *earth* happened?"

"He went to London before sailing for Europe, met with Anne, invited her to Devon and …" I ended with a shrug.

Julia reached for the teapot. "Anne told you this?"

I nodded sadly and accepted a steaming cup from her hand.

"Have you heard from Patrick?"

"No one has. He's in Europe."

"So he won't know."

"That Anne's pregnant? I suppose not."

"Well, I don't believe it," she said defiantly and calmly sipped her tea.

"Believe it. Anne admitted everything." I too sipped my tea and found comfort in its distinctive flavour. A moment slipped by when the only sound was the crack and pop of the fire. Julia put down her cup with a soft clink. "What will she do?"

"Gerrard found some nobody-knight in the Midlands. It's all arranged, though she's not happy about it – she always expected a match with Pat, but no one knows where he is."

"It's war – I don't suppose we're *meant* to know. Anyway, I still don't believe it. It's simply not possible, particularly after that set-to Patrick had with your Mother – remember that? No, I won't believe he did it."

"Well, he did," I said miserably.

"But he loves *you*, Alex."

"Not enough it would seem."

"Listen to me. I don't know Anne all that well, I've only met her once or twice before she went abroad …" she searched the ceiling for the words. "I'm trying to be diplomatic here … There *has* to be some … other explanation."

"Anne's no liar," I said tightly.

"Saints alive, Alex! You can't –"

"Don't, Jules."

She glared at me rebelliously. "Please don't marry Hamish – there, I've said it!"

"I have to." I gave a snort of contempt. "Patrick does not love me. He went straight from me to my sister, and now she's pregnant."

My friend leaned forward, her face intense, "You … did you … you know … with Patrick?"

I nodded. I could feel the tears welling in my eyes. "We spent a night together. The night before he departed for London."

Julia's pretty face hardened. "It's not his child, I'd wager Amberley on it – and you know how I love that horse. I don't know *how*, I just feel it. Nothing's changed for him – he's coming home to you … don't marry Hamish, Alex, *please* don't."

"Stop it, Julia!" I cried suddenly. "It hurts enough as it is. Simon has a feeling too – everyone has *feelings* about it, but at least Simon realises I must marry Hamish for no matter how many *feelings* we have. Anne is pregnant and Pat's the father. She has no reason to lie," I finished softly.

She flared her nostrils belligerently. "I think you're wrong."

"Then you're calling my sister – who, by your own admission, you hardly know – a liar. I'll not have it."

She studied me for a moment then shook her head with disappointment. "Very well. Be an ostrich. I only hope you don't wake up one morning and say, *What on earth have I done?*"

Simon had recently attained his majority and had officially taken over his inheritance and title. Accordingly, he signed the betrothal agreement between the minor knight in Coventry and our sister. George Penshurst, virtually penniless, would happily accept a pretty young bride with a bastard child, providing the price was right. And it appeared that the price, a manor house in Cheshire, complete with a parcel of land near Warrington, and two conscientious tenants raising cows and producing the local variety of cheese, was conveniently for sale.

The families agreed that Anne's marriage would take place during the week after my own and Anne was not impressed. She stormed about the house snapping at everyone and growing increasingly difficult. Her pregnancy was well advanced now, and the family lawyers were instructed to move quickly. The Cheshire property was purchased, and George moved in immediately to prepare for his new bride.

Time seemed to gain momentum and suddenly Hamish arrived. He came riding up the drive on his fine horse, escorted by Grahame and another groom. We greeted one another like cool acquaintances – a world away from the husband and wife we would soon become – and stood on the porch discussing the weather and commiserating over the damage a mole had done to the lawns.

In our peripheral vision, Janet and Grahame greeted each other with the enthusiasm appropriate for a couple planning their lives together. We both pointedly and uncomfortably ignored them and Hamish spoke in his soft burr, "I am looking forward to your coming to my home."

I did not believe him for a moment and thought how terribly awkward living with this man was going to be. Now, he said with more sincerity, "I was very sorry to learn of Simon's injuries. At least he is safely home now."

"Thank you. Yes, we're very glad to have him returned to us. But you haven't met Maria. She's lovely."

He offered his arm, "Och then, you'd best be making the introductions."

❧

Hamish met Maria, and handled Simon's disfigurement with unexpected aplomb. Rather than pretend everything was normal – as *we* all had – Hamish boldly asked questions, drawing Simon gently into a conversation that had us all feeling more comfortable, for in the talking, lay the acceptance.

And that evening, sipping plum wine before the parlour fire, Simon and Hamish discussed the running of their respective estates, enjoying an easy flow of conversation.

Maria and I talked of our hopes for children, and Simon, overhearing, commented bawdily that he was willing to practice as was necessary. Hamish affected a rather – I thought – forced laugh which doubtless was pre-wedding nerves, but it occurred to me that he may yet be virgin. If this was the case, I couldn't help but wonder what our first night would be like.

I retired for bed feeling more positive about my impending marriage than I had for a long time.

Perversely, just as I felt I was growing stronger and could face my future, thoughts of Patrick encroached and I began to dream of him, often waking to find my pillow wet with tears. The worst of these nightmares came two nights before my wedding. I dreamed that Patrick was imprisoned in a cage and, dressed in my wedding gown, I crawled through a layer of broken glass and crockery to find the key. My dress was torn and my hands and knees shredded and bleeding, and all the while from within the cage Patrick was angrily shouting, "Of course you have the key – *you* locked me in here!"

I didn't understand his anger and my tears and panic were making my task nigh impossible. A sense of impending doom closed over me and I knew I had to free him before it was too late.

"But I don't have it – it isn't here!" I cried hysterically, when suddenly the brittle rubble on the ground began sprouting thick green foliage. Trees grew to full size before my eyes, and serpentine ivy wove its way in and around the bars of his cage. Vines with large, leathery leaves crowded me, blocking Patrick from sight and eclipsing the daylight. Growing increasingly frantic, I screamed, "Where are you? Oh God it's too late!"

Though he was out of sight, his voice was close by, "It's not too late, Alex! Don't give up!"

I tore at the creeping tendrils with my raw hands, but his voice grew distant, becoming an echo from miles away, "*Alex … Alex …!*"

"*Nooo!*" I screamed in horror. "*Patrick, don't go!*"

"*Alex …!*"

"*No … please …!*"

"Alex, wake up!"

Anne leaned over me, shivering in her nightdress, holding a candle.

"You were crying and screaming out. Are you alright?"

I gave a sob as the last thread of dream evaporated. She placed the candle on my side table and I saw how her nightdress was stretched across her bulging stomach.

"It's cold – let me get under the covers."

I shimmied over and she climbed in beside me.

"Want to tell me about it?"

She listened as I gave a brief sketch of the dream and finally she said, "You know, when we sleep, our imaginations run amok."

"But it was so compelling. Oh Annie, what if I'm making a terrible mistake? What if Patrick and I … what if we're bound together?"

"Feel this," she commanded. Taking my hand, she placed it on her taut abdomen. "You don't think Patrick and *I* are bound together? I dream too – we all do, but I don't let it rule me – I'd run mad otherwise." She sighed deeply. "And so will you if you keep on like this."

My pulse was returning to normal and the sense of panic, so acute in the dream, was dissipating.

"Alex, the reality is he used us both terribly, but look on the bright side: by the week's end you'll be embarking upon a new life with everything to look forward to."

I wiped my eyes on my sleeve and took a deep breath.

"I'll be alright."

"I know you will," she said, softly. "We're strong, we Broughtons."

She snuggled further beneath the bedclothes. "Come on now, go to sleep, and you'd better not snore."

Mother's friends from Leeds and London began arriving for the wedding and suddenly our house was bursting at the seams and alive with the gaiety of anticipated celebrations.

Hamish and I stole some private time the evening before our nuptials, sipping plum wine in the library by the fire. I felt a strange eagerness to have it all over with so I could put the tatters of my old life behind me, and consequently told my husband-to-be that I'd like us to have our first Christmas together in my new home. He seemed surprised but readily agreed saying, "I know my father would be happy to see us home."

"Does he continue to ail?"

"Aye. He daily grows weaker and seems to become thinner before my eyes. His doctors say they can do no more than treat the pain. The doses of laudanum they prescribe are getting stronger. Are you nervous about tomorrow?"

"Yes," I admitted.

"And you're over your little … infatuation?"

His question took me by surprise.

"Don't look like that!" He snapped irritably. "D'you take me for a fool? How could I not know? He's the devil's own charm and you've lived beneath the same roof for years, though there's not a drop of common blood between you."

I was stunned into speechlessness, but he was undeterred.

"I trust you've not made a fool of yourself."

I bristled at his arrogance but he didn't seem to expect a response. "Well, now," he continued. "We've a big day tomorrow. I suggest we both retire for the night."

His kiss on my cheek was cold and I wondered again if I would live to regret marrying this man.

I remained staring into the dying embers of the fire and lost track of time. Eventually something made me look up and there before me, *was the lady*. I hadn't seen her in some time and had almost forgotten her, but now she appeared anxious, moving her mouth as though trying to speak. But all I could hear was a sound like wind rushing through a tunnel.

"I can't hear you," I said in agitation, but suddenly her image shimmered as though reflected on rippling water, and she was gone.

Shaken, I stared at the spot where my visitor had stood and wondered at her stress and the meaning behind her visit, this night of all nights. It gave me pause to review my situation, unfailingly arriving at the same inevitable conclusion I always did. Suddenly tired, I yawned and rose from my chair.

❧

The morning of my wedding dawned grey and dull – how apt, I thought wryly. I'd tossed sleeplessly all night and had the kind of vague headache that results.

Lacking appetite, I picked absently at some dried fruits then bathed and stood patiently as Mother, Janet and Anne smoothed rose-scented crème over my entire body. They dressed my hair and Mother hooked pearls through my ears and strung them through my hair before slipping my wedding gown carefully over my head. They secured the headdress and bade me stand before my mirror.

I was beautiful – even to my own critical gaze – and acknowledged a sly regret that Patrick would never see me thus and lament his foolishness.

I attended the ceremony as one in a trance, parroting words, and kneeling quietly in an attitude of prayer though my mind was dead. At length Hamish took my hand and slipped a gold filigree band on my finger, obeying all the demands of ritual, and then it was done. We were man and wife.

The food kept coming: platters, trays, bowls; of cold meats, hot meats, vegetables, breads, cheeses, puddings, custards, fruit and wine. It was lavish and unending, but I could not eat.

And there was music and laughter; people – many of them strangers to me – congratulating me and toasting my health, and I was kissed, passed around the room, my dress admired, and my ring, and there were touches to my stomach accompanied by sly winks.

The hours seemed interminable but at last, just beyond midnight I found myself propped in bed like a marionette. I waited as the lines of communication running the length of the hall passed word to Simon that I was ready.

Hamish was admitted.

Dressed in his nightshirt and robe, my husband looked more nervous than I felt. "Go on man," Simon encouraged from the hallway, "once you get started you'll never want to stop!"

"Be gentle with him Alex, he looks terrified," Anne giggled in my ear – as well she might for she and I both knew Patrick would never have been so afraid – even on the occasion of his first time.

Mother and Anne left the room, closing the door softly behind them. Hamish stood in the middle of the room, looking uncertain. Slowly, he took off his robe and discarded it over a chair before climbing into the bed. As he pulled the counterpane to his shoulders I saw the cords in his neck were stretched tight as violin strings.

I could almost smell his anxiety as we lay stiffly side by side watching the drapes on the canopy jump in the flickering firelight.

After a long time I said, "What do we do now?"

He was so silent I could hear my heart thudding, then he said, "We don't have to do anything."

"I'm afraid, Hamish," I offered, hoping to ease his nerves. "Is it your first time?" I was prepared to lie if he asked me the same. But he'd been to court – surely it was not possible that he was virgin.

Suddenly decisive, he rolled towards me and kissed my mouth. Not brotherly like he'd done in the past, but lingeringly, with experience and I relaxed slightly, thinking to find some enjoyment. But unexpectedly he began to paw at my nightdress, almost tearing the flimsy fabric with his hurried groping. He didn't touch or stroke as Patrick had, and any hope of pleasure evaporated. When he hovered above me, I squeezed my eyes shut, wishing that it could be done quickly for both our sakes, and knowing I'd feel nothing akin to the dizzy passion I'd experienced during that other encounter, for all I felt now was a gaping void where love and desire ought to be.

He placed himself between my thighs and pushed forward urgently. But I felt his desire failing. He pressed again.

It was no use.

With a grunt of annoyance, he flung himself away and lay with his back to me.

I stared into the dark, confused and upset, and after a long painful pause, his voice came bitterly, "You laid with him, didn't you?"

Betraying tears gathered on my lashes and I swiped them away. I could not answer.

"I know you did. And your sister carries his child. Servants talk, you know. Is that why you finally acceded to our marriage?"

Bloody Janet, I thought, and gave an involuntary sob. Without warning, he turned and dealt a stinging slap to my face.

I yelped and raised my arms against further attack but he had rolled away declaring, "I have been played for a fool, as I suspected. Little wonder I'm having difficulty with you."

Swallowing tears of fury, I pressed a cool hand to my burning cheek. I would not be held responsible for his evident lack of physical desire and his inability to consummate our marriage. My brief experience in Patrick's arms taught me what a man's desire was, and my new husband exhibited none of the signs.

"Don't look for excuses," I snarled. "You've a tongue in your head! You could have spoken out earlier. We didn't *have* to marry."

"Well we did marry, didn't we, and your family has duped mine well and truly."

"And yours profited very nicely out of it, so I think we're even!"

We fell silent, chests heaving angrily, and thus was my wedding night.

CHAPTER 2

"You could have warned me," I said softly. My new husband and I were strolling along a rain-washed terrace, my hand on his arm as any happy bride and groom the morning after their wedding. Over breakfast Hamish had announced to my family that we'd be leaving for Scotland the following day, and though it made sense to travel before the worst snows, I'd have appreciated forewarning. We were barely on speaking terms since the humiliations of the night before, and having experienced his unexpected violence, I now regarded him warily.

"We had discussed it. What difference does it make?"

I watched his face, the stubborn set of his jaw, the angrily pinched lips, and wondered desperately how I could salvage the situation. "We did discuss it, but I didn't think we had decided."

"*We* didn't decide. *I* did."

We walked on in silence and our path led us past the rose-bed, naked and dormant after autumn pruning, and into the desolate orchard. I remembered the trees with their summer finery, green and bright. Now they looked so forlorn.

We passed my particular tree – the scene of … I closed my eyes.

"I apologise for striking you last night," Hamish said stiffly.

I looked into his face but saw no genuine remorse there. "You did deserve it though," he went on. "You have lied to me."

I shook my head ruefully, but this was no start to our life together. "I think Hamish, that we made quite a hash of it all yesterday. I rather hope we can put it behind us … begin again?"

He drew in his breath and raised his eyes to watch a sparrow hawk wheeling above. Her beautiful striped breast stood out boldly against the dove-grey skies. "It's not easy for me, Alex, living in the shadow of your previous lover." He managed to make me feel quite amoral.

"It was only the once," I said gently, "and should never have happened. He said he cared for me. You see Hamish, I've been duped too, for he said so many things, yet it's true: Anne does carry his child."

He drew his eyes away from the bird and looked at me with something resembling sympathy. "You truly loved him, didn't you? I can understand that, you know."

I chewed my lip to assuage the sting behind my eyes and nodded. "And I believed he loved me in return. You, though, have always known that ours was an arranged match. Love was never promised."

"And now? What do you feel for him now?"

"Nothing," I lied with conviction.

He studied me for several heartbeats. "Good. We may start afresh."

I frowned at his magnanimity but kept my peace, and that night, I lay in the dark and endured again his humiliating fumbling, only this time he completed the act, quickly and aggressively, with no care for my enjoyment.

And when it was over, he rolled away, tugging his nightshirt down. "There," he declared, triumphantly. "Let us hope this night bears fruit."

I silently cursed my previous lover for awakening me to the delights of a man's touch, and unappeased by the realisation that our joining was as unpleasant for Hamish as it was for me, I also hoped we proved fruitful, and thus could avoid further nightly encounters.

ॐ

The morning of our departure Janet was beside herself with excitement. She chattered like a demented sparrow and flew about gathering last minute items and issuing instructions to the footmen carrying our things.

Until the moment my family and servants assembled in the drive, our departure had felt rather surreal and I'd managed to smile throughout. But when I stood before Simon and he curled his arm about me and held me to his heart, I wilted and the tears came.

Anne stood slightly apart. She had an unreadable expression on her pretty face. Her belly had grown tremendously and she rested her hand on it, absently stroking Patrick's nestling child. She watched as I approached and her mouth opened as though about to speak. And when my arms went about her, she drew a great shuddering breath.

"Annie, what is it?" I stepped away so I could look at her.

She smiled slightly, "Oh … just sad you're leaving. We were finally becoming sisters. Take care of her, Hamish," she added, turning to my husband as he mounted his bay.

Then, we were gone. I watched despondently as the frozen dales of Yorkshire rolled by. Snow laden clouds hung low over the Pennines as we journeyed north. Rumbling along, the carriage Gerrard had presented as a wedding gift was a new and very modern contraption with excellent suspension, velvet seats, and a box in the floor to be filled with hot coals for warmth, beside which Jemima curled and slept with great contentment. Janet continued her incessant prattling and I let my head fall back against the padded seat, trying to block her out, and wondering when I'd see my home again — *if* I'd see my home again.

CHAPTER 3

Hamish's estate, my new home, hunkered just beyond the busy port of Greenock where the Firth of Clyde cut its course past Dumbarton to Clydebank. We were expecting the trip to take three to four days providing the weather held, which it did initially, but as we moved further north, the dampness in the air crystallised and fell in a soft flurry, dusting the landscape in a fine white powder.

Huddled within the coach, with coals beneath our feet and woollen blankets on our laps, Janet and I were reasonably comfortable though the windows ran with condensation and blurred our view of the countryside. It took five nights in total to reach Greenock for the roads became boggy and difficult the further north we went. Each night I shared a room with Janet; my new husband – apparently undesirous of my company, for which I was grateful – took a room for himself, while Grahame and the other groom occupied a third.

❧

We arrived late in the afternoon of the sixth day of our journey, just as the snow began to fall in earnest. The castle, for that's what it was, was a huge stone monster, grey with moss and lichen and complete with curtain-wall, towers, battlements and arrow-slit windows. The grassy ditch that had once been a moat, was spanned by a wooden bridge over which the horses clattered.

Sliding down the window, I stuck out my head as we passed through the gatehouse where the stone still bore the grooves of the old portcullis, which long ago lairds had used to resist raiding enemies.

The coach emerged into a large cobbled bailey. On our right, two indeterminately bred hunting dogs hardly raised their heads as they dozed in a doorway, and half a dozen chickens, supervised by a conceited rooster, scratched at a pile of scraps beside the kitchen door.

To the left, the shabby remains of a once imposing residential building stood with its ancient studded door propped open, even in this chilly weather, by a heavy stump of wood.

Hamish pulled up his horse and we lumbered to a stop behind him. Flinging open the door and lowering the steps, he offered his hand to assist me. As I stood gazing about, he announced with what I considered misguided pride, "Welcome to your new home, Lady Elginbury."

Upon entering the hall it was the smell that hit me first: that damp, musty odour that comes with aged furnishings and wet stone. The second was the gloom. The bare stone floor was gritty beneath my feet and I tried to hide my dismay – inadequately it seemed, for Hamish said, "Since Father's illness there's been little work done, but now you may add a sorely needed woman's touch. I understand some of your dowry was put aside for the purpose."

He waited for my response but I had no words. "It is not all like this," he said sharply. "Your rooms, for example, have been refurbished and are quite luxurious."

Just then two carroty maids burst through a door and stood before us, one hiding a feather duster behind her back. Hamish introduced the girls, explaining they were twins whose names were

Beth and Aggie. Though I'd heard of twins, I'd never known any, and their looks fascinated me for I truly could not tell them apart.

They bobbed to me and their faces split in great, gap-toothed grins. "Welcome my Lady Elginbury," they spoke in unison in gravelly Scots voices.

Our luggage was unloaded by a pair of burly men, whom I took by their clothes to be local farmers. It was only later that I learned the Elginbury staff wore no livery and that these were footmen.

Hamish issued instructions, "This one goes to my room, and Aggie will show you where to take the rest. They belong to your new mistress," he turned to me. "Dear, if you would follow Aggie to your room, you may bathe and rest before supper. I must attend my father now, but shall present you after we have eaten."

I clucked to Jemima who was busily investigating a gloomy corner, and followed Aggie up a stairway that was worn from the passage of many feet and had a precariously creaking bannister. At the landing, a pair of double doors on my right was, Aggie told me, the library and adjoining it was Lord Hamish's study.

I followed the maid down a confusing series of rambling corridors that saw no natural light, making it difficult to discern the features on the ancestral portraits lining the walls. Halfway down the corridor an alcove appeared on our left which seemed to be a tiny sitting room with an empty fire-place, table and two overstuffed chairs. We turned a corner, up three steps, and arrived at my room. Aggie threw open the door and stood aside.

It was a large but sparsely furnished room showing signs of having received some recent decorative attention. The writing desk, chair and dresser were all new, as were the deep green velvet drapes, and matching curtains and counterpane on the bed. The stone walls were hung with a green and gold tapestry, which complemented the drapery, and there was a lovely gold and green rug on the floor.

Being a corner room, it faced the back and side of the castle. The side window offered a view of the great, grey waterway where a fishing vessel rode anchor. The rear window looked over the Scottish landscape whose rugged contours were not yet fully hidden beneath the snow.

A welcoming fire roared in the grate with a tapestried armchair and footstool beside it. A half-moon table stood against a wall and on it was a crystal decanter containing a dark, amber liquid and a pair of chunky-cut crystal glasses. I lifted the stopper and met a strong alcoholic fragrance, reminiscent of, but less sweet than, brandy.

Aggie opened a door, and explained in her heavy Scots voice that this was my dressing room where my clothing would be stored. A second door adjoined my husband's rooms. Trying the door, I found it unlocked and peered cautiously in. Hamish's room seemed comfortable and contained more furniture, including a long leather settee, though it bore no signs of refurbishment. Given the state of the rest of the house, my room certainly exceeded my expectations.

"Does the lady find everything to her satisfaction?" Janet said coldly, coming in behind me.

I turned in surprise. "Yes … it is quite nice."

"Is there anything you need me to do?'

"No. I think Aggie will take care of my things when the men bring them up. Do you need to rest?"

"No. But I would ask your permission to leave the castle. Grahame would take me to visit his parents over in the village."

"Very well," I said without hesitation. Since her betrayal, things had been strained between us, and having spent our journey at such close quarters, I was only too happy to see her off. Nevertheless, I responded cheerfully, "Far be it from me to stand in the way of your love."

Instantly I realised my mistake. Unveiled contempt crossed her face and she said, "No, that would not be at all like you." As a final insult, she turned her back to me and slammed the door on her way out.

The flush of anger reached the roots of my hair. Now, but for Jemima, I was alone in my new room, in my new home, and felt lonelier than I could ever have imagined. Sitting on the bed, I sank into the thick mattress, and reflected on the changes in my life. Only half a year ago I was in love beyond words and happily anticipating my future with the most wonderful of men.

Now, wrenched from my beautiful dream, I was wife to a Scottish lord and mistress of a crumbling, ancient castle. I had hopes though, and motherhood was among them. This role I would play, for it was all I had and I would make the best of it, pushing aside the persistent vision of my future extending as an endless road through a desert, the markers of changing seasons and the births of children posted along the way.

～

I must have dozed in my chair by the fire for I awoke when Hamish knocked on our shared door and suggested we go downstairs to supper.

The dining room was long and narrow and dominated by an enormous rustic trestle. Mullioned windows looked onto the courtyard below where the snow was steadily falling. The chairs were ancient and solidly fashioned from sturdy, black timber, evidently designed for the backsides of brawny Scotsmen.

We were served a soup thick with fine-cut vegetables, followed by a platter of rich and succulent meats and a round of coarse but fragrant bread. It smelled glorious and I realised how hungry I was.

As we ate, Hamish said he'd visited his father and the old man was eager to see me immediately we'd finished our meal.

"Do like your room?" he asked guardedly. "It was refurbished especially for you."

"Yes, I do," I said with sincerity. "Did you oversee the decorating?"

His face brightened noticeably. "Yes, with the help of a friend, Richard Kintyre. Still, I expect you will find it rather basic here."

"One thing that is definitely not basic is your cook. This meal is delicious."

"Yes, we enticed Monsieur le Petit from Belgium many years ago and Father swears he weaves magic in that kitchen. Further, he's a rather friendly fellow – unusual for the trade."

"Certainly. Patrick's chef in Waterville – Monsieur Chartrain – is entirely the most fearsome …"

My voice trailed off. Hamish's face had darkened and his black brows drew together. "I'm sorry, Hamish," I said, silently cursing my stupidity. "But he *is* my brother –

Hamish rose abruptly. "He is *not* your brother, he was your *lover*. Come, Father's waiting."

I was ushered into an overheated room from which the great fire burning in the grate seemed to suck all breathable air. A young, black dog lay in a corner panting heavily and eying me unhappily as I waited.

My father-in-law received me with kingly arrogance, having me stand patiently beside his bed while he perused a document. I took the time to study him.

He was a wizened, stringy man, with a halo of white hair and a clean shaven face. Loose-lidded, faded brown eyes squinted at a sheaf of paperwork while he, supported by a mound of pillows, reclined beneath the bedclothes with a knitted rug spread over the top.

Two full minutes passed while I silently simmered at the rudeness of it before deciding to approach. I hadn't even taken a step when Hamish's hand shot out, forestalling me with a shake of his head forcing me to resume my soldierly position.

Finally, the old man gathered his papers with hands that were crooked and stiff, and placed them on his nightstand before turning his watery gaze upon me. "You haven't filled out much since you were thirteen," he commented hoarsely.

"No, my lord."

"Why God created slim-hipped women I'll never know. Not productive – no point to 'em."

"Father –" Hamish began.

"Leave us! I would talk privately with your wife."

I watched in surprise as Hamish bowed his head submissively. The old man waited until the door had closed then demanded, "Come here, peepers aren't what they used to be – ache like hell if they work too hard."

Clasping my hands before me, I silently fumed and tried not to squirm while Lord Hamish's eyes travelled up and down, assessing my suitability as one would a brood mare.

"Would you care to examine my teeth now?" I said, and leaned forward to present my open mouth.

A look of surprise crossed his face before he barked a laugh that quickly turned into a hacking cough. Recovering at length, he stared at me slyly and said, "You'll do."

"Thank you, my lord," I said brightly as if he'd paid a great compliment.

"Don't get cocky with me, girlie. You have no understanding of what you've ahead of you. That son of mine … Let us say he needs the touch of a woman. A *real* woman, if you know what I mean."

I didn't, but nodded anyway.

He continued, "You must produce an heir. I've not long left and there must be an heir."

"But, you've Hamish –"

"A sad comment on masculinity is that boy … him with his perversions and all." His sunken eyes sifted over me again and came to rest on my small bosom, "Believe me, if I still had it in me, I'd do the job myself."

Appalled, I drew in my breath but his eyes returned to my face, "Before I leave this earth there must be someone to carry the name of this family. It rests upon you for if my son had his way, he'd never put his cock anywhere near a woman!"

My eyes widened at his words.

"I shocked you," he remarked with malicious satisfaction.

"You'd like to," I responded smartly.

"Girlie, I care not for pretty words. I say what must be said and if you don't like it I make no apology." He shifted uncomfortably and gestured towards a pillow on a settee. "Bring that here."

Plumping it behind him, my hand came into contact with his shoulder and I felt the bones hard and angular beneath his nightshirt. I moved to step back, but his skeletal hand shot out and gripped my wrist with surprising strength.

"My son's preferences," his breath was aged and reeked of rotting teeth and I tried not to wrinkle my nose, "do not conform to marital requirements. I've given up trying to change him, make him see reason. Now, it is your job. You must produce a bairn, a boy preferably, though a girl would be no worse than the son I already have."

I tried to pull my hand away but his grasp was firm. "Do you understand?"

I didn't. I was confused and more than a little afraid.

"Do you understand?" he demanded. I nodded mutely.

He released my hand and I restrained myself from rubbing my wrist. "Had I not pushed the issue all these years, he'd never have married at all. You're here now and you *must* conceive and bear an heir before my time is up. You must … *ah* …!" he winced suddenly and gripped his stomach, leaning forwards with the pain. Perspiration broke on his liver-spotted brow and his breathing came in short gasps.

"My lord …" My hand hovered uncertainly. "My lord … can I get you anything?"

He groaned in response and seemed to have difficulty breathing. Flinging open the door, I yelled, "Hamish!"

My husband leapt from where he lounged against a wall and strode over, "What is it?"

"Your father …" I stepped aside pointing.

He pushed past me and stood at his father's bedside.

"Shit and damnation!" the old man growled as the spasm seemed to recede.

"Is it getting worse?" Hamish asked. "Can I get your tonic?"

"What do you think, stupid arse! Of course it's getting worse … and no, you can't get my fucking tonic – 'tis useless! That thrice-blasted doctor … should be taken out and thrashed … prescribing such …" another pain gripped him and he clawed at his abdomen, panting.

"Father …?"

"*Get out of here*! Take her to bed … get your cock wet … in a woman for a change instead of … those filthy sodomites you …!"

❧

I sat on my bed. Aggie, or someone, had unpacked my clothes, and my brush and other toiletries were laid out on the dressing table, my pens, knife and ink jar sat on the writing desk.

The world beyond my window was empty but for a dot of light from a cargo ship moving slowly along the oily, black ribbon of the river. I wondered who sailed her and what she carried in her holds over so many waterways. And I thought of Patrick and saw again his green gaze, sometimes bright with mischief, sometimes dark with desire, and I knew he must have had his reasons. Even though I wanted to, I could not hate him, for despite his betrayal, I loved him still.

And here I found myself, in this decaying fortress, married to a man accused by his diseased old father, of oddities I didn't fully understand.

A quick knock at the adjoining door startled me and before I could respond Hamish entered, smiling. "Hello dear, not yet abed? I thought to wish you a pleasant night."

I smiled, though his father's urgent desire for an heir hung heavily between us, he continued, "I thought to share your bed but you're doubtless tired after our journey."

"It is up to you, Hamish," I said, and he made pretence of weighing up the options though we both knew I'd be sleeping alone, and were glad of it.

∾

I did not sleep well that night and was tired and grumpy the next morning when Janet returned, fairly glowing with excitement. Grahame's family had adored her and the happy couple planned to wed. Grahame sought permission from Hamish, who became very excited at the prospect of a party and immediately announced we'd host the event at the castle and the bride and groom could celebrate with their friends and family at our expense.

I wondered, mean-spiritedly, how much of my dowry would be paying for it. The date was set for the middle of January to provide enough time for the three requisite banns to be read, and it was all Janet could talk about, so I avoided her whenever possible preferring the services of Aggie or Beth – I still couldn't tell them apart.

My days were spent with Jemima in lonely exploration of the castle grounds and I tried as much as I could to find some small excitement, some spark of colour in this interminably grey and lifeless landscape. And, each evening after supper, Hamish and I visited his father, enduring again the evil old man's bitterness as he raged against his illness, and insulted his son in language that tested my imagination.

Winter deepened, and though I was used to the snow and cold of Yorkshire, Scotland was more intense somehow. The snow fell with dedicated severity and the winds screamed about the castle for days on end, finding gaps in masonry and beneath doors, creating icy draughts in the rooms.

And I was miserable.

CHAPTER 4

Christmas came and went with no acknowledgement from Hamish or me other than to exchange small and hastily arranged gifts, and to allow time for the servants to visit their families. The year became 1814, and then Janet married Grahame, and Hamish allocated a double room to them as a couple.

Since arriving at the castle, Hamish had visited my bed only twice – both hurried and humiliating couplings that were quickly over and saw my husband immediately return to his own chamber.

Thus was my new life in Scotland.

February gave way to March, and the snow lay in mounds against the castle walls, glistening wetly in sunlight too weak to melt it.

And in my quiet moments – those moments just before sleeping, or when I lay down my sewing to stretch my neck – the memories of Patrick came, unbidden, and always with the power to evoke intense emotions. In time I hoped they would fade to snatches of conversation or secret kisses, to be hidden away in a dusty, rarely explored corner of my mind. But when they appeared without warning, like glittering gemstones, they were so exquisite that I forgot the hurts and betrayals and saw only the beauty so briefly enjoyed. And despite having been deceived in the worst possible way, I remained haunted by a fleeting and impossible love affair.

Each evening Hamish and I took our meal together, though mainly in silence as increasingly we had nothing to say to one another. However, one night, I asked about the castle's history, and Hamish spoke at length and with a great deal of familial pride. Explaining the confusing network of corridors, he described how they were designed to disorient intruders and protect the laird.

"In thirteen-ten the castle was stormed by a marauding clan from the north-east," he said, laying down his spoon. "The raiders were unable to breach the curtain wall. It began to rain, fiercely, but the laird fought valiantly beside his men on the battlements. They would have won but for a servant, loyal to the enemy, who raised the portcullis. The laird ran, escaping down one of the twisting corridors into a hidden room at the end, but they found him."

I'd listened intently with my spoon poised. Now I asked, "How did they find him?"

"They followed the trail of water from his rain-soaked clothes. When they found him he was trapped in his own labyrinth and slaughtered."

I shivered. "How horrible."

"Depends how you see it. My family were the assailants and have held this castle ever since. It has only been in the last fifty years or so that the portcullis was removed and the moat drained."

Hamish's face glowed with satisfaction as we visited his father that evening and I thought how sad it was that he could be so proud of his heritage, yet his father regarded him with such distaste.

As we emerged from the sick-room he said, "I'd best make haste, or be late." He touched my cheek with his cold lips, and then he was gone, as he often was of an evening, and I wondered where he went.

His behaviour was baffling. It seemed that our having a child was important to him, if only to quiet the relentless harangue we endured while attending his father. But he didn't enjoy our attempts at conception any more than I, clearly preferring to avoid the undertaking altogether. I could count on my fingers the number of times he'd visited my bed in the five months of our marriage.

From the blatant comments made by his father, I now understood that my husband was one of those men who enjoyed sexual encounters with other men. Having spent my life surrounded by men like Simon and Patrick, and even Gerrard – men who clearly enjoyed and actively sought the attentions of women – it was confounding that Hamish was not like them. I could not understand it, and since I couldn't imagine how the act of love between men was performed, I effectively put it from my mind.

What a quandary – the pressure to bear a child, while reluctant to engage in the necessary act. As the weeks passed however, I became annoyed with Hamish for his infrequent visits to my room and could no longer keep my peace.

One evening, I sat moving the roasted parsnips around my plate while I thought about our situation. Hamish seemed oblivious to my distraction and ate with his usual enthusiasm. He was dressed in evening wear – the third time this week.

"Are you going out again?" I asked as pleasantly as I could.

He nodded, his mouth full, then swallowed and took a sip of his wine before answering. "Aye."

"Where do you go, and why do I never go with you? I am, after all, your wife," I spoke carefully, modulating my voice inoffensively.

He met my questions defiantly. "Where I go is not your concern, and why you remain here is because I prefer it." His tone was challenging, and his expression as mutinous as a child's.

I stared at him. He took a deep breath and tried again, more passively this time. "You do not join me because I don't believe you'd enjoy yourself. It is all men, and we gamble and drink and so on. I'm doing you a favour by leaving you here."

"Are you also doing me a favour by not visiting my bed?"

He smirked mischievously, "Do you miss me, wife?"

"It's not a game, Hamish. Your father is desperate that we produce a child. I myself would like one. Do you anticipate an immaculate conception?"

He sobered but said nothing so I continued. "You are required to contribute, you know. Each time I visit your father he is relentless. I am forced to lie to him and I won't do it any more, Hamish."

"I didn't know you *wanted* a child," he said contritely.

"What else do I have in my life? I've lived in this castle for five months and I've seen no one, gone nowhere. I'm bored and lonely. I don't even have my husband's company!"

He said nothing, and we sat, both of us examining our plates. "Do you find me so repellent?" I whispered.

He looked up quickly. "No Alex. It's that I am busy … Father's business … I have so many obligations …"

"What about your obligations to me?" I cried. "I'm your *wife* but I don't feel it."

"I don't know what you want me to say," he mumbled sulkily.

"Then don't worry yourself about it!" I snapped, pushing my heavy chair back. "This isn't what I was expecting our marriage to be, Hamish. It is *worse.*"

I stormed out and up to my room where, ever faithful, Jemima awaited my return. Her tail thumped in greeting and when I sat beside her, she rested her head in my lap, and rolled her eyes to look up at me.

"Thank God for you, girl," I said kissing her brow.

∿

My father-in-law decided we would take tea together each afternoon and I was to read the newspapers from Glasgow to him. He rarely failed to enquire if the signs of a child had revealed themselves. I persisted with excuses, constantly apologising, and was thoroughly, *thoroughly* tired of it.

The dog that Lord Hamish kept in his room was an enormous creature of mixed breed that looked like he'd been thrown together from oddments. Bony was his name, after Napoleon Bonaparte, because as Lord Hamish liked to tell me, "Don't much care for the little emperor myself, but anyone giving the English a difficult time of it can't be all bad." Though only about a year old, the dog sat in a corner bored and panting in the airless room, and I felt sorry for him. He was too young a dog to spend his life in a sick-room, with only five minute comfort breaks with Lord Hamish's grudging valet. He needed to run and play and be free, as all creatures do.

Lord Hamish bade me feed biscuits to the dog off my lord's plate. Inappropriate food and lack of exercise had taken its toll on Bony who was overweight and clumsy, and desperately in need of affection. As I visited frequently, the dog grew used to me and I suggested to my father-in-law that Bony could spend some time outside in the courtyard with Jemima and me. Setting his jaw stubbornly the old man snapped, "No!" and the subject was closed.

I grew to loathe this man and dread my daily visit. Nerves would contract my stomach into knots as I measured my steps to his room, never certain of his mood. He could be argumentative, accusatory, or just plain nasty, and his attitude on any given day was directly proportionate to the amount of pain he suffered.

Days when his pain was intense he was impossible to reason with. His arguments were illogical for he accused his son of impotence and insisted I was barren in one breath. Further, he claimed that if I were more attractive his son would be less inclined to seek male company.

In his more lucid, less aggressive days, he explained his son's preference and warned me about an infatuation Hamish held for a certain Richard Kintyre. I frowned for I remembered this man had helped refurbish my room.

"If only you produced a bairn – I'd not care," the old man said one day, but as a spasm of pain gripped him, he turned on me, raving irrationally that I was ugly, a dried-up useless whore, worse than a bitch, which was at least capable of conceiving.

By the time I left, a very long hour later, I was shaking and close to tears.

∽

I was having difficulty sleeping – so out of character for me – and each night I sat reading by a candle, waiting to grow tired. One such night, my glance fell upon the decanter of liquor on my table. Hamish called it usquebaugh and I'd tasted it briefly but hadn't particularly liked it. Nevertheless, as I sat in the hollow hours of the night, I decided a small glass might help.

Sitting on the floor before the hearth, Jemima's head on my lap, I sipped from a weighty crystal glass and eventually found my eyelids growing heavy. And thus began my evening ritual – a glass of usquebaugh before bed. But as Lord Hamish's sickness progressed, I began taking a glass each afternoon after returning from my visit to him.

Through my window, glass in hand, I watched the last traces of snow melt, and breathed deeply, willing my trembling to subside and my stomach to relax. I knew not how Hamish spent his nights, or his days for that matter, but I knew he had his business interests, and he was a member of some club in Glasgow. We saw each other only at supper, and those sporadic occasions when he visited my bed.

Janet had been married less than two months when she announced she was expecting a child and, since Aggie had been assigned to attend my needs, Janet was thankfully employed elsewhere in the rambling old castle and I rarely saw her traitorous face.

A steady correspondence with Gerrard ensured I kept abreast of the news from home and so it was April when I learned that Maria was with child.

Gerrard declared he'd never seen a man so overwhelmed with pride and happiness as my brother. I replied to Gerrard's eager questions that, though I'd not yet found myself with child, Hamish and I remained hopeful.

I knew that Anne had married her knight shortly after my own marriage and now lived in Cheshire. It seemed that theirs may prove a good match after all since the two were ambitious for court positions and were planning a move to London. Mother was in Cheshire with them and would join them at court when George took Anne there. Prinnie had been made Prince Regent in 1810 and Mother was relying on her old friendship with him.

Reading this, I was pleased that things had worked out reasonably well for Anne since it must have been so much worse for her than for me, but then Gerrard's letter took another turn.

Now Lass, I take this opportunity to announce that your sister Anne has produced a daughter. As you know, your mother is residing with Anne and Sir George. She was present at the delivery and reported that although the child was born in January – rather earlier than anticipated – Domenica, as she is called, is healthy and quite pretty.

Your mother has described a somewhat swarthy babe with very dark hair and eyes, resembling in no way, either of her parents. However, since my own cousin John was olive-skinned and dark-eyed, Domenica doubtless inherited her complexion from him.

Your sister experienced a short travail and recovered quickly – only four days abed – and your mother reports that she and Domenica are doing well.

The letter fell to my lap and my eyes drifted unseeingly to my window.

So Patrick was now a father and my sister a mother. Though I'd known from the first that this day would come, nothing could have prepared me for the tangible reality of Patrick's betrayal – a living, breathing, product of deceit, conceived in lust and perfidy, innocent and unknowingly unwelcomed by her inconvenienced mother and procured father.

I could pity this poor child, but I envied my sister. Oh how I envied the delirious passion delivered at her lover's clever touch, his tenacious seed that grew in her belly, and that violent, ecstatic agony, that culmination … that precious child.

With my head in my hands, I wept for my loneliness and childlessness. And long after the fire had burned out and my decanter run dry I sat, insensitive to the chill of night settling within my room.

It was the morning of the twenty-second of May; my twentieth birthday, and Hamish was leading me across the bailey to the stables. The early sun moved along its arc in the spring sky, casting tower-shaped shadows on the ground. As we walked my husband drew a linen scarf from his pocket and tied it over my eyes, then taking my hand, guided me into the ancient stone building. The smell of horses and hay was strong and caused my nose to itch, and my sightless eyes visualised the dust floating in the air. Hamish placed his hands on my shoulders, adjusting my angle. "Ready?"

I nodded.

The blindfold was removed with a flourish and I paused, staring into a gloomy stall, and as my eyes slowly focused I saw, all angles and knobbly knees, a young horse.

She was a deep rust colour, with patches of dark, baby fluff on her chest and flanks. Her mane and tail were black and she regarded me curiously from liquid brown eyes. "Her name is Ember," Hamish said with contained excitement. "She's yours – happy birthday."

I turned and impulsively threw my arms around his neck in a gesture so genuine it took us both aback. He caught me, laughing self-consciously. "She's only three months old. I thought you might like her for a riding horse. The stablemaster is very good. He will break her for you when she's old enough, perhaps a year from now – what do you think?"

"Oh Hamish," I whispered, "she's beautiful – I love her already."

He smiled happily.

❧

One afternoon in the middle of June, I was gazing at the marshy riverbank from my window. It was covered in little, white flowers that bobbed on long green stalks, which Aggie explained were bog-beans and common to swampy areas. Seated at my desk, a cup of usquebaugh at my elbow, I decided I was tired of the lies. Perhaps the drink caused my hand to flow so, but I poured out to Gerrard my loneliness, childlessness, my husband's disregard, and my deficit of diversion. And when it was done, I sanded and sealed it, and left it for Mrs Twigley, the housekeeper, to give to the post boy.

That evening, at supper, I asked Hamish if I could look into the refurbishment of the castle to occupy myself.

"There is no money," he replied flatly.

"But … you said there was money left from my dowry."

"There isn't. What wasn't spent on Grahame and Janet Father has contributed to an investment venture … it's all tied up. You're lucky I had your rooms done when I did," he said smugly.

"I don't understand –"

"It's not your business to understand. Anyway, ask him yourself. He wishes to see us immediately after supper."

We stood side-by-side, hands clasped behind our backs like naughty school children, and endured, yet again, the old man's abuse. He attacked Hamish in the foulest, most descriptive language I'd ever heard and listed my numerous failings as a wife and woman, bellowing with a strength I never suspected he had.

"The pair of you – nothing but scroungers. What's the matter with you, boy? Too busy shooting your seed up the arse of some stable-lad rather than your wife's cunny! And you …" he aimed a bent finger in my direction. "Any pox-ravaged whore can stoke a man's interest but not you! What do you think you were brought here for?"

And it went on, unendingly – one, great, lengthy tirade.

My face flamed with disgust and humiliation – I could not bear to look at Hamish and to my eternal disappointment, I began to cry.

"Both of you get out of my sight!" the evil old fiend shouted while Bony cowered in his corner. My knees were weak and I shook with the strength of my loathing for this man.

Wordlessly, Hamish led me from the room but though I longed for comfort, I recoiled from his touch. The imagery, the accusations, the language, all appalled me. Hamish was … unnatural, his desires repugnant to me, and this sodomite was my husband, and the despicable creature in that bed was my father-in-law.

In my room, Hamish poured us each a drink from my decanter and sat on my bed, his evening plans aborted. The furrows drawn between his brow and beside his mouth showed his own pain, and I wondered how he'd lived with this so long.

"Why does your father speak so, Hamish?" I asked at last. "Do you truly share your bed with men and … boys?"

So finally he told me. Over the course of several hours my husband described his early youth, his growing awareness that he was not attracted to women. He confided his fear of discovery, self-disgust, and his profound relief as he met others of his persuasion.

We reached the bottom of my decanter and continued talking into the night as he told of his time at court, where all manner of debauchery was indulged behind the King's back, and Hamish kept company with a group of like-minded lads.

"It was at court that I first saw Patrick, and you see, I understand your attraction to him – perhaps I'm jealous too. Though he moved in a very different circle, everyone knew him for his wit and charm … I doubt he even knew my name. Shall I call for wine? It's not yet midnight."

We drank and talked and for the first time, I felt a stirring of understanding between us. Though my revulsion for his preference had not lessened, I began to know him better.

"So tell me," I said. "Why did your father choose me as your bride?"

"It was my mother actually. She believed it was my choice that I am … this way." He gave a rueful shrug. "She thought you would be a good match since you met the financial and social criteria, and you were slim, small-breasted … boyish. Do you know the first time I saw you, you were wearing a pair of your brother's breeches and I thought you really were a boy."

I played with the stem of my glass, staring into the bloodlike liquid – it was like drowning in a ruby – as he continued. "But of course you are a woman, and through no fault of your own, I'm simply not attracted to you."

"Hence the difficulty with our …"

"Our intimacy," he finished helpfully. "Aye."

"We must try, Hamish. We cannot endure your father like this. But not only that, I need something to look forward to. I feel so … trapped … so alone."

"I understand. I was thinking that you could invite a friend, Julia perhaps, to visit. Would you like that?"

"Of course I would love that. But it's imperative we appease your father."

He smiled. "It would be nice, Alex, if we could be friends. You're not unattractive, you know. It isn't your fault."

We had emptied the contents of the bottle of wine and were now more than tipsy, and as he leaned over to kiss me, perhaps aided by the drink, I felt a stirring within. We made love that night, and though it was not the pleasurable experience I'd have liked, Hamish was definitely more relaxed and willing. I hoped that henceforth relations between us would improve.

✺

Though he continued to go out most nights, when Hamish chose to remain at home, we spent the evening together. We talked, read, or played chess. We could cheerfully polish off a bottle of wine during games that endured long into the morning hours, often to be resumed the following afternoon.

Relations between us had definitely improved since our talk that night, and during this relatively congenial time, Hamish visited my bed as regularly as I knew he could. I had every reason to hope I would soon prove with child.

~

One July day, mail arrived from Gerrard. I opened it late in the afternoon, sitting by the window in my room. Gerrard was replying to my most recent letter – my torrent of self-pity and misery – with the only response he could reasonably offer; that I was no doubt beset by the homesickness and lonliness one could expect once the excitement and newness of my marriage had worn off. He could not know, of course, that my relationship with Hamish had improved slightly and that I regretted my impetuous outpouring. However, my disappointment was quickly forgotten as I continued to read;

> *Perhaps you recall a young maid employed in my service at Waterville, by the name of Sylvie? You'd have met her that summer we spent in Devon.*

Of course I remembered her. It was silently regarded that given her rather profound resemblance to Maeve, and Gerrard's obvious favour for her, Sylvie was his illegitimate daughter. Now, driven by some unknown compulsion, Gerrard's letter explained that he wanted to publicly acknowledge her, thus making her continued service impossible. He suggested I may welcome her as a companion – a suggestion I would most eagerly accept – providing Hamish approved, which he was very happy to do. Evidently, he nursed a guilty conscience over leaving me alone so often.

∾

August arrived heralding clear-skied days and balmy evenings. Hamish and I took to riding along the edge of the Clyde in the mornings. Gannets and gulls swooped low over the water searching for newly-spawned fish, and cormorants, their wings stretched wide to dry in the sun, perched on rocks on the banks. "Shag on a rock," I observed as Hamish's lovely bay gelding walked patiently beside my squat cob.

"That's where the saying comes from," he replied. "Have you ever seen a puffin?"

I shook my head and he continued. "They make nests in the ground around here … always in pairs. You might come across one. Odd-looking birds."

An excited shriek pierced the morning as a pair of lads, knee deep at the water's edge, netted a salmon. They clambered up the bank, chattering in an unintelligible brogue, gathered their boots and ran for home with their breakfast.

As Hamish kicked his horse into a canter I attempted to follow but my somewhat costive nag managed only a fart before resuming its walk and I was forced to watch as my husband became a smudge in the distance.

During these pleasant excursions, I could pretend all was well between us. But in truth, I struggled with Hamish's sexuality. In isolation I could perhaps forgive his infidelities since I knew that if Patrick walked through the door I'd throw myself at him without hesitation – regardless of his sins. But it was the nature of Hamish's infidelity that caused me anguish.

There were times when Hamish touched me and I involuntarily recoiled. Those infrequent evenings when, carrying a single candle and dressed in his nightshirt, he resignedly approached my bed and

I, fortified by a cup or two from my decanter, received him with revulsion. I pretended it was Patrick's mouth on mine, Patrick's hands parting my thighs, but the strength of my imagination proved incapable of breathing tenderness or passion into these encounters, for Hamish was rough and my experience painful. Then there were the nights when he roughly pulled me on all fours and took me from behind like a beast, and my tears would drip soundlessly on to my pillow, until he shuddered and cried out.

But such was my lot and it was futile to supplement an unhappy life with impossible dreams and I shaded my eyes with my hand to watch him returning at a gallop, black hair streaming behind him, his face alive with vigour. Returning his cheerful grin as he pulled his sweat-stained horse beside me, we turned towards the castle.

CHAPTER 5

As summer progressed, Janet resigned her position. Her pregnancy was advancing and she and Grahame decided to move to Glasgow to set up a bakery before the baby was born. In view of our soured friendship, I was glad to see the back of her.

One evening I threw open the casement in my room and breathed deeply. The air was still and heavy with the smell of coal and fish and industry from the port over at Greenock, and it occurred to me that I was drinking in increasing amounts – indeed, when Aggie came to help me undress each evening, I'd had at least two cups of usquebaugh. Often, I fell into bed rather tipsy and awoke most mornings with a coated tongue and vague headache. But I was sleeping very well and once I'd broken my fast, was able to ride and participate in my *very exciting* round of daily activities without any ill consequence.

Nebulous self-recriminations were pushed aside; I was not about to admit – even to myself – that I had a growing problem.

And then, one late August morning, everything changed and I didn't see it coming.

Hamish had arrived in the breakfast room before me and was already helping himself to a plate of oatcakes, warm and fragrant from the ovens and dripping with golden butter. The newspaper from Glasgow was waiting by his plate and I paused in shock as the headline leapt out at me:

Sons from the Peninsular – Home at Last

Snatching it from the table I shook it out, reading rapidly.

"What is it?" Hamish asked, but I barely heard him.

The story was following on from an earlier one that told how, on 10 April, Wellington had pushed the French troops out of Calvinet Ridge, near Toulouse. Two days later, Napoleon had abdicated, marking the end of six long years of bloodshed.

The paper made the happy announcement that after the signing of the Treaty of Paris on 30 May, our brave soldiers had begun returning to Britain in June, and for the most part, their withdrawal from Europe was now complete.

And as I read, the one thought clanging in my brain like a hammer on an anvil, was that Patrick was home.

More than a year since that heavenly night we'd spent together. Nearly two years since he was wounded, three since his enlistment, he was finally home.

I put down the paper and mechanically nibbled at an oatcake.

But it meant nothing. I was married to another, and my sister – mother of his bastard – was also married to another, and he was free. Free of me, Anne, his child – all the responsibility my mother would have forced upon him.

Hamish had picked up the paper and now took a deep breath. "Nothing's changed," he said firmly. "Just because it is over … nothing's changed."

I glanced across at him.

"Don't look like that!" he snapped. "I know what you're thinking. Remember your sister? Remember her bairn? Nothing's changed."

I bowed my head to hide my face. "I'm glad it's over, that's all. No more war."

Whether he believed me or not, he nodded in agreement. "What do you think your mother will do? She'd be out to crucify him I should think."

"I would expect so, but Anne's married – there's nothing to gain from it." I shrugged. "Who knows … I … I forgot something in my room – excuse me."

He said nothing but I felt his eyes on me as I left the table.

I lay on my bed and wondered, what *would* Mother do now? It was hardly worth making a fuss since Anne was taken care of and Domenica had an honest name. And what of me? If only …

Shaking my head to throw off such futile thoughts, my eyes lit on my decanter. I could almost taste the smooth, hot liquid. How tempting to obliterate my relentless regrets in its blissful, amber depths, and it was not yet ten in the morning!

But the devil on my shoulder whispered that if people took brandy for medicinal purposes, why not the usquebaugh? 'Tis certain the Scots did.

My hand shook as I poured – not surprisingly for I was quite emotional – and as I raised the glass to my lips the door adjoining Hamish's room slammed open and I dropped the glass in surprise. Hamish stood on the threshold, arms folded over his chest.

"What are you doing?"

"Wh … what do you mean?"

"What do you think I mean?"

The warm smell of spilt alcohol hung in the air like a cloud, expanding, filling the room accusingly. He strode across and snatched the decanter from my hand.

"I … I … don't know …" I stammered in confusion.

"This Alex!" he shouted shaking the bottle so its contents sloshed up the sides and threatened to spill out. "*This* is what I mean. What are you *doing*?"

"Nothing!" I cried, making a grab for the decanter. He flung his hand out to deflect me, knocking me aside, and in two strides was at my window. He threw it open and watching me, up-ended the decanter, draining the liquid onto the grass and rocks two storeys below.

I stared helplessly and heard the shattering of crystal as the decanter followed its contents. Then he turned to me.

I cried against his chest for a long time and had I been asked to name the cause of my pain, I could not. All I understood was my desperate unhappiness.

Hamish said not a word, merely stood with his arms about me until I grew weary and then he led me to my bed. He lay beside me and I slept – a true sleep, the first in many months that had not been induced by the drink, and when I awoke, he was still beside me, having forgotten any alternative plans he may have had for the day. The sun had moved overhead in a cloudless azure sky and in the stark daylight of my room, he slowly and uncertainly removed my clothing, and then his own, and for the first time in our marriage, he made love to me slowly and considerately.

Some time afterwards, we continued lying on my bed talking quietly and he ordered that I stay away from the usquebaugh – a directive I hotly declared was unnecessary.

"You have a weakness for it," Hamish said, idly drawing a pattern on my counterpane.

"I only drink it because I'm bored."

"You are susceptible."

I sighed resignedly. "Very well Hamish. But what of your weakness? Will you give up your men friends?" As soon as I'd said the words I wished I could take them back for his eyes hardened and I recognised the stubborn set of his jaw.

"I'm trying to help you, Alex," he said climbing from the bed and reaching for his clothes.

"Then be a true husband. Stop seeing those men."

He stood above me buttoning his shirt and said sadly, "Don't ask that of me, please. Easier to ask me to stop breathing."

"But you're my husband …" I blurted out. "It is distasteful what you do … I can't … I hate it."

"I try to give you a child, and anything else, if it's within my power, I shall give it. But that one thing – you cannot ask."

"Which is what I need of you."

"Then we're at a stalemate," he said flatly, tucking his shirt into his trousers.

"I can't endure it," I said softly as he moved about my room, gathering his stockings and shoes.

Suddenly he turned, glaring imperiously. "Ah, but you *will* endure it Alex, because I am your husband and you shall do as I say."

"Hamish!" I cried appalled by his attitude, but he would not back down on this.

He shook his head, effectively ending my protest. "You'll not question my behaviour or the company I choose to keep and that's the way of it." With that, he strode from the room.

A month passed, then two, and I'd not touched a single drop of usquebaugh. Inactivity was my greatest enemy and in an effort to occupy my mind and hands, I'd taken to gardening, and it was in the kitchen garden that Mrs Twigley found me, on my knees in the powdery dirt, armed with my weeding tool.

"The post for you, my lady," she said, handing me the travel-stained letter.

I tucked it away for later, when the loneliness of evening closed in.

Leeds
8 September 1814

My Dearest Daughter,

I trust this letter finds you well and pray your return mail will be announcing some happy news – well, you can't blame an old man for hoping!

Sylvie wrote that she plans to leave Devon in the middle of September and progress immediately to you. She was terribly excited that you would welcome her as your companion. Please have the two grooms accompanying her return to Devon as early as possible.

Maria grows larger every day and Simon suggested it may be more than one babe that she carries. Maria was rather horrified and Simon laughed. They are so truly happy Alex, I know you'd rejoice with them.

I hear from your mother than Anne and her babe are doing well. Anne and George are planning their move to London soon. Your sister hopes to be presented to the Prince Regent at the Christmas and New Year festivities. Your mother, of course, will accompany them.

Time grows short for me this evening and since I have a dinner engagement I must close. I remain your loving father,

Gerrard

So Sylvie was due to arrive very soon and in anticipation, Hamish had found a small sum of money to decorate her room.

It was my first day trip since arriving in Scotland. Aggie and I, in the carriage that was my wedding present, took the rugged road along the Clyde to a market on the outskirts of Glasgow where I purchased fabrics and furnishings in shades of apricot and brown. It was around this time that I suspected I may be with child. I said nothing to Hamish for the time being – I wanted to be sure – but as I selected what I needed for Sylvie's room, I mentally noted colours and items that may suit a nursery.

Sylvie's room was decorated with new curtains at the windows and complementary drapery around her bed. The chair at her desk was re-upholstered to match and an arrangement of dried lavender in a bowl on the dressing table scented the room.

The last time I'd seen Sylvie, she had taken me to meet secretly with Patrick, enabling us to make up after a disagreement, the result of which was a kiss that had warmed my heart for many months after.

Thinking of it now, remembering how it was to be in Pat's arms, and to hear him call me *darling girl*, brought a lump to my throat that I quickly swallowed.

❧

It was the first Saturday of October and Hamish and I stood in the bailey watching as the Thorncliffe burgundy and gold coach trundled across the bridge. Smiling, Hamish said, "Here she comes at last. Are you excited?"

"Oh yes," I replied sincerely.

Relations had been less fraught between us in recent weeks and I knew I could be contented – if only memories of Patrick would stop intruding. I must constantly remind myself of the womanising cad he was. And now, certain that I was with child, I had every reason to feel positive. I'd not had the opportunity to tell Hamish the joyful news yet for he'd been out every night. Tonight though, I knew he planned to stay in.

The driver pulled the matched greys to a halt as they drew even with us, and a Thorncliffe groom leapt to quickly open the door and hand down a small stylishly dressed woman.

Sylvie grinned shyly at me. She was just as I remembered: thin and delicate with her pale hair and elfin face, and I stepped up to greet her. "Sylvie, it is so good to see you again." My pleasure was genuine.

"Thank you, Miss Alex, it is good to see you too." She curtsied prettily and added, "I'm so very grateful to be here."

"We're equal now, you must call me Alex."

Reminiscent of Maeve's, her eyes tilted up at the corners as she smiled.

Hamish came forward then and upon my introduction she dropped a polite curtsy and said, "My lord," at which he grimaced.

"Please reserve all that for my father," Hamish said, setting her at ease. He seemed to have a talent for it, as was proven when he'd first seen Simon's disfigurement. "I understand in some convoluted fashion we are related by marriage, so please call me Hamish."

"Thank you," she repeated on the verge of another automatic curtsy when his hand shot out.

"And none of that," he said with humour. "My wife tells me your father has at last recognised you. You are an earl's daughter – you're a higher rank than me!"

My pride in the redecorating of her room was not wasted. Staring around the room in awe, she asked, "And this is truly my room?"

I nodded. "Surely when Gerrard acknowledged you as his daughter, you moved from the servant's quarters?"

"Yes, but not to anything like this," she said fingering the tassels on the counterpane. "There were some noses out of joint and Mrs Bath was keen to keep the peace. When Master Patrick arrived home –"

"Patrick's home?"

Her clear blue eyes watched me carefully. "He arrived on the last day of August. He hasn't sold his commission yet … he's planning to return to Europe."

"Does Gerrard know he's home?" I asked softly.

She looked at me quizzically. "Of course – they correspond

regularly. It was Master Patrick, while still in France, who urged my father to recognise me."

"The sly old dog …" I said slowly, with dawning realisation.

"I'm sorry?"

"So he has ever known where to find Patrick."

She frowned in confusion but I said quickly, "Never mind … please, go on."

"Master Patrick has certainly never treated me as a servant, but some of the maids were rather … disdainful."

"Did they treat you badly?"

She sat on the edge of her pretty bed. "Everyone suspected who my father was, and when Lord Thor – I mean, Father," she blushed slightly, "made the announcement, it was not really a surprise."

"Did he go to Devon?"

"No, he sent a letter to Mrs Bath instructing her to announce it to the household. When Master Patrick arrived home –"

"You must call him Patrick for he's your brother."

"I know, but it'll take some getting used to," she said, with a wry smile. "When *Patrick* arrived home, he offered me a better room but I had already arranged to leave."

"Have you always known your parentage?"

At that she laughed and the gay little tinkle was identical to Maeve's. "Oh yes! I've always known. My mother told me when I was very young but I was sworn to secrecy. You see, Father was terribly concerned that his wife in Ireland would find out about his liaison with my mother. When my mother died – I was only five – he made certain I received an education and a position where I would be secure."

"But Patrick and Maeve's mother died many years ago, why is he only doing this now?"

"I don't know … Patrick has pushed for it for a long time … in any case, Father wrote that he had been grateful for my discretion all these years. Afterwards though, it became rather uncomfortable at Devon. I could not have stayed and I'm not sure where I'd have gone had you not welcomed me here. Your mother would certainly never have had me in her home."

I grimaced ruefully. "Definitely not, but Simon would have. Regardless, I'm so very glad you're here."

"So am I."

We smiled at each other as the grooms arrived with her luggage. I left her to settle in and went in search of Hamish.

He was in the library, in a high-backed chair, adding a column of figures by the afternoon light streaming through the window. I sat on the footstool before him and gave him the news of my pregnancy.

There was no mistaking his happiness, including the obvious relief that crossed his face for we both knew he would no longer be obliged to visit my bed.

After a barrage of questions: Was I sure? How long? When did I know? He was satisfied and taking my hand, led me immediately to his father's room.

Lord Hamish's condition had worsened of late. His skin, stretched like yellowed parchment across the bones of his face, looked transparent and brittle enough to split open, and when Hamish announced proudly that we had news, his hands shook uncontrollably in anticipation as he bade us tell him at once.

Hamish obliged and his father acknowledged the news with a surly nod of satisfaction, then demanded, "When? When will the bairn come?"

"Early May, Father."

"Good, good. An old man needs something to look forward to."

Fortunately, I knew better than to expect congratulations. But I had not expected the news that followed and he explained it with overt relish.

It seemed that Lord Hamish, upon my marriage to his son, had amended his will so that in the event of his death we would receive no income from the Elginbury businesses until a legitimate child was produced. That child, and any legitimate siblings, would be the sole heirs to Glendenning Associated Importers. Until such time as the eldest child attained his or her majority, Hamish would receive income from the business but thereafter, continuing income would be at the child's discretion.

If there was no child at the time of Lord Hamish's death, the businesses would continue operation and the major shareholder, Trehorne Trading Company, would receive the total income. Hamish would only ever see a return from the business when a child eventually was born, or if Lord Godfrey Trehorne chose to sell the company, thereby freeing the capital, and returning the original Glendenning investment – without capital growth or interest – to Hamish.

To be written out of his father's will in such a way was a blow to Hamish, but to his credit, other than tightening his features, he made no reaction.

We left Lord Hamish's room, my husband's arm at my waist, and went directly to the parlour where we could discuss this new development.

"Old bastard," Hamish declared as we seated ourselves.

"Hamish!"

"Well, he is. You heard him. If not for this child, we would be destitute when he dies. And if something should happen to the bairn …"

"Don't even think it."

"But, it's irrelevant now, isn't it, providing everything goes well. Shall I call for tea?"

As I poured, Hamish said, "I hope it is a girl."

I looked archly at him. "I thought you'd have preferred a boy, particularly if he's to inherit the business."

The pain in his voice was terrible to hear when he said, "And have him turn out odd like me?"

"You aren't odd," I whispered.

"No, I was simply born with objectionable tastes. In truth, I really don't care either way, providing he or she is healthy."

"I hope that's not just because we'll need the income."

He clucked scoldingly. "Of course not! Haven't I always wanted a child too?"

I made a doubtful face but he went on. "Our marriage will bear fruit and …" he picked up my hand where it rested on my lap, "things will be alright now. Father will not be able to control us after his death."

He kissed my palm and I wondered if I could ever feel affection for him. I had found some small pleasure in his arms that last time, but I knew I could never love him. In fact I doubted I would ever know again that shattering, thrilling, all-consuming passion with which I loved Patrick.

Perhaps though, given time, I may come to know contentment in this marriage. My pregnancy was just the beginning and, despite the blow of his father's news, it was true when Hamish said things would be alright.

I was smiling as the door opened. Sylvie quickly apologised and made to back out.

"Sylvie!" Hamish and I cried in unison.

The door opened a crack, and her face peeked around.

"Join us," Hamish said, rising, "we have joyous news."

CHAPTER 6

I revelled in Sylvie's company. She was witty and intelligent, kind and honest, and moreover, she loved Jemima – who would not!

Our days fell immediately into an agreeable routine: a morning walk along the river's edge – for Sylvie wasn't a rider and it was considered best for my precious baby if I refrained. Afterwards, we breakfasted, then went our separate ways – Sylvie to enjoy her new-found leisure, free from the servile duties she'd performed all her life, and I to consult with Mrs Twigley as to how the running of the house fared, including meal planning and the pantry stores.

The housekeeper and I upheld a perfect parody of household management, both knowing that Lord Hamish maintained a tight control over everything – every penny spent, every morsel of food consumed or wasted, every movement of the staff – all from his sick bed. The details were recorded and presented to him each evening before supper. Upon the old man's demise I expected to inherit the duties and responsibilities that were generally a wife's role – probably quite soon by the look of him – so I treated this time as something of an apprenticeship.

Sylvie and I came together again for the midday meal, after

which we spent our afternoons in chairs in the courtyard of the castle, if the weather was conducive, or in the gallery, if it were not. We read poetry to each other, sewed clothing and knitted stockings to be bundled up for the poor, and chatted like old friends.

It was Sylvie who suggested we should begin making clothes and blankets for my babe and so we set to work, talking and laughing as we knitted and sewed; eating buttery Scottish biscuits and sipping tea. When Hamish returned from his visits to Glasgow, he found his home a nest of peaceful domesticity.

And now, relieved of the burden to conceive, he no longer visited my bed, lending our relationship a sibling feel, which proved quite satisfactory for both of us.

We paid regular visits to his father. That old curmudgeon had reduced his attacks on his son to financial matters, and his assessment of my worthiness had been deferred for the time being. Though I could never consider him a pleasant man, during these quiet, anticipatory months, Lord Hamish was definitely less loathsome. He regarded me as one might a prized brood mare and I was content with this.

After visiting his father, Hamish and I shared a pot of chocolate before the parlour fire and, as the seasons changed and the temperature fell, and evenings closed in earlier each night, we drew our chairs closer to the fireplace, talking quietly of possible names for our child.

"A boy must be named Hamish. It is our tradition." When I grimaced, he added, "Aye, well I don't like it much either, but it's what we do in this family."

"Very well," I said. "But if you get to choose the boy's name, then I shall choose if she is a girl."

"But I quite fancy Mary."

"That's not fair, Hamish. You can't have it all your own way."

He adopted his sulky-child expression but said with a sigh, "Ach, very well. What name would you choose?"

I made a show of thinking it over before finally saying, "I think if we have a daughter, I should like to name her … Mary."

"Oh! You're an impossible wife!" he cried and we laughed together.

❧

Little Marish – a combination of Mary and Hamish – grew within my belly, and as December approached I entered my fourth month of pregnancy. Hamish and I had been married a year when I received a letter from Julia. Some months back I had invited her to visit but I'd not received a response. Now, she was finally replying with an acceptance.

She arrived one afternoon a week before Christmas and I saw her considerable loss of weight immediately. Her freckled face was gaunt and sallow and the bones of her cheeks cast blue smudges beneath her eyes. Her once glorious auburn hair hung dry and limp, and when we greeted one another, she clung to me, shaking uncontrollably.

I led her inside and up to the room that would be hers, and after the servants had delivered her single trunk and withdrawn, she turned to me. Touching my stomach reverently she said, "I'm so glad everything has worked out for you, Alex – after Anne … You deserve this …" and then she seemed to fold at the knees, crumpling to the floor in the middle of the room, her green velvet travelling costume billowing around her, and she burst into tears.

I held her as she cried her heart out, and it was a long time before she could tell me that Deon had called off their engagement, moving to Essex to live with Celia, in defiance of both their families.

I spent that first evening comforting her. We ate together in her room and when Hamish knocked on the door to offer his welcome, I explained my friend's distraught state.

He made a face as he left, muttering something that sounded very much like, "Men can be such bastards."

I smiled to myself, but Julia, unaware of our state of affairs, merely stared after him.

After that first night, the Julia of old returned, teasing, making jokes, lively and spirited, and just as I was beginning to find contentment with my husband and my friends, Hamish and I were invited to a Christmas ball.

Lady Jane Trehorne, newly married to Hamish's neighbour and Lord Hamish's business partner, Laird Godfrey Trehorne, had moved into the district. Laird Trehorne had a huge tract of land on which he raised hairy highland cattle for their meat. Lady Catherine, Jane's unmarried sister, lived with them to keep her sister company – for her brother-in-law's other business interests regularly took him to Newcastle and Edinburgh and beyond. Since they lived reasonably close to us, I invited them for afternoon tea the week before the ball so we could get to know each other.

Catherine and Jane arrived promptly at four o'clock and sat in the parlour sipping tea with Julia, Sylvie and me. At first sight, I wondered why Catherine was unmarried for she was very attractive. Tall and stylishly dressed, she had rich, reddish-brown hair that was scooped on to her crown to fall about her head like a burnished cascade. Her sister, Jane, was smaller and rounder with perfect blonde curls that bobbed neatly about her pretty face.

The conversation flowed effortlessly, for the two women were lively and easy guests. We discussed their upcoming ball and as they departed, they extended their invitation to include Sylvie and Julia. It was as they were leaving that I noted Catherine's assessing gaze fall on Sylvie's hands and a small frown creased her brow. Immediately, with the skill of a courtier, she rearranged her face but Sylvie had also seen her look and self-consciously clasped her hands behind her back.

As the women's coach trundled over the bridge, I grasped Sylvie's elbow and marched indoors. "Come, Julia," I threw over my shoulder, "we've work to do."

In the kitchen, I requested a cup of lemon juice and added to it a spoon of valuable sugar to form a paste. Julia and I took a hand each and scrubbed the mixture into the former maid's hands. After rinsing in warm water, I took some balm that Mrs Twigley had made from lavender oil and we massaged it gently into Sylvie's skin. The change was remarkable and Sylvie beamed gratefully.

∾

The evening of the ball arrived and I wore a new, deep-blue velvet gown, my pregnancy decorously hidden beneath the loose fall of its Empire lines. My hand rested elegantly on Hamish's arm as we entered with Julia and Sylvie behind us.

We were received by Lady Jane and Laird Godfrey and, as Hamish drifted away to speak with an acquaintance, Lady Catherine waved to us. She was exquisite in amber velvet trimmed with black fur, and many heads turned in her direction as she glided across the floor to meet us.

"How wonderful to see you," she purred, but her eyes continually followed a pair of men deep in conversation across the room.

Leaning towards her, my words shielded by my fan, I whispered conspiratorially, "Who is it holds your attention?"

She started and heat flooded her face as she garbled an incoherent response. Stunned by her reaction, I looked to the men again and smothered an inappropriate urge to laugh when I realised she'd been watching Hamish.

As Catherine hurriedly excused herself and vanished into the crowd, my eyes returned to Hamish for I'd noticed something odd about his conversation. The other man's mouth was twisting angrily as he spoke – something one would not expect from a mere acquaintance – and from time to time the stranger's eyes slid in my direction, in a way that was very disconcerting.

"Quite arrogant, that one," said Jane appearing at my side and following my eyes.

"Who is he?" I asked.

She looked at me in some surprise. "Why, you don't know? That is Mr Richard Kintyre – a complete nobody, but one is always required to invite him to these little get-togethers because the ladies love to dance with him and the gentlemen enjoy his jokes – *and* he is your husband's closest friend."

"So that's Richard Kintyre," I murmured to myself, and remembered Hamish's father talking of him.

"Unmarried and disinclined to settle down," Jane continued, "but at the slightest sign he's on the market, I'll ensure Catherine's well away – no money, no name – dreadful match!"

I shouldn't be too worried, I thought to myself, as she turned to address a gardenia-scented matron at her side.

I studied the man. He was certainly attractive with his dark, shoulder-length hair and confident carriage. He stood straight and tall and surveyed the room rather haughtily in his dark green brocade coat, buff trousers and shiny black Hessian boots. He must have sensed my watching for he turned sharply and stared challengingly into my eyes.

Shocked by his bold gaze, I grasped Sylvie's arm so unexpectedly she almost dropped the wine glass she held. "Are you alright?"

"Oh yes, it was … it was the babe … kicking harder than usual … surprised me."

"You've been on your feet a long time," the matron said and Jane turned to me.

"Come, let us sit."

I allowed the fluttering women to lead me to a couch. "I'll be alright …" I insisted, stealing a quick glance over my shoulder, but thankfully Richard had disappeared.

"Nonsense," the gardenia-scented matron said, "Get a usquebaugh into you, good for the bairn – strengthens the blood."

"It is true," said Jane, as I protested, but she was already snapping her fingers at a passing servant.

They brought me a small glass of the fiery liquid and as I uneasily put it to my lips and breathed its fumes, the old anticipatory juices flooded my mouth.

Oh yes …

To the surprise of my attendants, I threw it back in two gulps and it was like welcoming a long lost friend. But I knew then with triumph, that friends came and went, and I was no longer a captive of this particular one. I did, though, continue to be haunted by the hatred on Richard Kintyre's face.

❧

Finally, Christmas arrived and we celebrated well. The castle smelled of roasting meats and spiced puddings and the snow piled high against the stone walls. It lay heavily like a pristine shroud over the land and the herbs and vegetables in the kitchen garden were taken into the greenhouse for protection.

Two weeks into 1815, Julia decided to return home. Though I tried to convince her it was a bad time to travel, she was determined. I understood her original need to escape while her pain over Deon was new, but now that she was stronger she was eager to return to Yorkshire. Sylvie and I waved her off from the bridge that had been cleared of snow, and I wondered when I'd see my friend again.

CHAPTER 7

I visited Ember daily and she came to expect me. Her alert little face peeked over the top of her stall and her whiskery nose nuzzled my hands, seeking a carrot or dried apple pilfered from our hoarded summer stock. I eagerly awaited the day when I'd be able to ride her.

Catherine and Jane called regularly; the four of us, including Sylvie, were quickly becoming friends. Occasionally, they were accompanied by Jane's husband, Godfrey. On those occasions, Hamish joined us and we made a cheerful party.

Watching Catherine laughing and sipping delicately from her tea cup, I decided that she must be enjoying an illicit liaison for I could not imagine such a vibrant, attractive girl having no suitor. I liked the dreamy notion of a secret lover and I smiled to myself.

"Heavens above, Alex," Catherine declared. "Look at you smiling away. If impending motherhood is so joyous a thing, I must consider it for myself. You're positively glowing!"

"Find yourself a husband first," Godfrey grumbled good-naturedly and she made a face at him.

Nevertheless, it was true, as my abdomen grew, I found myself in excellent health. Pregnancy suited me in a way I'd never expected.

My skin, generally quite sallow when forced to remain indoors over winter, had a rosy glow and my hair had become mysteriously tamed. Aggie could dress my hair before breakfast and I knew it would not have escaped its pins by mid-morning.

Hamish was beside himself with excitement. Eagerly attentive, he could not do enough to ensure my comfort. Even my miserly father-in-law opened his crusty old purse and agreed to prepare the nursery with new furnishings. But I was under no illusions for I knew the foundations of my marriage were unstable. The soundness of its structure, its financial stability, its very mortar, was the security brought by this child, and though Hamish and I would never be in love, we at least dealt amicably with one another, and I was surprised to find myself at peace.

❧

Perhaps the acknowledgement of contentment is what tempts fate to tinker with our lives. It happened one afternoon in late January, as Sylvie and I sat in the parlour. We were busily edging a blanket for Marish, our heads bent over our work, and Sylvie stretched to offer some relief to her stiff back.

"I've never seen snow this relentless," she commented. "It is not like this in Devon."

"I imagine not, being so much further south," I said. I tied off my work and put the needle aside, flexing my fingers.

"When it snowed, Monsieur Chartrain used to make iced-cream," she went on.

"Iced-cream?"

"Hmm. He'd take the fresh cream off the milk, whip it with finely ground sugar until it thickened, then bury it beneath the snow. Later, he'd remove it and whip it again. Sometimes he'd add spices or dried summer fruits. Then put it back into the snow to freeze again."

"Sounds delicious," I said, imagining the fruity, icy confection.

"It used to be Patrick's favourite but … he has been very moody since returning from Europe …" Her voice trailed away and by her reflective expression I knew she wanted to say more. I rested my hand on my protruding stomach, unconsciously reassuring Hamish's baby as my heart stirred for my lost lover.

Sylvie was pensive. "Did you know I met your brother Simon?"

"Really?" I was surprised.

"He arrived at Waterville a week before I departed."

"He and Patrick were always close."

Her brow puckered. "It didn't appear so. They argued terribly. They were down at the old summer-house and we – Mrs Bath and I – heard the shouting from the porch. Then, Patrick came striding up the lawn as though possessed by demons. He threw a porch chair through a window – it ended in the breakfast room, and another landed on the lawn. Briggs – you remember the gardener – he was pulling up weeds and the chair barely missed him. Mrs Bath was near tears. She took Master Patrick's arm but he pushed her away and went upstairs to his room."

I listened in horrified disbelief, for the reserved Patrick I remembered would never have behaved so violently, so demonstratively.

"Did you find out what caused it?"

She shook her head. "Your brother left the following day. The incident was not mentioned again."

I sat back in my chair. What on earth could have caused Patrick and Simon to argue so fiercely?

"Patrick had invited his cousin to visit. He'd offered Aden a position managing the estate. When Aden and his wife arrived, Patrick's mood improved, but one night, he became very drunk and … " here she paused and I gestured for her to go on. "Some time during the night, he went to one of the guest-rooms – the one you'd used – and he destroyed everything. He threw the wash bowl and ewer through the window, he smashed the mirror and the chair.

Do you remember the crystal trinket box and vase on the dressing table? He threw them out of the window also – they shattered on the drive below. We were picking up splinters from the gravel for a week."

Suddenly the room felt too hot. With an intense feeling of *déjà vu*, images from a forgotten dream came flooding back. I was crawling on a gravel road, my hands and knees bleeding from broken crockery and glass and I was crying, desperately trying to reach Patrick, and he, beyond my reach, was calling to me, repeating over and over, *it's not too late.*

"Alex …?"

"It's alright, Sylvie. I was reminded of a dream I had … an age ago." I smiled reassuringly though my heart was pounding. "Tell me …"

I was aware at some level that I was about to hurt myself, but continued regardless, "Does Patrick … has he ever mentioned me?"

"He has never mentioned you," she stated flatly. But as I'd grown to know Sylvie, I'd learned that when uncertain, her blue eyes seemed to crystallize like chips of ice as her mind worked over her indecision.

She looked like that now and I said, "What is it?"

Her gaze rested steadily on me and she said, "It's nothing."

"You must tell me."

"I don't think –"

"Sylvie!"

She sighed. "You know that old summer-house?"

I knew it alright. The scene of my swimming lesson, when Pat had pressed his body to mine and I'd thought he was going to kiss me. It had been the cause of one of our many arguments.

I gestured impatiently.

"Two nights before I left Devon, a maid saw an odd glow above the trees – the summer-house was afire. Aden and Briggs and two servants rushed down but it was well alight. I don't know how, but they found Patrick inside … unconscious. He'd have died had they not dragged him out."

My stomach shifted uncomfortably and dampness broke on my brow.

"Lenny, a servant, said the young lord was stinking drunk and delirious … he was mumbling a name that Lenny didn't recognise. He thought it sounded like, *Alex* …"

I breathed slowly through my nose as an appalling and unnamed realisation began to take shape and I stared at Sylvie.

Her face was very solemn. "You were close with him … you were friends … I thought … I thought that was why he would ask for you."

I spoke calmly though my heart pounded and my pulse raced. "We weren't just friends. Sylvie, Patrick and I … we were lovers. I loved him … he said we would marry and … and I believed him."

"But you married Hamish," she reasoned gently. "If you loved Patrick, why –"

"Because of Anne," I spat viciously, as the angry grief I thought I'd overcome now resurfaced. "Because he betrayed me with my own sister!"

"*Anne?*" Sylvie repeated and her pale brows shot up.

I made a derisive snort. "He met her in London and took her to Devon … seducing her at Waterville, and no one the wiser had she not fallen pregnant."

My eyes filled with tears and I slammed my fist into the arm of my chair, causing Jemima, sleeping at my feet, to start. But the pain to my hand felt good in my anger. "You ask why I married Hamish? The Right Honourable Patrick Washburn, future earl and philandering bastard, claimed to love me and wanted to marry me. He loved me so damn much he went directly from bedding me to bedding my sister!" I leapt to my feet and paced the floor. The tears coursed down my cheeks as though a dam had burst. I was incapable of calming myself. "*I love him!*" I cried. "I always have, but I hate him so much it hurts! And you ask why I married Hamish? *Why would I not?*" I dropped to my chair, and wept into my trembling hands.

Sylvie didn't speak. At length I calmed somewhat and fished a handkerchief from my sleeve. She rose and leaned on the marble of the mantle, staring into the fire below. When she turned a stricken face to me, her blue eyes were chips of ice again and her voice was a hoarse whisper. "Who told you that baby was Patrick's?"

"Anne …" I said, blowing my nose and attempting to regain my composure. "She returned to Broughton Hall … in disgrace. They had to … quickly marry her off."

"That child is not Patrick's," Sylvie said cautiously.

I exhaled in annoyance. "Not you too! Anne told me herself – told me everything."

"Then, she lied."

"That's not true and … there's an end to it."

She watched me impassively and repeated with conviction, "That child is not Patrick's. Remember one thing; I was there. I remember it clearly. Patrick had spent the spring at Broughton Hall. He made a brief visit to Waterville before returning to Europe. Anne arrived unexpectedly one night. She was already with child. I know it without a doubt – I know it because I brought them tea in the library and heard her telling him."

A loud buzzing had started in my head and I gripped the arms of my chair and stared at her in horror. "Do you know what you're saying?"

She nodded and crouched before me, taking my two hands in hers. "I heard her as plainly as I hear you now. She said her mother had always planned that they marry. It would be simple to tell the family it was his child. If they acted immediately, no one would know."

I must have been in shock. Perhaps I'd lost my senses, for though I was hearing her words, I was struggling to comprehend … and the buzzing in my head –

"Alex!" Sylvie's face swam before my eyes and her voice came from a great distance away. She shook me gently, "Alex, listen to me! I listened at the door; Mrs Bath and I both. He said he planned to marry someone else. She was crying, but she said he had no right to someone else. She threatened that if he refused her she'd tell the family that he'd seduced and abandoned her. He said, *you would not dare* and she said, *oh wouldn't I?* They argued … raised voices … but Alex, *he did not yield.* She claimed her baby's father was married already and wanted nothing more to do with her …"

The ringing in my ears grew louder and the room began to spin. Sylvie squeezed my hands gently. "Alex do you understand me? It is *not* his child – she didn't spend a single hour beneath that roof. He threw her out …"

∾

There was much scuffling and a cooling cloth was pressed to my brow. Aggie was speaking, her voice panicked, "What happened? Is the bairn a-right?"

"We were talking," Sylvie said, tearfully.

"A pregnant woman will oft swoon," Mrs Twigley said calmly. "Let us get her comfortable instead of blathering about it."

I stirred and Sylvie, close to my ear said, "Alex, can you hear me? Are you alright?"

Aggie brought water in a tall mug and they supported me as I sipped it gratefully. After a minute or two I turned to Mrs Twigley. "I'm much better now. Thank you … I think … I stood up too quickly or something. Please, don't worry. I shall rest awhile."

Aggie and Mrs Twigley exchanged doubtful glances but finally agreed to leave. As the door closed behind them, Sylvie burst into tears and could not apologise enough. "I shouldn't have told you," she berated herself. "A woman … in your condition … how stupid, stupid, *stupid!*"

I sat numbly, coming to terms with the enormity of what I'd just learned, unable to suppress an immediate and intense regret over my marriage. The innocent growing within me was suddenly a shackle, preventing an impulsive flight to my lover's side. Ashamed of my disloyal thoughts, because I did truly love this baby, I could not help wishing I wasn't pregnant, for my future was now clearly before me: a loveless eternity, whereas I could have been with Patrick. And Hamish – he hadn't asked for any of this, but in thinking of him, his inability to be a true husband, my resentment of him and his predilections bubbled anew within me.

Anne's face drifted before my eyes and with sudden intuitive clarity I knew – she'd been about to confess. That morning, as I was departing from Broughton Hall, she had wanted to admit her lie but could not bring herself to do it.

And then there was Father's letter telling me how Anne's babe bore no resemblance to Patrick at all, and was in fact dark-haired and swarthy. He'd said the child must be a throwback to a distant cousin, but he'd known the truth. His concerted effort to contact Patrick in Europe had been a great charade to appease my mother's outrage, to shield his son from the claws of his wife's and stepdaughter's avaricious grasp.

All the evidence was there, with Mother's quick condemnation, and Anne's convincing lies, and I, among his accusers, had betrayed Patrick in the worst possible way.

I was distraught. I spent that afternoon and the next day hunched before the fire in my room, weeping intermittently. They brewed laudanum, forcing me to drink the sickly-sweet potion, which served to calm me and aid my sleep, but my mind remained in turmoil.

Why hadn't I trusted him? *Why?* He'd begged me to be strong and true yet what had I done? At the first word of doubt I had abandoned him while he wasn't able to defend himself.

I said as much to Sylvie who, in trying to comfort me, insisted that I could not have known when it was my own sister's word. But I was inconsolable and my stomach was so tied up with emotion that I had no appetite, nor any inclination to face the day – preferring to linger in my nightdress at my hearth.

Hamish visited. He sat beside me, his face a picture of concern, but I could not tell him what ailed me. Confused and worried by my sudden, inexplicable depression, he pestered endlessly. With his expression set petulantly, he complained that I was endangering our bairn.

Finally, foolishly, I relented and repeated Sylvie's story. Did I think he would understand? Sympathise? Was there ever a more dim-witted woman than me?

Suddenly his patience evaporated. Grasping my icy hands, he dragged me into my dressing room and from my wardrobe, in a fit of temper, he tossed bloomers, stockings, petticoats at me. "Get dressed!" he bellowed ferociously. "How stupid I am, how *bloody stupid*!" He pulled a dress from its hanger. "You said you'd spent one night together ...*one* – put this on – you didn't tell me it was a full-blown love affair! And now I find out my wife's obsessed with another man. Oh, how the pair of you must have laughed up your sleeves at me!"

"That's not true, Hamish."

"I said, *get dressed*!" He paced up and down the floor as I began dressing. "You know what? I don't care what you think of me or our marriage, but that's my bairn! If it were not for your condition, I'd have you thrashed – it's all you deserve! Have you no conscience? How you must wish it were *his* brat."

I flushed guiltily and buttoned my dress. "You listen to me ..." he ceased his pacing and wagged his finger threateningly in my face. "We're married, whether it is convenient for you and your lover or not. You're *my* wife and you'll bloody well act like it!"

I bristled angrily and rounded on him. "Then act like a husband you –"

Before I'd realised it his hand had shot out and he'd struck my face so hard my head snapped and I tasted blood. Recoiling in horror, I backed against the dressing table but he was unrepentant.

"You're carrying my heir! You will conduct yourself accordingly!"

"Are you quite finished?" I made my voice contemptuous – he must not know how his violence had shaken me.

He strode to the door and turned with his hand on the latch. "Lady Jane, Laird Godfrey and Lady Catherine are coming for supper. You will behave as befitting the lady of the house or so help me, you think you regret your marriage now …"

Out in the hall he shouted for Aggie, "Go attend your mistress!"

But Sylvie appeared in the doorway, her eyes haunted. "Alex …?"

"I'm alright," I said shakily. "Please, I don't want the servants seeing me like this."

She nodded. As Aggie arrived, Sylvie whispered something and the maid disappeared. My friend closed the door and turned to me.

"Your lip is swollen."

"I can feel it." Rinsing a cloth in cool water, I held it to my mouth as she levelled her wise blue eyes on me.

"Say it!" I demanded.

"He was wrong to strike you," she said quietly. "But his pregnant wife pines for another man."

She ignored my contemptuous snort and went on, "It does not excuse him from striking you – nothing can, but … it is over, Alex. Whatever you and Patrick may or may not have had … it's over. *You are married.* You have a baby to think of and a whole life ahead of you – friends, more babies …"

I shook my head. "You don't understand. This is no true marriage. There'll not be other babies. This one is so precious …"

And then, with an immense sense of relief, I told her the truth about Hamish's preferences, and when I'd finished she nodded sagely. "I know. I overheard Beth once. Apparently he prefers them young – too young by most standards. Even so, railing against things you cannot change will only make them worse. Think of this child – there is your hope for happiness."

With no alternative, that evening I played the congenial hostess to Hamish's charming host, and our guests enjoyed an evening of fine food and wine and pleasant conversation. And that night, alone in my bed, I wept for my lost love, the pain I'd caused us both, and the hopelessness of my future.

CHAPTER 8

Deception is an easy art to practice. Determinedly, I erected a happy public façade that crumbled in the privacy of my room each night where I cried myself to sleep.

I became the perfect hostess, impending mother and doting wife, and I put Hamish's twisted infidelities, along with other unpleasant things, from my mind.

February arrived, as did a letter from Gerrard announcing that Maria had given birth to a large, healthy boy, named Dudley, for Simon's and my papa. There'd apparently, never been a prouder father than Simon as he beheld his son, and having only one arm did not preclude him from holding and playing with little Dudley. It was widely expected that this child would be spoiled rotten in no time.

I expressed my congratulations to my brother and his wife, but my letter was otherwise brief. I found it difficult to know how to correspond with my stepfather now that I realised his role in my situation. For even as I understood he had been protecting his son, I knew now that he'd been in contact with Patrick all the while. He could have trusted me. If only he had told me …

Meanwhile, my social engagements continued, and through

our connections with the Trehornes, our circle of friends widened, and during a soiree at a house in Paisley, we met an interesting young man by the name of Quinn Atherton. He was the archetypal Scotsman with a mane of carroty hair, stocky build and broad cheerful grin – and he took an immediate fancy to Sylvie.

Quinn began visiting the castle. Ostensibly they were social calls to Hamish, but his laughing grey eyes followed Sylvie's every move. She, herself, took it all in her stride, neither encouraging nor discouraging, and since we all enjoyed Quinn's company, he became a regular guest in our parlour.

I'd entered my sixth month of pregnancy and by all accounts epitomised domestic happiness, and since Hamish was eager to keep up appearances, he shelved his anger.

Even his father had brightened of late, no doubt anticipating his longed-for grandchild. His uncharacteristic affability extended to allowing Bony out of the sick-room and the young dog flourished. Finally allowed to stretch his limbs, he spent his days galloping through the castle grounds, chasing chickens, tripping up servants and getting into all manner of mischief.

One evening, Hamish and I sat alone in the parlour, as the fire reduced to orange coals. Enjoying the peace of the moment, I rested my head against his shoulder and felt him stiffen warily.

Ignoring his response, I smoothed the velvet of my dress over my stomach. "Look, Hamish." We watched in silence as our child stirred, the small movements made odd little bulges in my belly and Hamish sucked in his breath in wonderment.

Since Hamish's one outburst, provoked admittedly by my foolish confession, Patrick's name had not been mentioned. Perhaps he assumed it was over and I was absorbed in impending motherhood.

But though I loved Patrick, fiercely; my life was here, with the husband at my side and the child growing within me.

Given our choice, Hamish and I would both be with others. But while his choice was socially unacceptable – illegal in fact – mine was unachievable. We'd been reluctant participants in this marriage, neither having been consulted, but if we should find some respect and trust for each other … perhaps through this child …

This child – the manacle binding me to this marriage.

It was an appalling idea curling like an evil tendril into my mind, and I dismissed it for the perfidious notion it was. But it returned, a restless serpent slithering, insinuating its way into my thoughts.

It was inconceivable that I could think this way. I wanted this child. I loved this child. And accordingly my future was with Hamish, the father of this child, and with whom I sat sipping chocolate spiced with nutmeg while the snow drifted past the window and Jemima snored before the fire.

So with our child slumbering in my belly, I turned my face towards my future.

And perhaps in some way Hamish knew it, for that night, he came to my bed. Mindful of my burgeoning stomach, we slept – nothing more – cuddled like spoons, his body curled protectively around mine.

And my traitorous heart dreamed of my lost lover.

❧

As old Lord Hamish's humour continued to improve, Bony spent increasing hours roaming the castle halls. He trotted happily about, following besottedly in Jemima's wake and, having lost weight, his coat gleamed. Hamish and I spent our afternoons together in the parlour – reading and stitching baby clothes.

Quinn regularly braved the snow in his horse-drawn sleigh, and when the weather was not conducive to his return journey, he was forced to acquaint himself with our guest room. I secretly hoped he was more acquainted with Sylvie's room but that was no business of mine – unless, of course, his visits bore fruit, in which case Hamish was sure to press for their marriage.

He was an engaging fellow, Quinn. He could never be called

handsome, with his fiery, untidy hair and his wide face, but with his agreeable demeanour and lack of guile, he was quite endearing. He was managing to turn Sylvie's head rather effectively and they made a well-matched couple, for she was a small person and Quinn himself was not tall. Interestingly, now that Sylvie no longer wore her burgundy Thorncliffe livery, she chose soft shades of blue, which favoured her eyes and elfin prettiness.

She and Quinn often joined Hamish and me in the parlour, where they bent their heads over games of cards. Quinn had taught Sylvie to play, and their games extended for hours.

From our settee, Hamish and I observed the subtle signs of courtship, and nodded knowingly to one another, sipping our chocolate like a pair of indulgent parents.

One such afternoon, I must have dozed for I was startled into wakefulness by Sylvie's victorious shout. "There! I've beaten you again."

Quinn sat back and ran his hands through his tousled hair, "Och, but you set me up beautifully there. I taught you too well."

"My apologies," she said, insincerely. "Best keep your strategies to yourself next time."

"That I certainly will."

Hamish yawned and put his book aside. "I feel I've been set in stone. Anyone care to walk?"

Quinn and Sylvie said they would and at my nod, Hamish rose and pulled me off the settee since I could no longer rise from a chair with dignity or ease.

"You're huge, Alex." Quinn said. Hamish frowned, but Quinn had a refreshing propensity for plain speaking that I liked. "Are you certain you're not having a Mary *and* a Hamish?"

I made a horrified face. "Good heavens, Quinn! One at a time, please."

"Let's go into the outer bailey," Hamish interrupted. "They were shovelling the snow away this morning. It should be a pleasant stroll."

We followed him into the hall, and from somewhere in the vast castle, the sound of Bony joyously pursuing Jemima bounced around the halls. The two dogs played like youngsters, chasing each other around the labyrinthine corridors. I smiled at the sounds; the knowledge that Bony was finally free to enjoy canine affairs pleased me.

We approached the stairs leading to the entry hall, and the other three went first for I was slower. I gripped the banister to support my bulk and Hamish stood by the newel post watching from below. "Are you alright? Do you need my hand?"

I shook my head. "No, I'm slow, that's all."

Jemima, energetic as a puppy for all her ten years, galloped along the corridor and plunged down the stairs, barrelling past me in two or three leaps. I laughed out loud, for Bony's youth usually saw him in the lead, but Jemima had got away from him today. He threw himself down the stairs in hot pursuit.

I was about halfway down when, without warning, he slammed into the backs of my legs.

Somehow Bony had misjudged his path. Dog and I both yelped in pain and surprise. He tumbled, a squealing ball of fur bouncing down the stairs, but I barely registered his cries for my knees had collapsed beneath me and I fell, my belly dragging me forwards. The stairs rose up and instinctively I flung out my hands, bracing for the impact. I heard a sickening crack as my left wrist took the full brunt of my fall. I tumbled down the staircase, flailing and desperate, until I hit the stone floor of the hall with a loud smack.

My womb contracted in flooding, nauseating, relentless pain. And I could hear, as though from a great distance away, my own terrified screams.

CHAPTER 9

They told me that I slept for three days from exhaustion and blood loss. Doctor Gregor was called and they feared I might die – and I wished I had died.

I had lost my baby – a little girl – my Mary. Her tiny body had been crushed and wrenched from mine. Had I willed it? Had my unbidden and deplorable thoughts somehow provoked fate? I tortured myself with guilt.

When Lord Elginbury was informed, they said he'd roared with anger and grief. As Sylvie reported it, he'd clenched his fist at the heavens and cursed God for bringing such ill-fortune upon his house; an accursed, abnormal son, and a daughter-in-law incapable of holding a child within her – a woman's most basic function.

Hamish himself was distracted beyond reason. He took Bony into the yard and kicked the dog to within an inch of his short life. It was only through Quinn that Bony was saved. Summoning a stable boy, he forcibly dragged Hamish away and, scooping the broken, whimpering animal out of the blood-stained snow, took him home in his sleigh.

It was days before I was well enough to drink a bowl of broth. Sylvie and Aggie took turns at my bedside, and though Hamish visited, he sat in heavy, brooding silence, before drifting away.

My broken wrist was bound and immobile. It ached relentlessly and I was constantly fidgeting in a futile attempt to find relief. Mrs Twigley kept me on strong doses of laudanum, which helped the physical pain, but nothing could allay the cavernous wound created by the loss of my baby.

At times the grief was so great that I lay in bed wondering how it was I continued to breathe, how my faculties continued to function, how my heart continued to beat. My body slowly began to mend, but my soul remained raw and bleeding.

I cried often, great soundless tears that turned my pillow into a sodden lump. And all the while, Hamish continued to perch by my side like a stone sentinel. I wished he would say something. Finally, ten days after my fall, his voice was entirely without emotion when he said, "You called his name in your sleep."

There was nothing I could say. I stared at my wrist, itchy beneath its tight bindings. My hand was pale and bloodless, swollen with yellowing bruises showing from under the dressing. It lay limp and useless, throbbing vaguely on the counterpane. "You're free now. Isn't that what you wanted?" There was no acrimony in his voice, only a resigned weariness that brought a lump to my throat.

At that moment, I wanted nothing more than for him to take me in his arms and tell me it would be alright. "We …" it was a croak, and I reached for him hopefully. "We could … try again … when I'm well."

His face crumpled and he passed a hand over his eyes. "Oh, Alex …" He rose and left the room.

Once I was able to rise from my bed, Quinn visited. I was sitting in a chair beside the window with a knitted rug over my knees when he came in with Sylvie and handed me a posy of dried flowers. I was very pleased to see him, and told him so as he kissed my cheek.

"Thank you for rescuing Bony," I said. "How does he fare?"

Quinn's expressive face split with a grin. "Recovering. He had a severe break in a front leg, among other injuries, and will likely wind up with a limp. He will hate cold weather, but he'll be eager to play with Jemima again."

At that Sylvie and I exchanged glances and Sylvie touched Quinn's sleeve lightly. "Dear, I don't think the dog should be returned here. Hamish said the other day if he ever again sees the despicable cur – his words – he'd finish what he started."

"He means it," I added.

Quinn smiled ruefully. "Very well. I've just become a dog owner."

I was happy with that for I held no animosity toward the huge, clumsy clod of a dog, who was entirely without meanness or aggression, and certainly not deserving of the punishment Hamish had administered.

Meanwhile, the growing warmth between Sylvie and Quinn touched my heart. Honest and without pretence, it threw my relationship with Hamish into sharp contrast. Like a proud parent I watched their accord grow and flourish, averting my eyes if I intercepted a special glance between them. Quinn's wooing had lent a lightness to Sylvie's step and her eyes glistened happily.

It was several weeks before I was strong enough to write to Simon. I wished him well in his new role of father, and then gave a diluted version of my accident, though this was not entirely my reason for writing.

My discussion with Sylvie had disturbed me, so I decided to tell Simon what I'd learned of Anne's lies. I remembered he had not believed Anne's tale, though he suggested marriage to Hamish would be for the best. I wondered if he'd known more than he'd revealed. I felt the answer lay in why he went to Devon, and implored him to tell me the reason he and Patrick had argued.

Knowing Simon would give careful consideration to his response, I did not expect an immediate reply.

In the interim, I continued to receive letters from Gerrard. At last, finally admitting the worst kept secret in Yorkshire, he'd moved permanently to Mrs Jamieson's residence in Leeds, taking Meg with him.

Hamish had become very distant. He took the loss of our child much worse than I could ever have anticipated, though I was certain it was purely for financial reasons. He blamed Bony for bumping me, blamed me for falling, blamed himself for descending the stairs instead of remaining at my side, and he blamed God for letting it happen.

After having to be physically restrained from kicking the dog to death, he could not face Quinn, and he could not look at Sylvie without seeing the sympathy on her face.

Jane and Catherine visited to offer their condolences, and before them Hamish was caring and attentive toward me. Yet no sooner had their coach rumbled back across the bridge, he had withdrawn from me once more.

Aggie said that a little grave had been marked with an expensive granite headstone in the Glendenning section of the local kirk. Mary Elizabeth Susanna Glendenning had been lovingly interred in her miniature white coffin, inlaid with gold doves and lined with pink satin. Aggie brushed the tears from her eyes as she described the brief ceremony that had been conducted while I remained more dead than alive.

"Elizabeth Susanna?" I asked.

"My lord's grandmothers."

"Oh … of course."

❧

As March became April, my wrist healed and my body resumed its slim shape and, though I felt physically well, my heart still grieved and, strangely, I missed Hamish greatly. I had Sylvie's company, but it was Hamish I needed for Mary had been of us both — we should have been a comfort to each other at this time. Hamish was now an infrequent visitor in his own home. I sat alone in the parlour one evening, eyeing a decanter of usquebaugh from across the room. How I longed to obliterate the pain and loneliness and grief. What luxury! But I knew I would not succumb.

My memories were well alive – my lost lover, my unwitting betrayal, my dead child. And if that wasn't enough, the Gods had decreed I would witness the slow decomposition of the only source of hope remaining to me – my marriage. Though it was an obligatory and loveless arrangement, I had hoped to raise from these infertile grounds a companionable future with a family of my own.

The brief flutter within my womb had been a blessing but as it was lost, any chance Hamish and I had had was gone. So fleetingly sparking to life; so quickly and permanently extinguished.

Yet my dreams continued to be haunted by guilt. Never could I forgive myself for my disloyal thoughts – however unbidden – prior to my accident. Could I in some way have contributed to Mary's loss? Had those deceitful thoughts planted a seed in my subconscious?

Atonement perhaps, or a need to return to a place of hope, whatever it was, caused me to reach for my husband. If we were to have any future we must fill the desolate void in our hearts. I spoke with Hamish but his response was cold. Undaunted, I beseeched him to come to me but when I reached for him, he pulled away. His indifference tore me apart but I knew that to claw our marriage back from the brink I must become pregnant.

Then one evening I heard him come in late, moving about his room and settling for the night, and I thought longingly of those times, so few in number, when we'd slept in each other's arms.

When all was silent, I slipped from my bed and lit a candle. Holding it high, I tried the door adjoining our rooms. It was locked.

Stepping back in dismay, I stared at it – he was now locking me out? Well, I would not be deterred for, as he himself pointed out, I was his wife!

I padded along the cold hall floor on bare feet and paused outside his room. The latch lifted soundlessly and I pushed the door open.

He stirred in his bed behind the heavy velvet curtaining, drawn against the chill of the night. "Hamish?" I whispered.

There was a vague, muted response in the dark, a murmur, a sigh, and I crept closer, my candle held aloft. I pulled back the drapes.

The revealing yellow arc of candlelight illuminated two naked men, one on all fours, the other – my husband – on his knees, thrusting from behind.

Choking, I fell back in horror. Hamish looked up and as his eyes met mine, his lips drew back to bare his teeth in ecstatic release. With a frenzied cry and violent shudder, he collapsed over the other man's back in a gasping climax, intensified, I knew with disgust, by my presence.

Swaying in revulsion, I dropped my candle and it sputtered out. Darkness closed in like a suffocating blanket. I fled to the sanctity of my room, my fist pressed against my teeth to hold back the sickness flooding my mouth. My door slammed shut and my knees buckled. I lurched drunkenly toward my washstand where my stomach convulsed, violently expelling my supper into the pretty porcelain bowl.

When the retching finally subsided, I staggered to my solitary bed to lay trembling with shock, listening to the sounds in the hall; muffled whispers, a slammed door, urgent footsteps receding down the corridor.

Tears oozed from the corners of my eyes and trickled through the hair at my temples. My heart raced uncontrollably and every time I closed my eyes the appalling vision of Hamish's contorted face rushed at me.

ॐ

Hamish and I were never to speak of the incident. I could not endure the thought of his touching me again, I'd die of revulsion if he did for that image of my husband straining over a naked man was ever there to sicken me. Just to have Hamish look at me made me feel unclean.

I tried to understand my reaction, after all, I'd known his persuasion. But seeing with one's own eyes, and the pleasure he'd derived from my witnessing the act, was more than I could bear.

CHAPTER 10

Brightly-coloured wildflowers valiantly broke through the slowly thawing earth along the banks of the Clyde. From where I sat in my window, I watched their cheerful heads nodding in the early spring breeze and refused to think about a woodland floor somewhere in Yorkshire, where new spears of green were pushing through a layer of earth and forest debris, to blossom as irises in the shape of a heart. It was their second spring now but they existed in a different time.

The surface of the river shifted and drifted, its secrets hidden in its impenetrable grey depths. Some said the waters of Scotland were bottomless, that they were a series of subterranean channels linking sea to sea. They said that mysterious creatures of prehistory lurked within their colourless depths.

I should like to visit that place the monster was said to inhabit. Once, I could have asked Hamish to take me there and he'd have obliged. But now … now we could barely look at one another.

During this time, Sylvie was a true companion – thoughtful of my needs and protective of my emotions. And of course, there was my ever faithful Jemima. Daily, I gave thanks for their company, but my strained relations with Hamish were too overwhelming, so one afternoon I confided to Sylvie the event I'd witnessed. She listened quietly and showed no surprise, but her sadness was evident in her face.

Any germinating affection I'd entertained for Hamish had been seared from my heart by shame, disgust, and bitterness that night. There was no escape, and there was no turning back. I felt battle-scarred, emotionally lifeless. Even my throbbing love for Patrick lay still, for my soul was a wasteland of grief and deceit.

On those rare occasions when Hamish was home we were as enemies, for even strangers would politely acknowledge one another. Sylvie joined us for most meals, though she, too, was affected by the strained atmosphere as we mutely served ourselves from plates and bowls, eating in silence before Hamish left the castle for the evening.

The only words Hamish and I spoke concerned his ailing father and we practised a travesty of normality by paying regular visits, as though we were united, as though we were making every attempt to become parents.

If he was not fooled, the old man was beyond caring. Mary's loss had taken its toll on him, as it had on all of us. His fire and fight had gone, leaving a shrunken husk of a man reconciled to his fate. Hamish and I were as eager to be away from his father as we were to escape each other. Immediately upon leaving Lord Hamish's room, we went our separate ways.

Tensions came to a head one evening when Sylvie was absent from the supper table. Hamish broke his silence. "It is all your doing, you know," he said bitterly.

My spoon paused in mid air. I stared at him. "What is all my doing?"

"You're so completely obsessed with that … that … *Patrick*," he spat the name like it was poison on his tongue, "You willed our bairn to die."

"Oh, Hamish …" I cried. "You cannot possibly believe that!"

His sardonic smile twisted his ordinarily pleasant features. "That mongrel dog did you a service."

Tears sprang into my eyes. "How can you say this? I wanted that child, Hamish. As much as you; perhaps more. You knew this for I begged that we be as man and wife."

"No doubt missing the touch of your man – a *real* man, isn't that right? Isn't that what you were thinking?"

"I shan't listen to this." Gathering my composure, I pushed back my chair. My knees shook as I stood before him. "It was an accident, and I lost our baby."

"A rather convenient accident."

His words sliced into me with the knife-edge of guilt I'd been carrying, and blood began pounding in my temples.

"I'm a healthy woman!" I whispered viciously. "I could be with child again now if you … if you did not prefer sharing your bed with men! And boys," I added unwisely.

He flushed angrily and leaned forward in his chair. "You think I would touch you now? My bairn died because of you and your little love affair!"

"That's not true!"

"A perverted love affair with your brother. Any wonder I find men more attractive than you."

I made a face of disgust. "You're jealous," I hissed putting as much venom into the words as I could. "And you're right I do miss him, for he at least knows how to pleasure a woman. You don't even know –"

Lights exploded in my head. The force of his clenched fist to my temple sent my head slamming into the wall – hard. I crumpled to the floor, dazed, at his feet. To my horror, he lashed out with his boot. He kicked me once … twice … again and again … in the stomach, legs, head – until finally he grew breathless.

He glared down at me. The shock of what he'd just done was plain on his face, but as I cowered before him in fear and pain, he straightened and his chin jutted out with new empowerment. "Do not test me wife, or there'll be more of the same."

Without another word, he slammed the door as he left the room.

So now it was war and he was capable of greater violence than I'd imagined. Sick at heart, sore and bleeding, I dragged myself to my feet, gasping in agony, and slowly hauled myself up the stairs to my room.

CHAPTER 11

"Napoleon is back!"

Five heads swivelled to the door as Hamish entered with an air of great importance to make his announcement. Sylvie, Quinn and I were entertaining the ladies, Catherine and Jane. It was the first comfortably warm day since snow had thawed and they'd driven over in their new phaeton to invite us to Laird Godfrey's birthday supper. We gazed at Hamish in stunned surprise since the latest we'd heard was that Napoleon had abdicated and the allies had placed Louis XVIII on the French throne.

"He's back?" Catherine asked. She tilted her head coquettishly to look up at him from beneath her lashes. Hamish perched on the arm of her chair and smiled in return.

If you want him, take him — with my blessing, I thought scornfully as she touched his hand. "Please tell us what you've learned, Hamish."

Hamish smiled for her alone and said, "Well, Bonaparte quickly grew tired of exile on Elba, and last month showed up in the South of France with twelve hundred men."

"Must've been plotting for some time," I said, but only Quinn acknowledged my comment. He gave a thoughtful nod.

"Good heavens," Jane breathed. "What of the French king, then?"

"He panicked … fled to Brussels. Bonaparte marched right in and by the twentieth had arrived in Paris – in triumph."

"Are they talking war again?" Catherine asked.

"Wellington is calling for troops. Russians, Prussians, Austrians – they're all gathering in Belgium. And they're calling back all those just returned from the Peninsular War."

He turned to me then, and his mouth curled in a sly smile. "I imagine that means your brother, my dear. They say it will be a particularly violent clash. A fight to the death."

"Was your brother on the Peninsular?" asked Quinn.

"They both were, and they are Sylvie's brothers too," I said quietly, my eyes on Hamish.

"They have been lucky so far," Sylvie said.

"Ach!" Hamish scoffed. "You can hardly say that Simon was lucky."

"He could be dead," she responded hotly, then turned quickly to Quinn. "My stepbrother was wounded quite badly."

I clasped my hands together tightly to still the urge to slap the smug look from my husband's face.

Catherine and Jane, perhaps sensing the undercurrents at play, remained silent, their heads turning this way and that, following the discussion.

"How is it, Hamish, that news of Napoleon's return seems to please you?" asked Jane archly.

"Now, my dear lady," Hamish said smoothly. "Surely you, a Scotswoman born and bred, would welcome any event that inconvenienced the English?"

Catherine laughed gaily. "That we *all* would."

"Regardless of the loss of innocent lives?" Quinn asked. "The Scots were on the Peninsular too."

"Indeed," I said facetiously, "my husband would discount this, as he discounts his time at the English court, where he took full advantage of all the conveniences and privileges to be had there."

Hamish glared at me. "I was accompanying my father – he was on assignment – as you well know."

"The English–Scots rivalry is most tedious and outdated," Jane interjected. "One would think, since we've all been occupying the same island for centuries, we'd have grown more tolerant of one another."

She glanced at me, seeking and finding solidarity. I raised my tea cup in salute. Turning to Quinn, she said, "You're Scots. What are your thoughts?"

I didn't hear Quinn's response for Catherine, encouraged by the difference of purpose between Hamish and me, had thrown herself into the breach. Touching Hamish's hand with her manicured fingers, she said quietly, "I agree with you, Hamish." She'd positioned herself perfectly, affording him an excellent view of her bosom, and unaware of Hamish's true nature, the silly flirt parted her lips to show her pearly teeth.

I'd have laughed out loud had I not been so annoyed, for he was clearly torn between responding to her coquetry for the sake of taunting me, and turning away – his instinctive reaction to a woman's attentions.

For several undecided seconds, he held her gaze and I held my breath, the three of us unaware that Sylvie was watching. As usual, the foil to any awkward situation, she leaned forward and jiggled the teapot. "Would anyone like more tea?"

Later, as we farewelled our visitors, I turned to my husband. "How long do you intend leading Catherine on in her imagined dalliance?"

"Who says it is imagined?" he rejoined smartly.

Laughing aloud at his swaggering attempt to play the jealousy game, I said, "Oh, Hamish, don't be ridiculous. As if she could satisfy your oblique tastes. The least you could do is *warn* her."

"What would you know about it?" he asked smugly.

"I think I know quite a bit about it," I replied, equally smugly.

"Really? Did you ever consider that your experiences in my bed were unique?" He leaned conspiratorially towards me. "Perhaps my degree of interest is a comment about my partner."

Anger seethed within me and I gripped a handful of my skirt in my fist. "You're beneath contempt," I snarled between my teeth.

He laughed loudly, as though hearing the funniest joke and glanced around at the footman by the door as if to share it. Sobering, he leaned toward me, "You wish I were. But your problem is that you married me of your own free will … left your home and friends … too stupid or too prideful to discover the truth about your sister's pregnancy. Then you decided it was our bairn preventing you from fleeing to your lover. And now he'll be going back to the war – probably to die – and even if he wasn't, you know he'd never want you again because you condemned him without trial and married me. Now, of course, our marriage has been exposed for the pathetic opportunistic sham it always was, you're blaming me."

His uncomfortably accurate summation of our situation struck me dumb.

"In any case," he said brightly and, taking my arm, strolled with me into the castle like any casually happy couple, "I shall be going out tonight – but not to my usual haunt. Rather, to a pretty little inn on the road to Glasgow where a discreetly-disguised young lady has offered her comfort during a difficult time in my marriage."

We paused at the foot of the stairs and I stared aghast as his words sunk in. Bowing with exaggerated respect he said, "And you, my *dear* Lady Elginbury, shall sleep alone in the bed you've made for yourself."

As he ascended the stairs, his laughter echoing off the stone walls, and I hated him with an intensity that would see me happily pour spirits on the man and set him alight. And as for Catherine! She would not step foot in this house again. A curtly worded note to the girl's brother-in-law and benefactor would see to that!

❧

"She *what!*"

The roar jolted me into dazed wakefulness. It had been an unusually warm day for this time of year, and I'd taken advantage of it by going outside with a cushion and a book. Propped against the ancient castle wall to catch the afternoon sun as it dropped behind the stables, the warmth soon lulled me into a light slumber.

"Where in hell is she?"

I winced at the crick in my neck as Hamish burst from the main doors and glared about the bailey before spotting me. He marched over, face aflame beneath his black hair, brandishing a single sheet of paper.

"You see this?" he bellowed. "You see this, you bloody interfering bitch!" He waved the page an inch from my face.

Jemima whined beside me in concern and a pair of maids stuck their heads out of an upstairs window to curiously ogle the commotion.

"What d'you think you were doing writing to Laird Godfrey? Who d'you think you are?"

My brain remained foggy from my doze and my limbs were heavy and sun-drunk. He leaned over me threateningly as I struggled to my feet.

"Well …?" he demanded. "Shut up dog!" He aimed a boot at Jemima, who yelped more in surprise than pain.

Leaning against the wall, and slightly less intimidated, I said calmly, "What are you talking about?"

"This, you *blasted idiot!*" he screamed and spittle hit my face. He slapped the letter with his free hand. "*This! This!* Read it!" He grasped a handful of my hair and pulled my face towards the page.

"Hamish *stop!*" I cried, clutching at the hand wrenching my scalp. "I don't know what –"

"*Read!*" he roared, flinging me backwards so that my head struck the stone wall.

I gasped with the sharp pain. "Hamish, please calm down."

I touched the back of my head and detected wetness there. My hand came away bloodied but the sight of it did nothing to cool his temper. He scrunched the page up tightly and threw it to the ground.

"Read it and deal with it. *You're* responsible for this mess – you fix it, and in future, stay out of my bloody business." He hurled himself past a knot of transfixed stable-boys. "Show is over! Back to work before I flagellate the lot of you!"

I sank back to my pillow and stroked Jemima's head gently with a shaking hand. "It's alright, girl," I said, breathing with focus to calm myself. A dull ache had started in the back of my head and I hoped the wound would quickly stop bleeding.

Picking up the scrunched paper, I smoothed it out on my lap and read.

Glasgow 5 April 1815

My Laird Elginbury,

I regret my position, which without preamble I shall address. I have been forced to express my disapproval of your daughter-in-law, Lady Alexandra Glendenning.

Two days previous, I received, to my great concern, a missive from Lady Elginbury which does make grave accusation against my sister-in-law, Lady Catherine Eddington. It appears Lady Elginbury accuses her husband of engaging in a clandestine liaison with Lady Catherine, a woman of flawless morals, who, during her residence beneath my roof has conducted herself at all times decorously, and with dignity.

The accusations levelled by your daughter-in-law are intolerably insulting, and grossly offensive. Further, Lady Elginbury has indicated that she intends to make public the relationship between her husband and my sister-in-law. She aims to ensure that Lady

Catherine will no longer be welcomed in polite society and that she will personally facilitate the destruction of her husband's, your son's, reputation and that of my sister-in-law with it.

Laird Elginbury, I am sure I need not remind you of the backing the Trehorne Trading Company has provided the business ventures of Glendenning Associated Importers in the Orient. I expect you will not underestimate the import of our support of your cause as we are the majority shareholder. Nor need I remind you that without our patronage your organisation will be required to seek financial assistance elsewhere, a situation I trust you would be eager to avoid.

I do not believe our business relationship ought to suffer at the hands of a silly, irresponsible woman, whose rampant imagination has been allowed to run unchecked. However, I am a man of business and have a reputation to uphold. I do not anticipate maintaining business activities with one whose own household is outside his control.

My sister-in-law is quite distressed that she has been the subject of Lady Elginbury's fantasies. Make no mistake, this situation is dangerous to our business arrangement. My lawyers have already drafted documents that will bring about the dissolution of our arrangement – I need only sign them.

My sister-in-law requires that Lady Elginbury publicly offer her apologies at my birthday supper next week in order to stay my hand. If not, Sir, I shall sign the documents and my lawyers will submit them to yours.

Until such time, I remain your partner in business,
Laird Godfrey Trehorne

I clenched my fists in rage as I pictured Catherine's flirting, simpering face. And Hamish – odious man – had told me of their rendezvous himself.

Catherine, the scheming bitch, had not only convinced Godfrey of her innocence – enough to threaten his withdrawal from a business enterprise – but had accused me of *fantasising*, as though I were unhinged.

I could see the angered pounding of my heart through the bodice of my gown. Catherine's flirtation was genuine – of that I was convinced, but Hamish's response was borne of flattery and a desire to upset me. As was his declaration that he was meeting … *someone who has offered comfort during a difficult time in my marriage.*

He'd wanted to wound me, but he'd never have foreseen my writing to Laird Godfrey – that must have come as a huge surprise and was the reason for his fury.

My heart beat was returning to normal, though my fingers were stiff from being clenched into fists.

What to do …?

Why should I make a public apology when my accusations were made in a private letter? Neither did I wish to make a private apology, for I did not regret my letter. Perhaps I should speak with Lord Hamish – tell him everything.

Foolish idea – the man detested me and even if he heard me out, Lord Hamish would never believe his son capable of a liaison with another woman. He, who'd wasted no opportunity to throw his son's sexuality in his face, would never, ever, believe him capable of infidelity with a woman.

So, I'd been made to look a fool – worse, they thought I was crazed and given over to fantasies.

I could see I had no choice but to accept my defeat and make my apology, as the letter demanded.

Aggie had taken one look at the back of my head and declared that there was a fair-sized lump and a small cut – nothing that would kill me. She cleaned the wound and I swore out loud as she touched it with a stinky salve.

"Well, you will go bumping your head, Lady Grizzle-guts," she commented irreverently. Sylvie stood leaning against the wall, her arms folded, her mouth a grim line, saying nothing.

∾

That evening, I went to Lord Hamish's room. The elderly man was worsening daily and Doctor Gregor was certain he would succumb to his illness within weeks. Nevertheless, he still had the power to issue orders and send spikes of fear through the household.

My father-in-law was propped against his pillows, gaunt and yellow and glaring at me from beneath sagging eyelids. It always took me a few minutes to become accustomed to the taste of the fetid air in that room. Why did he not open a window? The smell alone was enough see him off to the next world.

Some nameless urge was driving me to tell this man the truth. He would berate me in foul language and I would be accepting for I'd been naive and impulsive in writing that letter. But for some reason I needed the old man to know *why* I did it.

He watched me as I pulled over a chair and sat beside him.

"Aye well … what have you to say for yourself?" he croaked immediately.

I'd not expected that and it took me a moment to think how I wanted to start.

"Spit it out. I know you for many things but I've yet to see the blockhead in you. That letter … I expect you had your reasons. So tell me, what's been going on?"

My sense of relief was profound. He actually *wanted* to know. I let out my breath and began.

I started at the beginning – with Hamish's reluctance to share my bed, and the old man surprised me by remaining silent. I talked on, explaining our joy at my pregnancy and the trauma of the loss, and when I described finding his son in bed with a man, he winced but waved for me to continue, pursing his dry lips when I told him that his son and I barely spoke, so disgusted was I, so filled with hatred was he.

Finally, I told him of the flirtation between Hamish and Catherine and how they'd sat side by side that afternoon, giggling and whispering together.

"I'm positive he was trying to make me jealous," I said. "He told me he planned to meet a certain lady at an inn – someone to comfort him in a difficult time. That's when I lost my reason." I sat quietly watching his waxen face.

After listening silently for so long, Lord Hamish now spoke, homing immediately to the crux of the issue, "Why would he wish to make you jealous?"

Here was the moment of truth. I looked directly into his rheumy, red eyes and said, "He's jealous because though he sees me as his chattel only and bears me no love, he believes I love another."

"And do you love another?"

Bowing my head, I hesitated for only a heartbeat. "Yes."

The long silence that followed was broken only by his raspy breathing. Then he spoke, "Does this man love you in return?"

"I don't know. It was a long time ago … I betrayed him by marrying your son."

My father-in-law watched me carefully for several assessing seconds. "We did a great wrong by you … bringing you here," he said plainly and I felt the familiar sting of tears behind my eyes. His voice was weary but he went on, surprising me with his frankness. "You weren't told of my son's … inadequacies. You weren't allowed your love."

I stared at him incredulously and he attempted a weak smile. His lips were cracked and he had several teeth missing so the result resembled the expression of a gargoyle, but I recognised it as an offer of conciliation.

"I loved his mother and she loved me," he said, surprising me; I could not imagine this man loving, or being loved. "We were fortunate to wed. Where is your lost love? Can you not go to him? Leave my son to his machinations and unnatural diversions." His voice was weakening and his breathing becoming laboured.

I'd come here expecting to have the skin stripped from my back but now I was confused. "What … what are you saying?"

"I've no doubt Hamish teased you with this woman – hoodwinking her as well, for he is spiteful as he is deceitful. Oh, he can charm when he's a mind … but ultimately he is selfish." He sighed with fatigue, and said in a hoarse whisper, "So unfulfilling … such disappointment."

His eyes closed wearily and he fell silent. I waited, listening to the crackling of the fire in the grate. At last, thinking he slept, I rose to leave.

"I am well aware that you two have not shared a bed in months," he said suddenly. "You think I don't know what goes on 'neath me own roof?"

I had no response and he continued as his voice grew faint, "There will be no bairn from your marriage – I will'na live to see my hopes realised. There is no point … destroying your life while you …. may find happiness elsewhere. I'm an old man and …" his voice trembled slightly, "I'm dying. I will'na spend the remainder of my allotted time … struggling against … that which … I've no power to change."

Tears suddenly spilled over my lashes, trickled slowly to my chin, tickling, and I scrubbed at them in irritation.

"But … what of my dowry … my mother … the marriage contract?"

"I'll be mouldering in … ground before … year is out. Why would I care?" He closed his eyes and lay there for a long time then suddenly they snapped open again. A film of mucous glazed them and he peered at me blindly.

"Are you finished …? I wish to sleep."

"I … they want me to apologise to Lady Catherine."

His laugh was like a congested bark and I caught a whiff of his foul breath. "Immensely foolish … sending that letter … but … I like your gumption. Tell 'em to *stuff off*!"

"But … the business!"

"Let them pull out … could'na give … tinker's cuss. The agreement states … if they want out … Hamish must purchase … Godfrey's shares … Hamish could'na … run the business … without me … even if … had the money. And … without a bairn … there is … for him … no business …"

Oh, how I'd love to tell them all to stuff off.

"My son is worthless," Lord Hamish continued. "Leave him … Start your life anew – you've … my blessing."

With surprise I realised suddenly this man was not the ogre I'd always thought. He was angry, frustrated and ill, riddled with disappointment as he was with disease; dying and leaving nothing but an ineffectual son – a son that he didn't trust to run the family business – hence his desperation for an heir. With this understanding, I knew a vague glimmer of respect.

"I must make my peace with the Trehornes," I said resignedly. "I can do nought else – Hamish hasn't the money to buy Laird Godfrey's shares."

"And … what of … your love?"

I smiled sadly and swiped at a wayward tear. "He's not my love any more. I forfeited that right when I betrayed him. This is my life for better or worse, as avowed."

He nodded with acceptance. "Aye well … Do what you … feel you must." Grimacing suddenly, he lurched forwards and held one hand to his chest, coughing violently and pointing to a cup. I held it to his lips as he sipped before collapsing weakly against his pillows.

"Leave me," he said and his voice was a hoarse whisper. "I would sleep."

❧

In the hall outside the sick room, I leaned heavily against the wall and wept into my hands. How had it all come to this? How could I halt the downward spiral of my life? Suddenly becoming aware of someone lurking at the end of the hall, I took a deep, shuddering breath and tried to compose myself. As I watched, Hamish's silhouette emerged from the dimness, striding confidently toward me. When he drew level, he peered into my face.

"Good," he said with satisfaction. "The old man gave you a piece of his mind – as you rightly deserve."

"Leave me be, Hamish," I said, pushing past him. I was eager for the solitude of my room. I needed to think after such an extraordinary meeting. I'd no desire to discuss it with Hamish, nor did I need his taunts. Unfortunately, he chose to follow me.

"So, now you've had your talking to, you'll be attending Godfrey's supper to make your apology? They want you to do it before their guests."

I stopped and stared at him incredulously. "I am your wife, Hamish. Why would you want me humiliated this way?"

"They're being very gracious. You read the letter – if they withdraw their interest in the company I'll have to come up with more money than I'd see in a lifetime."

"What difference is it to you? We have no child – your share of the company's as good as gone. Let them sell it. It's the only chance you'll get to see any return."

"Not while my father still lives and there's a chance to change his mind. You must apologise."

"Why, when their imagined insult was private, do they require a public apology? Beyond our two groups, no one knows of the letter –" I broke off suddenly as the truth dawned on me. As expected, he looked guilty.

"Ha!" I tossed my head at him. "Does it make you feel more of a man to go strutting about your club like a bantam cock telling your cohorts of your wife's jealousies over another woman?"

Anger darkened his face momentarily, but was quickly replaced with a look of contempt. "We shall leave at eight. Have your speech ready."

He was walking away when I said decisively, "No."

He whirled abruptly. "What did you say?"

"I said, *no.*"

"Don't think to play your little games with me, Alex, just be ready by –"

"I'm not going."

In two strides he had shoved me hard against the wall and I glared at him defiantly. Any violence he could do now would be nothing compared with debasing myself before all those people, and though my knees trembled, I refused to look away.

"*You … will … go,*" he said, enunciating the words very clearly. "You read the letter from Godfrey. Without that apology, the business … I will be ruined."

"Without a child you're ruined. Anyway, your father has no care for the business." I said firmly. "In fact, the words he used were, *tell 'em to stuff off* – and that's exactly what I will do should you force me to that supper."

The look of surprised disbelief on his effeminate face lent me strength, so I continued. "And if you really want to know, your father is happy for Laird Godfrey to demand you buy his shares for he believes you're incapable of running it without him. He does not care if you fail."

"You're lying," he said through gritted teeth. "He's worked for years to build it … all that time in China and India … making connections, raising capital. I don't believe you."

I shrugged indifferently. "Then you must take it up with him."

Worried into passivity, he didn't react as I pushed away and tramped down the hall and back to my room, where I bolted the door securely, my heart thudding in my breast.

CHAPTER 12

"So we're leaving, aren't we?" Sylvie asked eagerly. I'd just told her of my talk with Lord Hamish and her eyes were shining with excitement.

I shook my head.

"Why ever not?" she exclaimed. "He gave his blessing."

"Where can I go … really?"

"Waterville!" she cried, as though it were obvious.

"You know I cannot. It is unlikely Patrick's even there – he's probably in Europe getting himself killed. And anyway, by marrying Hamish, Sylvie, I betrayed Pat – he must hate me."

"Is it not worth a try?"

"You said yourself how angry he is … drinking, smashing things, and that argument with Simon … Sylvie – it's entirely my fault! He'll not want to see me."

She sighed sadly. "So you will continue to live here in unhappiness."

"There's nothing else I can do."

❧

The day of Laird Godfrey's birthday supper came and went with no word from Hamish. I assumed he'd spoken with his father and confirmed my story for otherwise he'd have scorched the rug in his rush to tell me I was wrong. Regardless, he'd left the house some days earlier, and was still absent when, in the small hours of Saturday morning, I was summoned to Lord Hamish's bedside. The old man had taken a turn for the worse. He was quite calm but drifted in and out of consciousness. Mrs Twigley had sent for Doctor Gregor, but not the local priest.

"He'd launch himself off that bed and throttle me if I brought a religious man into this room," she said wryly.

Doctor Gregor felt his patient's pulse, checked his pupils and pressed an ear to his chest.

"Better call the son," he proclaimed. "Our Laird is failing."

Mrs Twigley and I looked at one another. "We don't know where he is," I said flatly.

"Well, find him," Doctor Gregor demanded, passing a hand over his shiny scalp. "Does that dog have to be here?" He glowered at Jemima lying inoffensively in the corner.

"My husband is not within the castle, Doctor – and yes, *that dog* has to be here – Lord Hamish likes dogs."

"Then don't stand there gaping like a toad! This man is dying, madam! Send a boy out to whichever whore's bed your husband is in and tell him to get himself home immediately."

Bristling, I swallowed my anger and gestured for Mrs Twigley to follow me.

Out in the hall I said, "Do you know Richard Kintyre?"

"No, my lady, I do not."

"Damn!" I'd been swearing a lot lately. I pulled my robe tighter against the cold. "Rouse everyone, ask them all – someone must know where this man lives. Send a boy immediately with a message for Master Hamish to return home at once."

"Yes, my lady."

I watched her disappear into the shadows and released my breath in a frustrated huff. Returning to the sick room, I found Doctor Gregor slipping into his coat.

"You're not leaving?"

"What would you have me do?" he asked smartly and picked up his bag. "I've dosed him with laudanum to ease his pain. With luck he'll slip away in his sleep. I shall return in the morning to write the certificate."

"But what shall I do?" I felt the first clench of panic in my gut.

"Firstly, find your husband. Secondly, sit with the old man. It won't be long."

I sat in my usual chair by Lord Hamish's bedside. The stench was worse than ever and I suspected he might have soiled his sheets. Mrs Twigley will have to help me change them. What an undignified end for this imposing man. Long minutes ticked by and when the door opened I jumped to my feet hopefully. I would never have been so pleased to see Hamish in all my life. But it was Mrs Twigley and, at the look on her face, I deflated.

"Richard Kintyre was found in the taproom at the White Hart. Master Hamish was not with him." I nodded resignedly and bade her fetch clean sheets.

❧

Sometime towards dawn, I woke in fright as the old man gave an agonised shriek. I leaned over to soothe him and he clawed at my arms. "Hamish!" he cried. "Oh God … *my boy … my boy … so sorry … my boy, forgive me …*" His voice wavered and gave way to dry, hacking sobs. My own tears ran freely down my cheeks and I held my father-in-law's hands as he gripped mine with supernatural strength. My fingers were cramping in his grasp as eventually his sobs gave way to gasps, rapid breaths, faltering, slowing, and finally … nothing.

❧

Hamish didn't return home until Monday evening, puffy-eyed from lack of sleep and reeking of stale alcohol and tobacco smoke.

I met him in the courtyard as he dismounted and tossed his reins to a waiting boy.

"Greetings, wife! What a fine homecoming – you standing there so –"

"Your father passed away yesterday morning," I interrupted abruptly. "We couldn't find you. In his final moments he cried out for you … you weren't here. I hope you're proud of yourself."

I turned and walked away, unable to countenance him for a second longer. The pain of an old man's dying plea to make peace with his only son was still too fresh. I went into the house and up to my room where Jemima waited and once again, I bolted the door.

∾

By May, I was riding Ember. The stablemaster had broken her in beautifully. She was a gentle girl and eager to please, but she had a strange motion to her trot, seeming to flick her left foreleg out at an angle, which resulted in a side-to-side motion rather than forwards and back.

She was, nevertheless, smooth and relaxed, and with the soft, tooled-leather saddle the stablemaster had recommended, she was a very comfortable mount.

I described her trot to him, thinking perhaps she had an injury, but he declared there was nothing wrong with her physically. "It's just her way. I can talk to the Laird about it … get a decent quid for her at market … buy a better one."

"I'll not consider it, Mr Kennedy," I said. "I shall keep her as she is."

I'd loved this horse for her sweet nature from the first day I saw her, but more than that, she was a memory of the brief time when relations were still amicable between Hamish and me. I had known contentment then and was anticipating a brighter future.

As spring was well advanced, the weather was glorious and I rode often along the river with Jemima loping joyously alongside.

Soon it was my twenty-first birthday. Hamish left a small gift by my place at the breakfast table – a porcelain brooch in the shape of a Scottish thistle – a far cry from last year's gift of my beautiful horse.

Mrs Twigley baked her specialty apple-cinnamon cakes and delivered them to the parlour, still warm, with a pot of tea while she, Sylvie, and Aggie all agreed I looked nought but a day older than yesterday.

Wiping cake crumbs from her apron, Aggie said, "Oh, my lady, I forgot to give ye this – came with the boy this morn." She dug a letter from her pocket and handed it to me, then returned to her work.

Simon's distinctively angular scrawl leapt up at me and I fingered the envelope's stiffness thinking he'd had a lot to report for it was quite a thick letter, but then I hadn't heard from him in a long while. I slipped it into my pocket with a thrill of anticipation. I would read it in privacy later.

We ate cakes and little sandwiches, and drank tea infused with rose-hips, and as the afternoon wore on Quinn arrived with a bunch of sad-looking flowers in his hand.

He grinned sheepishly, "Sorry the flowers don't look terribly well – I picked them from my garden this morning but accidentally left them in the sun."

"They're lovely Quinn," I said gratefully and Sylvie, unable to completely relinquish her servile past, left the room, returning shortly with a porcelain vase.

With the flowers on a table and more tea poured we toasted my birthday.

"Now you're of age," said Sylvie. "What do you think of that?"

Shrugging, I eyed her with interest. "How old are you?"

She smiled coyly. "Can you guess?"

"Och now, there resides serious trouble," Quinn said with a laugh.

I knew that Sylvie was born to Gerrard when his wife was still alive, and I knew that she died when Patrick was seven. Patrick was now twenty-three, nearly twenty-four. That made Sylvie only a couple of years younger. "I think you're twenty-two," I said decisively.

Her laugh was light and evoked smiles from Quinn and me.

"What's so funny?" I asked.

"You – the expression on your face showed exactly how you worked that out."

"So I'm right, then?"

"Actually, you're not," she said. "You're out by a year. I'm twenty-three. I was, shall we say, a diversion while my father's wife was carrying Patrick. He's five months older than me."

"Old maid!" I said, with humour.

"I'm waiting for someone special to sweep me off my feet but he hasn't appeared yet," she sent a wink in Quinn's direction.

"See what a coquette she is!" Quinn cried. "Who would marry a tease like that?"

"I hear they make notoriously poor wives," I quipped.

"But exceedingly gratifying mistresses – *ouch*!" Quinn cried as Sylvie boxed him playfully about the ears.

"Good afternoon, everyone," Hamish said from the door. Despite his apparent congeniality, his presence effectively dampened our mood. The tension between my husband and me had made everyone uncomfortable.

Quinn swirled the contents of his tea cup contemplatively and Sylvie, falsely sweet, said, "Hello, Hamish."

Since he'd inherited his father's title, Hamish had strutted around like a rooster, shaking out his plumes and trying to prove himself. He stood before us now, legs wide and hands on hips in an attitude of affected maleness, incongruous in his suit of pale blue and lemon satin. I gathered, from their surreptitious smirks at one another, that the ambiguity was not lost on Sylvie or Quinn.

"I'm going to the club," Hamish announced. He'd been less secretive about his whereabouts lately, though I don't think it was for any reason other than his misguided sense that the masonry would collapse without his supervision. He'd conveniently forgotten that the groundsmen, tradesmen and squad of staff had, for the most part, been working here longer than he'd been alive, and very probably knew more about the running of the place than he ever would.

His absences were bearing fruit, for I knew he had several business irons in the fire and was succeeding in attracting a handful of financial supporters from among his friends at the club. And contradictory to Laird Godfrey's threat; after my refusal to apologise, he hadn't sold his interest in the business for after several break even years, Glendenning Associated Importers was finally starting to see a return for its investors. At the time of Lord Hamish's death, the old man's vision was proving successful – not that Hamish was receiving any of the income, which no doubt contributed to his sudden interest in making entrepreneurial contacts.

"I'll not be home for supper," he said almost defiantly. "I've a meeting in Glasgow early tomorrow so I shall stay there tonight."

He left quickly but regretfully our little gathering had now lost its sparkle. I glanced at Sylvie and she looked grim, her face plainly saying, *why do you remain here when you received the old man's blessing to leave?*

Her expression annoyed me. Of course I would love to leave – but how could I? I was no gambler and could not be certain of the outcome. The picture of myself living on my brother's charity, like Adrienne's aunt, growing to old age educating my brother's children in return for my board was intolerable.

Perhaps I could go to Leeds and beg Gerrard's permission to live in one of his houses, but how would he receive me? Now that I knew he'd been aware of Patrick's location when Anne had returned home, I questioned his regard for me. And supposing he did let me live in his house, I'd have no income and no means of producing one. I sighed.

"Alex …?"

Sylvie and Quinn were looking at me oddly.

"I'm sorry," I said hurriedly. "I'm feeling weary. I thank you for the little party this afternoon." I gathered up the book of poems Aggie and Mrs Twigley had given me, and the delicate, blown glass figurine that looked remarkably like Jemima, from Sylvie. "I shall rest before supper and see you then."

❧

In my room, I relaxed in my window-seat and took out Simon's letter. This was the reply I'd waited so long for. Now I would know if he'd been party to the deception − I would know the truth. I broke the seal.

To my surprise the envelope contained not one, but two letters. They were each folded in half and half again. The first one I picked up had TWO written on it. I took up the other which had ONE − READ FIRST scrawled in Simon's hand.

I unfolded it.

16 May 1815

My Dearest Sister,

Thank you for your letter, which I had, without warning, received just as I was planning to write to you. I must, however, apologise for my delayed reply but the reason will become evident as you read.

Firstly, Maria and I would express our deepest condolences for your loss. Having Dudley in our lives, we cannot imagine the pain you and Hamish have suffered. We wish you well with all our hearts.

But let us not linger here.

With respect to your question regarding Patrick – yes, I did visit him upon his return from Europe. Gerrard expressed concern for him since we knew of his return but he'd not made contact with anyone.

When I saw Patrick, he had newly arrived home from France but already knew of your marriage. He asked after his father, Meg and Maria. When I mentioned Anne, he said he'd seen her briefly and that they'd parted on poor terms, but he didn't elaborate.

We argued because he blamed me for allowing you to marry Hamish. I defended myself saying that if he cared for you, he should have remained in contact so that he could counter Anne's charges.

It was my mistake to try to reason with Patrick – in his anger he was quite beyond reason. He told me he hadn't fathered Anne's baby and was furious that we had all believed her. He claimed that his concern over your marrying Hamish was simply due to his belief that Hamish was not suitable for you and the match between you ill-considered. He refused to discuss anything further. After our quarrel we parted unpleasantly.

In any case Zan, I don't think you ought to dwell overly on him. You have a new life and a marriage that, in spite of our initial concerns, appears to be a happy, supportive one.

But, my dear sister, so much of Anne's story had never rung true, as you and I discussed on one or two occasions. When I received your letter, many of my own questions were answered, but you must understand that until I heard it from her, I could not imagine how it had all come to pass.

You may be displeased with me, but upon hearing from you, I knew I had to write to Anne directly, hence my tardy reply to you.

You will notice that there is another letter enclosed in this envelope. It is Anne's reply.

Zan, before you read it, please remember, it is all water under the bridge now and not worthy of an expenditure of emotion.

I know you entertained feelings for Patrick when you were younger, but you are a married woman now, as he is a jaded old soldier. It is clear that if Patrick ever felt more than friendship for you, it was merely a youthful infatuation. He is not lonely for companionship, so you mustn't continue to harbour guilt for believing Anne — we all accepted her deception, we have all lost him.

My brotherly advice to you is to read Anne's letter — it should answer all your questions. Then, it will be your decision as to whether you wish to maintain a sibling relationship with our sister.

Meanwhile, I remain your loving brother,

Simon.

I took a few deep breaths to brace myself. Simon clearly assumed my reason for seeking the truth was guilt rather than love. I unfolded the second letter and Anne's flamboyant handwriting stared at me. I began to read.

April 30 1815

Dearest Simon,

Thank you for your letter, which I admit was no surprise. I knew that sooner or later I would receive something of its type from you or Alex.

Before I begin telling my story I must say that never, at any stage did I intend to hurt anyone, and in fact I believed that if my plan failed, I would be the only one to suffer.

I will answer your two questions as honestly and directly as I can. The first question — did I go to Devon to ask Patrick to say my child was his? In one word: yes.

Your second question — why? — requires more words. I'd best start at the beginning.

The first summer that Maeve and I were in Italy was dazzling. It was filled with new and exciting experiences and was a wonderland to us. We loved it!

Maeve and I did everything together. We went everywhere together and shared every experience. Maeve was all I could have wanted in a sister that I did not have with Alexandra. Alex was always more adventurous than I and definitely more your type; she was the brother you did not have. Now finally, I had a sister and we were having a splendid time.

As you would be aware, Mother gave permission for us to remain indefinitely – she was never one to need her children about her.

Sometime in 1811, Maeve became involved with some explorer types. They called themselves archaeologists or something, and she developed a fascination for their work. She began spending more and more time with these people and I was left to myself. (In case you are wondering, Catarina was courting with some fellow and Grace was in London. I had made a few other friends but I was growing quite bored.)

Isabella suggested I study something, anything I had an interest in. Well, we were in Italy – the centre of the art world –so I decided to take an art course. It so happened she knew a fellow. He was extraordinarily talented, and Isabella believed, on the brink of success. He made an income by taking students, so I became a student of Domenico Rossolini.

I studied with him for only two months before he was offered a commission to paint the portraits of the children of some baron or other in Vienna. He left for Austria and I continued my lessons with his apprentice.

I seem to have a flair for it, Simon. I do not call it talent, but I can capture light and shade nicely and can depict a still life very well. The chemistry of mixing colours is quite beyond me however, so often my colours are a bit odd.

Toward the end of 1812, Domenico returned from Austria, with quite a name for himself and a deal more in terms of financial resources. He also brought with him his new wife.

Domenico thought my colours quite fascinating. He suggested we work with them and see what happened, after all, it could not hurt to experiment with different styles. Our affair began soon after.

To this day, Domenico's wife remains unaware, and Domenico had made it quite clear that if there was fruit from our union he would have none of it. I went into this affair with my eyes open. I loved him, you see. I loved him with the single-minded passion that any seventeen-year-old girl would, and I spent many happy hours in his company.

Though we were as careful as possible, in May I realised I was with child. Of course, I spoke with Domenico of this, and true to his word he would not see me again — in fact he had a footman forcibly eject me from his house.

You will think this foolish, Simon, for I knew the risks and continued regardless. Oh, I begged and pleaded for him to reconsider, don't think I didn't, but it was pointless and in the end I had no choice but to return to London. If Isabella guessed the true reason I left in such a hurry, she did not say. In any case, the timing was convenient because you were due home from the war and Mother had requested that I return to England.

When I arrived in London, I went first to Grace. She was the only person I knew there, and was living with her husband and her baby. I did not tell her my situation, but said simply I needed somewhere to stay until I found a coach to Yorkshire. Naturally she was most obliging.

When she told me that I had missed Patrick by a day, the mention of his name set me thinking. Grace said he was going to check on his Devon estate before returning to the war. So, instead of taking coach to Yorkshire, I went to Devon.

Please do not think badly of me, Simon, but everyone knew

that Mother had wanted a match between Patrick and me. I had no qualms about my plans, for when all is considered we were supposed to be together, and besides, I had nothing to lose.

I arrived at Waterville one afternoon. I must say, that place is all Maeve described and more. Even after all I had seen in Italy, it fair took my breath away! I made my plans on the journey, but when Patrick received me in his library and regarded me with that, do-not-play-me-for-a-fool look he gets, I spilled it all out. He listened without making a comment and then when I was finished he said simply: and so you want me to marry you.

I said: yes.

I think what I have not explained here is how desperate I had become. I was two months pregnant now and fearful of facing Mother, not to mention my future. I was only now realising the implications of what I had done — and all for a man who did not love me!

When Patrick said, no, I quite lost my composure. I cried, I threw myself (I feel so ashamed of it now) at his feet and I begged.

Still he said no. He said his affections lay elsewhere. I said I did not care — I was desperate. I told him he had no right to have affections elsewhere as his responsibility was to the family and that we had been matched long ago. We argued, but still he said no.

I could not bear the thought of admitting my baby's father was a married Italian painter, however fashionable he may be. Mother would be beside herself.

I explained this but he did not care. You see, Simon, I tried all I could by fair means. He forced my hand.

Finally, I told him that if he refused to marry me, I would go directly to Yorkshire and tell everyone he had seduced me and then abandoned me. The staff had seen me arrive and knew I was in Devon. I told him our parents would take my word before his.

I expected him to be at least a little concerned by my threat. Instead he laughed at me. After he stopped laughing he grew very angry. Lord, I've never seen him so angry! Simon, he was white faced and I thought he was about to strike me. He called me some unsavoury words and then threw me out of the house!

Oh, in fairness he called for a stable boy to take me to the nearest village in his coach, but he made me wait under the portico while they hitched the horses.

He said that had I not threatened him he might have pleaded my case with Mother, but he did not take kindly to ultimatums and I could say what I liked for all he cared, he wanted none of me or my child.

He ordered me to get out and never come back, and he used the most colourful language – even by Patrick's standards!

Well, he may have been angry, but I was also. I was so angry that I'm amazed my child has been born with such a quiet and gentle nature when she was carried in such fury. I went immediately to Exeter and I booked a coach to Yorkshire. When I told Mother that Patrick had fathered my child, she proved only too willing to believe me.

Please, Simon, please understand that I was desperate and I had no choice. Upon discussing with Alex her situation with Patrick, I wanted so much to confide in her, and also you, that it tore me apart inside. But I was in too deep. I could not back down for I was terrified of Mother's reaction.

I believe George only agreed to the terms of our marriage because Father assured him he would become a wealthy man by marrying me. Incidentally, George has become a good father to my girl and though her resemblance to her natural father is undeniable, he has grown to love her.

Julia Chapman had supper with my friend Margrethe Darlington who said that Alex is very happy in her new home with Hamish. Things have worked out very well for her so it was best that I did not muddy the puddle with useless confessions. Apparently Alex has recovered from her little infatuation with Patrick now she is settled as a wife and mother. She is very lucky indeed to be married to Hamish. I always told her as much.

I expect this means that despite my error of judgement with Domenico, Mother should be satisfied that her three children have married, if not as well as she'd have liked in your and my cases, at least we are off her hands and content in our situations.

Patrick said his affections lay elsewhere but I doubt he's capable of human emotions. Sadly, the boy we came to love as our stepbrother, who according to Maeve is the embodiment of God, has become a cold-hearted and self-serving brute. If he chooses to disassociate himself from this family, it can only be to our benefit.

Simon, if I sound bitter, it is because I am. Patrick and I were matched by our parents years ago, it was no secret. Who else could I have turned to under the circumstances?

I expect you will discuss this with Alex and you will both form opinions of me. I only pray you think of me with compassion and understanding.

Anne

I sat back and shook my head in wonderment. Anne actually believed that Patrick had a responsibility to her and her bastard child. Angry that he refused to marry her and tell the world the child was his, she told that enormous untruth and changed many lives purely from spite and to save her own skin.

Anne admitted that had she not threatened Patrick he'd agreed to support her case with Mother, but she nevertheless had the cheek to call him a *cold-hearted and self-serving brute.*

My reply to Simon the following day, expressed my disappointment in Anne's behaviour and my assurances that I had no desire to maintain contact with her in the future.

∾

Meanwhile, my relationship with Hamish had disintegrated entirely. Hamish ordered Mrs Twigley to have his things moved into a separate building in the castle – which meant I would not turn a corner and bump into him – but now, I didn't even know if he lived here. For all I knew I could be living as a spinster – indeed for all intents I was.

CHAPTER 13

June passed and became July. It was the height of summer and in Scotland that meant fine blue-skied days, lazy afternoons in the long grass and restful evenings. Quinn and Sylvie were my constant companions and, though they meant well, I felt pitied. Quinn practically lived here now and my presence became that of chaperone and served to quell local gossip.

I liked Quinn. He was good and decent and Sylvie's happiness was a balm to my heart. His home was in Glasgow but he only spent a few days there each week. After one visit in the middle of July, he returned with a selection of papers, all carrying news of the conflict that would become known as the Battle of Waterloo.

"This clash," he said to Sylvie and me, "will go down in history as being one of the bloodiest. So many men lost – from both sides – they're saying no battle has ever cost so many lives."

He dropped the papers on to a table. "I can't begin to tell you – better you read it for yourselves."

We each took up a paper and the story unfolded before us.

Napoleon had managed to rally about 124,000 men but, aware that the four European armies were amassing rapidly, he needed to act quickly.

Britain and Prussia were planning to gather in Belgium and he wanted to hit them separately to prevent them from joining and becoming a force he could not defeat. Therefore, his plan was to attack the Prussians and force them east into the Rhineland. He would strike the British and move them west towards Ghent, hoping that this would prevent the Austrian and Russian armies from meeting up with the other two.

Moving secretly and swiftly, Napoleon marched into Belgium. Wellington was attending a ball given by the Duchess of Richmond on the fifteenth of June when he heard the news and was compelled to sound the call to arms around eleven o'clock that evening. In the early morning sunshine, on the sixteenth of June the entire allied army marched towards the French border. They'd been rallied so rapidly that some of the officers were still dressed for the previous evening's ball.

Wellington commanded the Anglo-Dutch army. His second in charge was the Prince of Orange – generally considered a political appointment since his father was the King of the Netherlands so many were doubtful of his competence.

It had been a bloodbath. Over the course of this Battle of Waterloo, some 25,000 men were killed or wounded.

Lost for words, Sylvie and I turned to each other in horror – such annihilation, death and devastation. The waste of life – soldiers, many of them little more than boys, and the horses, innocent of human folly, noble creatures working man's bidding and falling at his side.

And I read in Sylvie's face the question neither of us dared ask aloud: if Patrick was there, as he surely would have been, where so many had lost their lives, what hope was there for his survival?

∾

As we moved into September, I spent long hours pondering the beautiful, rugged landscape beyond the ancient stone walls of the castle. The leaves on the trees were turning gold and red, and the flocks of grey and brown water birds on the Clyde were leaving for warmer climes. A cold wind had blown in across the Hebrides from the Atlantic sending a ripple through the reeds and grasses lining the river's bank.

The realm was as bleak and grey as my mood.

I'd received mail from Simon saying how sympathetic he was towards Anne since she'd lost her great love. How was it that the loss of her love was considered so tragic? How was it that the love I bore for Patrick was considered simply an infatuation? My pain was no less real, my grief no less debilitating. She at least had a child from her union.

I shivered, thinking how she had knowingly engaged in an affair with a married man, returned home to weave a web of lies and deceit, and was then fortunate enough to deliver a healthy child; while I was doomed to a hostile marriage, and a childless, interminable existence many miles from my home and friends.

I concluded that Simon must have grown soft as an ageing dowager since his marriage. He ended his letter by inviting Hamish and me to spend Yuletide at Broughton Hall. My heart had leapt at the thought but I knew Hamish would not go. He would not share a meal with me let alone a four-day journey.

Perhaps I could go without him. An idea began to take shape. Sylvie's relationship with Quinn was going so well that she may not wish to accompany me – unless I suggested Quinn were to join us.

My thoughts raced end-to-end and I made my decision: next time I knew Hamish was in residence, I would talk with him.

My chance to broach the subject with my husband came two days later. From the gallery window, I watched as he rode into the bailey and knowing that he would be bathing and reading his mail, I waited a few hours before going to his office. I had thought my argument through very carefully and hoped I had considered all the hurdles he was likely to throw up.

It had once been his father's study, but was now his. Standing at the door, I knocked and he bade me enter.

It had been over a month since I'd seen him and I tried not to show my surprise as I sat in the chair he indicated. He had put on weight and was looking quite unwell. His ruddy face evidenced an excess of wine and food and he sported a rather rakish moustache and little beard. They did look well on him and diverted attention from his growing jowls.

He was seated behind his great, carved desk and I waited as he put away his documents and regarded me narrowly.

"What brings you here?" he asked with an edge to his voice. He rocked back on his chair but unfortunately the legs appeared too sturdy to give way.

"Simon has invited us to visit for Christmas," I said. "I would like to go."

"Would you indeed?"

I nodded.

"Well, I would not. I have business to attend to, and there's this place …" he gestured to encompass the entire castle, which was evidently reduced to rubble every time he rode away.

So far this talk was going to plan. I nodded again. "Surely *I* could visit my brother and his wife for Yuletide. I've not yet met my nephew."

A flicker of superiority crossed his face as he contemplated refusal, but even he realised that to deny my trip to Yorkshire would be churlish in the extreme and impossible to rationalise. Still, he could not resist exploiting his position.

"How long would you be gone?"

"A month perhaps."

"And who'd be paying for this?"

"We would, of course."

"*We?*" His black eyebrows arched haughtily.

"You," I corrected with annoyance – he was such a turd.

"You'd take the coach, I imagine?"

"The one my father gave us – yes."

"But what if I need it? And you'll need a groom … some kind of escort," he pulled his brows together in a contemplative frown. "Expensive."

I held my exasperation in check and answered mildly, "I could ask Quinn. If he agrees, perhaps we could take his coach. It also has the coal-box for warmth."

He paused. He hadn't thought of that. "Quinn wouldn't agree to that."

"I think he might because Sylvie would accompany me."

"Then his groom could escort you." Hamish thought of that on his own.

"Yes, I suppose he could." I waited but he didn't seem to have any further obstacles.

Finally I said, "Well?"

"Well what?" he asked, continuing his little power game.

I clicked my tongue with irritation. I hated to say it. "May I go?"

He returned his chair to its rightful position and leaned forward. "You do plan to return, don't you?"

At this, I burst out laughing and he looked surprised. "Of course, Hamish, for we have such a loving relationship – so fulfilled is my life here." In truth, since Sylvie had mentioned it several months ago, I'd discarded the idea of permanently leaving as impossible. Now, however, I locked the thought away for later examination.

He curled his lip at my sarcasm. "What if I said you could not go?"

I stared at him sadly. "Has it come to this, then?"

"Come to what?" he asked, but he was no longer enjoying his power over me.

"You've no use for me as a wife yet you would keep me here as a prisoner in a tower. He is my brother, Hamish. Where is the harm in my visiting him?"

He let his breath out as a hiss between his teeth, and passed a knuckle over his moustache, all the fight drained from him. "I would not blame you if you left," he said not meeting my eyes.

"If I planned to leave you, don't you think I'd have done so already? It would be months before you even missed me."

He nodded. "You know I cannot deny you a visit to your brother's house."

∾

When I told Sylvie she was excited about leaving and very pleased with my suggestion that Quinn accompany us. "He'll agree, Alex. I know he will," she said.

"Good. I shall write to Simon this evening."

Sylvie was sewing a seam on a man's shirt. For Quinn, I presumed. "When do you expect we shall leave?" she asked, tying off the thread.

"November, but before the worst of the weather."

"I think this is an excellent idea!"

CHAPTER 14

By the time November arrived we had finalised our preparations for departure and at last, on the morning of the tenth, Hamish's cold, thin lips brushed my fingertips in a counterfeit display of husbandly affection. I held my face in a rigid smile lest my impatience for departure show.

Quinn had been pleased to join us and suggested we take his comfortable new coach before I'd even asked him. He arrived the night before with a groom and a driver.

Being reluctant to leave Ember behind since she was used to my riding her often, Quinn agreed to ride her while Sylvie and I travelled in his coach. I thought it would be nice to ride her myself for part of the way.

To my great pleasure – and Jemima's – Quinn had brought Bony with him but had kept the dog in the stable overnight, well away from Hamish. Consequently, our leaving was delayed as the two dogs engaged in a boisterous reunion. When at last they settled, they clambered into the coach and lay quietly together on the floor. Sylvie and I climbed in, pulled the woollen rugs about us, and waved to Mrs Twigley, Beth and Aggie, assembled in the courtyard.

Quinn nudged Ember's flanks, the coachman clucked to the

horses, the coach jerked forward with a clank of harness, and we were underway.

I am free!

The thought came unbidden, but rather than stifle it – I revelled in it and breathed a great sigh of relief.

∾

With good roads and unseasonably mild weather, we made excellent progress. That first day we stopped at midday to give the horses a rest and, as Quinn handed me out on to the grassy verge, I felt heavy and dull-witted from dozing.

Sylvie, who'd also nodded off with her head against the cushioned, wall panel, emerged blinking in the sunlight. Leaning against the side of the coach, the sun shining full in my face, I breathed deeply of the fresh country air. From beyond the verdant scent of the grass and hedgerows came the distinctive odour of cattle. They ranged contentedly on a nearby hillock, their faces turned curiously to look at us as they chewed their cud.

Sylvie was watching me carefully. I raised my eyebrows questioningly and she smiled. "Are we returning to Scotland, Alex?" she asked, in typically direct fashion.

I pushed away from the coach, avoiding her eyes. "What a question," I said vaguely and called the two dogs. "Come on you two … have a twinkle before you get back in."

Bony obliged, finding the nearest tree that satisfied his requirements, but Jemima was more discerning. She inspected various likely locales before settling on a spot that, to me, looked no better or worse than any other.

Quinn's driver had vanished but now reappeared from behind a hawthorn bush wearing a grin that expressed his relief.

Sylvie, fussing behind the coach where a wicker case was strapped, gave a triumphant shout. "I knew it! I knew Mrs Twigley would pack some honey cakes."

She offered them to all including the driver and groom, who were Bill and Jarrod respectively, and we washed them down with ale before continuing on our journey.

We travelled all that day, stopping every couple of hours to rest the horses and stretch our legs. Bony and Jemima trotted behind Ember for a time but Jemima tired quickly. She was getting on in years and her joints were stiffening. Unfortunately, if Bony was outside, she was determined to be with him. Eventually, I called both dogs into the coach, that being the only way to ensure Jemima didn't cripple herself.

As night came down, we settled at an inn just outside of Carlisle.

∾

The following morning found me ill-tempered from lack of sleep. My bed had been hard and lumpy and I'd slept badly. My impatience to see Simon again and to hold my young nephew was making me fidgety and adding to my irritable mood.

Quinn was also feeling off-colour and decided to tie Ember to the back of the coach so he could ride inside with Sylvie and me.

"Why should Ember be disadvantaged because you've a sore arse after only one day in the saddle?" I grumbled.

"Good thing we are only going to Yorkshire then, isn't it," Quinn remarked. "Let Jarrod ride her today. I shall ride her tomorrow."

As we drove through Cumbria, our way was blocked twice by farmers herding their sheep; adorable black-faced creatures that peered at us from gentle, brown eyes.

I walked beside the coach for a short distance enjoying the autumn sky while Bony gambolled along like the young dog he was, thankfully showing no sign of the thrashing he'd received from Hamish.

Over the next days, we passed uneventfully through the countryside and the weather stayed mild. Lying miles behind us, I soon began to recognise the rolling dales of Yorkshire and my impatience eased. Inside the coach, it was beginning to grow dark. Quinn had continued inside with us and Jarrod was riding Ember.

"Quinn? How much farther, do you think?" I asked. He looked pale to my eyes but we were all suffering from the tedium.

"Not sure," he said. "Bill?"

"Aye?"

"Where are we?"

"See if we can get there tonight," I urged.

"Fifty mile or so," Bill called down.

"That's not far," I said persuasively. I had visions of sleeping in my childhood bed this night. "We can keep going."

"That's too far," said Quinn. "Besides the horses needing to be rested, it is not safe at night."

"But Quinn, the roads are good – we could do it in three hours."

He shook his head. "Not with my horses."

I slumped sulkily against the padded leather and Sylvie reached across to pat my knee. "Alex, we shall leave early. You'll be home before midday."

Quinn instructed Bill to pull in at the next inn.

I awoke at the first sign of dawn, washed and dressed. Sylvie glared from beneath the counterpane as I packed my belongings.

"A girl needs her beauty sleep," she groused.

"You're beautiful enough … get up."

She stretched and yawned. "I swore when Father recognised me that I'd never get out of bed early again."

I threw her travel gown at her. "Too bad that you promised yesterday we'd start out early."

Leaving our room, I crossed the narrow hallway. The inn was in darkness, but I could hear the first faint noises drifting from the kitchens below. Someone was singing, cheerfully and tunelessly, keeping time with a steady chop … chop … chop.

I pressed an ear to Quinn's door but could not hear him moving about so I gave a quick rap. The door was thick as an arm so I knocked harder and listened. There was no response.

"Damn," I swore in annoyance. "Quinn!" I said softly, trying not to wake the entire establishment. "Time to get up!"

Listening again, I heard a sound, though it was muffled and unidentifiable. "Quinn – are you awake?" I spoke louder this time.

I heard it again – it was a moan – and I knew a flicker of concern. "Quinn?"

The moan came again, followed quickly by some very unpleasant coughing. I tried the door. It was locked from the inside. "Quinn! Can you open the door? Are you alright?"

I was making no attempt to be quiet now and Bony was whimpering, scratching on the other side.

Suddenly there was another moan, followed by the tell-tale sounds of someone being violently ill.

"Oh God … Quinn! I'll get someone … I'll be back." I leapt towards the stairs just as Sylvie opened our door,

"Wha –?"

"Quinn's ill!" I threw over my shoulder. "I'm getting help," and I plunged down the stairs.

The taproom was in darkness and reeked of stale wine and smoke, ale and greasy food, and I could not reconcile it with the lively and inviting room we'd dined in the night before. A slit of light showed beneath a door at the end of the room and I fumbled toward it as quickly as I could in the gloom. The chopping stopped and the clash of pans rang out loudly as I threw open the kitchen door.

A boy was turning two large joints of meat on spits in a corner and a rush of heat hit me. A large sweating man with a rather bovine physique stood at a bench in a grey and stained apron, scraping chopped vegetables into a cooking pot.

He glanced up and a frown puckered his broad brow. "Wha' you want?" he demanded more annoyed than surprised that someone was at his door so early.

"I … er … there's a sick man upstairs …"

"So wha'?" He took up a handful of celery stalks and began chopping with a rapid staccato rhythm.

"His door is locked, do you …" I looked around reflexively, "does someone have a key? I need to get to him."

"Dunno. Not th' first drunk we 'ad 'ere. Let 'im sleep it orf. Wha' you about gettin' the man up at this hour anyways?"

"He's not drunk. Look, I need a key."

He wiped the back of his hand over his sweating brow and flicked it behind him causing the fire to hiss. Something in my face must have made him relent for he jerked his head toward the taproom. "Check be'ind th'coun'er … could be summat there."

He returned to his work – I was getting no more from him. The door swung shut behind me and I was once again in darkness. I groped toward the bar, sliding behind to scrabble among the assorted scraps of rubbish and lord only knew what else.

No keys to be found. I trailed my hands further along as Sylvie's disembodied voice came from the foot of the stairs.

"Alex! Are you there?"

Just then my hand nudged a large cold ring accompanied by a distinctive jangle.

"I found the keys!"

"Please hurry – something terrible's happening."

I stumbled across the blackened room and bolted up the staircase behind her. She waited outside Quinn's door and I could hear his moans from within as I arrived.

"Number four," Sylvie snapped urgently and I fumbled through the keys to find the right one. Each of the dozen or so keys on the ring had a number stamped on it. I quickly found number four and thrust it into the lock and as the door opened, we all but fell into the room.

The stench hit us like a wall – vomit and sweat. Through the dimness, we saw Quinn, lying on his bed, curled on his side gripping his belly and groaning.

"Oh my heavens!" Sylvie cried and dashed to his side. Quinn had managed to drag the pot out from under the bed and had vomited into it, but had been unable to prevent getting it on his bedclothes as well.

"Quinn! What's wrong?" Sylvie was uncharacteristically panicked and her elfin face was made sharp by her distress.

Quinn's body convulsed and he heaved once more into the chamber pot while Sylvie held his head and when it was over, she brushed the sweat-darkened hair from his forehead. His normally cheerful face was white and drawn with large purple shadows around his eyes.

He was far too ill for embarrassment, though I was embarrassed for him and occupied myself pouring water into his wash-basin and rinsing a cloth for Sylvie to bathe him.

"What is it? What has made you so ill?" She was asking.

"I … don't know," he said weakly. "I know … I've been very … tired lately."

Bony had taken himself over to a corner out of the way, his head on his paws with the mournful expression dogs do so well. I pulled a ladder-back chair over and sat beside him and he shifted so that he could rest his great, heavy head on my shoe.

Sylvie was rummaging through Quinn's things. She pulled a clean nightshirt from his bag and I averted my gaze as she helped him from his soiled one and into the other, and I knew then that this was not the first time she'd seen him in a state of undress. Of course, he'd spent so many nights at the castle, I'd have to be quite naive to think they'd not been intimate. I knew as well as anyone how difficult it was to love someone and keep them at arm's length.

Sylvie rinsed the cloth again sponging him, talking softly and as I looked up, she wiped her sleeve across her eyes and my heart lurched.

Would I ever know that kind of belonging again? To be so wholly committed to someone who returned my regard? I felt my own tears sting the back of my eyes and looked around for something helpful to do. Getting to my feet and surprising Bony as I did so, I said, "I'll tell Bill and Jarrod they may enjoy a rest day."

Sylvie nodded without turning away from her patient.

I crept from the room, Bony sticking close to my heels, and collecting Jemima on the way, we went outside to find Bill and Jarrod.

When I told them the news they looked at each other and Bill said, "You'll get to see that Nancy again."

At least someone was happy with the delay.

Whatever ailed Quinn had a good hold on him for by that night I knew we'd be staying at the inn for quite some time. I'd never seen anyone as ill and Sylvie sat beside him, refusing my offers to relieve her, as he tossed feverishly in his bed.

A doctor had been called from the village. He took a whole day to arrive and departed just in the nick of time for Sylvie was about to throttle him with her bare hands, so chafed was she by his inability to diagnose Quinn's ailment.

"*Idiot!*" she declared watching from the window as he rode away.

Thankfully after that first day, Quinn had ceased vomiting but the painful cramps continued, causing him to curl up in agony. He reached for her in his fever and she sat with red-rimmed eyes constantly assuring him she was there – she would not leave, not ever.

I lurked around the inn bored and frustrated and trying very hard not to show it. Unable to endure the inactivity, I ended up in the kitchen with Spotter, the greasy cook I'd met that first morning.

He put me to work chopping vegetables and basting the meats as a boy turned the spits.

Despite my first impression, Spotter was a cheerful cube of a man with no definition between his back and his rear – the apron tied about his middle offered the only suggestion of a waist.

It turned out that Spotter's nephew was the village doctor. As he leaned over a pot slung above the fire, Spotter asked what the boy had been able to do for my friend.

"Nothing, unfortunately," I told him. "He was unable to diagnose the problem."

Spotter nodded with wry satisfaction. "Jus' as I tole me brother it 'ud be," he said tasting the contents of the pot. "Tole'm yers learns all yers needs 'bout med'cal things on th' farm. Woun't listen t'me. What'd I know?"

"My brother studied medicine," I said. "He didn't finish though. Went to the Peninsula … served during the war."

"Good at it then was 'e?"

I shrugged. "He seemed to be. Met his wife over there … we were on our way to visit them when Quinn took ill."

He lost interest in my conversation, too annoyed by his nephew. "David cost 'is da a arm an' leg sendin' 'im t' stinkin' school and fer what? Can't even fix a man wi' th'spits – cut 'em up smaller." He waved his wooden spoon at me. "Small – size o' peas."

I nodded, scraping my pile of onions together and chopping as he directed.

∾

Finally, after a stay of four nights Quinn, although not fully recovered, was able to travel. He said he was reluctant to delay us any longer and I supressed my urge to sigh with relief.

We drove slowly, which made a two hour journey take nearly five hours and Quinn slept the entire way – stretched along the seat with his head in Sylvie's lap.

I considered pointing out that had we continued instead of stopping that first night, Simon could have taken care of him, but after witnessing the aggression with which Sylvie was prepared to defend him, I kept my thoughts to myself.

It was no matter now anyway, for it was a glorious November morning and we rolled up the blinds so Quinn could benefit from the sun's warmth. Soon, I recognised the landmarks around my home and though I'd only been away two years, it felt longer. So much had happened in that time.

I was only twenty-one, but mature beyond those years by the accumulated experiences of love, heartbreak, and betrayal, marriage, pregnancy and loss. I'd witnessed my husband rutting with a man, and I'd attended another man's death. I'd been beaten and I'd been both foolish and brave, and I'd watched the inexorable disintegration of my marriage.

Before I left Scotland, I had told Aggie I would pack my own things, carefully deciding what items I could live without, what items I needed with me, never framing the words – not even in my own mind.

And now, I would not think about Scotland or my life there – they did not exist for me as we drove through the Broughton Hall gates and trundled up the familiar drive with its half moon sweep to the right, the lush lawns on either side, the rose garden, terraces and walkways.

Our approach to the house passed the magnificent Great Oak, which stood half a foot deep in leaves as it shed its foliage for winter. A family of squirrels, complacent and unafraid of our coach, frolicked on the ground gathering acorns. The furniture was still there, but there was also a collection of small wooden toys – the type a toddling child might play with while his parents enjoyed their lemonade on a warm day.

We halted by the porch steps and Simon was there. I threw open the door and was out of the carriage and clasped firmly against his chest, unaware that I was crying until Maria offered her handkerchief, and with my face against my brother's shirt, I murmured, "I'm home … I'm home …"

CHAPTER 15

Quinn was immediately carried upstairs. Maria allocated Patrick's old room and I turned my mind from that other individual who'd lain in this bed as I looked down at Quinn's inert form. He'd lost a terrible lot of weight and looked like a boy beneath the counterpane.

Simon bent over him and quickly diagnosed a stomach germ. Untreated, it had poisoned his system, hence the fever. Maria, beside him, nodded her agreement and, suggesting a potion found effective on the Peninsular, went straight to her still-room.

"However did you deduce this when that useless clod at the inn could not?" Sylvie asked.

"We saw all manner of gut problems and fevers in Europe. You'd be surprised how many men died without ever seeing action."

"But Quinn won't die?" Sylvie said anxiously.

Simon shook his head. "Oh, he'll live, but he'll be weak as a newborn for the next month or so."

Sylvie stroked her patient's forehead lovingly. "That's alright — I'll take care of him."

Maria returned with her concoction in a jar. It smelled herbaceous and looked like mud. "Have him drink as much as he can," she said in her warm, velvety voice. "It will settle his stomach and break the fever. Soon – a day, perhaps two – he may take some broth."

"He'll sleep well after this brew, Sylvie," Simon added, "so come downstairs for supper. You'll do no one any favours by making yourself ill as well."

Sylvie agreed reluctantly. Simon and I left her with Maria and went to the parlour where a footman had built a welcoming fire. Jemima, with Bony in tow, had immediately reacquainted herself with Cook and Emily in the kitchen.

Flopping on to the settee, I sighed with relief. "Oh, Sime, you cannot imagine how good it feels to be home."

"Oh, I think I can," he chuckled. "It's good to see you. And Sylvie too, a free woman, so to speak."

"I'd forgotten you met her at Devon. And how are you, Sime? You seem to have adjusted …"

"Would you believe I sometimes forget?" He smiled ruefully. "I go to pick up a glass or something only to realise my arm is gone. It is odd – if I close my eyes, I feel I have two arms. My body thinks it's still there."

I plumped one of Mother's velvet cushions behind my head as Simon pulled over a chair. Studying me from his good eye, he said, "Well?"

"Well what?"

"Ah, you don't think I know my own sister? You're different … what's been going on?"

I was spared from answering immediately, as Emily brought in a pot of tea and a plate of small cakes. It gave me a moment to decide how much I would tell and how much to keep to myself. But this was Simon, my brother and friend. He knew me better than anyone – there could be no hiding the truth.

All the while Emily laid out the refreshments, he watched me steadily and I thought that if I held a fan over one half of his face, you wouldn't know he'd been disfigured; for the other half was virtually untouched. Simon's had been a beauty that, tempered with maturity, would have seen him become a heartachingly handsome man. I smiled to myself and he watched without question until Emily closed the door with a soft click.

"Hmm?" he prodded again.

It would salve my wounds to tell him. I'd told Sylvie, but she had lived it with me. Simon knew only what I'd written in my letters, anecdotes about my new home and friends. More serious details had been diluted or omitted entirely. Now I needed to unburden myself to someone who loved me and understood me as Simon did.

I took a deep breath and the tea grew cold in the pot as I began with my wedding night – the failed and embarrassing attempts at lovemaking then and thereafter. I told him about cranky old Lord Hamish and my habit of drowning the isolation and loneliness in the Scot's liquor.

I described how, as time passed, Hamish and I attempted to mend our bridges but after learning the dreadful truth of Anne's deceit, I was haunted by my unwitting betrayal. Throughout I remained loyal to my husband and my unborn child, but after the devastating loss of our precious baby, Hamish accused me of willing it, even as I blamed myself. Our marriage foundered, while Hamish's father died, clinging to my hand and weeping for his son, and I suffered mixed agonies of anger and relief.

Simon listened without reaction when I told how I'd discovered my husband coupling with another man, my feelings of revulsion over the act and the pleasure Hamish had derived from my witnessing it. Finally, there was Hamish's physical violence toward me, all culminating in the inevitable, weary disintegration of our marriage.

And playing behind it all, like distant music, was the ache of a lost love – at times distractingly dynamic, at others dull and exhausting.

"It should never have happened," I finished, wiping my sleeve across my eyes as Simon watched. "I should not have married Hamish. I shall never regret anything more in my life. I should have married the man I loved – still love."

I blew my nose, noisily.

Simon sat silent and pensive. He was leaning forwards, elbow on his knee and hand cupping his chin. I wanted him to speak. I wanted his thoughts. I wanted him to tell me that everything would be alright … I could have my old room back and things would be as they were before I married … That they, and I – we all – had been wrong. *God* I wanted him to say *something*.

But he didn't, he simply sat.

"Simon …?"

Slowly he looked up and unbelievingly, he shook his head. "You are married to Hamish. Despite all, your place is beside him."

My mouth fell open. "You cannot mean that! Don't you believe me?"

"I believe you," he said, "but you and Hamish … you're married, for better or worse, your lives are bound together."

"But we *have* no life together," I cried. "You don't understand!" I stood up now, pacing before him and he watched me. He was looking troubled but his jaw was set stubbornly.

"Zan, I do understand but you cannot change the fact that you are married. Whether it was a mistake or no, in the eyes of the law that's the way of it and it can't be reversed."

"But it *is* no marriage. We shall never have a child – heaven knows, we never share a bed. We don't even *like* each other."

He rose stiffly and I could see the frustration colouring his face. He gripped my chin and forced me to look into his eyes. "What would you do, Zan?" he asked, gruffly. "Do you think to leave Hamish and live the adulterous life with Patrick? Is that your plan? What would you have Patrick do?"

"I don't … I don't know …" I stammered.

"That's right! You don't know." He released me abruptly and

turned away. "Hamish is all you have – you must realise that. *He* must realise that. The two of you have no choice but to resolve this."

He leaned on the mantle staring into the flames and I could hear my rapid breathing above the noisy crackle of the fire in the silence that followed.

"Let me tell you something," he said, finally. "You will never reconcile with Patrick. Even had you Hamish's blessing – for you know what will stand in your way?" He waited, and his anger seemed to drain away. His face, often difficult to read since his disfigurement, showed very plainly his sympathy. "Patrick himself."

He came forward then and smoothed the tears from my cheeks. "This may be hard for you to accept right now, but … come, sit down."

He led me to the settee and kneeling before me, his face compassionate, he explained, "There is no fairy tale ending for you with Patrick. You would be better served returning to your husband – no, hear me out. I've been to Devon … I've seen him. He has changed: too many experiences … horrors. He's not the carefree charmer you dallied with one lazy spring. That boy is gone. Now he's bitter and very, *very* angry that we all judged him. He does not wish to see you – he will not even hear your name spoken. Perhaps he held some affection for you once – but not any more."

"But I was deceived. If I could explain … it was Anne –"

"We were all deceived but it's not about that. How do I say this…? Look, Patrick was ever one for … varied female companionship. He loves women, *many* women. Do you understand? In reality, it has only ever been physical with him. Patrick's propensity for love affairs is well known – Oxford, Spain, even here in Wolstone – and he loves them all – as much as he can love anyone. With you it was different, only because there was friendship too, and perhaps for a time he fancied himself in love, but it was doubtless a *passing, youthful thing*. And fleeting, like all the others. It is over now."

I shook my head stubbornly and he sighed. "Zan, I tell you

for your own good … if you go there … are you prepared for his rejection?"

"If he's so bitter … does that not show he cared?" I said, doggedly.

"You know, when I was there, we had a fierce argument – he's angry with all of us because we believed Anne and judged him accordingly. On the basis of your friendship, he had expected you to defend him. You did not. That's all it was – it was nothing to do with love."

Simon remained patiently at my knee while I wept into my handkerchief.

"Zan," he said gently. "He does not love you, he never did – he told me very plainly. Now, stay here as long as you need, but then return to your husband and no one need ever know about this conversation. Go back to Hamish. Tell him you want to begin again."

I shook my head. "I can't, Sime, I could not endure a life with Hamish. And as for Patrick … You weren't there … no one was …. Patrick and I … we talked … made plans for the future … we …" I could not finish for the knot in my throat. I wanted to scream with pain and frustration.

That Patrick had no love for me I would not accept. That it all was a passing, youthful thing was impossible. Patrick and I had made promises … No one understood the depth of feeling between us.

Though I had only just arrived in Yorkshire, I decided in that moment, that despite Simon's discouragement, I would go to Devon – I had to know for myself.

∾

The following weeks passed in something of a fog. Sylvie was fully occupied with Quinn, who was beginning to show signs of improvement, while Simon worked with his lawyer and Papa's old steward, Collings. He was negotiating the purchase of neighbouring land – Jackson, whose fearsome, prized bull had long ago departed his earthly paddock, was moving to his daughter's house in Leeds. Simon had seen an opportunity to extend our estate, and a group of tenants had expressed interest in leasing parcels of it.

I spent most of my time in the parlour, entertaining myself with a good book. Sometimes Maria sat with me, sewing things for Dudley or Simon. I did a lot of brooding then.

Simon and I had revisited my situation with considerably less emotion the following day, but with virtually the same result; Simon reluctantly agreed that I may possibly not return to Hamish, but genuinely believed I should.

He could not accept that Patrick may have truly loved me and was confident that I would be happier in Scotland starting anew with Hamish, than pursuing some romantic fantasy.

Yet I knew how strongly I felt for Patrick, and I had faith that if he felt only a fraction in return, it would be worth fighting for. I believed in my heart that given the opportunity to explain to Patrick in my own words, I could make things right.

Simon said Pat had changed, but no one could change that much. Somewhere hidden deep beneath Anne's treachery, the condemnation of his family, and my betrayal, alongside his experiences in the most horrific war man had ever waged against man, the old Patrick lurked — I was convinced of it!

I kept my thoughts to myself — not even telling Sylvie — awaiting Quinn's recovery, making plans; how long the journey would take, how much money and so on.

One afternoon, I was daydreaming thus while Maria sewed beside me.

When she paused in her needlework, she interrupted my thoughts saying, "Dudley grows so quickly. I must always be making something bigger."

Grateful of the opportunity to take my mind from my troubles, I said, "You should see if there are some of Meg's old things stored up in the attic. You could alter them for him."

"I did not know there were any."

"I'm certain there are."

❧

The attic was dark and smelled stale and musty. The light from the lantern revealed various crates, trunks and items of furniture covered with dusty sheeting. We could stand upright in most of the space but towards the edges, where the roof sloped downwards, we were forced to stoop as we moved about. In the centre, I could stand on tiptoe and touch the clay roof tiles but there were too many cobwebs and one or two very old and derelict bird's-nests squeezed into gaps between the beams and the tiles.

"Have you Broughtons been hiding your family skeletons up here?" Maria asked.

I hadn't been called a Broughton in a long time and I liked the sound of it. I grinned. "Only Mother has skeletons." I took up the lantern to begin my search. Immediately, the gossamer net of a spiderweb fell across my face. "*Phht!*" I spat, swiping at it. "I hope you're not afraid of spiders."

"Not yet," she said soberly and looked around. "Where to start?"

"Take your pick." I headed for a likely looking trunk on my left. Maria targeted an old wooden crate.

Dropping to my knees, I unlatched the lid. It was heavy and creaked on dry leather hinges and smelled old and stale causing my nose to itch.

"What's in there?" Maria asked. "I've only old books and papers here."

"Material, I think." I tugged at a corner of fabric and it came out shiny and slippery. "Oh, it's silk!"

Maria leaned over beside me. Reaching with both arms she extracted a great bolt of the stuff. It was magnificent, shimmering and exotic in ruby-red and emerald green shot through with threads of gold.

"It is beautiful," she breathed. "And so old – a wonder it has not been eaten by worms."

"There's a reason for that," I said picking up and smelling a ball of cedarwood. "Mother's trick for keeping nasties away."

"A good trick." Maria held the fabric before the lantern.

"You should take it downstairs – make a gown for a special occasion."

She chuckled. "We do not have special occasions – it would only be for Simon."

"Is that not reason enough?" I asked playfully.

"Pleasing Simon has never required fancy gowns. If I wore a gown made of this I would be too afraid for him to touch me."

"Then you'd have to take it off."

"Your brother needs no encouragement." We both laughed and she moved to another trunk while I put the bolt aside.

Continuing my explorations, I rummaged through oddments of dress material, lace and ribbon off-cuts. Suddenly Maria gasped. "Oh *Dios*! Come here, Alex!"

She was moving towards the back of the attic and had pulled a sheet away from a framed painting. I went to where she knelt in the dust and, holding the lantern high, I recognised a portrait that Gerrard had commissioned many years ago.

"It is all of you as children," she said tilting the large, heavy-framed oil painting to catch more of the light.

"Oh, I'd forgotten about this. Gerrard brought a painter up from London – I cannot recall his name now – just after Meg was born."

"Why is it here?" she asked, her eyes on Simon's likeness.

"Mother was never keen on it. Perhaps it captured us too honestly. She preferred something more pretentious."

We were both silent as we studied the painting. Simon stood handsome, tall and straight, laughing at something Anne had said, his hand resting lightly on Maeve's shoulder.

Maeve sat in the middle with Anne to her left and me on

her right. Her pixie-like face was puckered slightly in an attempt to suppress a laugh and the painter had depicted her dancing, mischievous eyes perfectly.

Anne, who I remember had spent the entire morning primping before her mirror, was dressed in her favourite, pale-pink satin gown as though about to attend a grand ball. When she had discovered the sitting would take many hours over several days, she insisted poor Janet sculpt her hair and help her into her gown each day. The result was that Anne looked out of place among the rest of us.

Naturally, Simon and I had teased her incessantly about it but she'd merely tossed her head to make the little jewels in her ears tinkle.

I sat to Maeve's right and for once, my unruly hair behaved obediently, restrained by a ribbon and multitudinous pins. I wore the forced smile of many hours in one position though I'd been admonished repeatedly for squirming.

Mother had insisted I wear my lemon muslin gown, even though it was slightly too small across the bodice and the air in the room was quite chilly. The dress's colour suited my brown hair and eyes, yet I spent the entire time fighting the gooseflesh on my arms and trying to sit in such a way as to hide the effects of the cold air on my young bosom.

Meg slumbered in Maeve's arms. The artist thought it a nice touch that the most innocent-looking held the newborn sibling. Meg was so young that all that could be seen of her was a pair of cheeks, fat and pink, buried in yards of cream linen and lace.

Inevitably, my eyes drifted to Patrick. Neither smiling nor frowning, his perfectly shuttered face stared from the canvas. I always thought the artist had failed to capture the intellect that lurked in his eyes no matter how blank his expression.

Maria watched me. "I've not met this Patrick. He was quite handsome in a … a distant kind of way."

"Handsome yes, but not classically so like Simon. He resisted getting dressed up, especially for the sitting. He said we should be captured as we really were."

"Such a long time ago. Were you in love with him then?"

The directness of her question took me aback and I laughed to cover it. "No, I wasn't in love with him then — I even hated him at first. He kept to himself and was quite surly. After I got to know him, I saw the person he was. That's when I began to love him."

She sighed wistfully. "Simon was truly beautiful, was he not?" I looked at the carefree grin and merry eyes of her husband as she went on, "When he first came to the hospital, the nurses all swooned over him. Not only was he handsome, but he was gentle and kind."

"Did you love him at first sight?"

She grinned. "I loved him from the moment he first said, *nurse could you direct me to the privy, please?*"

She mimicked Simon's English accent perfectly. We laughed together but she sobered suddenly. "Oh Alex, I am so happy with your brother. Do you think you will you return to your husband?" Once again she caught me by surprise.

"Simon thinks I should," I parried.

"Do *you* think you should?"

I turned to the canvas and looked again at my sister's face. Anne, so young and yet the signs were visible had we but known — the coquette's smile, the small upturned nose, the proud tilt of her head. She was only fourteen when this portrait was painted, yet already her cream and rose complexion and teasing lips hinted at the cunning beauty she would become.

And my heart shifted in my breast as I looked at Patrick. Pale shoulder-length hair tied with a cord, shoulders intimating the physique he'd develop in adulthood, loose-fitting white shirt rolled up to expose a forearm and strong hand. Long artistic fingers rested on the back of Anne's chair; fingers that in years to come would caress my body and awaken my womanhood. His lips, full and sensuous – even in youth – as capable of profanity as they were of delicate words of love. Thankfully the rush of blood to my cheeks was hidden by the dimness of the attic.

That he no longer loved me, I could not accept. He must still love me for how well I remembered his tender kisses, declarations and promises, the special glances only I could read, the secret brush of his hand, our one night together. And the familiar sting behind my eyes returned.

"No," I said, responding at last to Maria's question, blinking away the tears. "I cannot return to Hamish." In a rush I turned to her. "Maria, may I confide in you?"

"Of course, but –"

"Simon will be angry, but I am going to Devon."

"Simon only thinks to protect you."

"I know, but … oh, how to explain? There was something special, Maria; I cannot describe it. Something beautiful and honest, an acknowledgement that no one understands. I won't – I *can't* believe it did not exist for him. He *did* love me – must love me still, I'd feel it here if he didn't," I pressed my hands to my heart.

She sat back on her heels and regarded me carefully. "But marriage to another cannot be undone."

"Do you also think I should return to Hamish?"

She hesitated and I lowered my eyes with sadness, but at her next words my head jerked up.

"No. But you are Simon's sister. He does not see you as a lover would. Nor does he see Patrick as anything other than his friend. He does not understand that such a one as Patrick *can* allow love into his heart – though it is very private and can only be with great trust for it makes him vulnerable. Patrick does not despise you for believing Anne. It is more. He shared himself with you, he trusted you, but you took his secrets and rejected them by marrying another."

Her words were a revelation. Patrick, so reserved and private, had bared his soul to me. That is what I had destroyed — trust. Suddenly everything was clear and any lingering doubts dissipated like fog in the sun.

I smiled and she nodded knowingly. "Simon will not be happy, but we women are stronger than men — we will always fight for love."

~

"I'd wondered where this painting was," Simon said. The family portrait was now hanging above the mantelpiece in the library.

"It's a good likeness of Meg," I said jokingly.

"Swathes of lace and a button nose?" Simon laughed. "Actually, it's a rather poor likeness of me; I was much more handsome than that." He draped his arm lazily over his wife's shoulders.

"If you say so, *mi querido.*"

"All the girls said so, didn't they Zan?"

"And their mothers," I agreed.

Something bumped behind us and we turned as one to find Quinn leaning heavily on Sylvie.

"How's the patient?" Simon asked.

"Better ..." Quinn said breathlessly.

"Better sit down," Sylvie corrected, gasping with the effort of assisting him.

Maria slid from Simon's arm and went to where Quinn had flopped on to the settee. She held his wrist and checked the watch Simon had offered wordlessly.

"He will live," she pronounced.

"Unless I kill him," Sylvie said dryly. "He's becoming so bored he's driving me insane."

"If boredom is taking me around the twist, I'm taking you with me," Quinn said reaching for her hand and smiling lovingly at her. "Will you tell them?"

"Tell us what?" I asked, taking a fair guess. Their mutual affection was obvious, intensified by Quinn's illness and Sylvie's worry. I had expected for some time they would make an announcement.

Sylvie's eyes glistened happily and we held our breaths. "Quinn and I … are to become parents."

This was not what I'd expected.

Momentarily stunned we stood open-mouthed, uncertain as to how to react. Maria was the first to recover. She stepped forward to take Sylvie's hands. "That is wonderful news. We are all very happy for you."

Simon frowned. "Yes, we're very happy, but … er, Quinn?"

"Yes?"

"You will be … you know?" Simon nodded toward Sylvie meaningfully.

"Ah … not sure what you're getting at, old boy," Quinn responded puzzled, and Simon flushed uncharacteristically.

"Oh, stop it, love," Sylvie interrupted, her eyes shining. "Simon, of course Quinn has asked me to marry him and I have accepted."

Simon released his breath in a rush. "Oh, thank God. I thought I was going to have to call him out."

"Will you wait until after the baby comes to tell Sylvie about Devon?" Maria asked the next day. I was in the morning room arranging some late roses I'd salvaged from the garden before Alcott, Simon's new gardener, pruned them in preparation for winter.

"I don't know now," I confessed. "I cannot go alone, but I expect they'll want to remain here until the baby is born." I stepped back to critique my work.

"You could always take a pair of footmen with you," she suggested helpfully.

I adjusted a couple of flowers then turned to her. "Simon would never agree."

"I could talk to him."

I shook my head. "No. I'll not cause a quarrel between you – we both know where he stands on the matter. I'll talk to Sylvie when the time is right."

"Would that time be now?" Sylvie came into the room. Her face hadn't lost its happy glow since her announcement the previous day, and now she looked questioningly between Maria and me. "I've been looking all over for you, Alex. I have something to ask, so if you've a favour to ask of me, this would be a good time."

"Mine can wait."

She shrugged. "Very well. I would be very honoured if you would stand beside me as matron-of-honour at my wedding."

"Oh Sylvie!" I rushed into her arms. "I'd be so proud." We hugged while Maria looked on, hands clasped delightedly at her chin.

When at last Sylvie released me, she said, "Now, what would you ask of me?"

Maria tactfully made for the door, murmuring something about seeing Cook.

"Honestly, it *can* wait," I said.

"Come on Alex. Whatever it is surely it can be accommodated."

I sighed heavily. "Let's sit down."

We settled ourselves before a gently glowing fire and she prompted, "Tell me."

"Alright – I'll be direct. Sylvie I'm not returning to Scotland. My mind is made up – I'm going to Devon."

I watched her closely and waited for the words of caution, doubt, warning, but to my surprise a slow smile spread across her face and she reached for my hands. "Of course you are. Quinn and I depend upon it."

"What?"

She nodded happily. "So, when shall we leave?"

"But … your wedding? The baby?"

"There's a tiny chapel at Waterville, and as a little girl I always dreamed I'd marry there. When I told Quinn he said he'd be happy to marry me anywhere – so that's settled."

"But Simon?" I asked hardly daring to hope. "He offered to hold the wedding here."

"I know, but Quinn explained everything and he understands." She gripped my shoulders. "You see? Quinn and I will be married in my pretty chapel. It will be easier for Quinn's brother in London to attend, and I can ask Patrick to give me away."

"It is truly what you want?"

"Yes!" she cried, her eyes glistening happily. "It's what I have always wanted – but Alex, there is another thing. We told Simon – we explained that I want you with me and though he's not happy, he promised he'll not stop you going to Devon."

I leaned into her arms and we hugged again and she whispered in my ear, "You must go, Alex. It won't be easy but you must try, and I would not dream of your going alone. So you see, it all works perfectly."

Never had I known such friendship – I was speechless. I tightened my embrace as she whispered, "And we shall tackle Patrick together."

∾

My second wedding anniversary passed, irrelevantly, as Christmas approached. It was the week before Christmas and I was sitting in the library window, Jemima beside me, watching the snow lay a sugary dusting over the gravel drive when a carriage rounded the bend and pulled up beside the porch.

Julia alighted looking very pretty in a burnished-gold velvet dress and fashionable black and gold bonnet. She saw me in the window and waved her black fur muff enthusiastically. My heart swelled and I left the library at a run.

I found Emily and asked her to bring tea and cakes into the morning room.

Julia was shown in and immediately we launched into each other's arms while Jemima danced eagerly around our legs. We had corresponded by mail, but we hadn't seen each other since her visit to Scotland a year ago, and she was certainly unaware of my marriage breakdown.

We sat before a cheerful fire and exchanged news. Aglow with vitality, her peach-coloured complexion had a healthy vigour not present last time I'd seen her. She tossed off her bonnet with an airy flip and shook out her polished-copper hair.

"You look gorgeous," I remarked. "So alive."

She dropped her muff beside her bonnet and waved my comments aside. "I've resigned myself to life as a spinster. I'm twenty-four now – too old for a London season and certainly too old for anyone but the poorest of ageing land-owners – and that all lends one a certain freedom."

"You're definitely happier than last time we saw each other – you're shining like a beacon."

She laughed gaily. "I am feeling well – but Alex, what has happened to you? You're so thin and pale … like you've been washed too much and all the colour has run out."

"I've been indoors a lot … you know I hate the cold."

"Oh yes," she said, wilting slightly. "But you lost your dear little baby. I grieved for you, truly. So tell me – how are you now?"

I drew myself up in my chair and took a deep breath. "I've left Hamish."

"Good," she said firmly, showing no surprise.

"I'm going to Devon to see Patrick."

"Better." And she grinned. "Saints alive, why aren't you leaping about with excitement?"

I shrugged. "Worry, I suppose. I've hurt Patrick terribly – I'm told he'll not see me."

"Then stay until he does – it's quite simple, you know. I have never doubted the depth of feeling between you."

"I wish I had your faith."

"Gloomy-guts! If you had my faith you'd never have married Hamish in the first place. Remember when I –"

"Don't say you warned me," I cut her off quickly. "It's all in the past now."

"Hello Julia – so good to see you again." Sylvie joined us and the two embraced. I called for another tea cup to be brought while Julia regaled us with all the district gossip, including the fact that Celia and Deon had returned to Leeds two months previously – married.

"And the juicy part ..." Julia leaned forward conspiratorially, "they have an eight-months-old boy – she must have been with child when they ran away."

I sat back and regarded my friend curiously. "How do you feel about that, Jules? They must've been ... you know ... while you and Deon were still betrothed?"

"Oh, you know me," she said, too breezily. "I'm over it now."

I nodded, unconvinced.

"So," she cheerfully changed the subject, "where are Simon and his lovely lady?"

"Visiting the Salisburys ... Will you stay for dinner?"

"Thank you, but I promised Mother I'd be home to help her plan a menu. She's giving a supper on New Year's Eve."

Later, Sylvie and I waved her off as flurries of snow settled on our shoulders and, with a sisterly arm about Sylvie's still trim waist, I wondered again at Julia's exuberance and suddenly I knew.

"She's having an affair," I said in wonderment.

"Hmm," Sylvie mused. "I spotted that too."

CHAPTER 16

For those surrounding me, it seemed that 1816 would be a year of great promise. Simon and Maria were expecting their second child in February. Then there was Sylvie and Quinn's wedding followed by their babe – due late in July. I alone eyed the horizon with trepidation. As Christmas approached, I wondered where I would be this time next year. Would I be loved and secure in Patrick's arms? Or would I be living on the charity of relatives? I quite fancied the idea of sleeping the year through like some enchanted princess and awakening when it was all over.

And suddenly Christmas arrived. We five adults, plus Dudley and his nurse, enjoyed a quiet meal and an exchange of gifts. But Boxing Day guaranteed a lively celebration as Simon finalised preparations for the traditional party for Broughton Hall's tenants, servants and their families to enjoy feasting, music and dancing.

He was a generous man, my brother; strict when the need called, compassionate when required. He was strong, dependable, astute and above all, he was fair – as was evidenced by the contentment and lack of conflict on his lands.

I watched one of his tenants breaking a bale of hay for the cows in the newly acquired paddock. The library window gave an excellent view across the seamless, white landscape, and I could see the trestles being readied on the snow-covered lawns by excited, laughing and chattering servants.

On the gravel just below my window, Collings was building a fire to keep the revellers warm, while one of the stable boys had contributed a wheelbarrow laden with wood.

Just as well, for where I stood in the library, the fire beside me roared in the grate, yet I could feel the chill from the glass seeping through the wool of my gown. I turned from the window, massaging warmth into my fingers, and came face to face with *the lady*.

The last time I'd seen her had been before my wedding when she'd seemed to be trying to warn me – advice I'd ignored.

"Can you hear me?" I asked softly.

Her brow puckered and she cocked her head. I repeated, louder this time but her expression was vague.

"Can I touch you?"

Feeling brave, I stepped towards her, my questing hand outstretched and she watched. Another step and I had my answer for suddenly a wave of heat sent a rush of blood to my face and perspiration broke above my lip. Swaying dizzily, I gripped the back of a chair, but in a heartbeat, the sensation was gone and I was alone once more.

❧

Simon found me a short time later. I was still in my chair watching the preparations below. The fire had slumped low and he took a poker and stoked it into life before dragging a chair over. He sat beside me and smiled his handsome half smile.

"It all works out, you know," he said, taking my hand. "You may think, how did I end up here? But it's all part of some grand scheme, and so is the outcome."

"If only I knew what the outcome would be," I said.

"Would you still go to Waterville if you did?"

"You're assuming the outcome will be an unhappy one," I pointed out with a smile, at which he shrugged. "So what are you saying, Sime? That I should not hope?"

"If it was me, I would not go."

"Yes, you would," I said quietly. "Because you know what it is to love. I know what Patrick and I had. It was special and precious, even if you dismiss it as inconsequential."

"Perhaps."

"Then you've relented?"

He laughed lightly. "Let's say I'm gracious in defeat. You have three ranged alongside you. I am only one."

His hand still held mine and I stared at it lying in my lap. It was a strong hand, brown and calloused from hard work. I said, "Sime, not everyone has your perfect marriage. Marrying Hamish was the greatest mistake of my life – probably his greatest mistake too. If things don't work out with Patrick … well, I cannot think of it because if Patrick will not accept me … I cannot return to Hamish."

"You know I'd never turn you away."

"But you'd prefer not to have me here."

"It's not like that."

"Then what is it like?" I was suddenly angry. "You'd have me ensconced in a castle in Scotland with a husband who loathes me, beats me and prefers the company of men? No children, no friends and nothing to look forward to? Is that what you want for me, Simon?"

"You know I don't."

"Then what *do* you want for me?"

"I want you to be happy – like Maria and I are happy. I just don't think you'll find that happiness with Patrick."

"Why not?" I demanded.

"Because I know what I saw. He is … changed … bitter. He no

longer sees you as a friend — much less a lover — and he drinks and womanises with no thought to —"

"So he has returned to his youth," I remarked flippantly.

"He was never bitter — damn it, Alex!" he cried suddenly in frustration. "I am your brother. I love you dearly and want only your happiness. But as I see it, there are two men in your life. With one, you enjoyed a brief dalliance. The other you are bound to by law."

There it was again, a *brief dalliance*. Why did everyone believe it impossible that Patrick could truly have loved me? Internally I seethed but it was pointless repeating myself. I sighed heavily.

"I would never turn you away from my door, Zan."

"But …?"

"But nothing." He gave his half-grin. "Hamish is not a proper husband to you. This is your home — now, as it ever will be." He leaned in and kissed my cheek. "Come, let's join the party."

∿

The Boxing Day celebrations were in full swing when we emerged from the house. I stood in the snow beside Simon, smiling at the sight of our guests all drinking, feasting, enjoying themselves — particularly the children, their small faces lit with laughter, their eyes shining and mouths stuffed with all the delicacies their parents ordinarily could not have provided.

Some had brought musical instruments, crude pipes and fiddles, and there was dancing and merriment in the snow. The men competed in arm wrestling competitions while their women exchanged gossip. Maria sat among them, chatting happily and sharing stories of her childhood in Spain.

The children made a family of snowmen beside the rose garden and Cook supplied walnuts for eyes, carrots and turnips for noses and stalks of rhubarb for mouths. Emily produced an old hat of Simon's and a clay pipe commandeered from Alcott, the gardener.

Towards the middle of the afternoon, a familiar port-wine carriage bumped along the snowy drive. One of the stableboys broke away from the party to take care of the two well-matched greys, snorting in the icy air. A liveried footman unfolded the stairs and handed out a charming child in a red travelling costume trimmed with white fur. Her blonde curls bounced gaily and her tinkling laugh rang out as the snow crunched beneath her shiny black boots. Turning toward the inside of the carriage she said in a lilting voice, "Look Papa, a party!"

"Meg!" I shrieked and fairly flew to her.

Whirling about, the girl responded with a joyous squeal and closed the distance between us.

Gerrard stepped gingerly down from the carriage, leaning heavily on a silver-topped cane. In the two years since I'd seen him he'd grown ruddier of face and rounder of belly, but his leonine hair remained thick and blonde.

Our eyes met over Meg's shining head and I gently extricated myself from my youngest sister and approached him.

"Hello Lass," he said kissing my cheek. "So glad to see you here."

Simon shouted from behind us and Meg immediately ran to her brother – no trace of the frightened little girl she had been when he'd first arrived home.

He clasped her to him strongly with his one arm and spun her off her feet. "And aren't you all decked out like the Christmas pixie," he exclaimed, and she giggled happily.

"Who are all those people?" she asked when Simon returned her to the ground.

"They're our friends who work in the house and the fields. They're having a Christmas party. You may join them if you like."

"Papa?" Her father nodded and she ran toward the celebration.

"Gerrard, good to see you. I assumed you'd be coming," Simon said clapping his stepfather's back.

It was then that I noticed Sylvie standing on the porch with

Quinn beside her. She stood with hands demurely clasped and her face blank. Quinn's hand was resting lightly at the small of her back.

"Father?" I said. He turned to me and I nodded to where his daughter waited.

He followed my indication and paused. He may have made a written recognition of her, but as yet there'd been no public demonstration. Although her hands were relaxed in their clasp, the tautness around her eyes showed that Sylvie was acutely aware of this fact. Instinctively, Simon and I both moved aside for there must be no hindrance to this meeting.

Gerrard's hesitation was only momentary but must have stopped Sylvie's heart. From where I stood I saw the softening of his expression and the slight dampness in his eyes.

"My girl," he said simply, and held out his arms.

Sylvie, ever dignified, moved gracefully down the porch steps with Quinn at her side. None could have doubted her noble ancestry as she calmly paused two yards from her father.

"Hello Papa," she said before sinking into a curtsy, but her father grasped her hands and pulled her into his arms. I dashed the tears from my eyes as I watched father and daughter, who'd for so long denied their relationship, come together. When finally Sylvie broke away, she turned to Quinn. "Papa, may I present my affianced, Quinn Atherton. Quinn, my father, Gerrard Washburn, Earl of Thorncliffe," she announced proudly.

Quinn stepped forward and gave a formal bow, "my lord."

Gerrard's face broke into a jovial smile and he pumped Quinn's hand enthusiastically, "Call me Father, Gerrard, Thorncliffe or whatever you damn well choose – just not *my lord*. Son, welcome to the family."

❧

It took the house staff two days to right the place after the Boxing Day party. Mrs. Grainger grumbled *about all them servants tramping their filthy boots on my fine rugs*, while wrapping her new green woollen shawl with its red embroidery and silver tassels – her Christmas gift from Simon and Maria – about her shoulders.

CHAPTER 17

Snow suppresses sound. Like a smothering blanket it captures, holds down, and absorbs all noise. There is no silence as complete as that of a morning after a night of heavy snowfall.

That January, I awoke to such a silence morning after frustrating morning. The deadened hush kept me huddled beneath my counterpane until well into the seventh hour – late for me – because I had no thought to walk in the park. Indeed, I had no thought for anything but to saddle Ember and ride south like the furies.

Though the house rang with merriment I champed at the bit, watching impatiently as the snow continued to pile around the walls and along the terraces.

The trees sagged heavily with it and the lane to Leeds was blocked.

It was the fourth day of January when Father took me aside and, with a glass each of Cook's plum wine, we settled before a comforting fire, and he bade me speak of my two years as Lady Glendenning, wife of the Seventh Viscount Elginbury.

The fire reduced to a pile of glowing coals while I told my tale, leaving out only the more sordid details, and his face remained diplomatic throughout. At no point did he express surprise, condemnation, or support; he simply fingered his ear lobe and listened.

For the first time I was able to tell him of my love for his son, how we had hidden it, the future we had planned together, and the truth – that we had not been intimate until that last night before Patrick returned to Europe. "He didn't seduce me, Father. I offered myself to him, in love."

Unlike Simon, he accepted that Patrick had truly loved me. And then I asked the question that burned in my heart, "You knew it was not Patrick's child Anne carried, didn't you?"

"I suspected," he responded.

"And all along you knew where he could be found?"

He sighed. "Not at first, but I traced him quickly enough. Sending mail back and forth took time though. It was months before he replied to my letter – by then you were married."

"And you told him?"

"Yes. He'd asked after you … but I didn't realise. I thought – *damn it all* – I did not realise! You should have confided in me – the pair of you – before he went away. When he asked after you, I thought he was merely asking after family. Had I known, oh Lass … you'd never have married that Scots boy. I'd have done everything in my power, spent any sum extricating you from that contract. I knew you and Patrick were close. Looking back now … You see Lass, I know my son … I knew he felt more than a passing regard for you. I even spoke with your mother about matching the two of you, but she was adamant it had to be Elginbury – such an excellent match – and she wanted Anne for Patrick. In the face of Anne's story … well, I could not call her a liar without the facts. By the time I'd heard from Patrick it was too late."

"I cannot return to Hamish – even if Patrick won't accept me."

He nodded his agreement. "You know that my son is a very stubborn man, even if he loves you still."

"It's a chance I must take."

"More than that," he smiled gently. "I must tell you – you've a rival for his affection."

My heart gave a sudden jolt. Why had I never considered this possibility?

"I receive regular mail from Mrs Bath – always have. She keeps me informed of affairs at Waterville. She wrote just after Patrick returned from Waterloo. She said he'd taken up with a former mistress – Kate or Kat, or something – daughter of an old associate of mine. He's known her for years. Mrs Bath didn't say much, but he's been seen publicly with this girl. Perhaps he feels it's time to settle down, get an heir … I don't know. But I would welcome any woman who could quell the wandering spirit in him – get him to sell that commission."

I digested the information slowly. How could I have not considered competition, for he was titled, rich, attractive? This was the girl from Astor – how well I knew his liaison with her!

"I only tell you this to prepare you. What I haven't told you is that you have my full support. I want more than anything for him to leave the army and make a home and family. Rather you than some tarted-up chit any day."

"Thank you," I murmured. "But there is still the problem of my marriage. Every time I think of him, I remember I'm a married woman – I cannot give him heirs, I cannot even respectably live with him."

He touched my knee. "Go and win him over first, then we shall deal with the question of your marriage."

❧

The snowmen remained in place for almost four weeks. It wasn't until the end of January that the sun strengthened enough to slick their surfaces into a watery glaze, and form a muddy slush at their base. Squirrels stole their noses and eyes, and the clay pipe hung from the mouth of one making him look something of a drunkard.

From my window, I made my daily assessment of the situation and determined that the lanes were clearing sufficiently to begin planning our departure.

The park glittered in the morning sunlight and I decided to take Ember out. The horse was in need of exercise and I also was tired of being cooped up indoors. Jemima must remain behind. Her ten years were telling on her in stiffened joints and slower movements.

Sparrow, so called for his small stature, was surprisingly wiry and strong as he saddled Ember for me. Cook had given me two lemon biscuits wrapped in linen and a carrot for Ember. They were in a bag that Sparrow tied to my saddle. Wheeling Ember's head around, I walked her out into the snowy courtyard.

Sparrow had threaded a string of tinkling bells through her harness and I recognised them as the ones Anne's pony used to wear. With each step Ember took the bells jangled merrily.

The Great Oak stood like a faithful old companion, and I remembered the many happy hours spent beneath those huge boughs. Now she was grey and bare, her skeletal limbs burdened heavily with snow. The wrought iron furniture lay abandoned and snow-covered at her feet.

I let Ember walk where she would after her days of confinement in the stables. Her feet left tracks behind us and I twisted, my hand on her rolling rump, watching behind to see if the oddity of her gait showed in her tracks. In any case, Ember was very special to me – a remembrance of a brief window of time when the pain of losing Patrick had lost its edge and Hamish and I still had a future.

We neared the border of the park and moved through into the forest. The canopy, bereft of its summer greenery, arched overhead like fleshless ribs and I relaxed in the saddle, holding the reins merely for the sake of holding them and letting Ember pick her own way. My mind drifted beyond the delicate tinkling rhythm of the harness bells.

What did Kat Wheeler look like? Was she pretty? Thin? Plump?

Gerrard said, he thought Pat might be thinking to settle down. Did he love her?

But surely he must still love me! How could I feel this way while he felt nothing? Was it possible? A little germ of uncertainty crept into my brain. What if he'd been too hurt? What if he truly didn't love me? What if he never had …? I pushed the treacherous thoughts away, for surely no god would delight in such cruelty.

Ember stopped and I looked around. We were in a small clearing. A tree had fallen and its trunk formed a snowy seat so I slid to the ground and looped Ember's reins over a branch and, untying the bag of food, placed it on the log. My riding gloves were leather and very warm enabling me to brush away the snow.

Ember's inquisitive nose immediately detected the scent of carrot and I giggled as she nudged and snuffled at me. I snapped it in two and gave her half. Small splinters of it dropped from her mouth and stood out brightly on the snow.

The woods were tranquil and hauntingly pretty in their wintry dressing. I sat contentedly eating my biscuits and gave Ember the other half of her carrot. A small red-breasted bird perched lightly on a branch nearby, its quick eyes darted hopefully in search of crumbs.

Inspecting the snow around me, I decided that it was definitely melting. Some parts of it, particularly here in the clearing, were very sparse and brown patches of frozen ground were showing through. It wouldn't be long now and …

My eyes lit on something foreign. Its pale yellow colour contrasted boldly on a patch of bare earth. I went over and picked it up curiously.

It was the stub of a candle. Its wick was black, its top partially melted – and I knew instantly: this was our clearing, the site where Patrick and I had promised our love for one another.

I dropped to the ground and began scraping away the rimy earth and fallen leaves. There it was – a heart-shaped scar in the ground. Resting on my heels, I stared at it. The season was still too young for the spears of green to break through, but the frozen, dried, brown remains of last spring's blooms were quite evident.

He had loved me then. There was no doubting it for this had been his idea. The pretty purple flowers were my favourites, but the plan to come here in some private pre-dawn ceremony was his. If he had loved this much, there *must* be something left.

I wiped my damp eyes and nose on my sleeve and scrambled to my feet. I would take it all on – his anger, his disdain, the other woman, everything – I would face them with strengthened resolve.

I used my log seat as a mounting block and, settled in the saddle, nudged Ember into a walk. As we left, I remembered that other occasion when I'd looked behind and seen the candle in the early morning light sputter and die. I had been disturbed by that. I'd wondered then if the candle's premature extinction had held a warning of things to come?

Yorkshire, England
30 January 1816

Dear Hamish,

I write to apprise you of some news that you will not find surprising – Sylvie and Quinn are to be married. It will also not surprise you to know that Sylvie has asked me to stand with her as matron-of-honour. It has ever been Sylvie's desire to be wed in a private chapel on the edge of the park at Waterville Place in Devon where she grew up. Consequently, we shall be departing from Yorkshire on the morrow, to make our way there.

When the wedding and subsequent celebrations are over, we shall return to Yorkshire, for I have decided that I shall not be returning to Scotland or to you.

Alexandra

There – it was written.

Though it was my fervent hope that I would remain in Devon, I dared not even think it let alone write it lest I tempt the perversions of fate.

I signed my name at the bottom of the page without the usual formalities, and lay down my pen. Reading it over, I knew it was clumsy and cold but I didn't have the will to write it again. It was all I could do to document that I had left my husband.

❧

Finally, the morning of our departure dawned clear and crisp with a cloudless, mother-of-pearl sky. I watched from Ember's back as Sylvie made a final check of everything she needed before boarding the coach. I had decided to ride Ember with Bony trotting happily at our heels, while Quinn, Sylvie and Jemima travelled in Quinn's coach. As before, Bill drove and Jarrod rode beside him.

Simon and a very large Maria – for her child was due any day – Father and Meg, turned out to wave us off. There were hugs and kisses all round and Maria's urgent whisper in my ear, "Do not forget, your home is here if … just do not forget."

I smiled and thanked her but I would win Patrick over. It may take time but I would succeed because failure was unthinkable.

❧

The road was good in some places, but in others the going was sluggish. The melting snow had created gluey quagmires of mud that caused the coach to become bogged on more than one occasion over the first few days. On the morning of our fourth day, Ember was hock-deep in icy mud that sucked and squelched with each step she took. I directed her on to the grassy verge beside the road, thinking it would be easier, but was dismayed to find her lame.

I dismounted immediately as Quinn's coachman halted his pair and Sylvie's face appeared at the window.

"Ember's lame," I called, struggling to bend the horse's front leg at the knee to inspect her foot.

"Let me see." Quinn was coming over.

"Might be a stone in the shoe." Jarrod echoed my hopes as he hovered over Quinn's shoulder.

"No such luck." Quinn released Ember's foot. "She's lost a shoe. It was probably coming loose anyway. The mud must have —"

"*Damn and blast!*" I swore with unladylike fluency. "What'll we do now? We're too far from the last village to turn back, and we're still miles away from the next."

"She'll be alright if you're not riding her." Quinn said. "Tie her to the back and ride in with us. Bill, drive slower for now."

"I think Jemima would prefer that, Alex," Sylvie said with a chuckle. "She thinks she's missing out on something with you out here."

I shrugged, thoroughly piqued.

For the rest of the day the going was gallingly slow and when we finally arrived at a village, Quinn enquired after a blacksmith only to be told the nearest was some seven miles further along the road.

"How ridiculous," I grumbled to Quinn. "What village worthy of the name has no smithy?"

"Apparently this one."

Despite my tension and grumpiness, the slow rhythm of the coach lulled me into sleep. Shortly after midday Sylvie lightly touched me awake. We had arrived at the village of Medhurst where we found two inns, two churches, a school, a common and — *thank you, God* — a blacksmith.

Ember was attended to while we ate a light lunch and I cheered considerably at the thought that we would soon be underway. Having collected my horse from the smithy's yard, Quinn dragged over a mounting block and I climbed into the saddle and arranged my skirt appropriately. We set off once more.

The further south we progressed, the better the roads, and the rest of the journey was relatively uneventful; but for Sylvie beginning to feel ill with her pregnancy. We were forced to allow time after breakfast each morning for Sylvie's stomach to settle, during which I found some solitary pleasure walking with Jemima and Bony. Bony's energy was boundless, but Jemima, ageing and slow, enjoyed the opportunity to leisurely investigate new sights and smells as we followed sheep trails and streams.

Our morning explorations of these little villages became my private time for contemplation. I would not allow myself to consider failure. Instead, I levelled my meditations on a happy reunion with Patrick; visualising, imagining, believing, as if by the power of my positive thoughts, I could influence the outcome.

Finally, three weeks and four days from the day we left Broughton Hall, our small party crunched up the long, freshly-raked drive of Waterville Place.

My heart settled in my mouth as the magnificent mansion appeared before me. In the six years since I'd last been here, it had changed little. The trees in the park were taller and fuller but the gardens were the same, laid out in the French style with intricately patterned flower-beds, gravel walks, and private alcoves – sanctuaries for secret lovers.

I dismounted Ember beside the fountain, centrepiece of the circular drive, and the coach pulled in behind us. The small boy who came at a run with his face split in a big toothy grin took Ember's reins and led her away to the stables just as the main door swung open and Mrs Bath stood smoothing her hands down her apron.

She stared at me remembering, but not quite, my face. Stepping forward, I was about to reacquaint myself, when Sylvie leapt from the coach and threw herself at the surprised housekeeper.

"Sylvie!" Mrs Bath cried her arms instantly going about her former colleague. "You're home, Lass, and Miss Alex too!" She made the connection.

Quinn was introduced and Sylvie glowed under Mrs Bath's felicitations.

I was becoming increasingly nervous and was having difficulty paying attention as Mrs Bath enquired about our journey. My throat was dry and my eyes darted furtively towards the house, the drive, the stables, and back to the house, all the while twisting a wad of my riding habit in my hand.

I was, consequently, the first to notice when an unknown man and woman emerged from the house and, by the time I was introduced to Aden and Amelia Rourke, I was visibly trembling.

I'd heard their names before but my brain seemed to be swimming and I couldn't recall where, until Sylvie explained the copper-haired man was Patrick's cousin on his Irish mother's side. Then I remembered the tales Patrick had told over the supper table – colourful, childish adventures with his cousin that had had us falling about with laughter. Now, I studied this man who occupied a special place in Patrick's life. Aden was only slightly taller than me – and I was not tall – with a strong, square jaw and cleft chin. He smiled quickly, his face softening pleasantly and he welcomed me in a musical Irish lilt. It was easy to imagine his pranks by the glint of mischief in his grey-green eyes.

Amelia was even smaller than her husband but endowed with the same ginger locks. Beneath her country flush, she was freckled and her hazel eyes were welcoming. She hugged me with sincerity and asked Mrs Bath if our rooms had been prepared.

"Same room you had when you stayed last, though I'd no idea when you'd be arriving," the housekeeper told me.

"Thank you."

The empire lines of Amelia's grass-coloured gown fell cleanly to the ground, so it was only when she hugged me that I noticed she was with child. I was surrounded by impending motherhood – hopefully a good omen!

Aden and Amelia led the way into that breathtaking atrium. I paused in the centre absorbing it all over again, while Quinn, seeing it for the first time, let his breath out in a low whistle.

Sylvie smiled knowingly. "Takes a moment, doesn't it?"

∽

My room was almost exactly as I remembered; the writing desk, the chair and footstool by the window, the night-stand – everything unchanged until I stood before the polished, antique dressing table where once the beautiful crystal objects had resided. Gone were the elegant trinket box, the vase and clock, and in their place was simply a china bowl of dried rosebuds.

Jemima flopped on to the rug while I drifted to the window that looked down to the gravel drive, recalling Sylvie's description of Patrick's anger – how he had thrown everything from the window in his passion. Even the pretty porcelain basin and jug were gone from the night-stand. Instead there was a heavy, blue ceramic set, quite unsuited to the otherwise feminine furnishings of the room.

I turned as a pair of burly men brought up my trunks. A young maid was directing them from the doorway and after the men left us, she turned to me.

"Lady Elginbury, Mr and Mrs Rourke ask if you would care to join them for tea when you're ready?"

"Thank you. Please tell them I'll be down shortly."

"Yes, milady." Her footsteps receded down the hall and I slumped on to a chair, knowing I wasn't yet ready to be sociable. After the years of heartache and longing, I needed to find my balance, breathe the air and let the dust settle around my feet before I came face to face – with him.

I looked at the bed – the same bed where Patrick and I had sipped tea together – and tried to control my erratic breathing.

I had come here for this, so my heart must cease its tortured flip-flopping and my stomach its churning. Eventually, I rose and mustered the strength to remove my stale travel clothes.

༄

"So, Lady Elginbury, what brings you to Waterville?" Aden's shrewd gaze settled on me.

"I … we …" I smoothed my clammy palms over the skirt of my dress.

"Is Patrick here?" asked Sylvie, plunging in headlong and mercifully drawing Aden's attention from me.

"No, he's not," Aden responded cautiously.

The urge to throw up – from relief or disappointment, I could not tell – flooded me.

"Is he due home soon?" Sylvie probed, "You see, Patrick always promised to give me away at my wedding and, as I mentioned when I wrote before Christmas, Quinn and I are to be wed."

She waited but Aden didn't respond. It was his wife who spoke. "Yes, you did and I spoke with Patrick about that. He will be very happy, 'tis certain he will, but we weren't to know when you were arriving."

"I could not give a date," Sylvie explained, "it depended on when the roads would be passable."

Aden's face had relaxed and now he nodded his understanding. "You'll be standing beside her, then?" he asked me.

I smiled and attempted to look at ease, "Yes. I was very honoured by Sylvie's request."

"And I've had my heart set on that chapel at the edge of the park since I was a girl," Sylvie continued. "There was so much to do before we travelled, I barely had time to write – I hope you received my letter."

Aden waved dismissively." Aye we did, and 'tis proud we are that you've come here to share the big day." He slid her a sidelong glance, "That assumes, of course, you're intending to share it with Millie and me, not just Paddy."

"Of course," Sylvie assured him, "But if Patrick has not returned …"

"There's no tellin' when he'll tire of his little sojourn. All we know's he went to London. He'll be back when he's back. Have you a date decided?"

"March the seventh."

He pursed his lips. "In two weeks. He's been gone for three weeks already."

"He's generally not away for more than four weeks," Amelia interjected.

"Then I expect he'll be here," Sylvie said. "I hope you don't mind, Aden, but I shall have various sewing women, and others, coming and going over the next week."

"Mind?" Amelia answered for him. "'t'would not be a wedding without."

Aden rolled his eyes at Quinn in solidarity. He said, "And I know how you colleens get yourselves into a lather over wedding preparations."

As the conversation relaxed, I took the opportunity to sit quietly and drink my tea. It was strong and sweet, and knowing now that Patrick wasn't about to appear on the threshold, the fluttering of my stomach grew still.

But Aden would not let me off so easily. "So Lady Elginbury, 'tis very nice to meet you at last. We've heard a lot about you."

"And I of you," I replied archly. "Patrick has had us laughing fit to explode with the tales of your exploits."

"Has he indeed?" he grinned suddenly, exposing a gap between his two front teeth. "I could tell a few tales of my own but 't'would only be fair to have my esteemed cousin present to defend himself."

"Sure I'd love to hear any story you have about my mischievous husband," Amelia said, "and the juicier the better. It affords me great riposte when he's in a teasing mood. Do tell us one."

I smiled, the soothing quality of the tea doing its work. "Only if you promise to call me Alex."

We settled down to pass a pleasant afternoon filled with shared reminiscences. Aden sat with one of his wife's russet curls twirled absently about his finger as the afternoon drifted seamlessly into evening. Supper was served, and we moved into the dining room.

Somewhere near half past ten o'clock, I was growing tired and more than a little tipsy – the effects of sampling Waterville's extensive cellar. Amelia had retired an hour earlier, having been unable to keep her eyes open, and as my own eyes became heavy, I bade everyone a goodnight.

Unsteadily, I made my way up the great sweeping staircase to where the gallery created a corridor between the two wings of the house. Pausing briefly, I looked wistfully towards the west, the family wing, where Patrick's room was. A longing pulled at my heart but fortunately my common sense was not so dulled by wine, and I turned towards the east.

Mrs Bath had assigned her new maid, Bea, to assist me where needed. So, when I arrived in my room, I found the young girl dozing in a chair by the window. Her broad thighs were overflowing the arm rests and her hand rested mid-stroke on Jemima's black head.

At my entry, the startled girl leapt to her feet stammering an apology for sleeping.

"You should have gone to bed, Bea," I said, as she scurried to where my nightdress was laid out.

"No matter, milady. Miz Bath told me *wait up for Lady Elginbury an' when she come, you look after her,* so here I am." She suppressed a yawn. "I'm only new here, milady, and tryin'a do the right thing an' all."

"Actually, I'm quite used to taking care of myself. There's no need to wait in future. I'll let Mrs Bath know tomorrow. If I need you, I can always call."

She bent her knee in a curtsy of acknowledgement and her chubby cheeks wobbled. "Nice dog, milady. Nice 'n' friendly."

"That's Jemima. I've had her for ten years now." Jemima lifted her head briefly at her name, but quickly returned to her doze.

"Always wanted a dog, but me da says they's no good. This one looks good though."

"She is, and always available for a belly rub, so feel free."

She smiled and bobbed again before bidding me a pleasant sleep.

Alone, I changed into my nightdress by the light of a cheerful fire and as I snuggled beneath the heavy counterpane, Jemima crawled into her basket on the floor beside my bed.

༄

The sun had not yet risen when I slipped from bed and took up a poker to stir the fire. The previous night's logs had all but turned to grey dust, though as I prodded I roused a small yellow flame and quickly piled a few sticks of kindling on top. The fire took immediately and I dressed in its small warmth.

Making my way directly to the kitchen garden, I unearthed two young carrots, working quickly since I knew Monsieur Chartrain would be merciless should he discover my crime. Jemima was intrigued by her new surroundings and conducted an investigation of the new smells.

The hem of my dress quickly became sodden from the dew-damp grass as I skirted the house and headed towards the stables. I crossed the wide forecourt between the hitching rail and mounting block, and entered the old stone building.

A strong horsey smell filled the air and though the sky was lightening, it was still quite dim inside. I could hear a pair of lads going about their morning activities in one of the adjoining rooms, and the four-legged residents shuffled, snorting curiously at my unfamiliar scent. I moved slowly over the uneven cobbled floor, feeling my way along the wall, groping and identifying lead-ropes, harness and blankets. I located Ember and stroked her nose affectionately before moving on.

"Nella," I said softly. "Are you there, girl?"

There came no answering nicker from the old grey horse, but it had been so long. Perhaps she was in a different stall.

"Nella?"

I peered over the half-door into the gloom where the bulky outline of a horse showed blacker than the darkness and I proffered a carrot hopefully. The horse in the shadows gave no response. It wasn't Nella. *She* could smell a carrot a mile off and would have immediately thrust a questing, velvety muzzle into my hand. A sad knowledge inched into my brain, and as it grew, I knew its truth, for how many years had it been? Six? And she had been aged even then.

"Nella?" I tried once more but in my heart I knew.

Jemima, nose to the ground was on the trail of something outside. She looked up as I emerged from the stable and followed my path down the lawns, and as I walked, the sky moved through shades of rose to mauve to green. Without intention, I found myself wandering the narrow path to the lake where the swaying curtain of weeping willow gently brushed the gravel, concealing the place where the summer-house had once stood.

The air smelled clean and earthy as I rounded shrubs, thicker than I remembered, and pushed aside dripping branches as I passed. Scampering sounds came from the undergrowth – stoats or rabbits or mice – and Jemima's collie-ears cocked upright and alert, their tips folded forwards, though these days she was disinclined to give chase.

The rustling in the underbrush gave way to a cracking of branches and much less delicate sounds and, just as her image formed in my memory, a large blonde dog leapt from behind a shrub to land cheerfully on the path before us.

Jemima offered a warning woof that was completely ignored as the other dog bounded forward.

"Hullo Tess," I said brightly. The gangly pup of my previous acquaintance was now an adult dog. She paused and gave me a quick looking-over, surprised that I'd used her name, then dutifully addressed Jem's tail.

Expecting Briggs to appear at any moment, I looked around and caught a whiff of tobacco smoke only moments before the rangy old man appeared around a bend.

"Miss Washburn," he said, saluting with his pipe as though we'd seen each other only yesterday.

"Hullo Briggs," I said with genuine pleasure.

"You bin up the stables?" he said, nodding toward the carrots still dangling from my hand.

"She's not here, is she?"

He puffed his pipe and watched the two dogs before answering. "Took herself off t'other place winter 'fore last."

I nodded and blinked back a sentimental tear. "She was old though."

"Aye, that she was. And sadly missed too. Even the young lord turned out when we 'ad a little ceremony for 'er."

"You had a funeral?"

He tilted his head back and blew out a curl of fragrant blue smoke. "Part of the family that old girl was." He jerked his chin to where Jemima and Tess were still greeting one another. "That your dog?"

"That's Jemima."

"Old too."

"She's ten, and a bit stiff in the joints."

He nodded. "Age'll do that. Got it meself — stiff joints. Yer looking well though, Miss. All growed up now."

I smiled and said nothing.

We turned then and fell into step following the path bordering the lake. The two dogs trotted ahead as though Tess was showing Jemima around.

"I brought another dog with me," I said. "Not *my* dog – a friend's. Bony – still up at the house."

"Hmmph – still abed. Animals get ruint when yer pamper 'em," the old man said gruffly.

"You'd never ruin Tess, would you?"

"Nope," he replied very matter-of-factly.

Companionably we strolled, enjoying the morning bird calls and sporadic *plop* as fish and frogs leapt from the lake to feast on insects hovering low over the water. We passed among the drifting willow branches and followed the path around its wide girth. Emerging from beneath an ancient tree, I stood on the path staring at the site of the old summer-house. In its stead was a new building, modern and newly constructed with walls in a similar blushing stone to the main house.

Briggs watched wordlessly through narrowed eyes and pipe smoke as I moved closer and looked through the new French doors. Inside, the dark wooden floors were polished to a high gleam with a scattering of thick rugs. A settee reclined against one wall with two matching chairs angled opposite. A recently-used brick fireplace dominated the room and a sideboard occupied the wall across from where I stood. A pair of decanters, one containing a blood coloured liquid, the other with what appeared to be brandy, rested on a silver tray. Leaded glass doors in the front displayed the crockery and glassware within.

I lifted the latch and went into the building.

The interior had the clean smell of newness about it. Pretty palm-frond patterned curtains hung at the windows and matching cushions were scattered about and, as was evidenced by the open book on a table next to the settee, this place was used more frequently than its predecessor.

From where I stood, I could see the jetty that overlooked the water and my eyes lingered involuntarily at the spot where so many years ago, I'd closed my eyes and waited to be kissed.

Briggs was squinting into the lake's dark depths. He turned as I emerged and we silently resumed our walk.

Navigating the shrubbery, we came out on the lawn and made our way towards the house. It gleamed rose-gold in the new sunlight and I drew in my breath, as I always did, when beholding its beauty.

A short sharp bark of greeting sounded before we saw the large brown dog hurtling like a giant fur-ball in our direction.

"That's Bony," I said, and Briggs puffed his pipe impassively as the dog skidded among flying divets before Tess. They then engaged in the usual canine introductory routine.

Bony and Tess, closer in age and energy, began a chasing game around the lawn.

Briggs watched for a moment, then with his customary pipe-salute, he drifted off to begin his day's work.

Amelia and Aden were sitting at a glass-topped cane table on matching cane chairs as I mounted the porch steps. Aden rose as I approached. Plates of fruit, bread, cheese and cold meats were before them, as well as a pot of steaming, strong-brewed coffee.

"Good morning," Amelia greeted brightly. "Been out strolling?"

"Yes. I have such fond memories of this place."

"Including the vegetables?" Aden quipped with a grin and I realised I was still holding the pilfered carrots.

"Oh these?" I said with an embarrassed giggle. "What can I say? I'm a garden bandit."

They chuckled, but when I explained Aden nodded with understanding.

"And didn't we all have a tender spot for that horse," he said. "Paddy's mother brought Nella over from Ireland, you know. I learned to ride on her when I was a lad."

"Sure Pat was quite upset when the old nag gave out," Amelia added.

"I heard," I said, still standing and feeling quite awkward at the mention of Patrick's name.

"But we're so rude," Amelia said, "please Alex, share our breakfast. We thought we'd eat out here this morning, 'tis so lovely."

I took the seat Amelia indicated and looked around for Jemima. She was panting happily on the lawn at the foot of the porch, watching as Tess and Bony capered like spring lambs in the sunshine.

"I'll ask Cissy to lay a place for you," Amelia said. She pushed back her chair and disappeared into the house.

Aden and I sat opposite each other and he offered a pleasant smile. "How long since you were last here?" he asked.

"About six years, I think."

"You'll be noticing a few changes then?"

I glanced down the lawn and took a thoughtful breath. "Some – the gardens are grown and the summer-house … that's new."

His friendly smile faded slightly and he reached for his coffee cup. "Yes. The old one was destroyed in a fire an' all." He took a meditative sip of coffee as his wife returned, followed closely by the most unattractive girl I'd ever seen.

My heart went out to the young woman whose wide mouth and small, close-set eyes seemed to throw her face off balance. Her complexion was sallow and her thin, non-descript hair was tied in a knot at her nape drawing more attention to her unfortunate, bovine face.

Cissy laid out the crockery and cutlery before me with large masculine hands and ducked a quick, clumsy curtsy before leaving. Aden watched the maid return to the house. "Good girl, that one. Her da raised her on his own –"

"Girl came up to the house during a terrible rain-storm," said Amelia. "Her da had been crushed when his plough horse slipped and fell in the mud."

"And wasn't her da one of Paddy's best tenants an' all," Aden added.

Amelia nodded. "Good tenant, good man – please help yourself to breakfast Alex – Pat offered her a position here. She'd no place to go – not a soul of family left."

Aden propped his elbows on the table and steepled his fingers. He watched as his wife leaned from her chair to pluck an early daffodil from the garden bed beside the porch, but his words were addressed to me and came without warning, "Now Alex, I'm thinking 'tis a good time for you to be telling us the real reason you're here."

My heart leapt in my chest and my fork hovered in the air above the meat platter.

"Sure you're a subtle man, Aden Rourke," Amelia admonished, but Aden's eyes were now fixed on me and his smiling mouth had become a firm line.

But they were right to ask for I had rested beneath their roof, eaten at their board. I drew a deep breath and forgetting my hunger, repeated my tale, focusing on my relationship with Patrick and leaving out the more lurid details of my marriage.

When I was done, Aden sat back and regarded me with a new expression.

"That would be explaining a few things," Amelia said to her husband.

"Indeed," he agreed, "He's very changed, Alex. 'Twas a different Paddy Washburn came home from that war. You know he went back last May? He was there at Waterloo. After that second Treaty was signed in November he came home, though I'd be surprised if he stays."

"But the war's over," I said.

"The terms of the treaty require a fairly large number of men to continue manning the French borders. I get the feeling Paddy will go back. He hasn't resigned his commission yet. But you just never know with him."

"He never talks about his feelings at the best of times," Amelia interjected. "'Tis not surprising he's close-mouthed about you. But perhaps we can help," she added brightly.

"Millie, Alex is married. What would you be suggesting we do, darlin'? Aid her in pursuing an adulterous liaison?"

"Oh don't be so sanctimonious – sure no one is suggesting anything of the sort. But she's here now. The least we can offer is support. Neither will need any self-righteous behaviour from us. And if it turns out Alex can … if she can pull Pat out of his black mood we should thank her. It'll not be for us to be judging."

As his wife spoke, I studied Aden closely. For some reason his opinion mattered to me. He contemplated Amelia's words, his thoughts showing in the ruminative furrow between his brow and the doubtful pursing of his lips. Finally, he reached for her hand where it rested on the table. "I cannot imagine losing the one I loved."

She blinked hard and smiled at him.

"But you must prepare for disappointment, Alex," he added, turning to me. "I fear your memories of your time with him may be very different from his own. He never talks of you so we cannot be telling how the wind truly blows."

"But for what it's worth, we welcome you here," said Amelia.

"Thank you," I said humbly, "but it is not my intention to involve you. I … I really only want to talk with him, to explain."

"Be sure we shan't be involved," Aden was quick to point out with a warning frown at his wife, "and let it be clear that we'll not be taking sides. But we welcome you here as our guest – if not my cousin's."

"Thank you," I said sincerely.

❧

The days that followed fell into a slow and comfortable routine. I walked each morning with Briggs and the dogs, watching the witch hazel bursting with golden flowers among the shrubbery and early bluebells appearing in the garden beds. The air was clean and spring-scented and I was filled with a sense of eager anticipation.

Those days when the weather prohibited outdoor activity, Amelia and Sylvie sewed baby clothes while I applied my limited needle skills to the household mending. Quinn accompanied Aden on his rounds of the estate and could generally be seen with his sleeves rolled up assisting with various jobs around the property. Fully recovered from his illness, his robust Scottish constitution had prepared him well for heavy work in comparatively mild conditions.

It was still very early spring and the weather prone to inclemency. One afternoon, I stood by the parlour window staring at the low, leaden skies hovering over the lake. With each passing day, the tension of waiting for Pat – never knowing from one hour to the next if he would appear – had affected my appetite so that I could barely eat. I sighed.

Amelia stretched on a chaise, absently stroking her swelling abdomen. "For heaven's sake Alex, you've been prowling like a caged animal all afternoon."

"It's the weather," Sylvie said, raising her eyes from her needlework. "Alex hates being indoors."

"Mistress Millie," Cissy's ill-favoured face appeared at the door. "The Dowager Duchess of Chasseby is in the atrium. Shall I show her in?"

"Thank the heavens above – a visitor! The Duchess will liven you up, Alex, she is quite a character. Bring the Duchess in here Cissy, and fetch some afternoon tea please."

"Yes Ma'am."

Being in a grumpy humour, I wasn't inclined to sociability, but I fixed my smile and turned toward the door as Cissy announced with great dignity, "The Dowager Duchess of Chasseby."

Amelia rose to meet a diminutive elderly lady who strode briskly over and placed smacking kisses on each of the younger woman's cheeks.

"Hello child, how are you faring? No don't curtsy, you're too big to get back up again."

"Thank you your grace," Amelia responded affectionately, "and so glad you're here to relieve the boredom of a dreary day."

"Dreary alright," the older lady agreed. "Here, take these, there's a girl." She had stripped off her gloves and bonnet with brisk, birdlike movements and handed them to Cissy. Turning, she saw Sylvie and me.

"Why Millie, you've visitors. You should have said …"

"Oh no, please allow me to present my house guests, Lady Alexandra Elginbury and Miss Sylvie Washburn."

Summoning rarely employed etiquette, Sylvie and I greeted the Dowager Duchess with correct curtsies, but the lady gestured our formalities aside saying, "A pleasure – let us sit, I'm all done in."

She smiled as she took her seat and closer inspection of her face revealed a subtle application of cosmetics.

"So, Lady Elginbury – formerly Alexandra Washburn, am I right?" she said assessingly. Quick grey eyes ran over me. "*Stepdaughter* to Gerrard? You're Mim Broughton's daughter."

"Yes, your grace," I responded, curious as to how much she knew.

"You're the one they married off to the Scotch lad – yes? And your sister to Sir Knight Irrelevant?"

"Yes, your grace," I answered dutifully, failing to suppress a smirk at her description of Anne's husband. She raised a single eyebrow darkened with khol.

The door opened, and Cissy entered, followed by another maid, bringing a silver tea service and plates of petits fours.

The two serving girls departed and Amelia poured the tea and added slices of lemon. Sylvie and I sat stiffly on chairs beside Amelia's chaise wondering what to make of this tiny woman whose personality filled the room.

"And you," the Dowager Duchess abruptly turned to Sylvie.

"You're Gerrard Washburn's by-blow aren't you? Raised as a servant – I believe I've seen you here – finally acknowledged … about time too, if you ask me. Yes, I can see the resemblance to Maeve."

Sylvie looked uneasy beneath the duchess' forthright appraisal, but suddenly the older lady leaned over and patted Sylvie's hand. "It is not shameful, you know, to be who you are. Your father … a bit of a rogue in his day, is a good man."

Neither Sylvie nor I knew what to say under such rapid-fire critique but Amelia's calm voice interrupted, "Don't worry about her grace. She's direct but she's honest."

The duchess' laugh was a hoarse cackle. She said, "I like it if we can know each other quickly, for then friendship will follow. So Millie, tell me, how's your stomach?"

Amelia said her pregnancy was doing well, and the dialogue moved on. The Dowager Duchess' conversation was as entertaining and quick as her mind, dodging and weaving as swiftly as a sparrow chasing a moth. She was worldly, knowledgeable and ready to laugh, and when she did, it was like everything else about her – short, sharp and to the point.

I learned that she lived on a neighbouring estate and had known Patrick and Maeve most of their lives. She'd also known their mother.

The Dowager Duchess' visit lasted exactly one hour, and by the end of it Sylvie and I had thoroughly warmed to the lady. She departed as she arrived – like a wind-storm – and after she was gone, I felt dazed.

"You'll get used to her," Amelia said as she closed the front door. "She's a remarkable lady – a true friend. And Alex," she placed a hand on my arm to emphasise her point. "It may interest you to know, that if there's one person on this known earth Patrick actually respects, 'tis that woman." Amelia excused herself then, retiring for her afternoon rest.

CHAPTER 18

It was raining. I watched from my window as it dribbled down the glass in rivulets that puddled on the sill outside and brightened the spring colours of the gardens. There would be no walking in the park this morning.

I slipped my nightdress over my head and dusted lavender and rose-scented powder under my arms and between my breasts then slipped into my chemise.

Downstairs, the house was coming to life. I could hear thumping activity as I dressed in my dusty-pink velvet dress – this was my favourite and best gown, and I liked it for the way its colour brought out gold highlights in my chestnut hair and added a healthy glow to my complexion.

The dress fell smoothly over my hips and the silver filigree buttons on the bodice made my bosom appear rounder – it needed all the assistance it could get for I'd lost weight. I turned on my reflection and held my hair up. Perhaps I should have Bea dress it for me today.

Footsteps were coming up the hall – good, I would not have to call her. They paused outside my door, and I thought I heard Amelia's voice. I hummed a little tune while adjusting the lace at my bosom, and had just turned from the mirror when, without Bea's usual discreet knock, the door suddenly crashed open with such force that it slammed into the wall behind it. My cheerful hum was cut off abruptly and the smile froze on my face.

Patrick stood in the open doorway, legs astride and arms folded over his chest. Aden and Amelia were behind him, but I hardly noticed his cousins, having eyes only for him.

In the bright, revealing light of morning, I could see that Patrick had changed. Life and experience had matured and lent a worldly sophistication to him, though the casual untidiness of his attire plucked fondly at my memory. He wore a linen shirt the colour of new cream, rolled up at the sleeves, open at the neck and only partly tucked into tight, black trousers that hugged his narrow waist and flat stomach – the hard-muscled body of a professional soldier and routine horseman, clothed as a rather dishevelled gentleman.

All this in a split second, for it was his face that held my attention. The attractive youth I'd fallen in love with, had grown into a handsome man. His dirty-straw coloured hair was longer on top but cropped short at the sides and back and his fathomless eyes were thickly fringed and as deep a green as I remembered.

Yes, this was the boy who'd been my friend, the man who'd become my lover; whose wit had charmed me and whose love had enthralled me – my companion, confidant, my lodestone.

The brief seconds that we stood thus, examining each other, were enough for my heart to react with the old familiar longing.

He, too, seemed momentarily adrift, though his face was closed and unreadable. I searched it desperately for any flicker of sentiment, but it was as cold and unmoving as stone. As one approaches a nervous animal, I took a step towards him, a hesitant smile on my lips. "Hullo, Patrick …"

His movement was explosive. With military swiftness he raised a single hand and effectively froze me where I stood. "*What* are you doing here?"

The soft timbre of his voice sprung straight from my dreams and it took a moment to absorb his words.

"What are you doing here?" he repeated and this time there was no misunderstanding either the words or the tone of their delivery, and my stomach slipped to my bowels.

"I … I came to see you," I stammered inadequately.

"Well, now you've seen me you will leave my house."

He turned towards the door and my throat constricted in panic.

"Patrick!" I lunged to follow but he whirled abruptly, once again halting me, and his distaste was written clearly in the curl of his lip and the smouldering anger in his eyes.

I could feel the blood draining from my face as he snarled with undisguised loathing, "You are not welcome here − you will leave my house immediately." His voice was strained with the effort to maintain his control. I remembered his talent for cruelty and knew he meant every word. I knew also that this could become very ugly.

But Jemima chose that moment to make her move. With great effort, she heaved herself from her basket and tottered on her stiff legs to greet her old friend. Only then did Patrick's expression soften. His eyes shifted to the aged dog, and she nuzzled his hand when he dropped to a crouch beside her. My heart was in my throat as I watched him stroke her brow and he raised his face to mine, his eyes flashing fiercely. "Have you no care for anything but yourself? She is old and you dragged her here for nothing."

He stood and strode from the room without a backward glance. I stared after him, frozen with horror. This was far worse than anything I'd imagined. I had been prepared for his anger and harsh words, but not this … this total dismissal, this overt hatred, and I trembled with emotion.

"Patrick …" Amelia pushed past her husband, "now, don't be so hasty …"

"Millie, stay out of it, darlin'," Aden said, taking her arm.

Like a foolish statue, I remained in the centre of the room.

"*Patrick Washburn*," Amelia shouted angrily, "sure the least you could do is talk with her – hear what she has to say." Certainly the servants wanted to hear – they had paused in their work, their eyes agog.

"*Patrick!*" I cried, suddenly jolted into action. I ran from the room but Amelia was already waddling after him down the corridor and I could only watch in distress as he shoved Bea and another maid out of his way.

"*Millie …!*" Aden shouted, and, if I'd had a full stomach I'd have lost its contents, as unexpectedly Patrick turned and marched towards me. His face was the hue of a thunderous cloud and his fists clenched in fury.

"Go to your husband," he barked at Amelia, practically gnashing his teeth, but Amelia, though she was barely five feet high, stood her ground as he hurled himself past her.

"*You!*" he bellowed, pointing his finger and advancing upon me. "Out of this house before nightfall. You are *not* welcome here. You will *not* spend another night beneath this roof."

"But Patrick …" I pleaded, oblivious to the tears now coursing down my cheeks, "Can we at least talk?"

"*Get out of my house!*" he roared. I visibly shrank beneath the force of his fury. Flinging himself away, he stamped down the hall roaring over his shoulder, "Go back to your damned husband – today! And you lot get back to work," he tossed at the stunned servants.

❧

I huddled in a chair in my room with my legs curled beneath me and my head pounding, fit to kill. A cool cloth was pressed to my eyes – they were hot and gritty from crying. Sylvie, in a chair bedside me, was holding my hand, promising to convince Patrick to let me stay. "At least until the wedding," she said.

"A week." I sniffed hopelessly. "By his reaction today, I expect he'll draw a sword on me if he sees me again."

"I doubt you'll run into him for a while," Amelia said. She was lying on my bed, pillows at her back to support her weighty stomach. "He went directly to the stables and galloped that black horse of his down through the park – didn't even saddle her."

"I didn't know he was home," I said. "If I'd been prepared …"

Amelia shook her head unhappily. "I'm sorry, Alex. He saw Ember in the stables when he arrived last night and this morning he asked Aden if we had a house guest."

I shrugged. "It's no matter. Nothing could have made it any better."

Sylvie's voice was soothing, "Alex, he was in shock. He'll cool down."

"I hope so," I mumbled, miserably doubtful.

"I shall talk to him," she promised.

ॐ

"Probably went to that Wheeler whore's place," Amelia said over breakfast the following morning. She met her husband's warning look without contrition. "Well, she *is* a whore and none can deny it. She'd offer herself to Briggs if she thought there was a new gown in it for her."

"Leave it alone Millie, darlin'," Aden said. He turned to Quinn. "Many thanks for your help yesterday – couldn't have done it without you."

Sylvie had been quite angry with Patrick, and Quinn, grateful of any opportunity to avoid the conflict, had been helping Aden repair a wall that bordered the property. The two men embarked on a discussion about the lambing season since many of Waterville's tenants had ewes about to deliver.

"She *is* a whore," Amelia hissed, leaning conspiratorially towards Sylvie and me, "and Patrick keeps company with her. She should prove no competition though for she's no more than a peasant."

I sighed sadly. "Millie, you saw what he thinks of me. Cupid himself could not change his opinion."

Sylvie touched my arm. "Alex, if he felt nothing for you, he'd not have reacted as he did."

"Exactly," Amelia added enthusiastically. "You know how very proud he is. I think he genuinely loved you and was hurt for his trouble. Any wonder he is wary."

I looked at Sylvie, "And you agree?"

"Yes."

"Good," said Quinn and Aden in unison and we three conspirators looked up in surprise.

"Sure I've had enough of these feminine machinations," Aden said with a laugh. "Quinn, old boy, we must do something manly in the garden before I go crazy."

Patrick returned that afternoon, but for the following days we ran parallel; he managing to elude me whenever I had a mind to approach. Sylvie was more successful and I was sitting beneath a silver birch in the early spring sunlight when she came to tell me. The tree was showing off its pale, new growth, affording little shade – which suited me well.

Jemima dozed at my feet and Bony was investigating the garden beds, while the bees buzzed about the new blossoms and I wondered if, in a little clearing in Yorkshire, a heart of irises was breaking through the thawing earth.

I watched as Sylvie approached, stepping lightly despite her growing pregnancy. "I spoke with him," she said simply. She dropped to the ground beside me and absently stroked Jemima's head. I grimaced apprehensively but she smiled. "He agreed you may stay for the wedding. He was very reluctant, but he did agree and that's the main thing. We must be content with that for now."

I sighed through my nose. "Did you have to beg?"

Her smile turned rueful. "Yes, but he cannot give in too easily, can he? In any case there is good news – of a sort. Quinn received a letter advising that Andrew, his brother in London, shan't be able to come for the wedding and asked if we would visit him instead. So, Quinn and I have agreed to go. We shall leave after the ceremony and will need Quinn's coach. That means you'll not be able to leave until we return."

Her mischievous smile was an echo of Maeve's. "What do you think?"

"I think he's likely to hurl me out anyway. Besides, he knows I have Ember – he'll demand I ride her home on my own and he'll see me off the property at gunpoint with fixed bayonet."

Sylvie grinned. "Perhaps, but he wouldn't do it to Jemima. I think you'll be safe for a while."

We sat quietly for a few minutes, then she said, "Millie has invited the duchess for tea tomorrow."

"Oh? I liked her."

"So did I. And Millie told Patrick his attendance was required since Quinn and Aden would be there."

"Hmm," I said, thoughtfully. "How was that received?"

"We shall have to see."

The duchess was due to arrive at four o'clock, and just as the parlour clock struck its first note, she blew into the room. Patrick was nowhere to be seen but Amelia and Aden, Quinn, Sylvie and I rose respectfully, made our various bows and curtsies and were impatiently waved to our seats. An assortment of small cakes and finger-like sandwiches, and two pots of tea were arranged on gleaming, silver trays wheeled in on trolleys. Quinn was presented and after being sized up for marriage suitability, the duchess decreed that he seemed acceptable and Sylvie was duly congratulated.

Stiff and uncomfortable, I picked disinterestedly at a cake, my ears constantly alert to any sound from outside, and struggling to follow as the duchess recounted the story of one of her servants falling down the stairs and breaking an ankle.

"Poor girl. Cried more from fear I should dismiss her than the pain. But when I assured her to the contrary, she started a deafening bawling out of gratitude. Finally, I was forced to tell her to shut up before I changed my mind."

"That ought to've done it," said Quinn.

"One might think, but it ended with my sending her home to her father with instructions that she return *only* when recovered." She cackled briefly before changing the discussion in her flighty fashion. "Tell me, Aden, shall you attend Lady Locksley's ball next week? I believe Sir Christopher Thorpe intends to be there."

"Thorpe, you say?" Aden glanced at Amelia. "We were thinking to decline since Millie's condition …"

The duchess regarded Amelia's protruding stomach for a moment. "Yes … though such an opportunity for you. Perhaps Lady Elginbury would enjoy the outing. You do still have that idea you wanted to try on him?"

Aden assured her he had and glanced my way.

"Let us discuss it later," I said, reluctant to commit without further information, and the conversation moved on once more. Eventually, as it became evident that Patrick would not be joining us, I relaxed and began to enjoy the duchess's wonderfully entertaining company. Her repartee flowed vivaciously and humorously, and we were a very gay gathering.

After a time, she leaned towards Aden and said, "Is your cousin not favouring us with his presence today? I've not seen him for some time."

"I should not dream of missing your scintillating company, Dragon-lady," Patrick responded from the door. I had not seen him arrive and suddenly my mouth grew dry. I swallowed hard.

He sidled over to the small woman, bent and planted a kiss on each of her rouged cheeks.

"You have the devil's own nerve speaking to me in that manner, boy. I've a mind to gather my things and go home."

"Ah, but you won't because you know the truth of it," he rejoined smartly with a wink.

I exhaled slowly in an effort to calm myself, and clasped my clammy hands together in my lap. In dark-blue trousers, crisp white shirt and yellow and pale-blue striped waistcoat, he looked so fine that it tore at my heart. I forced my eyes away, realising at that moment the only vacant seat in the room was beside me.

The fire in the hearth was leaping enthusiastically and the room suddenly felt very close. Dampness broke on my hairline and I fought a rising urge to flee as involuntarily, my eyes slid back to him. Amelia dropped a slice of lemon into his tea with little silver tongs and passed him the cup.

The pain in my chest was real.

Patrick stood at the hearth leaning on the marble mantle. I could have been invisible as far as he was concerned, for which I was at once relieved and unnerved.

The conversation continued and he participated with typical ease, while I distractedly sipped my tea and prayed I'd not spill it all over myself.

After a while the duchess suggested Patrick be seated.

"I have been riding all morning, your grace. I'm content to stand for now."

"As you wish, though you make the place look untidy, standing there," she said, unhappy with his resistance. "Here, sit beside Alex."

She jerked her pointy chin my way. Amelia was innocently performing a close examination of the pink roses twining among green leaves on her tea cup and I cursed her silently, she had doubtless said something to the duchess. *Please don't let him sit beside me. I shall faint if he does.*

Aden chuckled softly, "Yes, untidy. So I have been telling him for years, your grace, but he never listens to me."

"Untidy you say?" Patrick's eyes gleamed at the prospect of a verbal thrust and parry with his cousin.

"Certainly," Aden confirmed. "Sure you should see him sometimes, lounging about, shirt-tails flapping, unshaven – your grace would be appalled."

"Your good mother did not raise you to be slovenly, Patrick Washburn," the duchess said. "You are a gentleman born and bred – you would do well to remember that."

Patrick grimaced across the room at Sylvie, and she shook her head quickly in response. "Do not look to me for support. I have lived under this roof all my life and have seen the truth of it."

"I see I have been ambushed," he said arranging his face to engender sympathy. "Millie, will you sit on your hands as they dissect my character?"

She smiled sweetly. "Having enjoyed your hospitality nigh on a year, I can safely say the argument goes not in your favour." She added innocently, "Particularly since one is judged by the company one keeps."

My tea cup gave a slight rattle but no one noticed. All faces were turned to Patrick whose eyes narrowed while he gave his cousin's wife a long, searching look. She raised her chin defiantly and suddenly the bantering tone of the afternoon became something else entirely.

"Really? And what pray –"

"Now, now," the duchess interjected quickly, her face a carefully painted mask. "All Amelia means is –"

"I know what she means," Patrick's hard eyes were on Amelia, "and she would do well to be less meddlesome. Such attacks are not unfamiliar to me."

"Then you will know that we have a care for your reputation," the duchess responded.

"Your grace –" Aden began.

"You have a social position to uphold. Your *companions* are –"

"This is nothing to do with your concern for me," Patrick said dangerously low, his eyes flashing. "You clearly labour under the misguided belief that you have a right to interfere in my life. Since your grace's disapproval of *my companions* has been made abundantly clear on many tiresome occasions, I've no doubt you are now enjoying a pleasant little conspiracy with my cousin's wife here."

His blazing eyes moved from the duchess to Amelia, and then, to my acute humiliation, he continued, "And before you launch yourselves into a campaign to orchestrate some kind of alliance between this …" he turned and looked at me for the first time, "*woman* and me, let me advise that her unsolicited visit, her presence, is merely tolerated. The sooner she leaves the better, and any of you seeing fit to pass judgement on me or the company I keep, will go with her."

As humans, we seem impossibly attracted to horror. Thus it was, as everyone in the room fell into an awkward silence, I found myself unable to drag my eyes from him. His intense gaze locked with mine and I understood his profound contempt of me. Placing his tea cup precisely on the table, his movements tightly controlled, his frozen, emerald eyes never left my face, and he said in a low voice, "A season of youthful experimentation, a lifetime of penance."

Rounding abruptly on the duchess, he executed an overtly mocking bow, and stalked from the room.

For the next agonising moments we each stared at the rug between our respective feet. Finally Aden spoke, "Millie darlin', what's going on?"

"She told me about Lady Elginbury here, that's what!" the dowager duchess responded sharply.

"Patrick's right – his affairs are his own business," Quinn uncharacteristically entered the fray.

"Quinn!" Sylvie exclaimed. "What about Alex? We promised to help her."

"Help her by alienating Patrick? We cannot help if he thinks we're all plotting against him."

The duchess rose causing the two gentlemen to scramble to their feet. Intimidating by the sheer force of her will, she said, "This is out of hand, and Alex I sincerely apologise for it. Patrick is quite familiar with my tirades against his libertine lifestyle. However, he is correct in that whatever may come to pass between you is none of our affair. I suggest we all simply stay out of it."

I had been struggling to keep myself together for the last thing I wanted was to dissolve in tears. Now I nodded miserably. "Millie, I thank you for your concern, but … her grace is right. You must all let me deal with this alone."

The duchess gave a clipped nod of her head. "In any case, I believe this little gathering is at an end and I thank you, Amelia, for your hospitality, once again."

❧

That evening, I sat alone but for Jemima, and watched the reflection of my candle flicker hauntingly in the night-blackened window. Jemima's steady, slumberous breathing beneath the crackle of the fire in the grate lent my room a peaceful and meditative ambience.

My head ached and my eyes were gritty from the intensity of my grief, for he had been very deliberate with the words he chose: *a season of youthful experimentation*. It was a well-aimed dagger plunged into my heart.

The following morning, my head throbbed mercilessly but I had determined my course of action. I lingered abed, deciding against my usual turn about the garden. With no appetite for food I took only tea for breakfast and spoke quietly with Aden. In reply to my enquiry, he gave a doubtful shrug but told me Patrick was in his office going over estate business.

It was just after eleven when I tapped hesitantly on the door, to which Patrick responded with a snapped, "Come!"

I turned the polished knob and pushed the heavy door open. He sat in an antique, leather wing chair near the window reading a letter, his hair falling over his eyes. He did not lift his head, but asked directly, "What do you want?"

Though his voice was impassive, his face had darkened angrily – he was not going to make this easy. "Spit it out or go away – I am busy."

His rudeness irritated me, as it was designed to. "For Christ's sake can you not even look at me?"

He sighed deeply and made a show of reluctantly lowering the page. Raising his eyes, he regarded me haughtily. "Get on with it."

"I'd like to call a truce," I said quickly. "I mean … can we at least be friends?"

"We cannot. I've no interest in being your *friend*." He said *friend* as though mocking me.

Not to be deterred, I placed my hands on the oak between us. "Pat, I had no idea Amelia and the duchess … I didn't know … oh God, I just want to talk to you – to explain."

He sneered nastily. "Why do you imagine anything you say could be of the slightest relevance to me?"

Oh, he was exasperating! I chewed the inside of my cheek, throwing about for another tack. "Then, at least while I'm here … it's not pleasant this –"

"Do you find your stay here unpleasant?" He lifted an eyebrow. "You are not a prisoner. My fervent wish is that you return to your husband immediately. Since you refuse, the least you can do is to cease your boring supplications and leave me in peace – I have work to do."

He watched with insulting arrogance while I remained standing foolishly, irresolutely, before him. Suddenly he groaned and passed a hand over his hair, "Christ, woman! What must I say to get it through your dense skull? I wish to neither see you nor speak with you. Now, will you *please* stop hounding me!"

"I don't believe you," I said with feigned calm.

"You don't believe you're hounding me?"

"I don't believe that spring meant nothing to you."

"That's your problem."

"After everything you said back then, how can you feel nothing for me now?"

"I told you. I was experimenting – weren't you? God, we were both so young and … when did you become such a shrew? Does Hamish have to put up with all this whining? I could pity him for marrying you."

I overlooked the bait. "What about the irises? The heart we planted … our pact?" For some reason I thought the pretty, purple flowers were my trump card, but he gestured dismissively.

"I vaguely recall some silly, sentimental game."

"*No!*" I cried, unshed tears stinging my eyes.

"Damn it, woman!" Abruptly, he leapt from his chair and strode around the desk. A pulse beat rapidly in his temple. "If I led you to believe you meant anything to me, I apologise. It's true what they say of me: I'm without a shred of honour and always out to lift a skirt." He turned his palms upwards in an attitude of helplessness. "What can I say? You provided diversion during an otherwise monotonous convalescence."

Flinching, I whispered, "No Patrick, *that* I will not believe. I came to you remember? I gave myself to you when you'd have us wait."

"Yes, I remember that well enough. I was not interested in bedding you but your persistence would have worn down a saint. Even then you showed signs of the whore you would become."

I recoiled and my hands flew to my mouth. "You know that's not true. I gave myself to you in love – we loved *each other*."

His mouth twisted derisively. "Look, I've told a lot of untruths in my time, but I am being honest with you now. I have never loved you and there is nothing for you here. Go back to your husband, *Lady Elginbury*." He spat out my name contemptuously and made to turn away.

"*I can't*," I shouted, exasperated. "I've left him … I left everything to come to you! I cannot believe you feel nothing!" Hot tears were coursing freely down my cheeks now, but he was unyielding.

"That was quite presumptuous of you." His nostrils flared as he inhaled angrily. "Now, get out of here – I've no desire to continue this … discussion."

Decisively, he moved forwards. Grasping my shoulders with bruising firmness, he bundled me roughly towards the door. Wrenching it open with one hand, he gave a savage shove with the other.

I stumbled into the hall as the door was loudly slammed behind me, a powerful message of contempt echoing off the panelled walls of the corridor.

◈

It was somewhere past midnight. The groans of the house and the depth of darkness beyond my window indicated it wanted at least another four hours before Monsieur Chartrain rose and stoked the kitchen fires.

The wind howled around the house and the stars were intermittently blotted by scudding clouds. What a glorious sight the sky would be from the observatory on the roof. I had not been there since Patrick's guided tour all those years ago. Then, I was simply infatuated with my stepbrother and had not learned how painful loving him could be.

Jemima snored contentedly in her basket, but I was too wakeful to sleep. I lit a candle from the smouldering remains of my fire and wrapped a large shawl about my shoulders, crossing it over my chest and tying it at the back.

My velvet slippers made barely a sound on the hall runner and my shadow danced eerily on the wall beside me as I descended the stairs. The windows of the gallery running the length of the house became black mirrors bouncing my image at me until I took the staircase up to the resident's wing.

Pat's door was at the end of the hall, and drawing near, my heart thudded loudly in my breast and I was struck by the humiliating vision of his discovering me lurking outside his room like some pathetic wraith.

Hurriedly, I continued past his door and turned the corner at the end of the hall. Despite my candle, the darkness in this narrow section of corridor was suffocating, but I trailed one hand along the wall for guidance. The spiral staircase loomed out of the dark and with my candle held high and my nightdress bunched in my free hand, I climbed.

The stairs creaked loudly in the dark and I cringed and held my breath. Nothing in the house seemed to stir and eventually I arrived at the landing. The trapdoor and pull-down ladder were as I remembered. I wondered how long it had been since anyone had been up here. Would the ladder's mechanism be too stiff for me to operate? Rusted and squeaky?

It extended easily on well-maintained rails and I locked its hinges in place effortlessly and started up. Upon reaching the trapdoor I pushed. Nothing happened. It seemed stuck. It was too dark to see if there was a catch so I felt around with my hand – nothing. I tried again.

This time it moved slightly. Heartened, I made another attempt, wincing as it moved aside with a raspy protest. Still nothing stirred in the house behind me, so I quickly addressed the remaining rungs on the ladder to emerge into that clever glass room.

The candle's flickering light served to convert the observatory into a large opaque mirror so, after replacing the trapdoor, I took a seat on the bench that circled the room, and snuffed it out.

Immediately plunged into near perfect darkness, it took some seconds before the outside world was revealed in a magnificent panorama of indigo velvet studded with a million glittering pinheads. Puffs of cloud floated above the woods, and the moon hung like a golden sickle casting shimmering splashes of silvery light on the roof of the house and the gardens beyond. The trees in the park and forest were lightly frosted as though a painter had touched his gilt-dipped brush to their limbs and foliage. I drew in my breath slowly, overawed by the inexpressible beauty of the night.

A loud sound echoed sharply off the glass and I leapt to my feet in alarm as the trapdoor moved. Under any other circumstances I'd have laughed at the comical way Patrick's silhouette appeared in the hole, but instead, I pressed my lips tightly together as he climbed into the room.

"Who's there?" he growled, peering blindly in my direction.

I moved back a step and resumed my seat. "It's me, Alex."

His white shirt gleamed in the darkness, hanging loose over his trousers as though he'd shrugged into it. Something in his hand sloshed suspiciously as he waved his arm and spoke in an inebriated drawl, "What'r you doin' here?"

"I couldn't sleep … I … I wanted to see the sky at night."

"You've no right … prowlin' round the house at this hour." He lurched unsteadily across the floor and threw himself on to the bench beside me with a grunt. "Drink?" He thrust the bottle into my face.

I caught the smell of strong alcohol and wrinkled my nose. "No, thank you."

"Suit yourself." He took a long swig and squinting at me through the dark he demanded, "What?"

"You're drunk," I said with amusement.

He shrugged, "An' you, madam, 'r' five kinds o' bitch."

We sat quietly for several minutes, and though his nearness caused my heart to leap, he seemed unusually calm. After a time, I could stand the silence no longer and said, "So, why are *you* here in the middle of the night with a bottle in your hand?"

He didn't answer immediately. He seemed to be slipping into a drunken stupor, his chin sinking to his chest, the bottle propped precariously on his knee. He sighed and mumbled, "Could'n' shleep."

His hand slackened and the bottle began to slip. With uncommon reflexes, I caught it deftly and placed it a safe distance from his bare foot. By the steadiness of his breathing, I knew he slept.

I blinked away the wistful tears, and before my nerve could fail me, I leaned in and breathed deeply his sensuously familiar clove and citrus fragrance. "I love you," I whispered against his unshaven cheek, but he was well asleep and beyond response.

CHAPTER 19

The day of Sylvie's wedding dawned with pleasing, blue skies and only the slightest breeze. The bride entered Waterville's lovely chapel on her brother's arm and was exquisite in ice-blue silk, overlaid with delicate silver lace. Her pale hair was caught in a coronet of ringlets, with a silver gossamer veil held by a garland of early spring flowers.

Patrick smiled proudly beside her, uncharacteristically formal in azure trousers, white shirt, and an exquisite waistcoat of cloth of silver. The neckcloth he so despised was a starched, white perfection, and he wore a heavy brocade coat in the same ice-blue as Sylvie's gown. My heart caught painfully in my throat at the sight of him so tall and handsome beside his sister.

Upon arriving at the altar, they joined Quinn who was dressed similarly to Patrick, except that he had a froth of lace at his cuffs and he wore a magnificent diamond and sapphire pin in his neckcloth – a gift from his new brother-in-law.

The ceremony was a quiet affair attended by only a small group of us. I stood beside Sylvie in my gorgeous matron-of-honour gown of silver and blue. My hair was pinned up at the back in silver clips leaving a cascade of chestnut ringlets to tumble between my shoulder-blades. I knew they suited me – the dress and hair arrangement – but I was too involved in my inner turmoil to fully enjoy the feeling of being pretty; since such proximity to Patrick was breaking my heart. My trembling hands caused my nosegay of white roses and blue forget-me-nots to shiver and I could see my heart thudding beneath my bodice.

Patrick seemingly had no recollection of our early morning encounter on the rooftop and acknowledged my presence with only a curt nod and very formal click of his heels.

The ceremony over, Quinn and Sylvie were declared husband and wife and a great celebration was held to honour Sylvie's long history at Waterville; the invitation extending to staff, tenant farmers and their families. Trestles of food were laid out in the park and musicians from among the gathering ensured the dancing was lively. An army of caterers, recruited from the village children on promise of a silver coin each, kept the platters of food coming in trains from the kitchen while casks of wine were broken open, the better to enthusiastically drink the newly-weds' health amid much backslapping and ribald laughter.

Wishing to avoid the tumult of emotions that Patrick's presence always engendered, I remained within the house, where the strains of music and merriment drifted through the open porch windows. Holding aside the heavy, velvet drapes, I watched as Sylvie and Quinn were passed around the gathering, accepting cups of wine, hugs and blessings. Patrick moved easily among his people, sharing their talk and encouraging their revelry. His coat and neckcloth had been discarded immediately the ceremony was complete, and he stood now in a group of farmers, in his shirtsleeves and that magnificent silver waistcoat, a large cup of wine in one hand, the other casually slipped into his trousers' pocket. As I watched, the men threw their heads back in shared appreciation of a joke and I caught myself smiling reflectively.

"That's her," the dowager duchess whispered at my shoulder.

I'd been unaware of her approach and now I dropped a quick curtsy and made room for her beside me. She pointed with an age-spotted hand to a slender blonde woman in a rather more expensive dress than that of her friends, and I knew that I watched my adversary.

By the flickering light cast from the braziers, strategically placed on the lawns, I estimated that Kat Wheeler was perhaps a year or two older than me. She lifted her skirts high and showed much petticoat as she skipped and twirled through the vigorous country dances, surrounded by a gaggle of appreciative males who encouraged her with cheers and whoops of delight. A bright yellow kerchief held her abundant gold hair from her face. It swirled and bounced about her waist in time with the music and, even at this distance, she radiated vitality and self-assurance. She was as opposite of me as night was of day, and his adamant denials of love for me gained momentum.

"He is a fool to spend his attention on that slut," the duchess remarked dryly.

"His father thinks he may marry her."

"Bah! Patrick Washburn is not *that* dull-witted. He'll not wed her. She's a peasant – common trollop. Dress her up he might, but a woman like that is good for one thing only – and it's not serving tea in a drawing room!"

"Heirs," I murmured. "Patrick has been pestered endlessly to marry and get heirs." I studied the capering woman, noting her healthy robustness, and my eyes shot daggers. "She could give him heirs."

"He will not marry her, mark my words. I know his father very well – too well," she added with a glint in her eye, "and while Gerrard Washburn may allow his son certain freedoms, he'll not countenance the boy marrying *that* far below his station. The Washburn blood is blue – cannot be diluted."

"I wish I had your faith," I said doubtfully. "My mother would have it that way, but Gerrard would never gainsay his precious son."

"Hoo-hoo!" the elderly woman cackled in her dry voice. "Indeed, Mim Broughton could torment Lucifer himself." She patted my arm. "Anyway, don't give up hope, eh? You looked very pretty at the ceremony, and I may be an old fart, but I know admiration in a man's eye when I see it. Your charms did not go unnoticed."

I snorted inelegantly. "Perhaps, but Patrick has ever been over-sexed. If he found me attractive it doesn't translate to love, and I've no desire to be his mistress."

"Patrick Washburn has been tumbling the lasses since he worked out his cock did more than just piss," she gestured impatiently at my shocked expression. "Amelia told me he did not importune you. Is this true?"

I nodded, flushing at her directness and wondering what else Millie had told her.

"Right! Then as I see it, you meant more than a mere tumble. The question is, what does he feel now?"

"Loathing," I said glumly.

"Possibly, but I suspect the opposite. In any case," she turned to leave, "one does not accumulate my years without the equivalent accumulation of wisdom. That boy is angry and, I suspect, very hurt. Methinks his pride will disallow any reconciliation between you. Soon enough you needs must decide how long you continue banging your head against a brick wall."

"Then I'm wasting my time?" I asked, but her retreating back gave no response.

❧

I stood on the porch in the crisp, spring morning surveying the remains of the party. Many of the revellers slept where they'd collapsed on benches, beneath the trestles, or even crumpled on the lawn, heedless of the damp of night. The smell of wood smoke hung in the air, and ashes mixed with dew to form a grey sludge, layering everything from leftover food, to a lovingly entwined couple, while a pair of ducks applied themselves to a furtive breakfast from a trencher of roasted vegetables.

To avoid the shambles, Jemima and I wandered the less familiar side of the house, opposite our usual route. We followed a meandering path along the edge of the woods, which wound its way behind the stables, coach shed and towards Briggs's cottage. Since the old chap had been at the gathering last night, I assumed I'd not see him this morning, but as I skirted a lush clump of dogrose in new bloom, I spied him resting on a bench against the whitewashed wall of his cottage, stuffing tobacco into his pipe.

"Hullo." My breath plumed before me as I spoke.

"'Mornin'," he responded. "Not feelin' any 'ffect of las' night?"

"I didn't drink a lot – unlike some."

"Hmmph! Don' know wha' yer mean," he commented dryly.

"Not out walking this morning? Too much dancing?"

"Don' call wot I did dancin', but that's prob'ly wot did it. Young lord knows 'owta throw a turn, thass fer sure."

I chuckled, visualising Briggs' scrawny legs going this way and that in something approaching a country jig. "Hmm … Then, I shall leave you to your pipe."

He nodded and clamped the pipe between his teeth with a soft click.

Continuing, Jemima and I tracked the path beyond Briggs' cottage around an ancient elder to where the thick greenery gave way to a meadow dotted with mushrooms and pink-capped toadstools. Jemima caught the scent of something intriguing and nosed her way into a cluster of plants to investigate.

The birds were thick in the trees here. Their nests, sheltered in the dense foliage, were a flurry of activity as the spring hatchlings made raucous demands for food and disturbed the otherwise stillness of the morning. As I passed they became alarmed, and a parent bird took a dive at me. Quickening my pace, I rounded a tree, only just escaping a pecking, and found myself before a decrepit old shed the size of a small barn.

It seemed to consist of two rooms. The shingle roof of one had caved in, leaving the stone walls supporting a couple of rotting beams and nothing else. The second room seemed reasonably intact, and from what I could see, housed a plough and other rusting farm implements.

Curiosity drew me inside and as my eyes adjusted to the dimness, I made out a small stack of hay piled against one wall and another bale broken up and scattered about on the dirt floor. No doubt some animal had discovered it and was treating it as his private eating-house.

Just then something stirred in the corner, and I stiffened warily. Perhaps the creature was still here, but as I turned to flee, the beast emitted a low, human-like groan.

Frowning, I cautiously crept closer and was somehow not surprised to discover Patrick sprawled face down in the middle of the hay. His beautiful waistcoat was nowhere in sight and he wore only his shirt and trousers.

Groaning again he rolled over and I retreated slightly, catching my bottom lip between my teeth. His trousers were unbuttoned, as was his shirt, and he was displaying a liberal amount of muscled abdomen. A long, pale pink scar snaked along his chest below his collar bone, and a line of gold hair trailed from his navel to become a thatch where his trousers only just managed to preserve his decency.

The blood quickened in my veins at the sight of him, so masculine, so vulnerable, so …

He groaned again and flung an arm over his eyes against the daylight. "Who's there?" he drawled in a thick voice.

"Me, Alex."

He moaned painfully. "Christ … not you again. Can't get away from you." With a growl, he dragged himself to a sitting position and raised a trembling hand to his head. "Shit, that hurts – get that smug look off your face."

"You look dreadful," I said, but my satisfaction faded suddenly with the bitter-sweet memory of the gentle care he'd dispensed during my own raging hangover years ago. Smiling nostalgically, I hunkered beside him. "Can I –" The words almost choked me. Crumpled in the hay beside him was a yellow kerchief.

Swiftly, as though burned, I stood. "You can rot here for all I care," I declared coolly, and with a dignity I shall be proud of for the rest of my days, I left him to his well-deserved suffering.

How he made his way back to the house I shall never know, but evidently he had, for later that afternoon I was surprised to find him in the drawing-room. Clean and freshly shaved, and sadly showing no ill-effects of his night's debauchery, he lounged on a couch in the last rays of the afternoon sun. In one hand he held a cup of steaming coffee, in the other a London newspaper and when I came in looking for a book I'd left, he lifted his eyes. Upon seeing me, he returned immediately to his paper.

My plan to take my book outside was quickly discarded. "Do you mind if I sit here?" I indicated the couch opposite.

Without looking up he said, "I mind very much that you loiter in my house, but since that does not seem to bother you ..."

"I was trying to be polite." I took a seat and opened the book at my ribbon.

He turned the page of his newspaper and shook it out, and we sat in silence for a long time, though his presence was so distracting I could only stare at my page, the lines of print blurring into illegible worms. The very air between us was taut and vibrating with everything we had and had not said, and the silence amplified each pop and crack from the fireplace.

"Why do you remain here where there's nothing for you?" he

broke the silence. Folding the paper he placed it on the table before him. His empty coffee cup beside it, he levelled his emerald gaze upon me.

"I told you – I left Hamish." I slid forwards on the seat, my book forgotten. "Patrick, *please*, I made a terrible mistake. I loved you so much – imagine how I felt when Anne said she carried your baby."

"Oh stop it," he cried melodramatically, "you're breaking my heart."

Foolishly, desperately, I was suddenly crouching beside him. "You *must* listen. I married Hamish because I was being pressured from so many sides – even Simon thought it best. Not even *he* understood what we had."

"You should have listened to him. Simon knows better than anyone how I value my freedom – get off your knees, woman!"

"Oh, *why* do you deny it now? Look – there's no one else here – you don't have to pretend."

He shook his head in bewilderment. "You really are relentless."

"I *never* wanted to marry Hamish!" I cried in frustration.

Explosively, he leapt to his feet and his eyes shot green sparks. "Then why did you?" he roared as though trying to shake the rafters. He was breathing hard and I cringed beneath his fury and willed my trembling knees to support me as slowly I rose to face him. Though I'd learned violence from Hamish, Patrick's anger gave me hope.

"They were pressuring me – *all* of them." I forced calmness into my voice that I didn't feel. "Anne was with child and she said it was yours. Then, Lord Hamish decided he was dying and needed an heir. Before I could catch my breath, Mother had it all arranged and … and …" I clasped my hands together to lend me strength. "I've made such a hash of things – so many mistakes. I am *so sorry*, Pat … I cannot tell you how sorry …"

He was watching me impassively and I held my breath, then slowly his mouth curved into an unpleasant sneer. "So where is this precious heir then?" he asked nastily. "Though I expect it's somewhat difficult to get a babe on a woman when you're busy fiddling with boys."

I stood very still and stared at him, horrified, and completely lost for words.

He squared his shoulders and stared back with satisfaction. When finally I found my voice, it was a hoarse whisper. "You *knew* about that?"

He smiled cruelly. "Everyone knew – your mother, my father, *everyone*. Why do you think you were chosen in the first place? You were slim-hipped, straight like a boy – they hoped he would take a fancy to you. Do you know the first time he saw you, you were wearing a pair of Simon's breeches? Quite ironic don't you think?"

I could not believe my ears and continued to stare dumbly at him for this revelation, coming after so much pain, burned me to the core. I'd never have married Hamish had I known, yet he – they all – had known and kept it from me. "You *knew*?" I repeated incredulously, and a surge of mad, consuming rage possessed me. "Do you have any idea what I went through?" I cried and my voice went up an octave. "You knew and you said nothing! You may not have loved me, but at the very least you were *supposed* to be my friend. You said *nothing*!"

Fuelled by hurt and disappointment, the words tumbled forth in a torrent of loud, incoherent accusation and anger. He held his ground, unruffled, with a bored smile on his face, and hands lazily in his pockets.

When finally I paused, breathless and shaking, he regarded me with mild amusement. He was clearly enjoying my distress, and not at all concerned by the storm that had broken over his head, and I should have remembered then, the callousness he was capable of.

"What's the matter, my Lady Elginbury?" he grinned maliciously. "Could not get an heir because my lord was shoving it in the wrong –"

With a scream that drowned his words, two years of pain and grief erupted within me and I lost all reason. I leapt upon him, screeching like a banshee and swinging wildly. My balled fist connected with his jaw with a gratifying *thunk*. I hauled back and was preparing a second assault when he burst into action. Grasping my flailing wrists, he clamped them as in convict irons.

By now I was sobbing with fury. He pulled me towards him, our faces flushed with emotion and our breathing ragged. His mouth twisted into an ugly distortion of his good looks and he whispered dangerously, "Do that again and you shall live to regret it, *my fine Lady Elginbury.*"

"For God's sake, man …!"

Aden had burst into the room, followed immediately by Amelia who gasped in shock, "Oh Pat, *no!*"

But still he held me, and the tears dribbled over my cheeks as I struggled against him. "Do not test me," he warned in a voice that was raspy with suppressed anger.

"C'mon now, let her go," Aden spoke calmly.

The pressure of his vice–like fingers was excruciating and I wondered fearfully if my wrists, weakened since the fall that killed my baby, would be crushed in his grip.

"C'mon, Paddy," Aden said wheedlingly. "Let her be, and we'll go have a drink, eh?"

I stared into Patrick's face, which was now so disfigured with wrath that I hardly recognised it. A pulse throbbed in his neck and his eyes were hard like chips of green onyx. Without warning, he released me, throwing me aside, where I hit the pitiless rug, all the wind knocked from my lungs.

"Take this fucking virago from my sight!" He shouted at Aden before slamming the door as he left the room.

❧

I sat in the chair by my fire, absently fondling Jemima's ears and staring into the jumping yellow and red flames. Sylvie leaned over my writing desk with her back to me. She was laying out a steaming bowl of soup and a hunk of crusty bread for my meal. "He wasn't at supper," she said. Her back was straight and slender, showing no evidence of the child that protruded from her front. She wore an apron over her pretty cotton dress and I frowned slightly, thinking how unconsciously she fell into servitude.

She turned and smoothed her hands over the apron. "Probably hiding out at some inn like a —" she broke off, her expression darkening. "Oh Alex, your wrists!"

My wrists were already turning interesting shades of violet and rose — Amelia had gently rubbed a rather effective balm into them to draw out the bruising.

"I know, but they'll heal."

She compressed her lips and went to stand by the window. A gathering of swollen, grey clouds hung low over the forest and a gusty wind was causing the treetops to sway and pitch. "Millie says a storm is coming. If Quinn and I leave for London soon we should get ahead of it." She turned quickly to look at me. "Alex, will you be alright? I don't feel we can leave you."

"Of course you can," I said convincingly. "Things cannot go on as they are or Patrick and I will end up killing each other."

She nodded and her face was grim. "I have suggested to Quinn that we take you back to Yorkshire."

"*Oh no!*" I was quickly on my feet. "Sylvie, please go to London. Quinn's looking forward to seeing his brother. You *must* go."

"Eat your supper," she said non-comittally, and sat wearily in the chair at my desk, watching the approaching weather.

"We cannot leave you here," she said at length.

"Sylvie, my dear friend, I doubt I shall even see him — we'll be avoiding one other like the plague. You must go, and don't give me a thought. I shall be alright — Aden and Millie are here."

"We can return early, perhaps in a —"

"No," I said firmly.

❧

Quinn and Sylvie decided to depart the following day. Over breakfast Quinn discussed their route with Aden. Sylvie was following the plans excitedly though I knew she continued to worry for me.

Patrick had returned home the previous evening and had broken his fast alone very early, lending weight to my argument that we would be at pains to avoid one another. This fact seemed to please not only Sylvie, but also Aden, who frowned thoughtfully at my bruises.

As the two men discussed the roads and suitable inns, I noted Amelia's absence and interrupted at the first opportunity.

"Where's Millie?"

"She's not feeling well. 'T'is the babe stirring and keeping her awake at night." Aden gave a helpless gesture. "Cissy has taken up a tray but she is sleeping."

He helped himself to bread and ham and looked across the table at me as though he had something to say. His carroty hair had recently been trimmed and it made his face look wider than normal, wider again when he smiled carefully and asked, "Alex, now you know I would not be asking but …"

"Yes?"

"You remember the duchess mentioned the Locksley's ball? 'Tis tomorrow night and a gentleman, Christopher Thorpe, whom I've a desire to talk with, will be in attendance."

"And you would like me to accompany you?"

"Millie does not wish to attend and would be happy for you to go in her stead."

"But I wasn't invited."

"Lady Locksley will not mind. She would rather the numbers of ladies match the gentleman for dancing and so forth."

I glanced at Sylvie who nodded eagerly. "Go on, Alex. It should be good for you."

"But my wrists … they're so unsightly.

"If you wear the dress you wore to my wedding you can wear the long silver gloves that go with it," Sylvie suggested.

I sighed, undecided. "Her grace will be there too," Aden coaxed.

I was still reluctant but denying Aden the opportunity to speak with this Thorpe chap was selfish in light of Aden's hospitality. "Very well, I shall go."

Upstairs in my room I threw open my wardrobe and took out the beautiful matron-of-honour gown. It was the best gown I had but was somewhat crumpled. I would ask Mrs Bath to have it pressed. I leaned into the wardrobe for the silver slippers that went with it and as I straightened, Sylvie's tinkling laugh floated up from outside.

Bea had left the window open slightly to air the room and the wind racing ahead of the storm, billowed the lace curtains. Moving them aside, I saw Sylvie below, sitting on the edge of the fountain, her hand tucked into the crook of Pat's arm. I let the curtain drop, but remained standing where I could observe without detection, my conscience pricking slightly as I eavesdropped.

They were looking up at the sky and Pat was saying how the clouds were too high, he doubted the storm would come today.

"Quinn agrees. That's why we shall leave this afternoon."

"And so you should – you ought to already have been on your way."

She smiled up at him and her resemblance to Maeve was plain. "Yet, I worry about leaving Alex here with you. Why do you squabble with her so?" she asked gently, and I stiffened – I had no further qualms over listening-in.

"Why does she refuse to leave? She must return to her husband – it's where she belongs."

Sylvie's smile faded. "She has left him."

"Then to Simon."

"Simon will send her back to Hamish, but neither you nor he understands what she endured while in Scotland."

He shrugged disinterestedly.

"No Pat, listen to me," she twisted around to face him. "Alex never wanted to marry Hamish but she had no option."

"Arguable, since no one forced her to the altar."

"Certainly, but since Anne's lies were so convincing … there was nothing Alex could do. You see, Janet betrayed you both … she told Lady Thorncliffe everything about the two of you."

"*Everything?*"

At the strange note in his voice I leaned forward to see his expression. Typically, it was unreadable but he was watching Sylvie closely.

"Yes – *everything*," Sylvie said meaningfully. "Her mother decided that since you had seduced Alex it was fair to believe you'd seduced Anne too. There was no argument Alex could offer … she married Hamish. Oh, she tried to make the best of it but there was no rapport between them – no common ground until she was pregnant and –"

"There's a *child*?" he exclaimed and his words seemed strangled. "She had his *baby*?"

"There is no baby," Sylvie said evenly. "There was an accident and the baby was lost. Any unity they had disintegrated entirely after that."

They fell silent for a short time until Sylvie continued cautiously, "Pat, one afternoon, Alex and I were talking and she confided her disappointment in you and Anne for she truly believed you had left her own bed and gone directly to her sister's. She honestly didn't know." She touched his arm for emphasis. "I told her what I knew – about that day Anne came here."

Patrick nodded. "Anne argued that since our parents had planned our marriage it would not be unwelcome. When I refused, she tried blackmail. I thought to call her bluff – I didn't think she had it in her."

Sylvie sighed and absently trailed her hand in the trickling fountain. "It's Anne you should be angry with. The only peace Alex had in that marriage was for a month or two just before she lost the baby. When that happened, Hamish accused her of somehow willing it so she would be free to come after you." She shook the water from her hand. "But they are married after all, and she really wanted to make the best of it. She wanted that baby so badly Pat, she was devastated – in fairness, they both were."

He said nothing, and Sylvie went on. "Hamish continued with his men friends. He became so disdainful of Alex he didn't even care when she discovered him with one of them. There were so many; even one of the stable boys." She shook her head.

I caught my breath at her last words, this new information crystallised further my loathing for my husband.

"He used to taunt her with them, and he beat her. And you know, she never stopped loving you. Even when her Mother would draw and quarter you, she'd have defended you to the death. And now you lock her out. Why do you deny your feelings?"

"I don't," he stated firmly.

Sylvie sat back and crossed her arms so they rested on her distended belly. "You're a liar."

"Little sister, I should have advised our father not to recognise you." He grinned and tweaked her nose. "You were a lot less trouble before."

Impatiently, she swatted his hand away. "If you never loved Alex, why are you so angry all the time? And that argument with Simon – what was that about?"

"That was about something else."

"I don't believe you."

He continued to watch her with amusement. "Simon visited because the experience of war can only be truly realised by those who have endured it. We disagreed over some minor detail." He rose, indicating the discussion was over.

"I still don't believe you," she said, standing beside him.

He laughed and pulled her into his arms. "Did our father know you would torment me so? By recognising you is he punishing me for my many horrendous crimes?"

"Exactly how many horrendous crimes have you committed?"

"Oh, that's an entirely different discussion."

They laughed together then, and turned, arm-in-arm, toward the house, disappearing from view.

Sylvie and Quinn departed that afternoon as planned. Travelling lightly for speed, they took only those items necessary – including Bony, for Quinn would not hear of leaving the dog behind. I stood beside Amelia and Aden waving the couple off as their carriage rolled around the gaily-bubbling fountain. And Patrick, thankfully, was absent.

CHAPTER 20

I sat at my dressing-table as Bea dressed my hair, and watched in the mirror as she pulled it into a knot, which she separated into three ropes. They were then coiled around each other and secured at my crown. Silver clips held sections of hair at my temples allowing a cluster of curls to frame my face in the latest fashion.

She stood back to critique her work. "What d'you think, milady?"

"You have a definite talent."

"Thank you, milady. Shall I 'elp yer with yer dress now?"

"Mr Rourke will be banging on the door at any moment — better hurry."

She slipped the dress carefully over my hair and pulled it to the floor and I turned so that she could fasten the little pearl buttons at the back.

"Oh milady," she complained, "it don't fit right. Yer must'a lost more weight."

The mirror showed loose folds at the bodice and sleeves and I sighed ruefully. "Well, I've nothing else so I shall have to grin and bear it." I snatched the gloves from a table and pulled them over my discoloured wrists while Bea watched wordlessly.

"Anyway, better than gaining weight and bursting my seams," I said with false cheer and, glancing up, I surprised a look of sympathy on her face.

"Yer look lovely, milady," she lied, generously.

"Thank you, Bea." I picked up a dainty reticule that Sylvie had left for me, and popped a handkerchief into it. "Don't wait up."

❧

The Locksleys' mansion overlooked the sea: I had visited years before with Gerrard and Mother. Unbidden, the memories flooded back and I recalled how carefree I had been back then, untouched and blissfully invulnerable. I shook off these thoughts as the carriage turned down the long straight driveway and Locksley Towers rose solid and imposing before us. The mansion was much older than Waterville Place, and to my eye, not nearly as attractive. A knot of horses and carriages clogged the driveway and we waited nearly half an hour before our turn arrived and a liveried footman flung open our door and handed me out.

Aden offered his arm as we entered the house and joined the receiving line. While waiting, I stared around me at the assorted guests. Other women milling about the house shimmered in a kaleidoscope of exotic colours. Silks and satins, lace and peacock feathers, all as could befit a visit to the royal palace were on display, while, glittering with so many jewels, the women tinkled musically as their heads turned to assess my gown and the pearls in my ears. Their voices whispered speculatively behind silk fans, as they conferred on my identity and dissected my character and merits. Is this what court was like? I felt truly out of my depth – definitely a country rabbit.

At length, the line moved forwards and I was introduced to Lord and Lady Locksley who expressed their polite concern for Amelia and welcomed me warmly as Aden's visiting cousin.

Strains of music floated in the air from a room to our left and couples were coming and going across the parquet floor. Enormous crystal chandeliers sparkled with the light of a thousand candles and reflected brightly in giant gilt-framed mirrors lining the walls.

Aden led me to a table where we helped ourselves, in the French *buffet* style, to iced champagne and strawberries. Feeling terribly out of place, I decided to drown my concerns in the champagne and quaffed my first glass rather quickly, immediately taking up a second.

"For certain you could be of Irish stock, Alex," Aden said, his eyes dancing merrily, "you take to the drink as well as any of us."

"Don't be so impolite, boy," snapped a familiar voice behind us.

Whirling, I dropped a quick curtsy and Aden bowed as the dowager duchess looked us over and smiled, the creases in her face deepening.

"How are you, child?"

"Well, thank you, your grace," I responded. "And you?"

"Marvellous. Now walk with me, will you," she said to Aden and, linking her arm with his, led us directly through the crowd. Immediately, I heard the sibilant whispers surrounding us, for since the duchess was the highest-ranking guest, her obvious friendship and my mysterious identity intrigued these bored people and gave them much to speculate on.

I was introduced to a range of guests, and as the evening progressed I danced variously with Aden – when he wasn't talking with acquaintances – and other gentlemen, or I stood primly beside the duchess, champagne in hand. Among the other women I met was a Lady Longhurst. Joanna Longhurst was an overweight woman, stuffed into a frilled and laced gown that did her no favours. Overflowing with the latest gossip, she kept me quite entertained.

The duchess snorted rudely. "Now Joanna, I am certain Lady Elginbury has no need of such information."

"Pooh! You know I'm right, Lucy, she *did* marry that fellow with the penchant for gambling and his poor father – how he would spin in his grave. I heard he had to mortgage his London house to pay the …" Suddenly her eyes widened, "Oh, Lady Elginbury," she held her fan to her face and pointed with her eyes. "See that gentleman over there? *That* is Sir Christopher Thorpe. I declare, the most perfect specimen I –"

"Heavens above, Joanna!" the duchess cried in exasperation. "Alex, you must tell Aden, Sir Christopher is here."

"Where?" Aden said coming up beside me.

The older woman nodded toward the champagne table while Lady Longhurst sighed dreamily, "Sweet Jesus, were I twenty years younger …"

"Were you twenty years younger you'd still double his age," the duchess quipped.

I followed Lady Longhurst's gaze, immediately identifying the object of her adulation standing casually with a glass of champagne in one hand, the other tucked into his trouser pocket.

He was well over six feet tall, immaculately attired in a rich burgundy coat, white and burgundy striped waistcoat and black trousers. His snowy neckcloth was intricately tied and his shiny black hair was thick and touched his broad shoulders. As he turned, even at this distance, I was startled by the intense violet of his eyes.

As one who'd grown up with Simon's devastating looks, I was nevertheless overwhelmed by the almost feminine beauty of the man, tempered by a truly masculine and overtly virile allure.

With feline grace, he moved towards a group of men in discussion, and I was struck by a sense of contained power.

"A completely arrogant bastard for a third son," Aden commented. "Women are captivated by him and men are in awe. He is unmarried and unrepentant, and highly decorated after his conduct in the Peninsular Wars."

"Perhaps, but I heard he is at odds with his family," Lady Longhurst remarked haughtily.

Aden turned to me. "He is also a very good friend of Patrick's."

"Did his arrogance rub off on your cousin, then?"

Aden laughed lightly. "Possibly, though I understand they fought side-by-side at Waterloo and earned each other's regard. Well … please excuse me ladies, I'd best be making myself known to our handsome Sir Christie."

He bowed gallantly and we watched as he made a beeline for the man who, seemingly unaware, had every silken fan in the room fluttering like so many butterfly wings.

"So, my dear," the duchess turned to me, "has Sylvie departed for London?"

"Yes, though only yesterday. But tell me, your grace, has your servant, the one with the broken ankle, returned to you yet?"

The older woman shook her head in bewilderment and the rubies, dripping from her ears like ripe grapes, tinkled prettily. "You know, that child returned a week later, still with the splints on, terrified she would be replaced should she be absent for too long. I could not convince her otherwise so now I hear her clump-clumping about the place on a crutch. Sooner or later she will break a Ming vase or something equally irreplaceable."

We chuckled together and Lady Longhurst rolled her eyes in sympathy. "You ought to have rid yourself of her, Lucy. I told you an age ago that girl would be troublesome – you never take my advice."

"Quite so, Joanna, but unlike yourself, I have yet to discover my best maid in my own bed with a footman."

I smothered a giggle as Lady Longhurst glared at her friend. Turning quickly to me she said, "Tell me, Lady Elginbury, I understand you are staying with Aden and Amelia Rourke. What brings you to Devon at this dreary time of year?"

"Lady Elginbury is young Thorncliffe's stepsister," the duchess said quickly. "She attended the wedding of the youngest girl, Sylvie."

"I see. And is Lord Elginbury with you?" Lady Longhurst

inquired politely. I absently touched my gloved finger where the bump of my wedding ring lay.

"Oh no," I said lightly, "he is busy with his estates in Scotland."

"Ah yes. In any case, your brother must be enjoying your – oh, there they are now!" She waved eagerly, "Oh, Lord Thorncliffe! Hello, Lord Thorncliffe!"

They?

I turned a stricken face towards the duchess who carefully arranged her expression and instructed me with her eyes to do likewise. I felt suddenly ill. I had – foolishly – not guessed that Patrick might be here, and with *her*.

I kept my face averted and focused my full attention on Aden who was deep in conversation with Sir Christopher and two other gentlemen.

"Greetings, my lord, we were just talking about you," Lady Longhurst purred, dropping a curtsy. "How nice, Lady Elginbury, 'tis your brother."

I had no choice then but to face him. He was resplendent in white trousers, lavender brocade waistcoat, purple coat and black neckcloth and as he rose from his bow to Lady Longhurst and the duchess, he levelled his impassive gaze on my face. Intensely aware of his partner, I avoided looking at her, and drew in my breath to say calmly, "Good evening, Patrick."

We hadn't seen each other since our brawl in the drawing room, yet I could count on his innate reserve and knew he would perform with cool dignity.

"Greetings, Sister," he responded in his quiet voice. His face was carefully blank but his eyes seemed to dart involuntarily towards my gloved wrist, as I held the now empty champagne glass.

Was he remembering, regretting perhaps, the punishment he'd administered? I scrutinised his closed face. To the left of his sensuous mouth, his skin was slightly discoloured and I felt the sting of shame for my violence towards him, but then he spoke.

"Your grace, ladies, may I present my companion, Miss Rebecca Renshaw."

My studiously assembled mask didn't slip despite my shock. This was not Kat Wheeler. This was another woman; dark-haired, beautiful, and sexually confident. She watched me as she rose from her curtsy with a slow, self-assured smile. Her gown was in soft lavender, perfectly complementing Patrick's attire, the bodice scooped low, exposing generous white breasts, and her hair was arranged to create a waterfall of ebony curls. She and Patrick were, to my chagrin, a handsomely-matched couple and, by the look on her face, I knew she sensed a rivalry between us.

"So," she exhaled, languidly, "you are Rick's little stepsister." Suddenly she chuckled low in her throat, "Oh – sorry, I understand you call him Pat. Only *I* call him Rick – it's just one of those pet things with us, isn't it, sweet?" *Rick*, to his credit, didn't respond, while she, being taller than I, studied my reaction down the length of her aquiline nose.

Feigning interest in the dancers, I chewed my cheek to quell the fury that tightened my chest. The duchess's hand lightly touched my back, and with a fortifying breath I turned back to our gathering and found Patrick's eyes on me.

"Your glass is empty, Sister," he said with unexpected gentleness. "May I bring you another?" I nodded in wordless surprise and he took the empty glass from me. "Your grace? Lady Longhurst?"

The two ladies declined while his bitch responded in a honeyed voice, "I should like another please, Rick."

Patrick bowed politely and strode to where Aden stood with Sir Christopher, and upon his arrival, backslaps were exchanged and friendly banter followed as the two friends, one fair and the other dark, greeted one another. These two unmarried men embodied every husband and father's worst fears and the hopes of every society matron; the room fairly vibrated with feminine admiration.

Drawing my attention to our group, the duchess said cheerfully,

"Now the pleasantries are over shall we move closer to the dance floor?"

"Surely you won't dance, Lucy?" asked Lady Longhurst, astonished.

"Good heavens no, Joanna. But that is not to say I shan't enjoy watching the young ones."

As we watched the lines of dancers, I glanced longingly over my shoulder, wishing fervently that Aden would decide he needed to return home to Amelia. Or at least, Patrick could bring back that champagne.

"Do you dance, Lady Elginbury?" his trollop's sultry voice cut into my thoughts.

"Yes. I quite enjoy dancing, Miss Renshaw," I asserted untruthfully. "My husband and I regularly attend balls at the homes of our friends in Glasgow."

"I take it then, that you did not bring your ball gowns with you to Devon," she said with practised innocence.

"Whatever do you mean?" Lady Longhurst lunged at the bait, and I winced inwardly.

"Merely an observation," the slut purred pleasantly, "Since Lady Elginbury's gown this evening is the same one provided by her *sister* to be worn at that by-blow's wedding."

Lady Longhurst gasped and to my eternal regret, I flushed to the roots of my hair, mortified by her rudeness, but her face was a study of ingenuousness.

Such was my outrage at Sylvie's denigration that I was rendered uncharacteristically speechless. But the duchess wasn't. She attacked with hackles raised and claws sprung for the kill.

"I challenge you to repeat those words before the young lord," she snarled.

"Oh, come now, your grace, everyone knows Sylvie Washburn is a bastard raised as a servant. And it cannot be denied the gown Lady Elginbury wears tonight was provided by her."

"You are quite shameless for one who snared herself a wealthy keeper simply by lying on her back. You bourgeois whore. You think yourself so superior while scraping the paddock grime from your boots like the shit-shovelling slattern you are!"

"Duchess, that is quite enough!" None of us had noticed Patrick's return.

"Pray do not stop me now, *Rick*. The cats have their claws out tonight."

"Then sheath them – all of you." He thrust the champagne glass towards me spilling half its contents indelibly on the hem of my beautiful dress. His doxy placed her hand coolly on his arm and gave a victorious toss of her great mane as he led her away.

While I struggled to compose my flaming face, the duchess's eyes glittered with fury. "Sow!" she spat after them.

"Is it true? Sylvie Washburn is a bastard raised as servant?" Lady Longhurst wondered in scandalised delight.

"Oh, do shut up, Joanna!"

The duchess marched us to a group of chairs where I sat in humiliated silence between the two older women watching the swish and sway of the dancers moving through their steps. I was beginning to feel ill from lack of air and the sickly scent of perfume, powder and perspiration.

Beside me, Lady Longhurst fidgeted annoyingly. Finally, she spotted her husband, and offered some babbled excuse, a perfunctory curtsy, and rushed off to join him.

"Can't wait to spread the gossip," the duchess remarked cynically.

I squeezed her hand where it rested on her lap. "Thank you for defending Sylvie, your grace. But I wonder how that bitch could have known. Patrick adores Sylvie; he'd never say anything against her."

"Servants, always the servants. I'll wager that whore knows why you're here too, and people like Joanna can't help themselves. Never mind, in any case, I enjoy a bit of a cat fight from time to time."

Before I could respond, Aden approached looking happy with himself. His gap-toothed grin was splitting his face in two as he recounted his conversation with Sir Christopher. "And he has agreed to come to supper next week so we can go over the details."

"Stupendous news, my boy," the duchess enthused. "But, I wonder if you would not mind escorting an old lady to her carriage now that you are done. Methinks I have been too ambitious mixing it with the younger set."

Concern furrowed Aden's brow as she fluttered her fan and affected a fatigued air. "Of course. Alex, you won't be minding if we leave, will you?"

I shook my head and tried not to show my relief.

"Very well." He offered his arm to the elderly lady, "Can you walk, your grace?"

She winked in my direction and said weakly, "If we go slowly, my boy."

CHAPTER 21

The morning started badly with Amelia leaning heavily on my writing desk. "Sure now I'd not be asking this of you if I could do it myself." She pressed her fists into the base of her spine and arched her back with a grimace. "But this babe … so large … and I am so tired all the time."

I cringed inwardly. "I only hesitate because … well, things with Patrick, they're –"

"I know, and understand. But he said it would be alright –"

"Alright for him – what about me?"

She sighed wearily. "He's prepared to do this for Aden. Couldn't you, please? It would mean so much to Aden and me."

I turned away to look out at the fountain; the way the splashes of water sparkled like droplets of crystal in the sunshine splintering the sunlight into dazzling shards of colour.

Her request, to dine with Aden and Patrick, adding the essential feminine ingredient when Sir Christie came to discuss the details of Aden's business venture, was not so difficult.

The thought of spending an evening with Patrick, exposing myself to heartache and probable public humiliation, was exceedingly unattractive.

"He promised, Alex. He said he would behave provided …" Her voice trailed off.

"Provided what?" It came out sharper than intended.

She smiled apologetically. "Provided you – his words – keep your moon-eyed bleating to yourself."

I opened my mouth angrily but she forestalled any response. "You'd be doing it as a favour to us, not Patrick. The meal would be so much more civilised if you were there to make conversation and … afterwards they will take their business elsewhere and you would be free to leave. Please say you will."

Her great hazel eyes were imploring. How could I deny her when she and Aden had been so good to me? I smiled resignedly.

Thus I found myself at Aden's side sampling the sherry Patrick had brought from Spain with him after the war. I sipped at the warm, sweet liquor and was formally introduced to Sir Christopher Thorpe. Up close, he was simply magnetic, and his incredible looks fair took my breath away. "Lady Elginbury, have I met your husband?" He asked in a melodic voice – the man was flawless.

"Perhaps, my lord. Though Scots, he has spent some time at the English court."

"Ah, Scots. Indeed, my nurse was Scots. It was she first called me Christie after the Scots fashion." Sir Christie's exotic purple eyes lingered on my face as though I were simply the most fascinating creature on earth. "I'm certain I know your brother though, Sir Simon Broughton … met him on the Peninsula … terribly wounded. Patched up this old soldier here," he said, with a nod to the door as Patrick entered.

"My brother ensured I received the best of care, for nothing has greater strength than the bond between brothers, Christie," Patrick said with a wink and the two acknowledged some private understanding with rueful grins. Dinner was called and Aden and I led the way into the dining room. The two war veterans followed, maintaining a light banter between them.

Sir Christie proved to be a charming and eloquent convers-ationalist. He and Patrick shared an obvious friendship, which saw my brother in good spirits, and though Pat's conversation was never directed to me, he honoured his side of the bargain. A pair of footmen served a meal of pheasant, venison, and herb-buttered vegetables, followed by cherry tart with clotted cream, and marchpane.

Patrick was a polite and congenial guest at his own table and, though I knew he behaved thus only to benefit his cousin, my earlier tension drained away and I started to enjoy myself. For the first time in many months, I basked in the attentions of a male who seemed genuinely entertained by my company and whose gallantry fortified my bruised heart.

As the evening progressed and dinner was completed, Aden threw a restless look in my direction. Playing my part as hostess, I called for brandy and suggested I withdraw and leave the men to their business.

Aden offered me a grateful smile and accepted the prompt, "Sure, that won't be necessary. If Sir Christie is agreeable, he and I may take our business to Patrick's office."

The brandy arrived on a tray and Aden asked for it to be taken to the master's study. Sir Christie bowed courteously in my direction. "You are most charming, Lady Elginbury. I thank you for your company this night."

"Thank *you*, my lord," I responded, rising from a formal curtsy and wondering how the man could ever be considered arrogant.

Patrick – who certainly was arrogant – inclined his head in his friend's direction, "Let us share a bottle before you leave tonight, Christie." The other responded with an approving grin.

Patrick and I remained at the table after Aden and his guest departed. He called for a second decanter of brandy and on its arrival, filled his glass.

"You're not joining them?" I asked tentatively. The first words I'd directed to him all evening and, without the moderating presence of our guest, I was wary of his response.

But he shook his head and drained his glass. Refilling it, he said, "It's none of my affair. Christie is my friend – that fact brought him here. The rest is up to Aden." He pushed the brandy decanter towards me. "Here, you're practically gasping for it."

I let my breath out in a rush and reached eagerly for the liquor, splashing it unceremoniously into my empty water glass. The strong flavour lingered on my lips long after I'd swallowed and I closed my eyes to savour its warm effects.

I heard Pat fill his glass again. My eyelids felt heavy as I opened them and sipped my drink. His chair was tilted on two legs, his arm hooked over its back, and he was regarding me fixedly. When he spoke his voice was unexpectedly civil. "I never said forever … back then. There were no promises."

Taken by surprise, I sucked in my breath and chose my words with care.

"You talked of marriage. Is that not forever?" I added in a whisper, "I'll never regret loving you."

He shifted uncomfortably and let the chair drop back into position.

His eyes slid to the flickering candles in the centre of the table. White, rose-scented and expensive, these candles did not emit curling ribbons of black smoke to discolour the walls and ceiling. Clear wax trickled down the wrought silver holders marring Bea's polishing efforts.

Without looking at me, he said, "Then I must apologise. I had newly arrived from the war and can admit my fear and disgust for all I'd seen and done. You were there … pretty and comforting."

His eyes returned to my face, his expression unreadable. "I took nothing you were not willing to give."

I bowed my head. My heart pounded and my face grew warm beneath the comparative gentleness of his tone and words.

"This is true," I admitted softly, staring into my glass. "But I loved you. You took advantage of that." My voice was steady though I quaked inside and could hear the blood pumping in my ears.

Looking up, I caught a mysterious look on his face but in a heartbeat it had vanished, replaced by his cruel smile. "As would any man, when a succulent little virgin crawls into his bed, eager as any gin-soaked whore."

I gasped involuntarily and hot tears leapt into my eyes.

He watched impassively as I shoved my chair away from the table and flew from the room.

I've always enjoyed the humbling power of the elements with its illuminating forks of lightning and deafening crashes of thunder. When the tension in the air builds over a series of days to finally climax in a violent heavenly display, I like to find a sheltered position where I can feel I'm part of it.

The storm that had been threatening would break this day, judging by the static crackling in the air and the rain-engorged, blue-black clouds piling in the sky.

It made my skin tingle and the birds and animals in the forest seemed to be bracing themselves, tight in their nests and dens.

And I felt that Patrick and I had arrived at an impasse; neither prepared to claim victory, neither prepared to admit defeat.

Whenever it seemed that I'd broken through his icy façade, he reacted with a torrent of malicious words that hit their target with unfailing accuracy.

Did he, in his quiet moments, consider as I did, that we had gone too far? I had struck him in a paroxysm of mad fury. And he had retaliated with equal violence.

These last weeks, I had endured such moments of exhausting grief and humiliation – for what?

I watched as the wind tore at the trees in the distance, whipping them back and forth, and imagined Briggs cursing around his pipe stem, for tomorrow he would be clearing away the broken branches.

I was keenly aware of how I had failed spectacularly to spike any sentiment through Patrick's shell. I was perceived by the household as some desperate, pathetic harpy – and what a hamper of sweet nothing it had achieved.

I have begged. I have wept at his feet. I have done violence. That I had arrived at the end of the road was clear. Retreat with my tail tucked beneath my belly seemed the only course available to me now. Today, I would talk with Aden and perhaps he would lend me a carriage so I could make my way to Exeter. From there I will take a public coach to Yorkshire and entreat bed and board from my brother, and in time, contemplate my future.

Resolved, I turned from the window and was startled by an urgent knocking at my door. I assumed it was Bea, but the door opened to reveal Amelia's face peering at me.

"Come in, Millie."

She closed the door carefully behind her, staring at me all the while from wide, luminous eyes. She licked her lips and placed a book she carried on my writing desk, but her hand remained protectively on its cover.

"This book," she began, hesitantly. "Alex, please you cannot be telling Aden, but …"

She removed her hand and I saw the title was, *Henry Hooka, A Novel by Charles Dibdin*. "I thought Patrick had this in the library, but I could not find it. Last week I asked him if I might read it. He said it was in his office … I could fetch it myself."

Her agitation was alarming me but the expression on her face forestalled my impatience.

"I only started reading it last night – oh, Alex, please don't be letting on that I've shown you. Aden will be so upset with me, but I'm thinking you ought to see this. Patrick must have forgotten it was there."

She picked up the book and shook it gently. A single page, folded across its centre, fell out. She handed it to me.

"You cannot keep it – I must be putting it back where I found it – he cannot ever know."

She turned and quickly left the room.

I held the page in my hand and sat in the chair by the window. Though it was mid-morning it could have been dusk for the weak light that was afforded.

Reverently, almost fearfully, I unfolded the page. Immediately, Patrick's restrained handwriting leapt up at me. It was a poem – untitled – and slowly, I began to read.

Oh moonlight pray release my soul
Great Spirit of the night
Weaver of dreams where she doth sleep
Bringer of the light

T'is all for nought – a maiden's gift
Her kiss, a star-bright lie
Gemini fickle young lover's heart
To thistle did she fly

Oh moonlight shed your silken beams
'Pon lover's plea to you
For tho' she prov-ed false in love
My foolish heart beats true

I sat still for a long time, serene and dry-eyed – a single thought ringing through my brain: at the time he wrote this he had loved me. If his love was deep as this poem implied surely he must love me still, though it seemed he believed I had passed him over for another as a result of my capricious youth.

And I knew then, I would try one last time to break through. If I should fail, there would be no choice but to finally capitulate.

Amelia came to my room just as I had finished copying the poem on a clean sheet. I returned the original, and she slipped it between the pages of the book and wordlessly was gone.

Patrick had not been at breakfast, doubtless having been out all night sharing the bed of one of his doxies. Much as his promiscuity pained me, I was relieved by his absence for I needed to prepare for our final showdown – to be clear about what I wanted to say.

Leaving the house by the rear door, I made my way along the gravelled path to the stables.

I'd not seen Ember for some days and decided to visit her and watch the storm – and think.

The wind clawed at my skirt and whipped my hair about my face. Today was not a day for riding, but my beautiful horse would appreciate my company, and the dried apples in my pocket.

A stable-boy ran up to me as I entered the dim building.

"You wantin' to ride m'lady?" he asked. His grubby face looked up at me with endearing concern for a lad who must have no more than thirteen years. "Weather not lookin' good. Mightn' be a good idea."

"What's your name, lad?" I asked, for I hadn't seen him before.

"Samuel, m'lady, but me mates calls me Blackie 'count o' me always being dir'y."

"Then I shall call you Blackie, if that's alright with you," and he grinned, showing agreement and crooked front teeth.

"I wasn't intending to ride today," I went on. "I thought to sit here, perhaps read and watch the storm."

"You like storms then?" Blackie said, incredulously. "Some folks are strange. Young lord rode out this mornin' and I tells 'im the storm's comin' but 'e says 'e got biznez on."

"The young lord went out this morning? What time?"

He shrugged. "Dunno, don' 'ave no clock, but the rooster down shed'd been crowin' for some time. Jimma was still abed but I took care o' it – was my turn an' all."

"I see. Blackie, can you drag over a chair or a bench, something for me to sit on?"

I stood in the doorway, watching the leaden sky and the weighty clouds that changed morning to evening. At the scraping sound behind me I turned and helped Blackie drag the bench to where I thought I'd have a good view of the storm.

The child touched his forelock and left me then, disappearing into his quarters in another room, and I sat, leaning against a wall, and opened *Jessica Mandaville, or the Woman of Fortitude* by Miriam Malden, at the first page.

Soon, a low rumble sounded in the distance and I scanned the sky for signs of lightning – nothing yet, but the clouds were boiling one over the other and the wind bent the backs of the trees in the forest.

The horses in their stalls stamped and snorted restlessly, sensing the imminent storm. Remembering the apples in my pocket, I went to Ember and gave her one.

Another horse, one I'd seen but didn't know very well, poked his head over his gate. He nuzzled my hand, his nostrils quivering. With a whispered apology to Ember, I offered the second apple to him. His cinnamon-coloured nose with its white blaze and russet whiskers bobbed up and down as he munched.

I was stroking Ember's head when the first drops of rain began to *clunk* sporadically on the shingle roof and I returned to my seat to watch the weather approach.

The first spear of lightning exploded behind the stables, momentarily illuminating the forecourt with a day-bright flash. I counted, *one cat and dog, two cat and dog, three cat and* – the thunder rumbled across the sky.

Rain pelted the roof and bounced on the ground in the forecourt. Lightning flashed behind the stables again. *One cat and dog, two cat and dog, three* – flying hooves sent a spray of gravel skittering across the cobbles but the sound was lost beneath a growl of thunder directly overhead. The horse's slender legs lifted high as she trotted past my seat, her rider leaning over her neck, trying to calm her.

I had not, in all honesty, expected to see him, for when Blackie said the young lord had ridden out on business I'd assumed he'd be gone for the day. As always, my heart skipped when I saw him, yet this time it was with renewed courage for I knew in truth he had loved me – once.

Horse and rider were both dripping and Patrick leapt from her back without so much as glancing my way, and stood stroking her head soothingly.

"Jimma! Blackie!" he called. Immediately Blackie was there taking instructions to rub Equus down and lay her stall with fresh hay.

Only then did Patrick turn and see me for the first time. Annoyance flickered across his face but he said nothing. He was wearing an oiled riding coat, which he shrugged out of and shook sending beads of water flying.

The rain was heavier now, and pools had already formed in the forecourt. Streams of water ran between them threatening to connect and make a lake. The lightning came again, this time cracking loudly above our heads and the thunder boomed almost immediately. I rose to lean against the stable door, exhilarated by the sight and sound, but intensely aware that he was only feet away – his eyes on me.

"I must say, you're remarkably tenacious in your pursuit." He took off his hat and his hair was plastered wetly to his temples.

"I came here to watch the storm," I responded evenly for it was the truth.

"Hmm …" He moved to stand beside me and looked out of the door. The rain fell in great sheets, blown almost horizontally across the yard. The sound on the roof was deafening and the horses twitched and whinnied in their stalls, rolling their eyes nervously.

My heart was pounding as though it was trying to break free of my ribs, yet I found the courage to turn to him. "Pat, since you're here, can we talk please?"

He cocked a mocking eyebrow at me. "What … again?" His expression showed amusement before shuttering and he added, "There's nothing to talk about. Your relentless quest has gone beyond tedious – it's time you went home."

"I don't want to go back to Hamish. Marrying him was the greatest mistake of my life. I love *you* – it has always been you I loved. Even when I thought you'd fathered Anne's baby, I did not stop loving you."

"So touching – now go home, whichever place you choose to call home, I don't care so long as you go." He spoke with finality and made to leave.

"Wait!" Something in my voice gave him pause and he stared at me. "I know you loved me once, Pat," I raised my voice above the din on the roof. "That's why you're so angry now. If only you'd let me –"

"Your voice is as grating as an old fishwife's," he shouted over the clamour.

"I could make it up to you!"

"No! Leave my house now," he growled through clenched teeth. "You've more than outstayed your welcome." His face was darkening as his anger rose.

"I know you've been hurt – *please* Pat, I thought –"

Now, he bellowed, "You have disrupted my house since the moment you crossed the threshold – I've had quite enough!"

"*Please*, I am begging you …"

Suddenly the thunder crashed so violently the building shook. The horses whinnied with fright and the wind shifted, slanting rain through the doorway, catching us both in its spray.

As though inspired by the elements, he similarly exploded, and his anger was fearsome. He took a menacing step toward me.

"I *don't* love you! Get it through your blasted head woman!

I don't *care* what you have to say to me, I don't *care* what your pathetic excuses are. Go back to your unnatural husband, you dreary bloody whore!"

At that he turned and strode into the storm.

"*No!*" I screamed but the wind whipped the cry from my mouth.

I took after him. The torrential rain and wind fought me, but I was determined for I really believed that if I could just touch him, surely, *surely*, I could penetrate that façade. I lunged and caught his coat. He spun around, breaking my hold and we both stood beneath the full force of the elements, soaked to the skin and breathing heavily.

The wind slapped my wet hair about my face. Coils of it caught at my mouth and were pasted to my cheeks.

"Don't touch me," he snarled. "Don't speak to me, and get out of my house – today!"

"I can't leave in this!" My sweeping gesture took in the flooded yard.

But he leaned into my face and shouted, "*Today*! And you can drown for all I care!"

I withered beneath his anger, cringing, ducking instinctively and raising my hands protectively – our recent violent clash all too fresh. My cheeks were awash with tears and rain and I trembled with cold, and grief, and fright, but he was oblivious in his fury.

He'd made no move to touch me, and now glared contemptuously as I whimpered before him.

"Don't worry," he spat the words out. "I'll not lay a hand on you – I cannot believe I fucked you!"

He did not hesitate. Neither did he look back, but strode toward the house leaving me where I cowered, sodden, humiliated and, utterly, unconditionally defeated.

CHAPTER 22

I've no idea how long I remained thus, crouching in the storm. Perhaps a minute, no more, but it felt longer until thin, thirteen-year old arms curled around my shoulders and directed me to the stables where I was wrapped in a dirty, horse blanket and handed a tin mug of strong, hot tea. My hands shook so violently the tea was removed and placed beside me.

My teeth chattered uncontrollably and my breathing was ragged, but I did not cry for my mind was numb and could only register that it was over – my surrender was absolute.

Aden ran into the stables and skidded in a slick of mud on the cobbled floor. He was quickly followed by a lad of about fifteen, whom I assumed was Jimma.

"What's happened?" he demanded breathlessly of Blackie.

"She 'ad a fight wi' th' young lord, sir." Blackie replied. "They was a-screamin' an' a-yellin' an' then 'e left 'er in th' rain. She bin like this since."

"You did right to come for me," Aden said. "When the storm's over, go round to the kitchen and tell Monsieur Chartrain I said you're to be having a hunk of fruit cake each."

"Thank yer, Mr Rourke," they chimed.

Aden turned to me. I was huddled into myself, trembling with shock and grief. "Alex," he said softly, "come on, darlin'. Let's get you to the house."

In the kitchen, I was divested of the horse blanket and led upstairs. Amelia and Bea stripped my wet clothes off and buffed me with a warm towel until my skin began to tingle and thaw. Finally, they slipped a nightdress over my head and rolled me into bed. Immediately, I curled on to my side and, as the enormity of my failure rose up, the dam within broke and I sobbed helplessly.

It was over. There was nothing left now, no husband, no child, no home, no lover. I had gambled and lost.

Amelia was distraught in the face of my grief. She sent for Aden, who sat on the edge of my bed and gently but firmly, instructed me to calm down and tell him what had happened.

At length, I quieted and explained haltingly that his cousin and I had quarrelled again; but unrepeatable, unforgivable things had been said and I had been unequivocally ordered to leave the house – and I would. At the end of it Aden said, "Well, you won't be leaving in this weather."

"We shall talk him round, Alex," Amelia said, trying to be helpful. "Sure it won't end like this."

I shook my head. Now that my tremors had subsided, I was more lucid. "It is over – I cannot fight the truth. There is nothing for me here and I have caused far too much trouble for you all. Aden, please may I borrow a carriage and driver? I shall go to Exeter and hire a coach to Yorkshire."

"No!" Amelia cried, turning to Aden. "She cannot leave yet."

Aden, ignoring his wife, nodded. "Of course – 'tis for the best darlin'. When are you thinking to be leaving?"

"Patrick said today."

He nodded again. "Tomorrow mornin' will do. You may use my coach and take Sid, the driver. Go all the way to Yorkshire. Bea can go with you for company, and Dan – he's that burly footman Paddy keeps – I'll give him a pistol to carry. Send them back once you've arrived safely."

"Patrick won't like me taking his staff," I suggested.

"Patrick, blasted fool, can go to hell."

CHAPTER 23

Thankfully, I didn't see Pat again before I left.

With Ember tethered to the back of the coach and my trunk strapped to the roof, I was ready to depart. Amelia cried and hugged me, and I stroked her belly and asked her to pass on my regards to the duchess.

Aden kissed my brow and handed me into the coach and with Jemima settled at my feet, I waved goodbye. Mrs Bath, Cissy and Briggs had turned out to see us off and I rested my forehead sadly on the glass window, watching as that magnificent house shrank away behind me.

The journey home was uneventful and uncomfortable. The storm on the previous day had reduced the roads to slush and opened pot holes large enough to break a horse's leg. Consequently, Sid was forced to navigate slowly and carefully.

Dan sat up on the box beside Sid, while Bea, Jemima and I occupied the inside. Bea had been all aflutter with excitement over her journey for, as she explained, she'd never been further from home than Tiverton.

Her enthusiasm lasted only a day, as the reality of endless hours of boredom and bone-jarring travel settled over her. Thus she promptly fell asleep, leaving me alone, and for the first time, I was able to analyse the events of these past six weeks.

If there was one thing Patrick could have said to convince me of his disregard – he had said it. For that one magical night we had shared, had lived in my memory like a glittering jewel. It had fed and sustained me and I had relived it time and again in my heart and in my dreams; always hoping – even when I believed Anne's lies – that he had treasured it likewise. Though I had no doubt driven him to it with my persistence, he had cheapened our honest lovemaking and me along with it.

I sighed. No point dissecting it. I must look to the future and the rebuilding of my life – and my health, for I had lost considerable weight in Devon, which showed in my loose clothes and dry hair. My frequent nights of insomnia had resulted in hollow eyes and drawn cheeks, and my usually robust appetite was all but gone while I succumbed to aberrant headaches.

I toyed with the idea of returning to Scotland – but only in a brief moment of insanity. My one hope lay in returning to Broughton Hall to entreat my brother's charity until I could reconstruct the ruins of my life sufficiently to move on.

Finally, after some three weeks of tortuous travel, Aden's coach rumbled around the sweeping curve of Broughton Hall's driveway. It was late afternoon and the Great Oak had thrown a long shadow over the lawn. As we slowed before the porch, Jemima sat up and showed a liveliness that had been absent during our journey. I stroked her head, smiling to myself, for I felt it too.

We had returned to where we belonged.

As the unfamiliar carriage pulled up before the porch, Simon came from the direction of the stables. He expressed no surprise at seeing me, though the physician in him frowned as he took in my sorry state. There was no need for words as he held me to his chest and I convulsed with silent sobs.

"Shh, it's alright. You're home now," he whispered into my

hair, while it occurred to me how starved I was of the touch of a human being who genuinely loved me as my brother did, and how desperately I needed to hear nice words.

We stood thus for a long time while Bea, Dan and Sid shuffled their feet and looked uncomfortable. Finally, we were dragged apart by Mrs Grainger's customary brusqueness suggesting we issue her with instructions for my escorts before they died of old age.

We placed them in the housekeeper's capable care and walked arm-in-arm into the house I loved, where we were met by Maria, whose loose spring dress evidenced the arrival of the child she'd been carrying at the time I'd left.

Though the bruises on my wrists had faded to an unsightly greenish-yellow they caught Maria's practised eye immediately. She arched her brows but I offered only a rueful smile in explanation.

When the inevitable questions were asked, I could not repeat how I had laid bare my heart before an indifferent Patrick, how I had learned the violence of love, and the heartbreak of rejection. I simply explained that Patrick did not harbour the feelings for me that I'd hoped, and that in the end it was best I return to Broughton Hall. It was the truth, if generously diluted.

They knew there was more, but nodded in acceptance and they all understood the subject was closed.

After I had settled in, I joined Simon and Maria for a glass of plum wine in the parlour. There, I was introduced to my new niece, Rosalie. She was a very pretty child, all pink and cream and with more than a passing resemblance to Anne at that same age. After an early supper, we retired to the parlour where they had surprising news for me – Maeve had returned from Europe. She had arrived unexpectedly one morning, strolled into the house and, unannounced, sat herself at the breakfast table and poured a cup of tea.

Apparently she caused quite a stir for no one recognised her. Her pale gold hair was bleached white by the southern European sun, and her skin was the colour of beer.

"Apart from that, she's the same old Maeve we know and love," Simon said.

"Where is she now?" I asked, expecting her to jump out from behind a chair.

"Leeds. Gerrard took her with him to collect Meg from school."

"Oh, so much has happened since you were gone, Alex," Maria said. "First with Rosalie arriving, only two days after you left, then Maeve coming home – such a surprise – and then one evening some peddler appeared on the kitchen doorstep begging a bed for a night. He ended up staying three nights and sampled a different maid on each. Cook discovered him the fourth day with Prudence, behind the butter churn, and called Atchison – he's the new butler – to throw him out."

By now I was laughing. "Right," I said, "so Simon has succumbed to pressure and employed a butler – not ahead of time, I might add. I was only away six weeks – what else has happened?" And before a pleasant fire, they shared all the local news.

☙

Later, alone in my childhood room, I could not rest quietly for thoughts of the last weeks churned round and round in my head.

At least now, there were no unknowns, no questions, for I knew that whatever my future held, Patrick would not feature.

But I continued to be racked with a grief that only time would heal.

Over the following weeks I became more restful, thanks in part to one of Maria's miraculous potions, though my treacherous brain ran rampant through the night, flashing images of Patrick angry, Patrick glaring disdainfully, Patrick ordering me from his life; all tumbling one over the other, interweaving with happier images of us kissing and laughing, until I'd awaken damp with perspiration and tears.

One dream that repeated itself almost nightly was staged in the summer-house at Waterville. Patrick was slowly removing my clothing, smiling and caressing me, and as he slipped my chemise from my shoulders and I stood naked and vulnerable before him, he raised his fist and smashed me to the ground. I lay inert on the wooden floor, staring up at him fearfully, and as he leaned over me, he changed from Patrick to Hamish.

During the day, I spent long hours wandering the park, alone but for Jemima. We strolled among the deer and the new spring fawns, and they became so accustomed to us that they lingered, their delicate noses twitching and their ears ever cocked for danger. I enjoyed watching them and began bringing bags of seeds for them purloined from Cook's supply.

Eventually, a young one, gangly and angular, showed an interest in the seeds in my palm. I had been coming to the same place each day and was triumphant when, warily, it ate from my hand. It was a small success for me, and I held my breath as its velvety lips sipped at my palm.

So, as my waking-self slowly corrected, my sleeping-self had a life of its own.

I had written to Sylvie advising that I'd returned to Yorkshire, and she responded immediately that she and Quinn would join me here for the birth of their babe. Amelia would pack and forward their things to Broughton Hall.

Thus it was, by the time May slid round and my birthday drew imminent, I had settled into something of a new life. And suddenly Maeve was there.

She bounced out of her father's coach with more life and energy than a person had a right to, and flung herself into my arms.

Rather than tame her, six years in Italy — and, I was later to learn, Northern Africa — had enhanced her. The mischievous and straight-talking child transformed into a young woman of worldly knowledge and unusual character, who no longer ate meat, and spoke in a slightly accented voice. Unlike Anne, Maeve had never been classically beautiful, but her complexion glowed, her hair shone, and her eyes sparkled with verve. Evidently, as seen in her brother, the adventurous life suited her well.

The Washburn siblings had been overshadowed by Anne's and Simon's good looks when they'd first come to Broughton Hall, but maturity and circumstance had seen them come into their own. Patrick was now a very handsome man, and his sister the possessor of striking, if unconventional, beauty.

On the day that Maeve returned, she arrived with Gerrard and Meg, and the group of us ate and drank, talked and laughed, until we were summoned to the dining table. The conversation continued and I listened enviously to Maeve's tales of the archaeological friends she had made, and the long, dry, dusty days in exotic locations. I learned about the marking of a dig area in grid format, the stringing of lines, the meticulously slow brushing away of accumulated soil and debris. And the result: often disappointment, always challenging, occasionally successful – a find, an artefact of untellable worth, untouched by another human hand for centuries or more.

Seven-year-old Meg was starry-eyed and hung off every word. I expected her to eventually grow bored with the conversation, but rather, she begged her father that she should be allowed to stay up later than usual, to which, of course, he agreed.

"You cannot possibly know," Maeve breathed, her eyes glistening and far away, "the emotions that run through you when you first hold something extracted from the earth. You touch it, and close your eyes and know that long, long ago, a person – with their own hands – made this. A *real* person, who lived and loved, who breathed and ate, who had hopes and dreams, someone of no particular consequence in their lifetime, left this broken fragment in the sand – a legacy, unearthed thousands of years later. I often fancy that part of their spirit has found its way into the shard of pottery, or bead or whatever, so that when I hold it, I can feel them close by. And then I make a solemn promise to care for their gift, to ensure it is respected and treasured and preserved for ever so they live on."

Though the others had heard her stories before, we all sat spellbound as at times she drifted trancelike, her small, almond eyes half-closed as she revisited those wondrous deserts and hidden valleys.

Eventually everyone drifted to bed, even Meg, yet I lingered, enthralled. Maeve, who was used to late nights, stayed with me, and we reacquainted ourselves, not as the girls we had been, but as the women we had become.

I sensed that for Maeve there would be no peace, for her appetite for life and experience could never be sated. Not for her a conventional settling down with a husband to breed children and run a household. She'd supped from the plate of adventure and would forever hunger for more.

When finally, I asked the question that had been on my tongue all evening, her small face, with its uplifted angles turned down.

"Missy followed me everywhere," she replied, as her eyes misted in recollection of the cat, who was as much her familiar as Jemima was mine. "I always tried to keep her safe in my tent, but she was so obstreperous she would never stay put. One day she snuck out and was bitten by a viper. We found her when we returned from the day's work – still alive, but barely. I held her to the last. I think – I hope she knew it was me holding her. We buried her in the sand and I marked the place with one of my hair-ribbons tied around a stone."

She took a deep breath and shook off the memory. "But I see you still have Jemima. Missy would be most put out to know the dog had outlived her."

❧

The days and weeks that followed were a wonder to me. I gravitated to Maeve for her warmth and vitality and the new strength I found growing within myself – my renaissance. Uninvited, she joined me on my morning strolls through the gardens and with her, I saw things I'd never seen before, despite my years of walking – like the intricacies of a spider's web with dew hanging like jewels from its threads. Pausing to examine the elaborate patterns of the web, and then the spider itself, she would say, "See, she always does her pattern with the gaps wider here, but narrower here. Hmm, very effective, don't you think, Alex? She has honed her art."

Maeve particularly enjoyed being outdoors when the elements were wild. If it was raining and I had decided to forego the morning's walk, preferring to watch from a window, she would march into my room and thrust a pair of boots at me with an urgent whisper, "Quickly. We should spy the squirrels running from tree to tree in this weather."

More than rain, Maeve loved fog. She claimed that, within its mysterious folds, unicorns and centaurs, faeries and tree-sprites, fed and frolicked, undisturbed and unseen by humans.

She plunged headlong into thickets of undergrowth, or skirted wide ancient trees, picking her way carefully around mushrooms and toadstools, ever respectful of the forest and its creatures, light as a wraith and leaving not a trace behind her.

Often she stopped, a finger to her lips, pointing to a nest of baby birds, a family of rabbits, or a young fawn suckling from its mother. With the dew glistening on her silver hair, she herself was a like a wood nymph embracing each day and experience. And I, captured by her contagious vivacity, discovered a renewed sense of life and hope. What her brother had taken away, Maeve began to give back.

But she was also a part of Patrick. He dwelt in her smile, her wicked sense of humour, her intellect. So while in some ways Maeve healed my wounds, in others, she ensured they remained open and raw.

One June morning, Jemima and I trailed behind her as she threaded her way through the woods. I was disoriented but happy to follow her path. The sun was shooting the first gold shards of light through the trees and the peaty fragrance of the forest hung in the air. The hem of her skirt was sodden with dew since she never lifted it as she walked. Then the trees thinned, expanding into a clearing, and in the centre was my heart of irises. We had approached from a different direction than normal and they appeared unexpectedly. I caught my breath in surprise.

Their pretty purple faces with yellow tongues bobbed merrily in the new sunlight and rivulets of dew ran like quicksilver along their sturdy green stalks. They were prettier than I'd ever imagined and my heart shifted as I beheld them, blinking at the old familiar sting behind my eyes. We had done our work well, Pat and I, for the heart was in good proportion; the bulbs were planted perfectly.

Maeve sat on the dewy earth, heedless of the dampness, and crossed her legs. The sureness of her manner intrigued me. I said, "You've been here before."

"I have," she answered tilting her head and gazing at the flowers. Then she settled her piercing eyes upon me. "Would you like to tell me about these?"

I was stunned for I'd never told a soul about that pre-dawn excursion with Patrick. How could she know this place? Perhaps she'd stumbled on it and guessed.

I decided to be clever. "What can *you* tell *me*?" I challenged.

A mischievous smile pulled at her lips. "I know that you and my brother planted these. I know that you loved one another. I also know that you married that Hamish fellow and it broke my brother's heart."

Broke his heart? To hell with dirt-stains! I hitched up my skirt and sat cross-legged beside her. "How do you know all this?"

"He told me. He visited me at a dig site in Morocco back in fourteen."

I let my breath out in a rush and said, "Are you angry with me too?"

"I am not your judge," she responded. "But I would like very much to understand *why* you married Hamish. He was never going to be what you wanted."

"Did you also know that … that he lay with men?"

She nodded. "It was known. I hinted to you once or twice – remember?"

I didn't. "You've no doubt heard what Anne did? She claimed her child was Patrick's. It was not possible to dispute her – how could we know? And when Mother found out about my involvement with Pat – she'd have lynched him for a taker of maidenheads had she the chance – she arranged my wedding immediately. I had no reasonable argument." I watched Maeve's face as I spoke but, like her brother, she gave no hint of her thoughts. "I did not want to believe he'd lain with Anne – your father tried to defend him, but Anne was so convincing, even *he* was at a loss."

She nodded slowly. "It was that you believed Anne which hurt my brother deepest. I doubt he'll ever forgive you for that – and marrying Hamish."

"He told you all this?" I was more than slightly put out.

"Patrick and I are, and always have been, in close contact. He first wrote of his love for you long before he declared it to you yourself – it was after you summered in Devon. He said he hoped to grow out of it – your both being so young – and, of course, love makes one vulnerable. My brother hates such weakness – particularly in himself. But oh yes, he loved you."

"I see," I said, ignoring the convulsive lurch my heart gave at her words. He had loved me. "So, tell me this – why does he deny it now?"

"Ah … You know Patrick has ever been a very private person. To declare himself to you, to do that … he took a great risk. I don't think you appreciate how deeply he loved. But now you know how effectively he can manage his emotions. He has exorcised you from his heart. It is over now, Alex."

"Oh, I know that," I said recalling the strength of his denials. But my foolish heart soared anew as I devoured this confirmation that he had once truly loved me. "Has he told you yet about my visit to Devon? He said some terribly cruel things."

She made a rosebud from her lips as she weighed her answer. Then she said, "I know. He said you attacked one another: Aden was forced to separate you." Her laugh was like a tinkling bell.

I smiled ruefully. "It was awfully ugly, those weeks I was there."

She nodded again, then reminiscent of her brother, sprang explosively to her feet and proceeded towards home, humming a little tune as she went. I scrambled after her.

"If you knew all this, why did you bring me here?" I asked as I caught up.

The humming paused. "Just curious." Then she resumed her song and effectively closed the subject.

CHAPTER 24

It was easy to forget myself for, infected by Maeve's youthful vigour, I was a girl again – carefree and energetic and eager. Maeve's return touched us all, lending new excitement to daily activities. Evening gatherings beneath the Great Oak took on the importance of a religious observation and, no matter where we had been that day, or what we had been doing, we all gathered beneath that tree as the sun hovered in the westerly sky.

By the middle of June, Sylvie and Quinn had returned, grateful to escape London. "I couldn't breathe," Sylvie complained beneath the tree's ancient boughs. "Never could I imagine such stench."

Quinn, like his wife, was unprepared for the assault to his senses. Their journey had been slow and painstaking due to Sylvie's advanced condition, but worth it at its end.

Earlier in the year, when Maeve had spent time in Leeds, her habitual enthusiasm for life, her love of society, and not in small part, the fact that she was an earl's daughter, assured her invitation to many fashionable gatherings. So, now at Broughton Hall, it wasn't long before two gentlemen of her social set came calling.

Richard and Hal were twins, and to anyone only recently acquainted with them they were difficult to tell apart. Both were well-built, nicely-dressed young men, with light brown hair and persuasive brown eyes, surrounded by smudgy brown lashes – attractive lads, and both entirely besotted by Maeve.

In Maeve's company, everyone was made to feel special, which led to much competition between the two, much mirth between Maria and me, and much consternation from Simon. After speaking with Simon, they were invited to stay the remainder of the summer and thus our ritual gathering was expanded by two.

I enjoyed the companionship of my family and new friends and, though I was disinclined to make great contributions to conversation, I was content to rest and listen to the gay chatter surrounding me, and my recovery was advanced beneath the influence of pleasant company, wine, food and laughter.

One morning, I was in the rose garden cutting some of the best blooms for a vase, when the crunch of hooves on gravel sounded behind me. Straightening, I shaded my eyes to see the rider – a female sitting astride like a man – cantering up the drive, skirts bunched up around her thighs and showing sturdy, brown riding boots. I knew her identity immediately and waved.

"*Halloo!*" Julia returned cheerfully. She reined in beside the porch and used a step to slip off her beautiful, sand-coloured horse with chocolate mane and tail. "What a lovely morning," she said, looping the reins over the handrail and coming towards me.

We met halfway and hugged affectionately, then stood back to admire one another – we hadn't seen each other for some months and I thought she looked very well. I carried my basket of roses over one arm and linked my other with hers as we entered the house.

"So," I poured two cool glasses of lemonade with sprigs of mint floating on top, "You look so well. What has been happening?"

"I'm pregnant," she said, without warning.

I stared at her in surprise. "Oh! ... And ... you're happy with this?"

"Now Alex, get that puritanical look off your face. I may not be married, but the father will support me – indeed *has* supported me for five months now. I don't care what society thinks. I have a townhouse in Leeds, with a little garden and a maid – yes, I am very happy."

And she looked it. Her russet curls were scooped up the back of her head to show off her pretty face, and her complexion was glowing with health and contentment. Satisfied that my friend's situation was pleasing to her, we chatted like twittering birds and she told me of the affair she'd been having for almost a year now. I admitted that I had guessed as much when last she visited, and since she didn't offer to identify her lover, I assumed he was married and asked no questions – though curiosity was near killing me.

Finally, we quietened to sip our drinks and draw breath. Leaning forwards in her chair, she said, "It didn't work out with Patrick?"

From the moment she arrived I knew this question was coming and was prepared for it. "No, and, difficult as it is to accept, the fact is he no longer loves me. But I am alright, Jules. I am getting on with my life."

"Good to hear. And you'll not be returning to Hamish?"

I shook my head decisively.

"Even better. Does Hamish know you're not returning?"

"Oh yes. I wrote to him before I went to Devon. I've not received a response."

"Will you seek a divorce?"

I paused, for the concept of divorce was so foreign as to be extraneous. "Um … I haven't thought … why?"

"I should think you would," she said quickly. "Especially given the attention you were attracting in the garden as I arrived."

I frowned. "What attention?"

"You don't know?" She slapped her thigh as though that were the funniest thing. "Saints alive, what have they done to you, these men in your life? Are you so used to being rejected that you've closed yourself off?"

I bristled slightly even though I knew she meant no insult. She went on, "Some young brown-haired blade in buff pants and blue shirt. Don't tell me you don't know who I mean?"

Still miffed, I said, "There are two such visiting here. Anyway, what was he doing?"

"Couldn't take his eyes off you. Looked like he was about to go and talk to you. Sorry, I think I ruined it with my arrival."

"Hmph, I'm a married woman and not given to flirtations. You ruined nothing."

"I counter that on two points. One, you have not been married to Hamish – not in a true way – for ever. And two, you'd be given to flirtations well enough if it were Patrick doing the flirting."

"Give over Julia, I told you it is done between me and him. It hurts to remember him that way."

"It may be over for him – which I doubt, incidentally – but never for you. It only hurts because it's so real."

"It is over for me *because* it is over for him," I said, growing irritable.

"As you wish – I didn't come here to argue with you. Anyhow, I should be keeping my eyes on that young fellow if I were you," she added a saucy wink, "perhaps he could remind you what your woman's parts are for."

I blushed but she was gathering her things. "Should you be riding in your condition?"

She laughed gaily. "Women have been known to do more and still bring forth healthy babes. But I'm staying at Mother's tonight, so I haven't far to go."

On the porch, we waited for her horse to be brought round and, despite my protests, she insisted I visit her in Leeds to share with her all the news about my new lover once he made his move. She rode happily down the drive, brandishing her crop in farewell.

❧

Mindful of Julia's assertions, that evening beneath the Great Oak, while Richard paid unabashed court to Maeve, I noticed that Hal had moved his seat closer to mine. How old was he, I wondered? He looked younger than I, but not by much. He refilled my glass with plum wine and as I took it, his eyes lingered on my face in the self-assured way both boys had. So, my admirer's identity was confirmed and I experienced a thrill of delight at the thought that a man could find me attractive – I hadn't felt the like in a long time.

Hal, the older of the two boys by some thirty minutes, had newly inherited a baronetcy and was trying it on for size. He smiled roguishly, and I responded uncertainly.

The days passed in summered indolence. I spent a lot of time outside, strolling with Jemima and Maeve, or simply sprawled on the lawn reading or staring at the sky. Hal began seeking me out each afternoon, and we talked and laughed, flirting wickedly until joining the others beneath the Great Oak.

I was enjoying the game, for that was all it was – all I would allow it to be – and I basked in his courtly flattery, doing nothing to discourage his growing desire for me, and feeling alluring in a way not even Patrick had made me feel, because Patrick and I had grown together over several years of friendship. This was different; a man was paying attention to me, showing off for me, and it felt good.

And soon it was July, and Sylvie was large and cumbersome and struggling with the warm weather. The summer dragged on, the days hotter than we'd experienced for many years. The trees in the park drooped wearily and some of the less hardy plants along the terraces wilted and browned as the heat rose off the flagstones. The roses seemed to thrive, providing a gloriously colourful display.

Evenings that ordinarily received a cooling breeze remained sultry and often a group of us ventured into the park after supper. This particular evening, Simon led the way, carrying a rug. Maria followed with bottles of wine, Meg next, the child happily swinging hands with me. Gerrard and Maeve, arm-in-arm, trailed us with another bottle of wine each, and Richard and Hal, carrying a second rug and a basket of glasses, bread and cheese, brought up the rear. Sylvie and Quinn opted to stay behind since Sylvie's advanced pregnancy made it increasingly difficult for her to move any great distance.

We walked down the sloping lawn at the back of the house to the edge of the forest where the rugs were spread on the cool grass, the wine poured, and we all reclined beneath the indigo skies.

This night, I was intensely aware of Hal's presence as he commandeered a place beside me. The moon was full and ribbons of cloud trailed like gossamer threads across the sky. Maeve had brought her sketch book and, as she worked by lantern light, a reflection of the velvet heavens began to appear on the page.

She drew fine lines and smudged them with the heel of her hand, and was, for a time, completely absorbed in her work. When it was complete she handed it to Meg saying, "Remember this night, for it is enchanted."

"How is it enchanted?"

"See the moon? It is a witch's moon. If you watch long enough you may see good witches on their broomsticks playing among the clouds. Only on nights like this, when the moon is full and there are wispy clouds, can you see them."

"What are they doing all the way up there?" Meg asked, her eyes fixed on the sky.

"In days gone by," Maeve explained, "wise women were called witches, and they used brooms to sweep away the bad spirits of the night. And then they danced for joy, jumping and leaping over their brooms, and the more they jumped, the higher they went, until they flew through the sky."

"Might I see one?" Meg asked.

"They are cunning – they know you are watching, but if you lie on your back and stare at the moon, you might be lucky."

Charmed, Meg settled herself on the rug and prepared to study the celestial vista before her, and soon, the wine ran low, and Gerrard carried the sleeping child to the house, returning with a further two bottles of wine.

Maria sang softly in her native Spanish and though I could not understand a word, its tune was quite beautiful.

Glancing at Hal, I found his eyes, warm with wine-fuelled desire, settled on me. I was lying on my back and he on his side facing me. Taking my hand, he opened it and pressed warm lips to my palm. A tiny flame flickered deep in my stomach, rekindling memories long suppressed, as his tongue traced slow circles. I drew in my breath and my eyes closed of their own accord.

"May I come to your room tonight?" he breathed into my ear so that I barely heard.

My heartbeat faltered and my eyes opened a sliver. He met them unblinkingly and I arranged my face into a picture of sophisticated boredom – as if propositions from practised courtiers were commonplace for me.

"You know I'm married." I had no intention of having him visit my room, yet the game was too enjoyable to quit.

He chuckled low in his throat. "I know it. But forbidden fruit is ever the sweetest."

The wine was fogging my senses and I struggled to clear my head. Reluctantly pulling my hand away, I said, "Perhaps not tonight."

"Your sister is not so coy."

Over his shoulder I saw Maeve's pale hair shimmering in the dark. She was in Richard's arms being thoroughly kissed. Father was snoring and Simon, his back against a tree, cradled Maria on his lap, his arm around her – they both dozed.

"I'm not being coy." In fact, I didn't know what I was being, except that I'd no desire to find a lover in my bed who considered me no more than another conquest. Yet, it felt so good to have a man desire me – my husband did not; the man I loved did not, but this man did, and he was here and now …

And he rolled towards me, placing persuasive little kisses along my throat. My head lolled to the side, and all the while I knew I ought to stop him, yet I had neither strength nor will. Moving over me, he pushed his knee between mine and pressed the bulge in his trousers against my groin. Dormant desires sparked to life and when his lips touched mine my traitorous body responded wantonly.

His kisses were insistent and his hot breath was deliciously wine-fragrant and I could no more resist him than I could resist breathing. His hands were cool and sure, delving into my bodice and roving beneath the summer silk of my dress. My breathing was becoming ragged, and I was only vaguely aware of Maeve and Richard disappearing further into the woods.

Hal pulled his mouth away. "Should we do likewise?"

Suddenly the fog lifted. I pressed a hand to his chest, holding him back, and sat up, collecting myself.

"Alex?" He reached for me but I firmly resisted.

"No Hal, not tonight … perhaps another … not tonight."

"But Alex," his voice was gravelly with desire.

"Hal, I'm married –"

"But he's not here, and I am." Annoyance made his voice a petulant whine.

"Please … it's all too soon for me."

"Alex –"

"My sister said no, Hal," Simon spoke quietly so as not to awaken Maria. "Please do not abuse my hospitality." My brother's eyes remained closed and he'd not moved, but his voice was definite.

Hal said nothing, but in the lantern light, he had the sulky look of a child denied a toy.

"I'm sorry, Hal," I said, and I was, but he was not to be placated. He got to his feet and strode through the night, back towards the house.

"Rather lofty opinion of himself, that one," Simon said, still with his eyes closed.

∾

I was unnecessarily wary of seeing Hal at breakfast the next morning for he acted as though nothing unusual had happened — and for him, perhaps nothing had — a testimony of his lifestyle. In any case, such events were overshadowed by Maria's entering the breakfast room and announcing in her unruffled way, "Better come now, Alex. It is Sylvie's time and she asks for you."

My feet took the stairs as though they had sprouted wings. Gerrard and Quinn were lurking in the hallway outside the door and as I approached, Quinn grasped my hands. "Oh Alex, she is terribly afraid. She is so small and the bairn is so large."

Gerrard conveniently forgot that his first wife had died in childbirth and said, "Now lad, women are made of tougher stuff than we."

"And Simon and Maria are attending," I added. "She could not be in better hands." I kissed his cheek, clammy with anxiety, and smiled at Gerrard. "Take him downstairs for breakfast."

I made to enter the room but Maria stopped me with a hand on my arm. She watched until Gerrard and Quinn had disappeared down the hall. "It is true, Alex. The baby is too big, her hips too narrow. It will be a long and painful labour. I hope you are prepared."

"She is in no danger?" I asked, uneasily.

"I should not think so but we cannot tell. I need — she *needs* you to be strong."

"I can be strong," I asserted, and entered the room.

Sylvie was propped on pillows. Damp hair clung to her forehead and her eyes looked haunted.

"Alex!" she cried and reached for me. I took her hands and sat on the edge of the bed. "God Alex, it hurts when the pains come. Was it like this with Mary?"

"I think not – my travail came because I had an accident, remember? Your pains are perfectly normal."

"Yes – *oh!*" Another contraction seized her and she squeezed my hands with bone-crushing strength.

Simon approached. He'd been preparing some evil-looking concoction. "Have her drink this. It will taste horrible but she must drink it all."

"Pooh! It reeks to high heaven."

"It will ease the pain." I looked sceptical and he added, "Just have her drink it."

Sylvie did drink the mixture, and in time her grip on my hands loosened. Soon it was midday and her pains were coming steadily and gradually closer together. Simon made an examination beneath Sylvie's nightdress and shot a grim look in his wife's direction. "She's not dilated enough," he whispered to Maria. "Yet the baby wants to come. Alex, fetch a pile of towels – thick ones, there will be a lot of blood."

CHAPTER 25

Over the next hours I held Sylvie's hands and bathed her face. The minutes between contractions were reducing and her moans of pain had become screams of agony. Simon and Maria tended her constantly; checking beneath her nightdress, massaging her stomach, moving her legs and mixing up solutions of painkilling herbs, gradually increasing the strength as the day wore on. Towards evening, Quinn came to the door. I opened it a crack and peered out. His face was pale, his eyes haunted.

"You will be the first to know," I promised him, but he craned his neck to see over my shoulder.

"Is she alright? Why is it taking so long?"

"Babies take their own time." I said, as if I knew anything about it. "Go back downstairs with Gerrard."

"Zan, let him in," Simon ordered behind me.

Surprised, I opened the door wider and Quinn pushed past, dashing to his wife. She smiled up at him through her tears, and he whispered to her. Simon let them be for several minutes before calling Quinn aside.

"There is something we can try," he said. "It has been known to be successful —"

"Do it!" Quinn demanded.

Simon held up his hand, "Wait, I must explain the process and ask your permission. It can sometimes be effective for saving the infant – often the mother does not recover, but I have to tell you, man, this is not looking good."

As Simon described the procedure, Quinn's face grew paler still. "No!" he shouted angrily. "Out of the question! I will not consider anything that may … may jeopardise her life."

"Doing nothing jeopardises her life," Maria said softly.

Quinn glanced at Sylvie and took a shuddering breath. "No!"

When Quinn left the room and closed the door behind him, I turned to speak with Simon but caught him and Maria exchanging a concerned glance.

They looked at me unhappily. "She's not wide enough, the baby cannot pass through," Simon stated.

For the next hour Maria worked beneath Sylvie's nightdress. Sylvie screamed and writhed in pain, and Maria's face was stricken. When she withdrew, I saw the blood on her hands and arms and the panic fluttered in my stomach, rising to my throat.

"*Dios, nos ayudan a,*" Maria murmured, and turned away before Sylvie could see her face.

The day dragged into night and Sylvie's nightdress had been changed twice as it had become drenched with perspiration and blood – so much blood. The sheets beneath her were sodden with it and horrific, long-buried images flashed unbidden before my eyes.

I remembered now, a young serving girl I'd known years earlier – Jane Carter – whose life had drained from her while I had stood by, powerless to stem the flow of blood

Quinn had knocked on the door twice more and each time Simon implored him to agree to the mysterious procedure, and each time Quinn refused. But as the clock downstairs chimed nine, Quinn's haggard face appeared at the door yet again and he asked to speak with Simon.

The two men conversed in quick whispers eventually coming to some kind of agreement, then sweet, gentle Quinn fell to his knees beside his wife, the tears running freely down his cheeks as he stroked her face. She was so small, and so exhausted she could not speak, could barely move her head to look at him and the tears trickled into her already wet pillow.

"God, Simon, I've been foolish …" Quinn said. "Please … do what you can. Save my wife."

"It may be too late," my brother said frankly.

"But she cannot continue like this. I should've let you earlier."

Simon turned away as Quinn wept. "Sylvie, my love, you must be strong … please, Sylvie, can you hear me?"

But Sylvie had drifted into merciful unconsciousness. Her face waxen, her skin stretched like wet, transparent, parchment across her bones. I looked at her and I thought of Lord Hamish – his skin had looked like that before … *Oh please God, Sylvie must live!*

Simon and Maria were talking quietly in the corner and Maria was nodding. Quinn took a last juddering breath and hauled himself to his feet.

"Very well, Simon. Do it. Her suffering is intolerable …"

"Then we must ask you to leave," Maria said gently and Quinn looked panicked.

"No," he said firmly.

"You must," Maria said. "Please," and she touched his shoulder significantly, "you must trust that we will do all we can."

Quinn placed a lingering kiss on Sylvie's forehead, before doing as he was bid. As soon as the door closed, Maria extracted a rolled pouch from the large leather bag she and Simon had been delving into. She unrolled it and spread it open on a table. My eyes popped at the surgical instruments lying there – sharp and shiny and gruesome.

Simon had watched my reaction and now he said, "If you cannot stomach this, you must leave now."

"Though we would prefer you stay," Maria added quickly. "We will need your help."

"I will stay," I said decisively. Sylvie, my truest friend, would do no less for me.

Immediately, Simon and Maria went to work with professional efficiency. What followed fascinated as it revolted. Carefully, Simon felt around Sylvie's abdomen, and satisfied he had the correct place, selected a blade from his armoury and with a quick glance at his wife he asked, "Is she still out?"

"Yes."

Then, with unflinching ease born of innumerable wartime surgical procedures, Simon sliced into Sylvie's stomach. He cut a large crescent flap of skin, sinew and muscle and literally folded it back. Blood poured immediately but he worked on, cutting further, and then he stood back as Maria reached both hands into the exposed cavern and extracted a slimy, purple form. She held it above Sylvie's stomach in both hands and Simon cut the cord.

"Zan, tie it!" he commanded, "I can't with one hand."

Overawed by their cool efficiency, I obeyed automatically, hardly even glancing at the tiny creature. The cord felt like a greasy sausage but it tied and I stepped back, strangely elated.

"A girl. She's not breathing," Maria announced and rushed to the desk where a supply of towels waited. I went to follow.

"Stay there!" Simon ordered. "You look after Sylvie. Here, clean her."

It's a girl … a girl … my heart chanted. *Oh please let her live.*

Using water and wads of torn sheet, I bathed around the gaping wound, then followed with the strong-smelling liquid in a bottle that Simon handed to me.

"Smells like you could get foxed on this," I said.

"You could," Simon replied dryly, sorting through his bag. "Here, thread this – and don't lick the end." He thrust a needle and silken thread at me. Suddenly from Maria's corner, came a cough and a gasp and the unmistakable whimper of a newborn. It was a weak, thin cry, but a cry all the same. She lived!

The needle and silk blurred before my eyes but I finished my task and passed it to Simon. Working first within Sylvie's stomach, he then replaced the flap he'd opened, sewing a better seam with one hand than I could ever have done with two and I observed my brother's composure and skill with stunned reverence. What broken bodies had he repaired, what lives had he saved, in that ramshackle hospital in Europe?

But looking at Sylvie's ashen face, fear shot through me again. It wasn't over yet.

"She will not be able to suckle the babe," Simon said. "Zan, go to Mrs Grainger, tell her to find a wet-nurse urgently."

"I will come with you," Maria said, more to Simon that to me, "Quinn ought to be here ..." her voice trailed off.

"She's not going to die is she?" I whispered fearfully as Maria and I marched down the corridor. "Please, Maria ..."

"She is very weak, has lost a terrible lot of blood. Had we not operated – they would both have certainly died. This way, we may have saved one – hopefully two."

It was nearly three in the morning by the time I sat in the parlour and poured myself a glass of Simon's best brandy. By the light of a single candle, I cradled my head in my hands and wept. They were the tears of the exhausted and the grieving, for in my heart I did not believe Sylvie could live – not after such struggle, such blood loss.

The door silently swung inwards and Jemima strolled in. Her legs were stiff and inefficient, yet her tail swung from side to side. She flopped down beside me and I absently fondled her ears while I drained my glass.

I slept where I sat, and awoke stiff and cold, hours later. The sun had long since risen but as the parlour faced north it was dim and cool. Jemima was faithfully by my side and as I stirred she attempted to stand. Her legs refused to obey and I felt a twinge of guilt: she should never have spent the night on a cold floor. I stood up and linked my hands beneath her belly to support her weight as her legs regained movement; my thoughts centred on Sylvie.

A maid burst into the room, feather duster aloft, and stifled a cry of surprise as she saw me.

"It's alright, Maggie, I'm on my way out. Go about your work."

Simon slumped against the wall outside Sylvie's door. His face was grey from lack of sleep, his eyes bleak, and the small scrap of hope I'd been nurturing trickled away.

"How is she?" I asked.

He shook his head. "She won't survive, Zan. Quinn and Maeve are with her now. She awoke briefly an hour ago, but could barely open her eyes – went right back to sleep."

He ran his hand through his unruly, dark hair. "I did so much out there in a flea-infested tent," he whispered hoarsely, "in the middle of nowhere, for men with limbs shattered and guts full of shot, yet I can do nothing here."

I swallowed the lump in my throat. "You did the best you could. They would both have died but for you – the baby lives, and she will survive."

"She is weak. Mrs Grainger found a wet-nurse – should be here soon."

"You must eat and rest," I said and kissed his cheek.

"I've asked Gerrard to advise Richard and Hal to leave. It's not appropriate they remain at this time." He offered a small smile. "You did well in there, Zan."

I nodded sadly and pushed open the door.

Sylvie lay small and shrivelled in the bed. It was difficult to remember her bulging with child and happy with expectation so few hours ago. Quinn looked drawn and ill. He had pulled a chair close to the bed and was leaning forwards uncomfortably, his head resting on Sylvie's pillow beside her pallid face.

He didn't stir as I approached but Maeve, who was keeping vigil over the silent cradle, came forwards and we hugged, each dampening the other's collar with our tears.

The cradle's occupant was less purple now, but she squirmed, her mouth working in soundless cries and her tiny face screwed up like an old man's.

"She's hungry," Maeve said. "Maria tried to take some milk from Sylvie, but there's nothing there yet. We gave the babe some water but she –"

The door opened suddenly and a buxom brown-haired girl about my age followed Mrs Grainger into the room. "This is Bette," the housekeeper announced.

Bette immediately went to the cradle, "Oh the dear little one. She's starving!"

"That's why you're here – get on with it, girl," Mrs Grainger directed, and Bette obeyed spiritedly.

Showing no regard for modesty, the girl scooped up the newborn and tugged at the laces of her bodice in a single effortless action. Releasing one enormous, milk-engorged breast, she expertly attached the tiny wimpering creature. As one, Maeve and I let out our breaths and new tears slid down our faces.

The door opened again, this time admitting Gerrard. He placed one pudgy hand on Quinn's head and clasped his daughter's hand in his other and then his face crumpled in grief. The night's worry had etched new and permanent lines into his brow.

Bette, at home in a chair overlooking the back lawn, was humming softly to the eagerly suckling baby. "She looks strong," I said, hopefully.

"Not as strong as she ought, ma'm. But Bette will make you

better, won't she, little one." She stroked the baby's forehead soothingly as she fed and continued her humming.

∾

Drained of strength and on the brink of emotional collapse, I returned to the quiet sanctity of the parlour and threw myself on to the settee. Maggie had finished her work so I knew I would have peace. I laid my head on a cushion, one arm flung over my aching eyes, and was instantly asleep.

∾

"Found you!"

Hal's voice startled me awake. I groaned audibly.

"Your father has explained the family's unhappy circumstance and asked if Richard and I might return to Leeds. I came to say goodbye."

He sat on the edge of the settee and took my hand in his. "I am so sorry, Alex, but it's not over yet. Try not to lose hope."

At his words, slow tears slipped through my lashes and spilled into my hair. "Don't cry my dear, you need your strength for Sylvie."

Suddenly I wanted nothing more than to be weak. I wanted to be comforted by his arms and lips, and reading my face, he pulled me against his chest, his mouth immediately seeking mine in a kiss that I responded to in desperate, clinging, misery. I tasted my own tears as his tongue opened my mouth, his lips bruising and insistent and he allowed himself to fall on top of me. I sobbed and moaned simultaneously, as passion fed by grief leapt within me.

He pulled his mouth from mine and whispered, "I shall return in a month or so, but in the meantime … a small gift to ease your pain."

I gave a surprised gasp as sly fingers reached beneath my skirt. Stealing up my leg, they quickly located the junction of my thighs. He pressed his hand there and I arched instinctively to meet him savouring the heat of his fingers through the cotton of my bloomers, reacting with thrilling, appalling eagerness.

With his mouth covering mine, and his tongue insistently probing, I groaned with desire as his free hand strayed to the buttons on his trousers. Fumbling and urgent, he released himself and with a moan against my mouth, he took my hand and clasped it around his firmness, held it there, and began sliding it rhythmically up and down.

"Oh Alex," he breathed frantically and his guiding hand worked faster, "Cannot hold on … I … wanted you … so long …"

Suddenly there was a derisive shout of laughter from the door and we sprang apart, and in the eternal seconds that ensued, I thought there was no possible way I could be seeing true. I thought I was going to die – I wished I could die – for slouching casually against the door frame, one foot crossed over the other, arms folded on his chest, and the most contemptuous look on his face, was Patrick.

CHAPTER 26

Dazed and confused, I leapt to my feet, garbling an unintelligible and utterly useless explanation. Patrick merely pursed his lips and regarded me with gem-stone eyes.

Hal hastily rearranged his clothing and mustering his dignity, introduced himself, making no excuse for our compromising position. "Sir Henry Smythsdale," he announced, importantly puffing out his chest, "and would you Sir, be so kind as to introduce yourself and offer your apologies to the lady for not announcing your presence sooner — as any gentleman would."

Patrick raised a mocking brow, and imperiously dismissed my would-be lover without a word. He turned to where I stood, dizzy with unspeakable humiliation.

"Where is everyone? Copulating in corners all over the house?"

"Now, see here …" Hal bristled. "Who do you think you are to —"

Patrick sighed and rolled his eyes. His attention swung back to Hal and he looked him up and down with undisguised scorn. "Patrick Washburn, your, er, *lady love's* clearly unheralded brother," he said caustically, omitting his title and correctly discerning from Hal's blanched look, the younger man knew of him.

Hal had, of course, heard from Maeve all about her brother, future earl and decorated soldier. In such circumstances, a man in Hal's position could expect to be called out. His eyes sifted over Pat's lean, impressive physique and he shrank visibly. I could have told him not to worry – doubtless Patrick considered my honour entirely negotiable – but Hal wasn't a gambling man.

"I … ah …" Without so much as a nod in my direction, he was out the door.

Patrick snorted and returned to me. "Well, doesn't that demonstrate your profound perspicacity?" The curl in his lip said more than his words. He hissed, "You disgust me. I'm right to call you a whore." He moved to leave but in no ordinary mood, I grasped his sleeve.

"Wait!" I cried urgently but he moved violently, flinging off my hand and opening his mouth to give me a thorough serve of derision when something in my face made him pause.

Doubt flickered in his eyes. "What is it? Where is everyone?" he shot a chary look towards the door.

"It's Syl … Sylvie … she …" and my control faltered.

I covered my face with my hands and stood before him weeping, my body quaking and overwhelmed by fear and grief. My knees threatened to give way but he made no attempt to touch me, neither did he leave me.

How I longed to throw myself into his arms and have him comfort me. That only minutes earlier I'd felt the same about Hal now seemed impossible.

Instinctively I swayed into him and he must have thought I was about to swoon for he grasped my shoulders to steady me. How soothing he smelt, all horsey and wind-blown.

"Stop this!" he commanded and his voice was gruff. "What about Sylvie? I've no care that you were conducting yourself like a slut on the settee. I want to know where everyone is and what's going on."

"They're … upstairs," I said, gulping and trying to calm myself. "It's Sylvie … the baby … Simon thinks – " and he was gone so fast I'd have thought the floor opened and swallowed him whole but for the pounding of his boots on the stairs.

Slowly I followed, hauling myself up the staircase and reaching Sylvie's door as Patrick knelt by her bed. The unguarded tenderness on his face caused me to draw in my breath. Quinn was still in his chair, and Gerrard and Maeve stood solemnly beside him.

Patrick was whispering to Sylvie and though her eyes were closed, her small, wan face was turned toward his voice. The baby was nestled by her side and someone had curled Sylvie's weak arm about her daughter. Patrick leaned forwards to look at his niece and when he spoke, Sylvie's smile was frail, and tears glistened on her lashes.

Gerrard stepped forwards and placed a hand on Pat's shoulder and for the first time in three long years, during which this family had experienced deceit and conflict, war and tragedy, father and son met. Pat pressed a loving kiss to his sister's forehead before rising to embrace his father.

Maeve approached then and Pat released his father to hold her, with an intensity of feeling he'd once shown for me. My heart turned over – I didn't belong here – and I slipped away, unnoticed.

❧

Alone in my room, I leaned dizzy and faint against my washstand. My great fear for Sylvie created a physical pain in my chest. I felt ill for Quinn and angry that so gentle a creature as Sylvie should suffer so. And then, of course, was my immeasurable humiliation; for how could I have allowed myself to succumb to Hal's persuasions? Had Patrick not interrupted, we'd no doubt have completed the deed and I'd have regretted it. Yet, with Patrick's arrival I knew such self-loathing I wondered how I had the audacity to continue breathing. The utter disgust on Pat's face rent my heart.

Leaning over my washstand, I splashed cold water into my face, then feverishly stripped off my clothes and scrubbed and scrubbed my naked body starting with those places Hal had touched. I took a ball of rose scented soap, lathered myself, rinsed and scrubbed again.

When at last I felt clean, I crawled naked into bed and slept.

∽

Patrick had come to Broughton Hall to see his father and sister before returning to Europe. Since the signing of the second version of the Treaty of Paris in November the previous year, 150,000 soldiers from the seven nations that made up the coalition against France would continue to occupy the French frontier fortresses. The salaries of these men and their associated expenses, such as food and lodging, were to be paid by France at a cost of some 50 million francs each year – a hefty penalty – and for many former soldiers it was an attractive option, particularly for those who'd made a career from soldiering.

And Patrick had decided to join them and was journeying to France where he was to be assigned a garrison.

Simon was perched on the side of my bed. He had come to my room to see how I fared after he had slept away the afternoon. "Gerrard and I spoke with Patrick and he told us his plans," my brother explained. He still looked haggard and the scars on his face were more defined in his fatigue. "Pat didn't know you were here. He assumed you had returned to Scotland."

"I told him I'd left Hamish."

He shrugged. "He assured me that had he known you were here, he'd never have come – he'd have met his father in Leeds or some other place."

Jemima climbed out of her basket and ambled over to him and he absently stroked her head. "Is there any hope for Sylvie?" I asked quietly.

He shook his head sadly and I felt the tears coming again. "You will need your strength, Zan." He patted my legs where they rested beneath the bedclothes. "Get dressed and come downstairs. I've asked Cook to prepare an early supper."

He left me then, and I dressed slowly. I was afraid to see Patrick and the aversion I knew would be in his face, and wondered if he had told Simon about my … indiscretion. I was not to wonder for long.

On my way downstairs, Simon's door was open and Pat's voice was audible from within, "… think it's only a matter of time?"

Pressing myself against the wall I knew with fleeting guilt that I could not restrain myself from listening.

"Her recovery is … doubtful." Simon was hesitant and I recognised the voice he used when he was reluctantly giving bad news. "I'd be amazed if she lasted more than a day, but she is fighting – she may surprise us yet."

"Quinn must be feeling terrible. If he'd agreed to the … operation? If he'd agreed earlier …"

"There'd have been a better chance … but we cannot know for sure. Sylvie was being torn apart. She'd already lost a huge amount of blood and she's not a strong woman."

Patrick was momentarily silent before he said, "I shall send a messenger to Hull … they can sail without me. I can catch up with them in Belgium later. I wish to stay if I could, at least while Sylvie …"

He didn't finish and there followed a heavy pause during which, Simon sighed. "There must be no trouble, Pat. Zan told me nothing of what happened between you at Waterville except that you sent her away. She has been hurt terribly by Hamish, and you, and now this …"

"She seems capable of finding diversion from it, judging by what I encountered this morning," Pat commented dryly and I groaned inwardly.

"Look, those two dandies … one was after Maeve, the other

followed Alex about like a puppy. She has rebuffed him all the while. I can only imagine what you saw this morning was a moment of weakness on her part. She did well in the birthing room – very brave, but I don't mind telling you she has changed. For someone who used to be so alive, she is … withdrawn, brooding. Something … some spark is gone." Simon paused. "Damn these new boots … so tight. Give me a hand?" Pat chuckled and I heard the squeak of leather as he helped Simon on with his boots.

"Listen, old boy," Simon went on, "you and I parted on bad terms last time but I expect we can put that behind us – we've been great pals in the past. But I'm telling you plainly, if there is any trouble, you must leave, is that clear?"

"I did not come to make trouble," Pat said, tersely. "I told you – I thought she'd returned to Elginbury. It is where she belongs."

"Perhaps, but you tread carefully. This house is grieving."

"Hang about," annoyance sharpened Pat's voice. "Sylvie's my sister – I grew up with her. You hardly knew her so be very careful when trying that tack with me."

Another pause, then Simon conceded, "You're right. But please, tread carefully is all I ask."

Pat also backed down with a sigh. "Don't be concerned. I don't intend associating with her at all if I can help it. As soon as we know what's happening with Sylvie … I'll be gone."

"Good," Simon said assertively and two pairs of boots started toward the door. "It is good to see you, though … after that last time. You should have …"

Quickly retreating, I scampered back up the hall, ducking into my room just as the two men emerged. I lingered for a suitable time, standing by my window and pondering what I'd heard before going downstairs.

❧

Supper was a sombre affair with undercurrents of grief and tension flooding the room, stilting conversation. Patrick never once looked my way, and I kept my eyes locked on my plate lest they stray towards him. Maria hardly touched her food and Maeve picked at some roasted vegetables without enthusiasm. She spoke to Patrick briefly, asking him where he thought he'd be posted and whether she'd be able to visit him there. His response was clipped and disengaged.

Emily came in and approached Maria. A supper tray had been taken up to Quinn but it remained untouched. She didn't know what to do.

"Leave it there," Maria said. "Simon, perhaps you could talk with him. He must eat."

Her husband nodded and Emily escaped with evident relief.

The six of us continued with our silent meal and at length, I could no longer endure the strain Pat's presence wrought within me, or the cloying sadness in the room. I excused myself and took a glass of wine out to the Great Oak.

Nine chairs stood haphazardly around the table beneath the ancient boughs. Was it only days ago we'd sat beneath this tree, sharing laughter and good company?

The sky was darkening, and the first stars appeared. The trees in the park became indistinct shades, black silhouettes against an indigo backdrop.

The house was unusually shrouded in darkness – only one light burning in the entry and another upstairs and I listened as disembodied footsteps crossed the lawn. Maeve was approaching, wrapping a shawl about her shoulders. In the darkness I couldn't see her face, but I didn't need to.

"You'd best come, Alex."

Wordlessly, I rose and followed her.

CHAPTER 27

Sylvie slipped away in the same manner she lived her life – quietly and without fuss. The babe who would never know her mother snuggled against her breast and her husband's hand caressed her cheek. There were no cries or struggles. She simply let out her breath and did not take another.

Maria and Simon stood by her side, holding each other and Maeve wept softly into Patrick's shirt. I stood beside Gerrard and could only guess at the enormity of his pain. Whatever Sylvie had been to the others I couldn't know, but to me she'd been friend, confidante, and above all else, my champion. She had supported me during my marriage, nursed me through my miscarriage and subsequent illness. She had travelled from one end of the land to the other buttressing my entreaty to Patrick. It was only in her passing, that I realised I may never again know such friendship.

That night I didn't sleep. I rose near midnight to take myself to the grotto in our garden where I listened to the sounds of the night. A sickle moon completed its sweep across the sky while I wept intermittently, and prayed. I was not good at praying, and was not even sure why I felt the urge, except that Sylvie had been such a special person, she was deserving of special effort.

❧

Sylvie was buried in the Broughton section in the grounds of the chapel where Hamish and I had been married. Patrick, Simon and Gerrard had ridden their horses, while the rest of our group travelled in a carriage. Quinn stood beside the grave with the unnamed baby in his arms, silent tears running freely down his cheeks, his gentle face made gaunt by the horrendous last few days.

Simon and Maria stood with Meg and little Dudley who was bewildered into solemnity by the grieving adults. Maeve leaned against her Father, while Patrick and I stood on either side of them. I longed to go to him, to give and receive comfort, but at the end of the service, it was to Maeve he turned and I remained apart.

As a group we moved toward the horses, the same minister that had said the words for Hamish and me, instructed his lads to fill in the grave. I walked alone, behind Gerrard, Maeve and Patrick. When Maeve stopped and turned to me, her elfin face was pinched and drawn. "Come, Alex," she held out her hand. "Walk with us."

She had an arm about her brother's waist and he, surprisingly, paused with her as she waited. His jaw was tight and his eyes cloudy with pain. He watched me approach and then we continued as a group in silence.

❧

Quinn seemed to have aged ten years, and lines of pain were scored into his face. He stood beside the breakfast table the following morning and announced his intention to take his daughter to his home in Scotland and raise her there. Bette had accepted a position in his household as wet-nurse and nanny. He asked if he could impose upon Simon's hospitality until the baby was well enough to travel. The difficulty of her birth had taken its toll on the infant, and while she daily grew stronger, she was still quite weak.

Naturally, Simon readily agreed.

Quinn's voice broke when he explained that while he would never recover from his loss, he remained eternally grateful to Simon and Maria for all they had done. He understood his decision had come too late to save his wife and he would live forever with that guilt. But his child had been saved. "Sylvia Kathleen," he told us. "Named for her mother and my mother, she shall be called Kathy."

And so it was, this family that rarely attended church, made its second visit to the local minister in less than a week, and little Kathy was christened.

Patrick lingered. He didn't say why, but I suspected he was struggling with his own grief and was stubbornly reluctant to admit it. He spent a lot of time with Quinn and Kathy, and I recalled nostalgically his attentiveness to the baby Meg.

When finally Simon deemed Kathy strong enough to travel we assembled on the porch as the feeble November sun first appeared over the trees in the park. Quinn ensured Bette and Kathy were comfortably installed in his coach before hugging me and kissing my cheeks affectionately. "Come visit us, Alex. Kathy must grow up knowing her aunt, and mother's great friend, and besides, there's this dog who'll miss you to pieces," he indicated Bony who was settled on a blanket on the coach floor.

He smiled, a vague echo of his former self, and climbed into his coach. "Drive on," he ordered Bill and Jarrod, and embarked upon his new life that I knew he would embrace as he did everything, kindly and honestly.

Gerrard decided to return to Leeds. He had taken Sylvie's death very badly and we understood he needed to bury his grief in society and the arms of Mrs Jamieson.

Surprisingly, Patrick chose to remain at Broughton Hall. I had expected he'd leave with his father and was irritated when he did not because the undercurrent of tension between us continued to reverberate throughout the household.

By unspoken agreement we avoided contact wherever possible,

but when circumstance threw us into the same room or situation, we circled one another like pugilists. His casual contempt kept me tense and guarded and, since I was well acquainted with his ability to attack with calculated cruelty, I maintained my own company more than ever.

Thankfully, he was often absent, and I could only assume he had resumed his drunken, libertine lifestyle and was frequenting the inns and whorehouses of Leeds and its surrounds. The sporadic occasions when he stayed in were the worst for me. The sociable activity of sharing food, wine and conversation had me anxious through the entire event and, though he did nothing to provoke my distress, his mere presence drained my strength and caused my appetite to evaporate. At such times, it was all I could do to force the tasteless food into my mouth. When at last he announced he would depart in a week's time, I welcomed the news.

Those evenings when he joined us beneath the Great Oak stretched my nerves to snapping point yet I could not stay away. I was irresistibly drawn to him, recognising my obsession, even as I eagerly anticipated his departure.

Every muscle in my body was tense with the awareness of his proximity. I wondered if he felt it too, but never did I feel his eyes linger on me, and when I did happen to steal a glance at him, his face wore its customary inscrutable expression, and his long, lean body sprawled comfortably in his chair.

One afternoon, I could stand the tension no longer and decided to hide out in the library. There were five days remaining before his scheduled departure and I hoped to avoid him entirely, if possible.

Unfortunately, he was there, lounging in a chair by the window, reading a large, leather-bound book. I stifled a grunt of annoyance.

His legs were stretched before him in dark grey trousers and black boots, his feet were crossed at the ankles. He wore a pale-blue linen shirt in his usual careless manner. The afternoon sun pooled on his shoulders and shone like a corona through the honey-blonde hair resting on his collar. I paused involuntarily — he took my breath away.

Gathering myself, I entered the room and glancing up, he saw it was me. "What do you want?" He spoke gruffly, as though he too, was hoping for solitude.

"I came for a book."

He cocked an amused eyebrow. "Thank Christ! I worried you planned to stand there staring at me."

I took a deep breath and made my way to a row of books; suddenly unable to bring to mind the one I'd thought to read. Trailing my hand over their spines a memory of another time came unbidden — Patrick and me, all those years ago, wrapped around each other in that same chair. What would he do, I wondered, if I slid on to his knee and …?

My face suffused with heat and my hand hovered, forgotten, over a section of leather-bound,. first editions. Would he eject me in an undignified tangle of skirt and petticoat? Or would my touch reignite those long ago flames we had at once sought and suppressed? Marking his page, he closed his book and placed it on a table. His enigmatic eyes sifted over me.

"Find what you're looking for?" he asked. At the mocking tone in his voice I turned and let my hand drop to my side where I gripped a wad of skirt in my fist. He laughed then and it was a surprisingly carefree sound. "Are you blushing? You're the colour of a plum."

To cap my embarrassment, my colour deepened. My heart was racing and perspiration tingled my upper lip. He seemed to be in a strangely expansive mood.

I spoke without thinking. "I was remembering a time when we … that chair …"

Upon saying the words I plunged headlong into certain disaster. His face darkened and I knew my mistake immediately. "We were kissing?"

I was unable to read the tone of his voice and simply nodded wondering if taking a knife to my tongue would hurt terribly.

"Did you follow me here so you could remind me how easily you offer your favours?" he drawled.

I stiffened, but forced myself to speak calmly. "No, I was looking for a book, some solitude – seeing you there … looked so familiar, that's all."

He took a deep breath and linked his hands behind his head and regarded me for a long time. Finally he spoke and his voice was … civil. "Yes. Being here, in this house, has brought back a lot of memories for me too."

My heart skipped a beat. "Good memories?" I asked, hopefully.

He leaned forward and rested his elbows on his knees, but his eyes had that menacing glitter that raised the warning hairs on the back of my neck. "Good enough. Care for a little afternoon dalliance?"

The world jolted and my throat grew dry. "What …?" My heart leapt with desperate hope yet I knew immediately his intention was to use me before casting me aside. As if to prove my thoughts, his expression grew wolfish and my stomach turned to liquid. Sudden anger coursed through me – the effrontery of him!

"C'mere," he whispered, invitingly. "As I remember you were quite eager back then, and from what I saw of you with your young friend recently, you've achieved a certain … expertise with your hands."

"How dare you!" I demanded indignantly. "I'm not one of your poxy trollops you can … you can –"

"Oh give over," His lip curled derisively. "There's no call to feign maidenly outrage. You're no virgin – we both know that." Lazily, he unfolded himself from the chair and moved towards me. "And you know I'm not discerning, nor opposed to a romp with you for old times' sake." He grinned fiendishly, "So – how about it? Have you any plans for the next hour?"

How I longed for a touch, a loving caress, a sweet word, however counterfeit, and cursing the social niceties that demanded my refusal – if only I had the ease of principle of one such as Kat Wheeler – I backed away from him. The situation was monstrously out of control.

"Don't you touch me," I hissed, my voice low, but his eyes glinted dangerously. I continued my retreat, coming up hard against a desk. Instantly, I grasped Simon's heavy, crystal ink bottle and weighed it threateningly as my one-time lover drew near. "I swear to God I will crown you if you come any closer."

His lips moved in that slow, disarming smile, and I knew I wasn't going to break crystal on his head. I wanted to throw myself at him, to have him drown me in kisses and take me here – on the rug, in the full glare of daylight.

I shook off the traitorous thoughts – oh I wanted him alright, but not like this. I wanted him in love, for eternity – not as a diversion one afternoon to be discarded as a whore when it was done.

He continued to approach, but something about me stopped him, and it wasn't the ink bottle for he plucked it from my hand and replaced it on the table. Staring down at me, his expression softened and he regarded me with something I'd have called regret … if I hadn't known him better.

His hand came up between us, strong and rough from handling weaponry and horse harness and he touched me, trailing a line of liquid fire along my jaw, and down my throat, to pause agonisingly at the cleft between my breasts.

With mounting apprehension, I fought to control my treacherous emotions but his fingertips casually caressed the rise of my bosom and I knew he felt my pounding heart. His mouth lingered just above my own; humid breath tantalising my lips and weakening my knees. My body was set to betray me with every sense alert to his touch – if he kissed me now, it was all over.

How I wanted him – I trembled with it – but not like this, and as the grief welled within me, my eyes filled with tears. I marshalled a supreme effort of will and whispered viciously, "*Go to hell!*"

Abruptly, he dropped his hand and I knew a perverse stab of loss. "You'd have agreed had I said I loved you," he said softly. "At least I'm being honest. Is that what your little baronet said? That he loved you? Or did you give yourself to him for nothing in return?"

"I never gave myself to him," I ground out. "And you know that. There have been only two men in my life and one was my husband."

He smiled scornfully. "Ah, the perpetual eavesdropper. I knew someone was listening that day outside Simon's door. Did he make all that up himself or did you feed him the dialogue?"

"I've said nothing to any of them since my return. What's the matter? Are you afraid they'll discover the cad you are? That you insulted me? That your whore insulted me? What is it Patrick?" My mouth twisted spitefully. "Or do you answer only to *Rick*?"

We stood so close that I was forced to lean backwards, pressed against the desk to avoid touching him. I could smell his exotic scent and it was making me giddy with need and my skin still burned from his touch. I could not offer myself – he would call me whore. But I loved him, *God how I loved him*, and I stood glaring up at him, recklessly daring him with my eyes and mouth to kiss me, for it would be no violation if he did.

Toe to toe we faced each other, breathing each other's breath, and in a rare moment of exposure, indecision flashed across his face. His lips parted and his tongue flicked across them.

He wanted to kiss me.

I had disarmed him and I allowed myself a fleeting wave of triumph. I may not have his love, but he desired me, and I smiled then, smug with my small victory and the knowledge of it made me strong.

But his transitory moment of weakness was gone, and in its place was a scowl, so contemptuous, that I withered beneath it.

He said slowly and precisely, "Not if you were the last woman on earth, you *slut!*"

He threw himself away so roughly that I stumbled, and then it all happened so quickly. I made to take a step but the heel of my shoe was caught in the hem of my skirt and in the briefest of seconds, as he strode to the door, I twisted, losing my balance. My fall was made all the worse by the fact that I was trying to release my heel without tearing my dress.

I fell hard. Flinging my hands out towards the writing desk to save myself, I missed, and took the full weight of my fall, with the side of my face, on the angled wooden corner of the desk.

Like a blow from a hammer, accompanied by an explosion of light and sickening crack of pain, I was suddenly floating in a warm pool, the temperature of blood, and then mercifully, everything went black.

CHAPTER 28

Disconnected sounds were coming from a great distance away ... a woman's cry, footfalls on wooden floors, urgent shouts. I rose upwards, weightlessly, through a swirling black fog.

A voice was pressing and insistent, and I knew with detachment that it was Patrick. Commanding ... issuing instructions ... trying to penetrate my senses, but his words washed in ... out ... in ... out ... ebbing and flowing ... waves of an ocean, "... Stop the blood ... Alex, darling girl ... where is Simon ..."

Disjointed, disembodied words that my brain snatched at and clung to, while all the rest swam beyond my reach.

And there was a velvety, accented feminine voice close to my ear, "... Not ... lose ... *Please* Alex ... Stay with me ..."

The voices were drifting further and further away and I was tired – so very tired. And the warm pool was irresistible.

I let it buoy me and I was dissolving into it, melting ...

"*Alex!*" Patrick's shout jerked me back to the hard surface of the floor. "Look at me!" he demanded. "Alex, open your eyes, damn it!"

Yet I could not, for the pain was too great

But he said my name over and over and I wanted to scream for him to stop as the memories rushed back – the humiliation, the grief. I had lost yet again, and I longed to return to the warm pool.

"Alex, look at me," he ordered and I twisted away from his voice. I could not look at him — it hurt too much. It all hurt too much.

"*Oh God … Oh God,*" my own voice whimpered as something cold was pressed against my forehead and I shrank from this new pain.

I was being lifted. Someone was carrying me and every jarring step seared my head with agony. When they laid me on a bed the cloying, inescapable pain eclipsed the room, and the voices grew distant as I returned … so gratefully … to the warm pool … the waves closing … over my head.

∾

Somewhere in the distance a voice spoke about blood and unguents, but the words connecting them to make sentences were whipped away as though snatched by the wind. I caught them, but could not make sense of them.

And I was hot. So hot, and Patrick was teaching me to swim. He held me in his arms and I was floating. Then from nowhere came a storm and we were torn apart. I screamed and clawed towards him, my mind a whirlpool of fear and panic. I called for him but he turned from me.

I was drowning, without his strength to support me I foundered and sank beneath the relentlessly beating waves. Sinking down and down to the seabed where mud oozed between my toes, my knees buckled and I came to rest on all fours.

Yet I was not alone — there was Hamish, naked and rigid and preparing to take me from behind. At my cry of outrage, he threw his head back and laughed and laughed. "So we meet in the depths of despair," he crowed, and then he screamed maniacally.

Squirming from his reach, I cried, "I should not be here with you, I was never meant to be with you," and he laughed until he cried, and then all was quiet, and I was alone in my bed, weeping and exhausted.

❧

Maeve's voice was angry, though she struggled to keep it low. "I never would have thought you such a fool."

I was prone in bed, my head bound and part of the dressing covered my eyes. The pair arguing in the room could not tell that I'd woken. I lay still and confused and my head persistently ached.

"We've been through all this – it's nothing to do with you," Patrick whispered viciously.

"You are wrong, it has –"

"– *nothing* to do with you."

"You're not the one who has watched her drift through her days as a ghost. You're not the one who hears her weeping in her sleep at night. All that time with Hamish, and then you, she is on the edge of collapse and she does not even know it. She is desperately unhappy."

"She seemed happy enough with that Hal fellow all over her."

"By God, you've a nerve! As one who unlaces his breeches for any slut drawing breath. *Merda, ti amo mio fratello, ma qualchevolte …* She married Hamish – so what! After Anne's little deception she had no option. That you were hurt over it – be man enough to say so."

Patrick muttered something indiscernible, and she responded angrily, "Look at her then." There was a protracted silence before she demanded, "I hope you're proud of yourself!"

Silence again, for a very long time. "If it satisfies your righteous outrage," he said finally, and then his voice constricted and faltered, "I have never hated myself more than I do at this moment."

His sister responded, mollified, "No, my love." The silk of her skirt whispered across the rug and her voice became muffled against

300

his chest. "I don't want you to hate yourself. I want you to be *true* to yourself."

❧

It was not really pain; it was a dull, debilitating ache at the front of my head. The bandage had been removed, and when I opened my eyes the room slowly came into focus.

It was my room, and it was evening. Maria had her back to me and was working on something in a small circle of light. An apron tied about her waist emphasised how slim she was even after carrying two children.

I tried my voice and produced only a croak but she whirled around, her face registering intense relief.

I tried again. "Have I slept all day?"

She approached the bed. "You have slept for a whole night and day. How do you feel?"

"All night and day …? I have the worst headache of my life."

"Here," she held a cup of water. "You must drink."

She helped shuffle me into position and put the cup to my lips. I'd never tasted anything so cool and sweet.

"I really slept all that time?"

She nodded. "You had a very bad fall. You split your head here —" she placed a hand over her temple and eye. "The worst possible place. A blow like that — it could have killed you. We were very worried. Simon stitched you up."

She peered into my eyes, felt my forehead, and seemed satisfied.

"You must eat something, though you may feel nauseous at first. And you have a visitor who is eager to see you."

"I'm so tired, who is it? Is Julia here?"

"Someone who has not left your side for a moment," she replied evasively. "Now, I must fetch Simon." She turned towards the door, but threw over her shoulder, "I shall not be far, and will hear if you call me."

It was an undisguised warning to my visitor, who moved from the shadows as Maria pulled the door to.

Patrick advanced cautiously. He looked terrible. His face was pale and unshaven, his clothes rumpled. Pulling over a chair he sat beside the bed and rested his elbows on his thighs, hands hanging loose between his knees.

He didn't look at me when he spoke. "How do you feel?" he asked gently.

I was wary. My heart hammered wildly in my breast and the blood pounded painfully through my skull.

"I'm alright," I said tightly, wondering why Maria would leave me alone with him.

He looked up and his eyes were the colour of the sea on a cloudy day. "How did you come to fall?"

So that was it! He was afraid he would be blamed.

"Don't worry," I snapped. "I shan't be telling anyone about our argument."

He frowned slightly. "That is not my concern. I'm trying to understand what happened. One moment you were standing – the next …"

Still suspicious, I relaxed my guard only slightly. "I remember my heel caught in my dress. As I fell I tried to grasp the desk but missed – I stopped my fall with my face."

He studied his hands again and in the silence of the room my head beat like a kettledrum. "It was bad, wasn't it?" I said at last.

He sucked his upper lip and nodded. "When I heard the crash I was in the hall. I yelled for Alice to get Simon. Maria was in her room. She came running and we got you to your bed … do you remember any of it?"

"Some things – shouting, people talking, none of it made much sense."

"Do you remember what I said?" He looked at me now, and our eyes locked intensely. *Indeed, I remembered what he said.*

But I hesitated in order to control my emotions. "You … you called me … darling girl – like you used to." My throat constricted as the tears began to well in my eyes. Turning my face away, I swallowed with effort.

He watched me steadily, saying nothing, and finally, after a telling silence, I pointed him to his escape route. Avoiding his eyes, I said, "I expect the sight of all that blood …" I paused. Still, he said nothing. "All that blood … must've scared you," I finished and looked up.

He nodded and took a long, shuddering breath. "It did – it scared the hell out of me. I … thought you were dying."

The pain in my head intensified. It felt like cannons firing and my stomach was beginning to turn over. I wanted him to leave. "I think you –"

"Alex," he interrupted, and I stiffened – he'd not spoken my name in so long. "I meant it – when I said that. All that blood … and you were in my arms drifting in and out of consciousness … I've never been more afraid in my life. And after Sylvie and the war … too much death … I thought, *she is dying in my arms and I have caused this. I have caused her death.*

"I have shouted at you, insulted you, I have called you whore and propositioned you as one. I have paraded other women before you – deliberately hurting you. I have hated you so much I've wanted to throttle you with my bare hands, yet I've never stopped loving you – not for a second. And I have been too mulish to admit it and stop tormenting us both."

His words came out slowly, and I sensed their honest plea. I even heard his voice break slightly, and yet there was no uplifting tide of emotion, no relief. So unprepared was I for this development that I simply stared at him.

"Alex, I have done some appalling things to you, too consumed by my own anger. I'd tried to tell myself I was happy to be free of you … drinking and whoring, taking everything life had to offer. But you appeared at Waterville and … and the truth is you brought back so many emotions I'd tried to bury. I resented you – determined to reject you as you had me. Anger was the only emotion I could safely express – and anger was easy. I was angry with you because you were, you've always been, my weakness. And then there you were … in my arms, unconscious and bleeding."

The blood pressure in my temples was increasing. I could feel its throb and hear its boom. I digested his words, and found my voice at last. "I told you I loved you – you turned me away."

"It is no excuse, I know, but … you accepted Anne's story. You married Hamish."

"What else could I have done?" I whispered hoarsely.

"You could have asked me."

"I did not know how to find you … your father did, but by then it was too late. Everyone believed you had used me – your reputation spoke for itself. No one believed your feelings for me were genuine."

"When Father wrote he asked about my involvement with Anne; naturally, I replied that she was attempting to blackmail me. When I asked after you he said you had married Hamish."

"I made such a mess of things," I said softly.

He nodded. "As I did. And you're married still – there can be no future for us – another reason for my anger when you arrived in Devon for what did you expect of me?"

"I never would have guessed you so esteemed the sanctity of marriage vows," I said scornfully, swiping the tears from my cheeks. "You are certain to have bedded more than one married woman."

"Well, I'd wager you wanted more than just an adulterous affair – as I would – and since Lord Whatsit is lurking somewhere out there, that's all we could ever have."

"Your father promised to help me obtain a divorce if we reconciled."

"A *divorce*?"

"Hmph!" I snorted bitterly. "Didn't expect that, did you!"

He sighed in exasperation. "Alex, I once told you I would marry you openly and honestly. I still would – if you could find it in yourself to believe me, and forgive me all the terrible things I've done to you. I love you – always have. Terribly inconvenient," he added with a hint of his old humour.

I desperately wanted to believe him. Tears spilled anew on to my cheeks and he lifted a hand to touch my face, but I stayed him. "Don't! You sit there saying all these sweet words but that day in the storm … The things you said … the way you described our one night together …"

"Oh God …" he ran his hands through his hair.

"I gave myself to you in love," I went on. "All the months I cried for you, believing you'd betrayed me with my own sister, I held that one night to my heart. I prayed I'd not been merely another conquest. And all the nights my husband preferred the attentions of his pretty boys, it was all I thought about. I thanked God for that one night with you."

While I spoke I watched his face. It was unusually open, leaving me in no doubt as to his true feelings. "I carried that night with me into battle," he said huskily. "I left England believing I'd be coming home to you and a lifetime of such nights. It was only one night but it sealed my fate – I loved you beyond reason, Alex. When Father told me of your marriage, I cannot describe what I felt."

"Similar to what I felt when Anne said she carried your child?" I suggested, and he nodded thoughtfully.

"When I left you out in that storm, after saying the most cruel things to you, I knew I had sunk to the lowest point in my life. You have ever been my Achilles' heel; you expose both the best and worst in my character."

We fell silent and I dabbed at my eyes with the sleeve of my nightdress. Jemima stirred in her basket – I hadn't realised she was there until that moment. My head was reeling with the force of his confession and I was afraid to be hurt again, but there was no malice in his face, only honesty – and love.

"I didn't know you had lost your baby," he said gently. "What I said, about you and Hamish … I didn't know."

"Would it have made any difference? You were hell bent on cruelty. Why did you never tell me about Hamish? About his … preferences?"

"I didn't need to," he answered. "You were supposed to marry me – your children were to be ours."

He laid his hand lightly over mine and I stared at it. It was a gentle hand for one so calloused and strong. "Please Alex? Could you ever forgive me?" My heart swelled. I gave a little sob and fresh tears ran down my cheeks. He stroked my hand soothingly. "You never used to cry all the time like this – my doing as well. Could you forgive me – one day?"

"You're a fool," I said thickly. "How could I *not* forgive you, when I love you as I do? But you must forgive me too."

"Of course. Don't ever doubt it."

I slid my hand from beneath his so I could mop my eyes. Gingerly, I touched the crusty lump above my right eye and saw him wince.

"Is it really bad?"

"You're quite bruised and all around the stitches it's red and angry looking. The scar will add fierce character to your face."

"Then I shall wear it boldly."

He laughed lightly, but his eyes were serious. "Alex, we must solve the dilemma of your marriage, so I can spend the rest of my life proving how much I love you. May I kiss you? I have wanted to for three long years, you know."

"You could have kissed me in the library before I fell," I pointed out.

"I know, and have berated myself for my perverse need to insult you instead."

"And you made that crude proposition to me – said you were not discerning."

"I didn't actually intend it to be crude. I'd rather hoped you might take up my offer but you went all puritanical on me."

"My thoughts were not puritanical. I was affronted because I knew you only wanted me for amusement. Had you kissed me, I'd not have rebuffed you."

"You would never have been *only amusement* – but I would have died rather than admit it."

"Nevertheless, I could not countenance the thought of your discarding me afterwards. I thought you were right in calling me a whore – except that it's only with you I've ever wanted to behave so."

"Sweetheart, I was playing with fire. It's highly unlikely I'd be able to discard you afterwards. Anyway, you're not a whore. And I knew exactly what was going on between you and that Hal fellow when I arrived that day."

"How?"

"Because I knew something was amiss when I rode up … everything so quiet. When I found you, you were crying and he was taking advantage of your grief. I wanted to plant a facer on him – and I wanted to brain you, for being so gullible."

"So, do you want to kiss me or talk about that Hal fellow?" I chided playfully.

"Need you ask?" His fingertips brushed my cheek, savouring the moment, and I revelled in his touch, my heart pounding once more as he moved towards me.

Suddenly there was a quick rap on the door and Maria's head appeared. "Oh good, you are both still alive."

She carried a tray with a bowl of something steaming on it. Simon, following closely on her heels, grinned at me. "Welcome back, Zan."

Pat's hand still caressed my cheek, and as Maria approached

she smiled. "It was so quiet, we thought you may have killed one another."

"Move aside, man, the patient is due for her check over," Simon said. He examined my pupils and pressed his fingers to my neck. "She still needs rest, Pat. A quickened pulse will not aid her recovery," Simon said meaningfully.

"She must eat too," Maria added. "And you must tidy yourself and go downstairs to eat something. She will be here when you return."

Pat squeezed my hand gently and rose from his chair.

"Your recovery is progressing," Simon remarked from the foot of the bed. "How do you feel? Any dizziness?"

"Well enough, thanks to you," I said, "though the dizziness could be for other reasons." I smiled shyly at Patrick: there were no secrets anymore. We could love one another openly, the way we'd always wanted to.

"Yes, I see reconciliation has taken place," Simon commented.

"Could you doubt it the way he has haunted her bedside?" said his wife.

"Hmm – there had best be no further problems caused by you two," Simon said, examining my stitches. "We have all grieved enough recently. Can you stand?"

"I haven't tried."

"Then, let's get you up and see how steady you are. If you are dizzy or ill, you must tell me immediately."

Maria helped me out of bed while Pat politely removed himself to gaze out of the window.

I stood comfortably, with no signs of weakness or giddiness and Simon was pleased. "I think you will live," he pronounced as I scrambled back into bed. "But remember, it was a very nasty crack, and the gash is quite deep. You may experience faintness for a few more days, and you may be wobbly on your legs. No over-exerting yourself," he added throwing a warning glance at Patrick.

Pat came and stood beside the bed. "Good, since I have a lot to make up for, if she's prone in bed she'll be unable to escape my repeated pleas for clemency."

Maria said, "Will you still return to Europe now?"

He nodded affirmatively and my heart sank. For some reason I'd forgotten he was leaving. He smiled at me as though he read my mind. "I shall be back here as soon as I'm able. It's very important that I come home."

"Perhaps," said Simon, "but for now it's very important you leave her alone. Alex needs to wash and eat her meal. You need to do the same. You may visit her later."

Pat nodded and looked at me, and I read clearly that he did not want an audience for our first kiss in reconciliation, and neither did I. Cocking my head towards the door, I remarked, "You had better obey the doctor. Come and see me after supper."

Pat and Simon left the room together and Maria helped me to bathe. She stripped off my nightdress and assisted me into another, then plumped the pillows behind me so I could eat my meal.

"Will I be able to get up tomorrow?" I asked hopefully.

"Provided you do not rush about."

I shook my head. That still hurt though my headache had eased. "I won't."

"Very well, you may come downstairs to breakfast, but if at any time you feel unwell, you must return to bed. Do not underestimate how dangerous such a knock as yours may be."

"By your fussing, how could I?"

"Good. I shall leave you now. Emily will collect the dishes later." She gathered up an armful of things and went to the door.

"Maria?" She turned. "Thank you for everything. Not just looking after me, but Patrick and … everything.

The bowl of braised meat and vegetables had cooled to eating temperature. I dipped my spoon into it and found it tasted good, and I hadn't realised until that moment how hungry I was.

When I'd finished, I placed the meal tray aside, and climbing carefully out of bed, took up the candle and tentatively approached the mirror. My face looked hollow and my eyes large. Pink splotches showed on my cheeks from the warming food I'd just eaten.

The wound was angry, as Pat had said. It was long and puckered and just missed my right eye. Simon had done a clean sewing job, and the stitches stood out black and spiky, a bristly second eyebrow, running diagonally across my brow, past the corner of my eye and extending to my temple.

Needless to say I was extensively bruised in otherwise pretty shades of rose and lavender all around the right side of my face and shadowing my cheek. As I moved, the flickering candlelight caught my wedding ring. It glinted spitefully on my left hand. Though I felt detached from my husband, I'd not removed it for wearing it afforded me a certain matronly respectability.

Now, it caused me to ponder its removal. After so many years of pining for Patrick, it was difficult to accept that I had attained my heart's desire; it seemed so surreal. Could it really have happened, or was I in the throes of some delirium?

As if cued, there came an efficient knock behind me and the door opened a crack. I stood before him in my nightdress as Patrick slipped quickly into the room carrying a three-branched candelabrum. He kicked the door to with his heel. He was freshly shaved and had changed his clothes and as he approached, his eyes dropped to where I toyed with my ring and he cocked his head to the side.

"Is something wrong?"

"I was wondering … if I should take this off." I watched him carefully.

"That depends on you. It might be more socially acceptable to continue wearing it for now."

"Do you know what I want?" I asked with a coy smile.

His eyes glittered with flecks of gold in the candlelight.

"Tell me," he said and he placed the candelabrum on the dressing-table and stood with arms at his sides, waiting.

I padded towards him on bare feet, until I could take his two hands in mine. Pulling him forwards and reaching up until our mouths were only inches apart, I whispered, "I want you to tell me how much you love me, and kiss me to seal it."

Abruptly, he dropped my hands and cupped my face in his palms. "I love you," he said and kissed my forehead. "I love you … I love you," he kissed my cheeks. "I love you so bloody much it hurts," and he kissed my mouth.

I clasped my hands behind his head and his arms encircled my body, pulling me to him as our mouths fused together. We savoured each other and inhaled each other and I tasted my tears on his lips as we hungrily devoured one another.

We spoke a million words and forgave a million hurts in that kiss, and the long suppressed need for him sparked to life, eclipsing the room, the furniture, everything, leaving me breathless and aching deep in the pit of my stomach.

Nevertheless, I was not the inexperienced girl I'd been when Patrick and I first found our love. I could name the fever that burned inside me, and I needed him within me to extinguish it. Yet, I would not be the one to initiate it. Was it a tiny shard that had not forgiven, or did not truly believe? But our kisses grew deeper, and his hand in the small of my back held me to him, and I longed to be as close as a man and woman can be.

At last, he raised his head and I stood in the circle of his arms, breathing heavily. I trailed my fingers over his face. "This isn't a dream, is it?" I whispered.

"No, my love," he too, was breathing hard. "We still have several days together, and I'm worried about hurting you. Come, you should get back into bed."

Disappointment bit hard and suspicion must have showed in my face.

"Ahh, Alex," he dropped a quick kiss on my nose. "I would love nothing more than to spend the night in delicious exploration of your body, and proving beyond doubt my depth of feeling for you. However, with a mere flick of his wrist Simon will divest me of a certain anatomical part should I interfere with your recovery."

Despite my misgivings, I smiled. He was right.

"Come, get into bed and I shall kiss you good night."

He pulled back the bedclothes and I snuggled down as he tucked the counterpane around me. Dragging over a chair, he sat close to my shoulder. "Maria said I can get up tomorrow," I told him.

"That's good. Shall I escort you to breakfast?"

"I would love that. Besides, we have only three days left to us; we must make the most of them."

"Alex, listen to me. I have ever been a poor correspondent. Had I written from Europe it may have quashed your sister's lies, and probably, you'd not have married Lord Whatsit."

"I definitely would not have married Lord Whatsit. You proclaimed your love, but you never wrote – not once. Yet, you corresponded very regularly with Maeve."

"Corresponding with Maeve is habitual, but I promise this now: I shall write to you as often as I can."

Beneath the covers I'd been working away at my wedding ring. Now, it came free and I reached out to show him.

"I shan't wear this any more."

He took it and turned it over in his hand distractedly. "What would you say if I called in to see Father on my way to Hull? He could see about arranging that divorce of yours while I'm in Europe. We can be married as soon as I return."

"I'd like that …"

At that moment someone knocked on my door. "Come in," I called.

Simon, Maria and Maeve entered. Maria looked satisfied and I saw her give Simon a playful punch on the arm.

My brother responded to my unspoken question, "I threatened to punish Pat severely if he was … disturbing you."

"And I said I would not let him," Maeve added mischievously. "I was rather hoping tha —"

"We don't need to hear it, Naughty Puss," Simon said with a laugh and Maeve glowed at his use of his childhood name for her.

"Well, *I* said Patrick would be more respectful," Maria said.

"Respectful of my manhood," Pat murmured, with a sly wink in my direction.

"How was your supper, Zan? Do you feel nauseous at all?" Simon became professional again.

"I feel fine."

"Good. You need your rest so we're going now — that means you too, Pat."

"Right behind you," Patrick said, rising from his chair.

He waited while the others filed out before leaning to kiss me again. "Sleep well, my darling girl," he said, with his lips against mine.

I did sleep well that night, wrapped warm and safe in a cloud of love, with Patrick's heavenly fragrance lingering on my skin, and my lips still tingling from his kisses.

CHAPTER 29

I've always loved early mornings, but autumn mornings are particularly beautiful. While spring bursts into vibrant, heady-scented life, the autumn is the winding down of the year, painting the landscape in fiery reds and burnished golds. If spring is the time of flowers, the autumn belongs to the trees.

I loved the crunch of leaves beneath my feet and I loved kicking them about as I strolled, watching the animals in the park; the birds and squirrels and deer, making ready for the colder months.

The morning following my reconciliation with Patrick, I awoke with a feeling of expectation. I was excited, eagerly anticipating the day, the months and years ahead. I was reborn, at peace, and in love.

I stretched and yawned and thought that if I rose now, I might join Maeve on her walk and enjoy the autumn morning. My eyes lit on the simple band that was my wedding ring, lying where Pat had placed it beside my clock.

Yes indeed, I was embarking on a new life. One in which I could, for the first time, openly express my love for Patrick.

I dressed slowly, mindful that if I became giddy Simon and Maria would insist I remain abed. Jemima's chocolate gaze levelled on me and I waited as she executed her stretching routine.

The house was still at this lightless hour, though I could hear early kitchen sounds echoing in the otherwise emptiness of morning. I descended the stairs and at their foot a shadow detached itself from the wall.

"What are you doing up? Do you feel alright?" It was the voice of my beloved and I immediately went into his arms and our lips met in greeting. At length we parted and I replied, "I feel very well. I'd planned to walk with Maeve. What are *you* doing?"

"Thought to do the same, but on second thoughts, let's jettison Maeve."

We left the house with Jemima trailing happily behind. She walked a lot slower than she used to, but still enjoyed the outing.

Pat draped his arm lazily across my shoulders and as we walked, he guided me over the lawns and through the park. We skirted the edge of the forest and then dropping his arm, took my hand and wordlessly conducted me into the woods.

I knew where he was leading me and though I'd expected our irises might be dying back at this time of year, I was unprepared for the sight of their gorgeous purple heads dancing slightly in the soft morning breeze. Crisp autumn leaves floated around us as he dropped to the ground and sat leaning against a craggy birch trunk. Positioned between his knees, I rested my back against his chest and he wrapped his arms around me. We watched as Jemima ambled away to examine a log. She sniffed, pawing at it investigatively before moving on to something else.

"I said something once about a sentimental game." He spoke in a soft voice. "That's just one other thing I deeply regret."

"It hurt me, you know. This place means so much to me."

"And to me – God Alex!" His chest heaved beneath my head. "I can't believe how foolish I have been."

I turned in his arms and looked into his face. His eyes were like shining emeralds, and I read in them his rare vulnerability. The Patrick that presented to the world a façade of independence and detachment, was showing me plainly, in this special place, the depth of his love.

"Your brother reminded me yesterday how I said I would love where I will and give my heart to no one. Ironic isn't it? When I said those words, so long ago, I was already lost in you, I just didn't know it. When you came to Waterville that summer I recognised the intensity between us. We were both too young to cope with the feelings we shared. I think that's half the reason we bickered all the time. Even so, I sought you out as often as you did me." He stroked my cheek affectionately, "After you left, I analysed myself and I knew then that I loved you … have loved you every day since. You're a part of me I simply could not cauterize, no matter how I tried."

And how I loved him in return – it surged through my veins and I wanted to shout and scream with it. I kissed him then, and he responded with a passion that was almost violent in its hunger.

Our breaths mingled, our lips and tongues tasted, and I breathed the wonderful citrus and clove scent of him. He had ever been an addictive assault on my senses. I would never be sated, for without him, as I'd already learned, I was soulless.

He pulled away and stroked an unruly tendril of hair from my face, curling it about his finger, and with a contented sigh he tightened his embrace.

"Ah darling girl …" he murmured. "Tell me about your marriage."

I hadn't expected this question and drew back to look at him uncertainly. But there was no malice in his face.

"I don't know what to tell you."

"Just tell me what you can. I'm trying to understand."

So I took a deep breath and he listened as I told him everything – the entire, undiluted story, including all the parts that for various reasons I may not have told Simon, or Gerrard, or even Sylvie.

When at last I fell silent, I held a large russet leaf in my hand.

I studied it in order to avoid his eyes. He had listened without reaction, but now he pulled me against his chest again and drew a ragged breath.

"I'm so sorry, Alex. Had I told you of Hamish's tastes … had I written to you … had I denounced Anne immediately she left Waterville – so many opportunities to avert disaster yet, as always, I was too stubborn, too prideful."

"Yes, there were so many things you could have done. Yet I am also to blame. I didn't trust you. At the first negative word, I leapt to condemn you like everyone else."

"And the biggest mistake we both made was not going immediately to my father to tell him everything. I know now he would have supported us."

There were no words I could add so I relaxed against him and we sat in silence for a long time before we called Jemima and began our walk to the house. Upon our approach, he took my arm and turned me to face him.

"You haven't asked," he said soberly, "but I want you to know that I have truly only ever loved you. Kat Wheeler and the others have never been more than bed sport. They mean nothing and I'll not see any of them again."

I looked at him calmly and felt his love coursing through me. "I didn't ask because I didn't feel I had to. But I thank you for saying it."

"This looks very serious," Maeve interrupted brightly, coming towards us from the direction of the orchard.

Our eyes lingered on each other a moment longer before we turned and she joined us as we entered the house.

CHAPTER 30

Patrick and I spent the remainder of the morning blissfully enjoying each other's company – we had three years to make up for. Simon had examined my wound and declared that it was healing nicely, and since I'd experienced no giddiness I could remain out of bed.

"Pity," Pat whispered roguishly, "I was hoping he'd order you to spend the day on your back."

It was wonderful to be open about our affection for each other. Simon alone seemed to have reservations and urged discretion, which I didn't feel was necessary.

Later, the two men rode over the land Simon had recently acquired from Jackson. My brother was keen to see what Patrick thought of his plans to build a handful of cottages and divide the paddocks up for new tenants.

In the parlour, Maria spread a rug across her lap and dozed while I repaired a seam in one of my coats. With one ear carefully cocked for sounds of the men's return, I was, therefore, the first to hear the carriage crunching on the gravel drive.

Maria stirred, "Did I hear something outside?"

"A carriage," I said from the window and watched as Julia and

Adrienne stepped out on to the drive. I hadn't seen Adrienne since my wedding and now my eyes sifted over her critically. She was beautiful – she always had been – but womanhood had applied a veneer of maturity, which was obvious in her walk, and the serenely confident tilt of her head and languid expression.

The two women moved towards the porch and the bell chimed in the hall. I turned back to Maria. "It's Julia and Adrienne – two friends of mine."

Maria sat up quickly and straightened her gown. "Good. It would be nice to have some company. We'll ask Atchison to bring them in here."

I greeted my friends enthusiastically and performed the introductions with Maria. Once settled, Julia and I fell into our old pattern of gossip and chatter, sharing our news. I noted that Julia's waist was thickening and I commented that she looked very well.

"I'd love to be able to say the same for you, Alex, but what on earth have you done to your face?"

"Oh," I giggled, and my hand flew self-consciously to the bristling stitches. "I had a fall in the library and hit my face on the corner of a desk."

"Luckily for Alex, her brother is an excellent surgeon," Maria stated proudly, "or she'd be bleeding all over the rug still."

As the conversation continued, I longed to tell Julia about my reconciliation with Patrick, but time and privacy were required for that. Consequently, where only minutes earlier I'd been watching the window eagerly for his return, now I hoped he would be delayed.

"You certainly seem happier than last I saw you," Julia said. "Under those bruises you are positively glowing."

"Thank you, and I must return the compliment for your condition seems to suit you well." I was eager to divert the conversation.

"For good reason," said Adrienne. Her black eyes sparkled with news. "Will you tell her Jules, or shall I?"

"I will," said Julia quickly. "Alex, the reason we came here today is to invite you to a gathering at Adrienne's house in Leeds – well, it's more of a celebration really. You see, when I told you I was with child, I neglected to identify the father …" she glanced uncertainly at Maria.

I nodded. "Go on …"

"The father of my child is Deon." She paused for my reaction. For some reason I was not surprised, and found a slow smile creeping across my face.

"So he realised he should've married you in the first place," I said smugly.

"Indeed," said Adrienne. "I cannot say I approve of their affair but they're both happy with the arrangement."

"What arrangement?" I said curiously.

"I said I'd tell her," Julia snapped. "Deon has left Celia, and we plan to marry. He is attempting to arrange some kind of annulment, or divorce, or something, on the grounds that we were betrothed for years and he ought never to have married Celia."

"My brother is not terribly constant," Adrienne huffed.

Maria frowned at Adrienne's caustic tone but Julia ignored it. "Don't worry about Adrienne," I commented to Maria, "she's always been outspoken."

Adrienne looked pleased, even though it was not said to flatter her. She turned to Maria. "And where is your charming husband, Lady Broughton? I've not seen Simon in years."

Before I could respond, Maria said, "He and Patrick are riding over the new land. We expect them home any time now."

"Patrick's here?" Adrienne snatched up that piece of news as eagerly as ever.

Julia grasped it for different reasons. "He's here?" she confirmed, with a weighty look at me.

I smiled quickly, my eyes shining, and she fairly squirmed with curiosity.

But Adrienne hadn't noticed. With undisguised eagerness she breathed, "I can't believe Patrick is home. Oh, I cannot wait to see him again."

"I expected them before now," Maria said glancing toward the French clock on the mantelpiece. "They will surely arrive at any moment."

"That should prove entertaining," Julia muttered, winking in my direction. She went on to tell us how she had embarked on her affair with Deon shortly after he and Celia had returned to Yorkshire. "Oh, it's marvellous, Alex," my friend beamed, "we'll be an instant family. Hopefully it'll all be arranged by the time our baby is born. Deon thinks we should ensure our baby knows his older half-brother and he plans to talk to Celia about how we can do this."

"I think it's so deliciously scandalous," said Adrienne, her eyes shining.

"Don't you just," Julia commented, looking as though she was sucking a bitter lozenge. "You simply thrive on scandal."

"Well, *I* think it is romantic," said Maria, "that true love wins in the end." She threw a quick look at me, "Don't you adore a happy ending, Alex?"

Suddenly the front door banged and the low timbre of masculine voices could be heard. Immediately Adrienne chewed her lips and touched her hair. Julia watched with a smirk.

"Better tell them we're in here, Alex," Maria said, but before the words had left her lips, Pat's head appeared around the door. His eyes immediately found me, but widened in surprise when he spotted our visitors.

Without ceremony, Adrienne leapt to her feet and grasped his hands, dragging him into the room. "Oh, Patrick … you're home … I'd been so worried about you over in Europe … and how well you look … so handsome …" She made a brazen fuss of him, greeting him as warmly as a long lost lover.

He managed to extricate himself and turn to Julia. Hugging her with genuine affection, he placed a kiss on each of her cheeks. Meanwhile, Simon watched with a rather bemused look on his face.

"Patrick, dear," Adrienne patted the seat beside her invitingly, "come, sit by me so you can bring me up to date with the war and all you've been doing."

Given little choice, he obliged and before long her small hand rested daintily on his arm and she was batting her long sooty lashes, talking rapidly and laughing gaily.

As the hour by which social visits were concluded approached, Adrienne lingered, obviously angling for a supper invitation, but Julia had had enough. Pleading fatigue, she rose, prompting Maria to have their coach brought round.

Adrienne continued her incessant prattling, hooking her arm through Patrick's as we walked on to the porch. I watched with amusement as she leaned towards him, her breast pressing his arm, and whispered into his ear – doubtless some kind of invitation. He smiled passively, unwound her arm and came immediately to my side.

It could have been the devil in him, Adrienne's invitation, or the novelty of no longer having to hide our love, that induced him to take my hand and raise my palm to his lips in full view of our visitors.

Julia grinned widely, her freckled face fairly splitting in two. "*I knew it*! I just *knew*, as soon as we arrived today that something had changed. You looked so different, Alex, so *happy*."

"I would have told you, Jules, but today is your day for news."

"Nonsense! Nothing's as important as news like this – and look, you no longer wear your wedding ring. Will you divorce Hamish?"

Simon cleared his throat uncomfortably. "No one has discussed divorce, and we'd prefer that you keep to yourselves, Julia, Miss Morehead, that my sister and Washburn are ... er ..."

"Why so stuffy, Simon?" Julia teased. "They're meant to be together. So what if she's married; we all knew *that* was a mistake." She giggled delightedly and hugged me exuberantly. "Saints alive! Mistakes happen – just ask Deon."

Julia slipped on her gloves and trotted happily down the steps, chattering all the way about the wonders of true love.

Meanwhile Adrienne was clearly seething. Her smooth brow furrowed angrily and two violent, red splotches spread across her pearly cheeks most unflatteringly.

Was she, perhaps, recalling other rejections from Patrick and suddenly understanding their meaning? Probably, judging by the *may-God-strike-you-down-with-a-bolt-of-lightning* glare she aimed in my direction.

"There will be gossip from that corner," Simon remarked as their carriage rounded the bend and disappeared.

"Oh Simon," said Maria. "I do not see the problem."

Simon ushered us all into the parlour before explaining. "The problem is that Zan's left her husband, and now these two are carrying on a liaison – under this roof."

"I can see it may cause a scandal but do we really care what society thinks?" Pat asked.

"Yes!" Simon replied. "I care very much when my children may be involved. They live here too, remember."

"Alex and I mean to be together and if that's too much for your suddenly starchy sensibilities, Sime, then we can remove ourselves."

My brother retreated immediately. "Now, that's not what I meant and you know it."

"So, what *do* you mean, for Christ's sake? You never used to be so straight-laiced. What's happened to you?"

"I don't want the talk and ... after your little display in front of that Morehead girl, the news that Patrick Washburn and his *sister* are ... it'll be all over Yorkshire before dinner tomorrow – London by supper."

"But I don't understand, Simon," I said, going to him and laying my hands on his chest. "Patrick and I are not brother and sister, and it's true, you've never been so squeamish before. In fact, I remember a time when you were –"

"I don't want the talk, that's all." He threw himself on the settee that Adrienne had recently vacated.

"Don't you want them to be happy, Simon?" his wife asked, going to him. "After all Alex's been through, don't you want her to be happy with the man she loves? Imagine if someone told us we could not be together?"

"Of course I want them to be happy but –"

"Provided we're happy in private, right?" Patrick stated bitterly. "Well, I love Alex and I don't care who knows it. We've wasted years – we shall be together regardless of public opinion."

"Christ! Settle down, man!" Simon swore irritably. "I just ask that you not show yourselves off so soon, and further, *think* before you fall into bed at any consequence. You're leaving for Europe – whatever legal battles, scandals, or anything else that erupt while you're over there, Alex'll be facing them without you. And if she ends up with child – what then? I don't want her hurt – and that's the truth. Who knows when you'll return? What if you don't?"

Understanding rose up to slap me back to earth while Patrick dropped to the settee beside Simon and frowned thoughtfully.

"Simon," I knelt before my brother and took his hand. "You are right – I've not seen it that way before. But you have ever been supportive of me – as friend and brother. I'm asking you now: don't think like a brother. I know this will be a battle, but I'm a grown woman. All I ask is that you stand beside me as a friend. I know there'll be talk, but they'll be talking about *me* and it's a price I'm prepared to pay."

Simon sighed. "And if you … I mean, I expect you'll be intimate. What if you become pregnant? What then?"

My face grew hot. Patrick and I had not discussed the possibility of such a relationship, but Maria quickly rescued me. "Simon, how can you behave so?" She stood beside me, glaring down at him with her arms crossed over her bosom. "Their private relationship is not our concern."

Simon groaned and ran a weary hand over his face. "You agree with all this?"

"Yes I do," she said firmly.

"Very well." He shrugged and smiled ruefully. "But I insist that you both be discreet, for all our sakes. It'll not do your cause any favours if you make a public display of yourselves."

"Agreed," Pat said, as Emily announced that supper was being served. The four of us, joined by Maeve, enjoyed a pleasant meal and afterwards we three women left the men to their brandy.

Much later that night, I lay alone in my bed, weary but intensely aware that Patrick's room was only a few doors up the hall. I wondered if he would consider Simon's concerns and not visit me.

I must have slept for I was awakened some time later as he slipped into the bed beside me – still wearing his trousers and shirt.

Immediately, he rolled me in his arms and his mouth found mine in the dark. This time, our passions would not be so easily laid aside. Our hands explored, our mouths tasted. I slid my hands between us and unbuttoned his shirt trailing my fingers over the firm contours of his chest.

He untied the ribbon on my nightdress, and slipping it over my shoulders, followed the brush of his hands with a trail of kisses, across the rise of my breasts then along the valley between them, before moving up to claim my mouth again. The blood raged in my veins and my lungs swelled with the fury of my breathing. My body was screaming for his penetration and I arched against him with a savage adult need I'd never known before.

At last he took his mouth from mine and searched my face through the dark, "Ah, darling girl, do you give me leave to pleasure your sweet body?"

"Oh yes!" I breathed, pulling his face towards me, but he resisted momentarily.

"If we do this," he said huskily, "and Hamish refuses a divorce, you will be consenting to become my mistress. I'll not give you up again. Can you live like that, my love, in a less than socially acceptable position?"

"Like Nelson and Lady Hamilton? Why should we care for the opinions of others? Now that we're reconciled, I'll not give you up either."

"You will come to Devon and live as my wife, in every sense of the word …?"

"But for the signature on the parchment – I am yours, and I will live with you on the moon should you desire it. Besides," I added glibly, "Hamish may well agree."

"Hmm, I doubt it. But tonight is not about Hamish."

He smiled then, and reached to unbutton his trousers. Slipping them off and adding his shirt and my nightdress, we created a pile of clothes on the floor.

And so, witnessed by the moon beyond the window, we consummated our love. The silence of the night was broken by our sighs and murmurings.

His hands and mouth took me to feverish heights of passion I'd never known existed, and I clung to him in a crescendo of crazed delight, crying out as I reached the pinnacle, pulsating dizzyingly as he met me there, held me aloft, and gradually eased me down to earth with caresses, kisses and whispered promises.

Later, we allowed our breathing to return to normal and I wept from pure joy.

He pulled his head back to look at me and, even in the dark, his own eyes were glassy with emotion.

"I think we should spend the days before my departure making love until we are delirious with it," he said. "So now you're an adulteress, my lady mistress, how do you feel?"

I thought about how unfairly I'd judged other women in my naive, inexperienced past, like Mrs Jamieson, Gerrard's lady in Leeds.

"Loved, wanton, strangely sophisticated," I replied.

"Any regrets?"

"None," I replied without hesitation. "It feels so terribly right to be with you – it always did."

Fulfilled after these long, long years of yearning, we talked until the moon had moved well beyond the window, filling the gap in each other's lives from our years of separation. Then we came together, and delighted in each other again, until finally sleep claimed our sated bodies an hour before first light.

I awoke the following morning to find him propped on one elbow, watching me as I slept. Dropping a light kiss on my forehead he said, "Good morning, my love. I did not know how appallingly you snore."

I grinned and stretched languorously. "I don't snore."

"Oh, yes you do. I could barely think for the din, and you're dreadfully off-key with it too. Come, let's get up. I'll help you dress."

We spent the day with Maeve, walking in the gardens, playing cards in the parlour, talking and creating memories to sustain us over the coming months of separation.

And that night, once again, we lay in each other's arms, whispering and loving well into the small hours. We were greedy for each other, and with each minute that passed, we clung together all the more tenaciously.

Our last morning before his departure dawned shrouded in mist. The sun was rising later now that winter approached, and I watched from my bed, as the inky sky paled only slightly and the ghostly shapes beyond the window became trees eerily swathed in fog. Patrick and I rose together and helped each other dress in the half-light.

It was still and grey outside and the sun had not yet risen. The fog lent an otherworldly quality to the morning; we could have been the only man and woman on earth as our walk led us to the orchard where it all began.

He backed me against that same tree and kissed me slowly; his mouth lingering on mine, his breath hot and his tongue erotically tracing my lips.

I veritably swooned with need – I ached with it – would I never have enough of him?

He pulled back and stared into my eyes – his own dark and stormy with passion. "We must wed, as soon as you're free."

"Three and a half years ago," I whispered against his mouth, "we kissed beneath this same tree. We should have married immediately."

"Yes – I was wrong to delay it. I should have spoken with my father."

Later that day in the parlour, I sat on the settee reading, while he rested his head on my lap, eyes closed. I stroked the strands of sun-drenched gold from his forehead and as he looked up at me; I wondered how I could ever have thought him reserved for his soul was laid bare in those green pools. I decided in that moment, my wedding dress would be the colour of his extraordinary eyes.

Rolling on his side, he wrapped his arms around my waist and kissed my abdomen. "Alex, what if you're already … what if our child is in there?"

"I hope it is – it may bring you home sooner.'

"I plan to be home as soon as I am able, regardless." He sighed and sat up, twisting to face me, and frowned thoughtfully. "I want to talk to you about something."

"Oh, don't let's be so serious," I said with a giggle.

"Shh. I have decided to call at Leeds on my way to Hull – I would see the lawyer, Archibald, about your divorce. But I shall also instruct him to make available to you any money you need – no, hear me out – should you decide to rent a cottage or something while you wait for me, or if you just need money for something, *anything*. You mustn't rely on Simon's hospitality."

"But he —"

"You are my responsibility now — particularly if you carry my child."

My stomach tightened anxiously. "How long do you expect to be away?" I dreaded the answer.

He shrugged. "It could be as long as a year — I don't know, it depends where they post me and what they have me doing."

"If I'm with child now —"

"I know   so I must ensure you are well provided for.'

"Oh, why did you agree to go? You must sell your commission. What were you thinking, Pat?"

He sighed in exasperation, "I was thinking I had nothing to remain in England for — Christ, Alex! Don't pick a quarrel on our last day."

"I'm not picking a quarrel, I'm just so ..." I made a helpless gesture. "I'm weary of being separated from you."

"I know — come here," he pulled me against him placatingly, "I know none of this is fair, and I'm expecting so much of you — again. If you prefer, we can wait until I've returned before I talk to the lawyer about the divorce. Then, we can do it together."

"Perhaps," I pondered, "but if there's a baby — I could enlist your father's help. We must be wed as soon as possible."

"Does it matter? We'd love our child no less if we weren't married." He touched my abdomen gently. "Could there be, my love, a baby in there?"

"It's possible," I said, doing a quick calculation in my head. "How would you feel? I can't give you heirs if we're not married."

"I'd only be happier if I could be with you to watch your belly grow and you blossom. And don't worry, you can give me heirs. I can recognise my children as Father did with Sylvie."

My heart stirred and my arms wrapped despairingly about his

neck. Part of me wanted so desperately to be pregnant, but the other part hoped I wasn't, so we could experience it together when he returned.

I turned my face slightly to kiss his temple. I'd never believed it possible to love as much as I did now. I felt vulnerable with it and fearful for his safety. I held him tightly and he chuckled, gently unwinding my arms from his neck.

"It is going to be alright," he smiled reassuringly. "It's not possible that we feel the way we do only to lose one another again, not now. Surely no God could be so cruel."

I felt the tears welling in my eyes and he quickly held up his hand, "Don't do that! Trust me; I'm coming home. And I'll not be so easily put aside this time."

❧

The evening meal was sombre. Maeve's eyes were often misty when levelled on her brother, but she smiled at me. Simon opened a bottle of his finest wine and toasted Patrick's early return.

I'm sure Maeve would like to have sat up all night, making the most of having her brother with us, but just before ten o'clock, Patrick pushed back his chair and took my hand. Maria beamed and Simon tried to feign ignorance when Patrick announced that he and I were retiring for the night.

Maeve let out a bawdy cackle that had me flush to the roots of my hair while Simon glanced sharply at her. "What?" she demanded of him. "Don't be such an old prude Simon, there's no one to know but us."

Simon sighed resignedly. "If you don't return to her Washburn, you'd better be dead, for if you're not, I'll hunt you down and kill you myself."

❧

Upstairs in my room, by the light of a single candle, we slowly undressed one other. Though we'd spent the previous nights together, we'd not paused to pay due homage to each other's body. His was beautiful – lean and muscular, slightly tanned and bearing the scars of battles past. I saw an answering appreciation in his eyes as he laid me across the bed. Kneeling reverently before me, he introduced me to the delicious torment of his mouth and lips, as his tongue flicked tantalisingly down the flat of my stomach and over my hips.

My breathing was ragged and my hands clawed at the counterpane as his mouth moved with agonising deliberation. I writhed under his teasing, opening like a flower beneath his tongue, and I cried out as the world exploded into tiny shards of coloured light.

Afterwards, my head still reeling, he moved over me. Welcoming him with a need born of looming separation we loved aggressively and urgently. In eight hours – less – he would be gone.

Restful in the afterglow of our lovemaking, I fought sleep, clinging avidly to consciousness, not wanting to miss a second with him. But unconsciousness arrived stealthily, and carried my exhausted body on a billowing cloud of serenity.

Was it only minutes later I opened my eyes? Rolling on to my side I watched as he bathed quickly in the cold water from my ewer. Then, wearing only military trousers, he shaved and I imprinted the sight of him on my memory to sustain me until he returned.

Patting his face dry, he saw my reflection in the mirror and smiled. "Like a baby's arse," he said, and came over to rub his fresh-smelling cheek against mine. "Are you coming to wave me off or have you already forgotten me?"

A short time later, I stood on the porch hugging myself against the chill of the morning. Maeve shivered beside me in her nightdress, a woollen wrap about her shoulders and her silver-blonde hair uncombed. We waited for him to come round from the stables with Equus saddled and ready.

Maria and Simon had said their farewells the night before, and Cook had already handed him a parcel of food and returned to her morning duties in the kitchen. She refused to say goodbye, stating stoically that he'd be back before we knew it, and she'd have to stand guard over her fruit pies in case he resumed his old pilfering habits.

The crunching of Equus' hooves on the gravel echoed in the still of pre-dawn. The pretty mare with Patrick astride appeared at the foot of the stairs before us, and I felt a warming inside at the way his hips moved in rhythm with her step, his legs, well-muscled from years of riding, gripped her flanks. She halted before us and he slid down her side.

Maeve let out a sob and rushed into her brother's arms. I remained, irresolutely, where I was. This was the first time in all our years of partings, where I could be honest about my feelings for him, and perhaps because of that, I knew not how to say goodbye.

He kissed his sister's forehead, his gloved hands holding her face, as he whispered to her. She gazed at him, her eyes great, wet pools, and nodded solemnly.

When he turned to me, one arm still about Maeve, he held the other out and I went to him. He drew me against his chest. "Ah, my two most precious creatures," he sighed, hugging us both. I was determined not to cry – it was all I'd done for the last year, and not the way I wanted him to remember our parting.

Maeve released her hold on her brother and stepped back to pull a handkerchief from her sleeve and blow her nose. He took both my hands in his heavy-leathered ones, holding me away so he could look at me.

"I cannot express how I feel," he whispered. "I've always loved you, I hope you believe that, but these last days ..." he uncharacteristically failed to find the words. Instead, he released me and stripped the riding-glove from his right hand. Reaching out he cupped my cheek and his thumb smoothed a wayward tear. "Alex,

I love you more than words, more than life itself. I will be coming home to you as soon as I can, that is my sincere promise to you, my darling *darling* girl. You humble me, you honour me …" he didn't finish for I'd begun to cry.

We kissed then and it was as demanding and aggressive, as it was filled with love and when at last we parted, Maeve's arm slid around my waist and I blinked away the tears to afford a clearer picture of him. He mounted his beautiful horse and nudged her into a deceptively cheerful trot, down the drive and toward the sweeping bend that would take him from our sight.

CHAPTER 31

He was gone.

And I was filled with such hope for the future, hope so reminiscent of that other time he went away, that I began to fear he would not write and things would be as they were before our reconciliation. Perhaps these last few days had all been part of a perverse game on his part.

Yet, each morning upon rising, I listened to my body, alert to the first hint that Patrick's child may dwell within me. I counted the days and trawled my memory to recall the early indicators of my previous pregnancy, but eight days passed and my body showed every sign that I could expect my monthly course.

Inclement weather dictated I remain indoors, so I drifted listlessly about the house, disinterested in my usual pastimes, eventually finding myself in the kitchen where Cook was busily preserving the last of the summer fruits.

Surprised but grateful, she accepted my help and for the next two days, I boiled and bottled, sealed, labelled and stored jars of plums and apples, and the wild berries Maeve and I collected in baskets during our strolls in the forest. The kitchen garden wanted some weeding and the winter vegetables some tending, so, whenever the weather allowed, I was on my knees, trowel in hand, pulling out weeds, aerating the soil around the stems of cabbages, turnips and carrots. I dug up a patch of potatoes and selected a handful to turn back in for the next crop, surprising myself by enjoying the activity. I thinned the rhubarb crowns, carrying the long red tusks into the kitchen by the armload.

"The leaves are poisonous," Cook told me, as I dumped the pile on her scarred work table. "Cut 'em off. I'll get Sanders to take 'em back out."

"I can take them," I volunteered quickly. "Where does he throw them?"

She regarded me speculatively. "Missin' the young lord, eh," she stated flatly. "Throws 'em down back o' t'garden. When they break down, he turns it all back int' ground."

I pushed the kitchen door open with the toe of my boot and the late November sun splashed over my face. The smell of wood smoke from Cook's oven hung in the damp air. As I followed the well-worn path, skirting the kitchen garden, I inspected the sky. Pale blue in its earliest phase of winter, with clouds like whipped egg-whites – the first snows were not far off.

Where was he right at this moment? Did he think of me, or had it all been a dream? Would he write as promised?

Evil serpents of doubt slithered into my mind and I was incapable of holding them back.

Only time would tell.

I found the waste pile and dropped the rhubarb leaves on top. Upon returning to the kitchen, I found Maria chatting with Cook about a menu she was planning for a Christmas dinner.

She turned as I came in. "I thought to invite your friend, Miss Chapman, Alex, would you like that?"

I shrugged. I wasn't being churlish for I recognised Maria's attempt to cheer me, but I didn't want to be cheered, in fact I was feeling quite odd, somewhat vague and distracted – perhaps I was coming down with a cold. I thanked her, saying I would enjoy Julia's company. "But I think I shall rest for a half hour or so, Maria. I didn't sleep very well last night."

"Oh, before I forget," Maria said. "A letter arrived for you. It is on the hall-stand."

The envelope was crumpled, and bore the grime of the many hands it had passed through on its way from the coast. Patrick's assured handwriting addressed *Miss Alexandra Broughton* and I smiled at his defiance in addressing me by my unmarried name. It was the first time he'd ever written to me – in all our years of knowing each other – and its arrival, sooner than I'd expected, suggested he had mailed it before leaving England.

Suddenly light as air, I trotted up the stairs to my room. Placing the letter carefully on my bed, I stripped off my garden-stained gown and as I washed, my eyes kept sliding to it.

Finally, donning a warm nightdress, I slid beneath the counterpane, took up the letter and slipped a finger beneath its seal. It was a single page, containing what appeared to be a song. I read.

Sing with me a song of colour
In shifting light and shade
Step with me through prose and rhythm
A hymn of love I've made

To look upon you – darling girl
With eyes so clear and new
Revive the barren love in me
Accept my pledge to you

For mine's the oath of honesty
In a bitter stricken age
My allegiance and my reverence
Unto you at every stage

Sing our song when times grow dark
In faith, when e'er you do
For trust and love will ever be
My legacy unto you

Two year old Dudley staggered besottedly around Meg's legs. His cheeks glowed like shiny pink apples and his eyes, so like his father's, sparkled merrily. "He thinks you are a fairy," Maria said, and Meg giggled and performed a little dance.

Simon was assisting one of the tenant farmers whose roof needed repair, leaving his womenfolk to enjoy the warmth of the sun streaming into the morning room. Maria held Rosalie in her arms and was humming softly while the baby slept and Maeve sat nearby making a sketch of mother and child.

Meg tiptoed through the shards of sunlight on the rug, fluttering her arms, dipping and twirling, and Dudley squealed in delight, clapping his pudgy little hands together.

Maria turned her serene face to me and her expression was thoughtful. "Are you feeling alright, Alex? You look pale."

"I am tired," I admitted.

She nodded. "Could you be with child?"

I'd expected the question would arise and managed to control my reaction, despite the hope that grew within me with each day that passed. "I don't know."

"Have you had your flow this month? You could be, you know."

"Perhaps, but I've been with child before and thought to know the signs."

She smiled encouragingly. "It can be different every time."

"Then, I shall keep hoping."

"If that is your hope," Maeve said, without looking up from her sketch-book, "I shall hope it too."

Impulsively, I squeezed her hand, then smoothed away the sentimental dampness at my eyes.

"Weeping? Afternoon sleeps?" Maria cocked a smooth black eyebrow. "And you say the signs are not there?"

❧

Later that afternoon, I stood on the only sunny path in the garden as Jemima sniffed and attended to nature's call beneath a tree. A light breeze carried the distinctive scents of wood smoke and distant snow, and fluttered my pelisse. I crammed my hands into the pockets of my dress and hoped Jemima would be quick. The beeches and birches in the park clawed their gnarled fingers towards the pale sky, while the roses and trees in the orchard were stumpy and pruned back in readiness for the winter.

I hadn't heard Gerrard approaching. I turned quickly when he said, "May I join you?"

He'd arrived from Leeds the previous day and seemed to be enjoying the slower pace afforded by the untroubled lifestyle of Broughton Hall.

He offered his arm and I tucked my hand into the warm crook of his elbow. We strolled and I remained silent, knowing he wished to say something. He began without preamble. "Lass, before Patrick returned to Europe, he visited me in Leeds. He explained that you are reconciled and would wed, and asked me to take care of several things. Firstly, to bring Equus here – which I have already done. He'd not wanted to take her with him to Europe. Then, he asked me to make the necessary arrangements to ensure your financial well-being – he would have you independent in his absence. This also is done. My son gave a clear directive that you should have unencumbered access to his finances."

I nodded. "I understand. But I don't need any money. I told him that."

"Nevertheless …" he shrugged, then frowning, he reached for his ear lobe.

"What is it?" His uneasy gesture troubled me.

"Alex, I've spoken to the family lawyer and I am advised that in order to divorce, the conditions of the separation must be outlined in a particular document. It is called a Deed of Separation and Hamish must agree to it. You see, common law does not recognise you, so –"

"Because I'm a woman?"

"Er … yes. Mr Archibald – he was your papa's lawyer, and it was he who drew up the original marriage agreement under your mother's instruction – has agreed to act for you. He will draft the papers, which must be signed by himself and Hamish."

"That seems rather simple," I said.

"It's not really because then we must petition the Court of Chancery to have it enforced."

"I see. And they may choose not to enforce it?"

"They may."

The path we strolled along meandered round the back of the house, where a barn accommodated the family's coaches, a cart and assorted farming equipment. The stables were nearby and the horses within could be heard snorting and moving about in their fresh hay.

"Can we not seek an annulment?" I suggested. "Surely that would be easier?"

"On what basis? You were betrothed for years. It was a legally drafted contract."

"He would not lay with me, he chose others – is that not grounds?"

He shook his head with a grimace. "What man would not seek his wife's bed? That a child was not produced would be deemed your fault. No, m'dear, I have to tell you, that even if Hamish does agree to the Deed of Separation, a divorce will be difficult."

I studied his profile as we returned to the house, growing jowly now as his years advanced, but still jovial and quick to smile, though at this moment he looked as grim as I felt.

We continued our walk in silence.

∾

With each morning that dawned, and the continued absence of a certain physical event, I grew more hopeful, until finally, six weeks after Patrick's departure, I knew without doubt that I carried his child – and how I rejoiced! Hugging the knowledge to myself – it being too precious to share – my spirit rested in a serene place while my thoughts centred on my lover.

By the second week in December the first snows had fallen. I leaned on the porch balustrade surveying the seamless white landscape before me. The Great Oak, twenty yards to my right, looked grey and skeletal in its winter nudity. Its sturdy boughs seemed to slump wearily beneath their heavy white overlay. The rest of the garden was dry and shrunken from winter's frosty caress.

I straightened as Simon approached, his steps measured to enable little Dudley's short, stumpy legs to keep apace. The child's rapid breathing pumped plumes of vapour into the frozen air.

"Well?" I blew into my chilled hands as I spoke and watched anxiously as Simon scooped up his son and balanced him on his hip.

He shrugged as he mounted the stairs. "I'm no horse doctor, but looks to me like she has some kind of chill."

"Can horses get such a thing?"

"Remember that old cob we had years ago – the one with the freckles and sway back? I recall his coming down with something similar, and that stableman of Papa's wanted to shoot it."

I laughed, emitting a damp cloud. "Until I made such a fuss that he finally agreed to treat its illness simply to shut me up."

"That's the one." Simon stood beside me now and Dudley was squirming to be put down. Running freely was still a novelty for the little boy and he took every opportunity to practice. "Careful Dudley, it's slippery."

In the weeks since Gerrard had brought Equus home, she'd gradually gone off her food, had developed a streaming nose, and her breathing had grown heavy with a rasping sound accompanied by a dry cough. I was desperately worried and had pleaded with Simon to help.

"Do you remember what the stableman did?" I asked.

"I do, in fact I made close notes – even then I wanted to be a doctor – stay away from the steps, Dudley."

"Then you'll be able to help her?" I said, hopefully.

"If I can find my old book."

"So, what are you waiting for?" I took my nephew's hand and Simon draped his arm over my shoulders, smiling at my anxiety as we entered the house.

"Don't worry, I won't let anything happen to that horse. Now, when you write to Patrick don't tell him about Equus. He's better things to worry about."

"I was planning to write this afternoon."

"And will you tell him your news?"

We paused in the entry hall. "My news?"

"It's not difficult to spot a woman aglow with anticipation." He stroked a stray hair from my cheek, "I'm not mistaken, am I?"

I flushed slightly and returned his smile. "I am the happiest woman alive. Now all I want is for him to come home. Do I ask too much?"

He shook his head. "Sometimes I look at Maria and Rosalie, and little Dudley here, and I feel truly blessed. No, I don't think you ask too much."

My smile turned sad and I gently touched his scarred cheek. "You have your happiness with Maria and your children, but there was a cost. What must I pay I wonder?"

"Perhaps you've paid in advance? C'mere." He pulled me against his chest. "May I be the first to congratulate you, Zan, on your expectancy. For all our difference of opinion, Patrick is a good man, strong and kind. I was wrong about him and I am glad it's you he loves. But it does not stop me worrying over you."

"I know," I breathed into his neck, "and I love you for it."

We separated to find Maria leaning against the newel post, smiling indulgently. "It is easy to guess what you celebrate," she said, coming forwards to embrace me.

∾

That night over dinner I told Gerrard and Maeve my happy news. Maeve, as predicted, was very excited. Gerrard, however, smiled politely and said all the right things, but his pleasure didn't show in his eyes. Later, while Maria and Simon attended Rosalie and Dudley's bedtime, and Meg practised her reading on Maeve, he leaned towards me, his fleshy face ruddy in the glow of the fire.

"Lass," he said quietly, "have you thought through the consequences of all this?"

I frowned in confusion. "I'm not sure what you mean."

"You're married to one man and pregnant by another. Considering there's doubt you will attain a divorce … Have you thought about this, is all I ask?"

"Of course I've thought about it, but … what else can I do? I must seek a divorce, for without it Pat and I shall never be married."

"Do you not think you and Patrick were perhaps … hasty?"

I shifted in my seat uncomfortably. "This is not the time for recriminations, Gerrard. Whether it was wise or no, we would deny ourselves no longer. We want to be together and if I cannot achieve a divorce we shall live together without marriage."

He sat back slightly. "You would do that? What about Simon? Have you not considered the dishonour you may bring to his door?"

"I wonder," my voice was sharper than intended, "do you experience such compunction when you visit with Mrs Jamieson?"

I made to leave but he stayed me with a hand on my arm. "I meant no offence Lass, I was simply trying to prepare you —"

"Patrick and I will be together," I stated vehemently. "With or without my divorce, and if that brings too much shame to this family … I'm sorry but for once I'm doing what *I* want, not what's best for the family. I did that last time and look where it got me."

"Good heavens, Alex, sheath your claws! I'm concerned for you. I doubt you'll obtain a divorce and once your pregnancy becomes evident people will begin to talk. Even if Patrick is beside you, it will be a very difficult time."

I calmed slightly with the sense of his words and he went on. "Mr Archibald sent word that he has drafted the Deed of Separation. He recommends offering a modest financial settlement to Hamish."

"I know Hamish. He'll require more than a modest settlement – at least enough to bolster his pride, as well as strengthen his business."

"Then I shall instruct Archibald to double his offer and have the document sent forthwith, if you are in accord.

"Thank you," I said adding contritely, "And … I apologise for my attack just now."

He leaned forwards and dropped a fatherly kiss on my forehead. "It's just that I worry."

CHAPTER 32

I stirred beneath the bedclothes and yawned. My breath froze in
the icy air and I shivered, pulling the coverlet close about my
neck. I guessed it to be somewhere around half-past-seven o'clock
by the weak and watery light from the window, and I could see
threatening, blue-bellied clouds hanging heavily in the sky. Spring
was making a valiant effort to impress itself upon the landscape, but
winter clung tenaciously, and the days, though growing gradually
longer, remained very cold.

With the advancement of my pregnancy, I was sleeping later in
the mornings. It was five months since I'd seen Patrick – though it
felt much longer – and my belly was larger than it had been at this
stage of my previous pregnancy.

The door creaked softly and Emily peered around it. "Oh,
ma'm, you're awake."

She came into the room and shut the door behind her. Simon
had assigned the maid to assist with my needs. She was cheerful and
diligent, and I'd grown quite fond of her – though it was difficult
to reconcile this efficient woman with the young maid I'd seen
dallying in the forest with a footman all those years ago. Emily's
disdain of idle gossip made her unique among her peers.

"Good morning, Em," I said from my cocoon.

"Ooh, it is cold in 'ere," she muttered and poked aggressively at the logs in the fireplace. Enticed from my bed by its warmth, I scampered across the rug and stood with my nightdress raised before the fire, as Emily left to fetch some warm water for my morning ablutions.

Jemima sighed in her basket and rolled creakily on to her back, eyeing me hopefully.

"There'll be no belly rubs until I'm warm and dressed," I told her as the door opened to admit Emily and two maids carrying pails of hot water.

I bathed as Emily straightened my room and made up the bed, then having completed my toilet, Emily helped me to dress. My distended stomach bulged beneath the Empire-waisted gown and I smoothed my hands down the front, caressing the firm roundness of Patrick's child, my child. This wonder swelled my heart with love for it and its father, in a way – to my deep remorse – I'd not experienced with my previous pregnancy. But that wasn't to say my little lost girl was not wanted or loved, for she was – terribly. It was simply that my love for Patrick eclipsed my love for everything else – and always had.

I looked up from my reverie and found Emily watching with a gentle smile. "It is good to see you so content, ma'm," she said, then quickly dropped her eyes self-consciously. "He's a nice lookin' man, that Master Pat. That un'll be a nice lookin' babe."

I was smiling as I joined my family for breakfast, passing the silver tray where Mrs Grainger left the mail. I gathered the six envelopes and flicked through them hopefully as I wandered into the dining room.

Simon was in the middle of reading an article from a newspaper to Maria, as she spread boiled egg on a slice of toast. Two-and-a-half-year-old Dudley was in his high chair, accepting spoons of fruit compote from his nurse, and Maeve was pouring coffee from the pretty silver pot Gerrard had brought her from Leeds for her twentieth birthday.

Simon peered over the paper at her. "How many's that then?"

She snorted derisively, "Only the second, if you must know."

"It is known to be habit-forming," Maria pointed out.

"I like it," Maeve said, deliberately hanging her bottom lip out in imitation of Dudley when reprimanded. "Besides," she added brightly, "it gives me energy. I feel I could run all around the garden, don't I, little man?" She leaned over to tickle Dudley's belly and the little boy gurgled happily.

"Run around the garden screaming all the way," said Simon. "'Morning Zan, brought the mail have you?"

"Three for Simon," I said, dropping the letters beside his plate, "one for Maeve and two for me."

"*Two* for you," Maeve said archly. "Aren't you popular this morning."

"Evidently." After five months of letters from Patrick, I recognised his hand immediately on one of them and put it aside to read later in privacy. The other I turned over curiously, but it gave no clue as to its sender, though the hurried script on the front seemed vaguely familiar and there was an ink splotch beside my name – Lady Alexandra Glendenning.

I took my seat and helped myself to toast and fruit, and a cup of tea. As I poured, I studied the mysterious letter. Curiosity bested me and I reached for it.

"Who is it from?" Maeve asked impatiently.

I didn't respond – I was too busy reading.

And as I read, my heart swelled with happiness. "It's from Quinn," I said at last. "He writes to tell me that little Kathy is doing well. She is over a year old now, of course, and he says she has her father wrapped about her finger."

"Well, that's not hard to believe," Simon said and Dudley showed a mouthful of stewed apple.

I smiled and exchanged a knowing glance with Maria, "As Dudley and Rosalie have *their* father."

My brother shrugged. "I don't know what you mean. Anyway, Quinn, by all accounts, seems a decent chap."

"He is. He doesn't yet know that Patrick and I are reconciled. I shall write to him this afternoon."

Later in my room, I tore open Patrick's letter and settled myself in the chair next to the hearth.

5 March 1817

My Darling,

I trust this letter finds you well and happy.

I have been posted to an ill-tempered garrison town near Bologne in the north of France where considerable labour is required. I have been given a small command, and our work is to assist the regional forces in maintaining order in these parts. Despite a harsh winter, small insurgent uprisings of mutinous locals, wanting us removed from the region now that Napoleon is defeated, from time to time erupt and our men are required to quell these, as well as assist with the building and repair of housing and roads destroyed by the armies.

But the Spanish are an ungrateful bunch. For all we did to support them, they are reluctant to assist us now. Such is the nature of humans; we must continue to battle one another even after the war is done. We are kept very busy with the whole business. Nevertheless, my thoughts return to you regularly, and I wish fervently that I could be holding you each night and weaving our plans for the future.

You have a lot to answer for, my darling girl, for up until this last tour, I've been eager to pursue the life of a career soldier, with all the excitement and stimulation that world offers. Now, I've tasted, however briefly, the contentment to be found in the quietude of life with the object of one's affection. I catch myself daydreaming of the future we shall build together, and I find soldiering no longer holds my interest. I long to come home to you, to the dereliction of my duties here — my heart, as they say, is no longer in it.

I have made my commanding officer aware of this fact, and have been advised that my commitment over the years has been held as an example to others, and my work duly appreciated.

Such model behaviour on my part was not planned but has proved rather convenient. As, therefore, a gesture of gratitude for past services, I am to be released from duty at the beginning of May. I shall surrender my commission and embrace the life of a landed gentleman.

My one love, I shall be home for your birthday — and what a birthday it will be! I cannot describe here what I intend your present to be — though I suspect you'll be able to guess.

And so, I shall leave that thought with you, for I am called away, and the sooner I get on with it — the sooner I return to you.

I remain, your own,

PW

He was coming home. He loved me and he was coming home. I pressed the crisp page to my breast and wept.

Simon was in his study when I told him the news.

"So all the pawns are in place," he said, grimly.

"What do you mean?"

He shrugged. "Do you never get the feeling that things were so out of your own control that some higher being, with a malicious sense of humour, was having himself a grand old time at your expense?"

"Aren't you the cheerful one!"

"Take you and Pat, for example. So much against you, you'd be forgiven for thinking the dice were loaded right from the beginning. So many events you had no influence over, yet they had immense impact on you."

"I hadn't thought of it. I never suspected you were so superstitious. Nevertheless, *I* always hoped."

"Yes you did, didn't you," he smiled at me. "Good for you, Zan."

CHAPTER 33

Finally, the weather turned and the heralds of spring burst forth in a glorious explosion of colour and industry. The white and pink blossoms in the orchard were abuzz with insect activity and the lavender, jonquils and freesias filled the air with their heady scent. I picked a path through the roses, a basket hooked over an arm and a pair of scissors in my hand. Selecting a half-opened specimen the colour of a ripe apricot, I cut it and touched it to my nose. Its fresh, distinctive fragrance filled my senses and I placed it in my basket before moving to the next.

Across the drive, Maria and Simon lounged in chairs beneath the Great Oak with Rosalie at their feet, while Maeve frolicked in the grass with Dudley, tossing a blue leather ball between them. The breeze lifted my hair with a chill reminder that winter had not quite done with us yet. It carried fragments of conversation, interspersed with Dudley's childish chortling and the merry jangling of the bells within his ball.

I cut the roses discriminately, planning to use a large, crystal vase to make an elegant arrangement. My eyes lit on a bloom, the colour of snow with a blush of pale-pink on its lips. Pausing irresolutely, I debated whether I ought to cut it or leave it as nature intended.

As I pondered, a bee arrived and delved within the flower's interior and I watched in wonder, my problem resolved.

"Alex!"

Straightening, I followed the direction of Maeve's extended arm as an unknown coach lumbered around the bend in the drive. A pair of sweat-stained bays drew the coach up to the porch, snorting and tossing their heads.

Maria, with Rosalie in her arms, stood beside Simon and Maeve, ready to greet the unexpected visitors. I joined them, watching curiously as a footman in unfamiliar grey livery threw open the door with brisk efficiency. He unfolded the steps and handed my mother from the coach.

I felt myself gaping in surprise for Mother, so attractive in my memory, was lined and thin, considerably aged these three years and more since I'd last seen her, though closer inspection revealed the unremitting steely glint in her blue-grey eyes.

Eleanor, in time-honoured tradition, followed closely behind, still wearing her pinched face and frighteningly red wig. She pointedly ignored our assembly and occupied herself by straightening her travelling costume.

Mother reached into the coach and extracted a small, swarthy child endowed with the thickest black curls of any child in creation. This small person could be none other than my niece and, through no fault of her own, the epicentre of my troubles.

Her wide eyes returned our stare and she demanded, in an incongruously mature voice, "Who are these people, Gran-mama?"

My mother was spared her reply as a third woman exited the coach.

Anne accepted the footman's hand with courtly grace and stood before us in an elegant, blue-velvet travelling gown. She cocked her head coquettishly to one side, causing a coiled rope of chestnut hair to tumble forwards over her shoulder.

"Hello everyone," she greeted brightly. "Mother and I decided it was well time we paid a visit … in spring. Broughton Hall is so beautiful in spring."

My stomach clenched and I fought the urge to be ill from the sheer effrontery of her. She was so sure of herself, so completely without shame or remorse. Sweat broke on my lip and my heart raced wildly. I opened my mouth to speak but before the words had even formed in my mind, Maeve shrieked and rushed at Anne in a passion of feline rage.

"How dare you show your face! After what you did to my brother … you spiteful, conniving, selfish bitch!"

"Maeve, that is quite enough!" Mother declared, but the feisty little elf stood three yards from my smug sister and hurled abuse in language that would have Simon's tenants blushing, including one or two choice expletives in Italian.

Anne, to her credit lifted her chin and eyed her erstwhile companion condescendingly. "How dare you speak so to me!"

She held herself arrogantly, so arrogantly that I could stand it no longer. Purposefully, I marched towards her and she turned to me in hopeful solidarity. Thus, she was facing me and unprepared when I raised my hand and slapped her so hard her head snapped and my palm stung with the impact.

Anne screeched with outrage and burst into tears, at which point Mother instructed Eleanor, with a barely contained tremor in her voice, to take the child into the house.

Eleanor, ever one to derive malicious pleasure from conflict, took her time gathering the little girl away. Shaking with the force of my anger, and an odd mixture of pride and horror at what I'd done, I stood firmly beside Maeve as her trembling fist grasped my hand.

"What is the meaning of this peasant-like behaviour?" Mother rounded on Maeve and me. "And you," she aimed her finger at Simon, "standing there like a tree stump, condoning this in the foreground of the family seat. Is this — oh, for heavens sake, shut up Anne – is this the type of behaviour you foster in those within your care?"

"I would disagree with their actions, Mother, but stand behind them for their reasons," my brother stated steadily.

"You're not fit to wipe … my … my boots …" Anne sobbed, "and … you have the … cheek to …"

"Shut *up* Anne," Mother insisted. "You, I can *almost* understand," she thrust a finger toward Maeve, "some misguided sibling loyalty no doubt, but not you … Alexandra, what has got into you?"

Standing before my mother, as fearful of her wrath as I had been as a child, my courage failed and I was unable to find words.

Her eyes sifted scornfully over me, "Why, look at you," she sneered. "You're pregnant. Pregnant and coming the fisticuffs like some taproom wench. Where *is* Hamish?" She looked around as though expecting him to appear at any moment. No one dared answer.

"Clearly, he's not been firm enough with you. Don't tell me this is all in defence of that degenerate whoremongering brother of yours?"

Maeve stiffened and I clung to her arm, wary of this unexpected anger in her. "Don't you speak about my brother that way! If it hadn't been for *her*," she flicked her hand disdainfully in Anne's direction, "he'd have married Alex. Instead he's –"

"I don't care!" Mother snarled. "What a fine homecoming this is! She marched towards the house, "Maria, order tea, I'm parched."

She mounted the steps to the house she'd been lady of for so many years, stripping off her gloves as she did so.

I turned to watch her and caught Simon's eye. "*Tell her,*" he mouthed.

Anne hurried after her as Mother strode into the house, my sister glaring at me as she passed, a distinct four-fingered welt reddening her cheek.

"You have to tell her," Maeve said beside me. Her jaw was

tight and angry; red stains marred her normally even complexion. "Come, I'll be with you."

Mother and Anne were in the parlour. Eleanor – never too far from the action – and the child were with them.

Simon stood in the doorway, his shoulder braced against the frame. He moved aside to allow Maria to enter. "Eleanor, perhaps you could take the child to the kitchen for cake," she suggested.

"Her name's Domenica," Anne said, wiping her nose with a scrap of lace-edged linen. "Go with Eleanor, now, there's a good girl."

"Tell Mrs Grainger to bring a pot of tea while you're out there," Mother ordered, as Maria followed Eleanor and Domenica from the room, gathering little Dudley on her way. "See that tea is brought quickly, Eleanor. One could die of thirst here."

To her credit, Domenica had remained unresponsive during the quarrel outside. Where other children may have reacted in fright or confusion, her great black eyes had observed with mute interest the behaviour of her two aunts and mother.

After the children and Eleanor had gone, I turned to Mother, but she forestalled me. "I want an explanation, Alexandra, Maeve. *What* is going on here? This is a family, Alexandra; you are a married woman, carrying a child no less. Is this any way to conduct yourself?"

"Alex." Simon levelled his gaze on me significantly.

"Mother –" I said, but broke off as Emily entered, settling a tea tray on a table. She bobbed politely, then closed the parlour door behind her.

I started again. "Mother, there's something … I must tell you that Hamish … he's in Scotland … I'm here without him because … because I have left him." I watched as her chin pulled back indignantly. She opened her mouth to speak but I leapt in pre-emptively, "I left him over a year ago. I will be, with Gerrard's help, seeking a divorce."

She rose slowly to her feet, angry colour flooding her face.

"*You what!* A *divorce?* And Gerrard's *abetting* you in this? Oh no, this family will have no such scandal, thank you very much. Oh heavens, Alexandra, you always were so air-headed. You must immediately take yourself back …" suddenly her eyes widened and she hesitated. "You left him over a year ago? That is what you said?"

I nodded slowly and breathed carefully.

She pointed to my belly. "Then … whose is *that?*" She blanched, suspicion stealing across her face. "Good grief," she whispered, collapsing into her seat. "Say it, Alexandra, just say it."

"It's … Patrick's baby," I bowed my head, not in shame, but because I couldn't countenance the anger I knew would be on her face. So, I was studying my hands when I heard it, soft at first, a low bubbling gurgle that grew, finally bursting from Anne's throat in the most undignified, hysterical laughter I'd ever heard from my elegant, pretentious sister.

We all watched wordlessly, as she doubled over on the settee, her eyes streaming, arms clutching her stomach. "Oh!" she gasped, "Oh! That's the funniest … oh my … I cannot believe it … he got at you again, did he?" She dabbed at her eyes with her handkerchief. "He did you again and … where is he? In Europe, I suppose … again! Just like the last time … Oh Mother … it's too funny …!"

"Enough Anne," Mother sounded very weary all of a sudden.

"But … Mother —"

"Enough, I said," she turned to me and sighed heavily. "Alexandra, how could you be so clumsy?"

I gaped at her. "*Clumsy?*"

"There are ways around accidents like these happening. I'd have thought a married woman of your age …"

"We were not clumsy, Mother. We love each other. We were happy for this to happen."

"Hmph," scoffed Anne. "He got you again …"

"You're just jealous because he didn't want you," Maeve hissed, her elfin face twisted viciously. "He never wanted you, but you set your cap at him because you'd ruined your own life and wanted his money and title to put it right."

"Oh, you know all about it, don't you!" sneered Anne.

"Shut up the pair of you!" Mother snapped. "Alexandra, start again. How long has this been going on?"

"We have loved each other for many years, Mother. That's why I never wanted to marry Hamish. That's why I was so upset when Anne showed up *claiming* to be carrying Pat's child," I shot a glare across the room at my sister. "Her lies changed everything."

"Love doesn't enter into it," Mother responded dully. "And how could you know love? You've not experienced anything of life. In any case, your marriage was contracted as a mutually beneficial agreement to suit two families. And so fortunate! Alexandra, I never dreamed I'd make such a match for you! You were never going to marry Patrick."

Her eyes scanned the three girls before her. "Don't any of you understand? It is not about love. Married love is for the lesser people. Love for *our* kind is for love affairs – Alexandra have your love affair with Patrick, if you must, but it was very foolish of you to get with child by him. You are married to Hamish, and that will not change. If a married woman is discreet, she may love where she chooses. Do you see?"

I wanted to scream with frustration; I wasn't having a love affair with Patrick. I was *in love* with him. I wanted to marry him, live with him, bear his children. Besides that – Mother was clearly forgetting her own unplanned pregnancy to Gerrard all those years ago … or maybe it had not been unplanned at all …

"Perhaps I can help," Simon spoke for the first time. "It appears that the depth of feeling between them is genuine and quite overwhelming. I've witnessed the impact of separation on both of them individually, and … Mother, I neither condoned nor encouraged their relationship, but to see them together … even *you* would be hard pressed to keep them apart."

All the while Simon spoke, Anne had the decency to study her lap, but now she looked up. "You do not honestly think he loves you do you?" she said to me nastily. "He's a lothario – only ever interested in the conquest."

Mother snorted rudely. "I certainly witnessed plenty of that behaviour when he was at court, I can tell you –"

"Why are we discussing this?" I cried. I got to my feet and stood looking around the room at them all. "I married Hamish because I fell for Anne's deceit and no other reason. If not for Anne, I'd never have married Hamish. It was a mistake; my entire marriage was violent and fruitless. Old Lord Elginbury was so desperate to have an heir, he even wrote Hamish out of his will unless a child was produced. To this day Hamish receives no income, but even the threat of destitution could not entice him to lay with me."

"Fascinating," Anne commented nastily.

Ignoring her, I addressed Mother, "I intend to live my life with Patrick; whether sanctified by marriage or no, it matters not to either of us. Maeve," I turned to my lover's sister, "I thank you for your support and am proud to have you stand beside me, but as for you, Anne," my own sister was regarding me with an expression of bored contempt, "I cannot believe we are related. You are selfish and deceitful and had I told Mother of your own exploits – with servants no less – she'd not have been so quick to believe your lies. I want nothing more to do with you."

The shock registered on Anne's face but I was not finished. "Mother, I know you've always tried to do what you felt was best for this family, and I have done my duty. Now it's my turn and in this I will not move. I will not be returning to Hamish."

Finally, I turned to my brother. "Simon, I cannot express my gratitude for your hospitality but I cannot impose upon you any longer, nor shall I remain beneath the same roof as Anne."

"Where will you go?" Maeve jumped to her feet. "Will you go to Waterville? I'll go with you."

"Wherever I go I shall appreciate your company."

"No, Zan, you've no reason to leave," Simon said.

"I'll not have to go far if I don't want to." I shot a smug glance in Anne's direction, "Patrick has given me unencumbered legal access to his finances. I may even rent a house of my own, if I so choose."

"Hmph!" snorted Anne, while Mother, for once, looked rather impressed.

"No," Simon repeated. "This is your home for as long as you want. It is Anne who's not welcome."

Anne gasped while Mother leapt to her defence, "Simon! Of course you're not serious."

"But I am," my beloved brother assured her. "I've not seen two people more destroyed by spiteful lies. She has a lot to answer for, does Anne, but she'll not be doing it here. Mother, you're welcome to stay, but Anne, I want you out by tomorrow evening."

"Oh, you've always sided with Alex," Anne cried, angrily. Her face became flushed and twisted into an ugly mask. "You and she have always hated me."

"That's not true," I said calmly.

"Of course it's true," she shouted with growing hysteria. "You were always having your games at my expense and … always laughing at me … your petty secrets and all …"

Mother went to calm her but Anne would have none of it. She was gathering her things and dropped a glove in her distress. Cursing colourfully, she retrieved it, all the while abusing Simon and me. "*Eleanor!*" she screamed at the full pitch of her lungs.

"Heavens Anne, don't shriek so," Mother said, frowning.

"*Eleanor!*" Anne bellowed, ignoring her. "Bring Domenica here." She turned to me. "Well, I suppose you think you've won. But I'll get you for this, don't think I won't."

"There was nothing to win," I said placatingly.

Eleanor appeared in the doorway holding the hand of my niece.

The child's black-velvet eyes, framed by long lashes blinked at her mother in bewilderment.

"Oh, you think you've won alright, you always do," Anne snarled. "You always get just what you want. You didn't consider that I could have married him and secured this family's fortunes."

"And Patrick's interests didn't factor?" Simon commented dryly. "You've never thought of anyone other than yourself, Anne. Money and position ran close seconds. Patrick never loved you, but …" he turned to me, "he's always loved you, Alex. I know that now and I saw the signs often enough … when you're young you don't think of things like that. When he and I first went to Europe he missed you terribly … I puzzled over the reason for it – at the time I assumed you were simply friends – he was so busy chasing whores that I didn't consider he could truly love someone."

My brother drew in his breath and straightened. "Anne, go upstairs to your old room and rest for the night. I'll have a meal sent up for you and your little girl. Then, you must leave tomorrow."

"Spare me your grudging hospitality," she snapped. "I would not spend one night beneath this roof. Mother, are you coming?"

Mother looked from Simon to me with a new expression on her face and slowly she smiled. A decade seemed to slip from her weary face. "Yes, I too saw the signs but stubbornly clung to the Elginbury match – I thought it a wonderful opportunity. I often questioned how it was the two of them rubbed along so well, but how easy it is to disregard the things that don't follow one's plans." She rose then and gathered her gloves and hat. "Good luck to you, daughter," she said, with uncharacteristic benevolence. "I shall go with Anne."

Maeve and I watched their departure from the porch, and she linked her arm through mine. "Thank you for your support," I said. Our eyes lingered on the departing coach.

"Thank you for loving my brother."

As we turned towards the house, I said, "I didn't know I was capable of such violence. Twice now, I've struck someone in anger, and both times Patrick was the cause."

"Anne today, but who was your other victim?"

"Patrick himself," I said with a sheepish smirk.

"Ah yes, he did tell me about that. I understand you delivered a fair wallop."

"Belted him. He would not admit he loved me – what was I to do?"

We both laughed at that, but she quickly sobered. "We burned some bridges today, Alex. Any regrets?"

"Only that I'll not get to know my niece; she looked a sweet thing."

"Yes, and quite undeserving of such a mother."

CHAPTER 34

I stared fearfully at the envelope. Patrick's handwriting stalked across its face and I could not bear to read it. It wanted only weeks, perhaps days, until his promised return and a letter at this juncture surely brought news that he'd been delayed. I was loathe to read those dreaded words so I sought Maeve.

Without difficulty, I found her stretched on a chaise longue in the morning room, her nose buried in an archaeologist's handbook. I stood beside her and thrust the envelope at her. Her pale brows came together as she stared up at me, "What's this?"

"A letter from Patrick. You must read it for me."

She made no move to take it. "Why?"

"Because it carries bad news – I'm certain – and I could not bear … you must read it and tell me what it says."

"Oh Alex …" she said with a sigh and took the letter. Breaking the seal revealed two pages, and I could see they were covered in writing – he'd evidently gone to great lengths to explain himself.

I watched as her eyes briefly skimmed the page. "Alex –"

"You haven't read it properly."

"I've no need to – no, listen to me – he writes that he misses you and … it's too private, here – read it yourself."

"I can't!"

"Don't be ridiculous," she snapped impatiently. "Any woman would love for such things to be written to her."

She rose and thrust the offending pages into my hand. "Start at the second page, cowardly-cat!" she said. She closed the door on her way out.

Separating the pages, I saw immediately the second contained what appeared to be a song – words accompanied by musical chords, and a warm tide of relief flooded over me as I began to read.

If only you could see me love, emboldened by the night
The stars grow bright, my heart's delight
And dreams hung from the moon my love,
and dreams hung from the moon

The sky belongs to you my love, my prayers will guard your sleep
And though you weep, my promise to keep
Your dreams hung from the moon my love,
your dreams hung from the moon

I chart a course to you my love, and tho' my aim be true
O'er distant lands and drifting sands
My dreams hung from the moon my love,
my dreams hung from the moon

To track the morning star my love, return-ed unto you
Love's beacon bright, my guiding light
And dreams hung from the moon my love,
our dreams hung from the moon

My gladdened heart throbbed with delight. Turning now to the first page, I read of his army discharge and travel plans and was vaguely aware of the bell at the door and Atchison going to answer it, as

I absorbed each word of love. In my mind I mapped his journey to Calais from where he would obtain passage via the first ship to Dover.

There were voices in the hall immediately outside the morning room door and though the belligerence of the caller's speech did not proclaim a casual visitor, I refused to be distracted from the sacred business of reading.

"*Alex!*"

I looked up distractedly. Maeve's small face peered around the door. She glanced furtively behind her and said in an urgent whisper, "You've a visitor. You'll never – *oh!*"

Suddenly the door was thrust open and she staggered into the room, shoved from behind. My mouth fell open as Hamish stood beneath the lintel in her stead. "Greetings, wife!"

The pages in my hand fluttered guiltily. He swept his hat off with a mocking salute and leaned casually against the door-frame, one travel-scuffed boot crossed over the other. His dark-blue velvet trousers and garish, blue-and-yellow waistcoat did nothing to hide his paunch, and his puffy face sat, corpulent with over-indulgence, above his high-collared blue coat.

"What's this?" he said in his old familiar brogue, "no loving welcome for the husband you've not seen in well over a year?"

I turned to Maeve, whose ice-blue eyes were bright with alarm. "I'll fetch Simon," she said pre-emptively and darted towards the door. Hamish, with deliberate slowness, moved aside to allow her passage.

"So," he moved into the room, "come embrace me, wife."

"Hamish … you … we were not expecting you," I said evasively and remained in my seat. Casually folding my letter and returning it to its envelope, I hoped to delay the inevitable moment of truth for I feared his reaction when he saw my pregnancy.

"Evidently," he said arching his brows. Coolly, though my heart pounded in my breast, I placed the envelope on the table beside me.

"Had you sent word we'd have –"

"I wasn't aware that I had to announce my arrival upon visiting my wife," he said, watching me intensely.

Oh God, where was Simon?

Somewhere in the house a door banged and Maeve's breathy voice sounded, followed by the urgent tramp of feet. Filling my lungs, I slowly rose, bracing for the storm.

He stood very still, his mouth falling open, as contempt leapt into his face. But his disgust was quickly followed by sadistic satisfaction and he said, "So it's true then. You're big as a cow!" Instinctively, he raised his arm and I prepared for the blow.

"I wouldn't do that, Hamish," Simon's voice came from the door.

Hamish spun on his heel, "And give me one good reason why I should not beat her senseless … not a court in the land would condemn me for it – look at her – *filthy whore!*"

"And beating her senseless won't change it," my brother reasoned calmly. Maeve stood beside him, her face pinched with loathing.

"*You!*" Hamish thrust a quivering finger at her. "That abominable skirt-chasing brother of yours is responsible for this." He took a menacing step towards her but she stood firmly, some eight inches shorter than he, and faced him squarely. "*Answer me!*" he bellowed.

"I've nothing to say to you," she responded through white lips.

"Where is he?" Hamish was breathing heavily and trembling with the force of his anger. Swinging once more to face me, he roared, "*Where is he?*"

"Not here," I said. I was unable to keep the tremor from my voice. "He's in … Europe, he's –"

"It is his brat though, isn't it?" he insisted.

"Yes," I said flatly.

And before any of us could react, he closed the gap between us and struck me so hard my lip burst with a spray of blood.

Maeve screeched like a wild creature and rushed at him, dragging at his arm. But her meagre weight was no resistance for him. As he heaved back to strike a second blow Simon calmly placed himself between us. Grasping my husband's throat, he slammed him against a panelled wall.

"There will be no further violence from you – Maeve move away – do you understand me, Hamish?"

Maeve's bosom was heaving and her pretty face distorted with fury. She stood beside me while I held a handkerchief to my mouth with a trembling hand.

Simon addressed Hamish. "Why are you here? You've no doubt received communication from our legal man – you know Alex seeks a divorce."

"Yes, I have your man's letters, and until last week, I'd given them the attention such absurd notions are due. Then, I received a letter from your sister advising that it would be to my immeasurable advantage to make all haste to Broughton Hall." He sniffed disdainfully. "I must say, dear wife, you are literally *bulging* with immeasurable advantage."

A flush of blinding anger towards Anne engulfed me, such that had she walked through that door, I'd have effortlessly strangled the life from her deceitful and traitorous body with my bare hands.

"You clearly went immediately to his bed," Hamish went on, "for all the good it did you. Such a convenient little war we had – does he know about the bairn, Alex, or did he abscond too quickly to know that his seed took hold in your belly?"

I stared dumbly, shivering with hate and he curled his lip in righteous distaste. "As I thought; he's no better than a rutting animal, perpetuating the species … and you left me for that!"

He turned to Simon. "I shall be returning to Scotland tomorrow. I request your hospitality until such time, in order to rest my horses. My wife shall leave with me."

Suddenly I found my voice. "I'll not go with you, Hamish – it's over." My swelling lip thickened my words and panic bubbled in my stomach. *Could he really force me to leave with him?*

His bloated face was damp with anger. "You don't seem to understand, *wife*," he emphasised. "That bairn is mine," he pointed to my protruding belly, "and it shall be born 'neath my roof."

"You're mad – this is not your child!" My eyes slid to Simon, pleading for support but the expression I saw there caused my palms to grow clammy.

"You are so desperate for an heir you would raise another man's child as your own," Simon said evenly.

The blood seemed to have stopped trickling from my lip. I removed the handkerchief. Hamish smiled slyly, adopting that cocky, confident stance that said he'd won the argument.

"I've no disagreement with you Simon, I merely come for my wife. But should you stand in my way, it will not go well."

Simon's face hardened and he sucked a breath through his teeth. "Let us all be reasonable."

The two men faced each other and as Hamish rested a hand on his hip his coat fell open to reveal a long pistol gleaming menacingly at his belt. He spoke with affected patience and a condescending smile. "How about this for reasonable? My dear, in the eyes of the law, any issue from your body is considered mine. I can, and will, do whatever I choose with that bairn. So I tell you now – all of you – I shall return home with my wife, and when the little bastard is born, the world will know me as its father. Should you choose to return to your whoring, adulterous life, you may do so, but the bairn shall remain with me."

"Why Hamish?" I cried. "You hate Patrick – why would you –?"

"Business – why do you think? I worked beside my father for years to build Glendenning Associated Importers and in the last few years it has taken off. I have been forced to stand by and watch that blasted Trehorne reap the rewards. Now, thanks to your adulterous nature, this bairn will enable me to claim my rightful income." He grinned spitefully, "And Washburn has saved me the distasteful duty of impregnating you myself."

"Simon?" I turned a stricken face to my brother who was staring at my husband.

"Alex cannot travel in her condition, Hamish," Simon said rationally. "Having already lost one unborn child, would you have her lose another?"

Hamish sucked his lip contemplatively as he pondered Simon's words. "Yes, that would be inconvenient, however … it's a risk I'm prepared to take." He grinned then and leaned so close to my face that I detected the Scots drink on his breath. "Besides, you remember our friend, Lady Catherine, don't you? You might say I've blossomed somewhat under her imaginative tutelage and look forward to demonstrating my new skills, my dear."

I shivered in disgust and shook my head. "I shan't go with you."

"Aye, you shall."

"Patrick's returning any day now."

"And you're expecting me to … flee in terror?"

"Hamish, let's talk this out properly," Simon interrupted. "I shall have a room made up so –"

"Such trouble is not necessary, dear brother. I shall happily share my wife's bed. It will give us occasion to renew our relationship. Lead the way, dear."

I remained unmoving and Hamish reached for my hand, "Come on love, show me your room," he said cheerily. "No need to be shy. We *are* married, after all."

"Simon!" Maeve cried. "Do something."

"He won't," Hamish sneered, "for he is smarter than you – he knows that to stand between a man and his legal wife would attract much scandal, not to mention the full force of the law, which, I might add, would be entirely on my side." He bowed mockingly, "Good day to you, Miss Washburn. After you, my dear."

Hamish wandered about, absently fingering trinkets and ornaments on my dressing table and writing desk. "Don't worry, Alex," he said distantly. "I've no desire to touch you – unless you slip that bairn as you did ours, and then I'll be forced to perform my husbandly duty." He added with a wink, "I was lying about Lady Catherine, of course."

"Simon is right, though Hamish," I ventured bravely, attempting to placate him. "It is unsafe for me to travel. If we stay here … just until the baby's born …" My voice trailed off for I'd no intention of returning to Scotland but was too cowardly to say it while alone with him.

Oh God, where was Patrick? Why wasn't he here?

Hamish was thinking and I held my breath. "When's Washburn due?"

"Soon – any day."

"Very well," he nodded slowly. "We shall stay – for now. And unless he's in some other doxy's bed and has forgotten all about you – I shall be ready and waiting to blow his fair head clean off his shoulders – the right true end for the cuckolding bastard." He adjusted his neckcloth before my mirror, regarding himself with satisfaction. "The right true end."

∾

The days that followed sprung directly from a nightmare. Hamish vacillated between jealous rage and gloating anticipation of the business profits he could claim along with the retribution he planned to mete out to Patrick. I spent hours in the library, attempting to escape his snipes and jibes and the unsettling sight of his brightly-polished Doune pistol. I lingered by the window, desperately watching the drive and praying for Patrick to round the bend, yet fearful that he would.

Hamish was exceedingly pleased with himself and, each evening as he joined us for supper, I sat ramrod straight in my seat, clenching my fists impotently at the sight of him. He made an exaggerated fuss of little Dudley who, uncharacteristically for so happy a child, eyed Hamish warily.

Around the table, we attempted to behave as normal and failed entirely. Maeve barely ate at all, for it's difficult to chew while making faces. Simon and Maria looked uncomfortable at their own board and I was constantly ill from the strain. Only Hamish happily stuffed food into his mouth like it was his last meal – no wonder he was running to fat. I derived malicious pleasure from comparing his flabby, effeminate body with Patrick's sculpted and virile physique.

If the days were bad, the nights were simply tortuous. When Hamish and I were alone in my bed, he would spend several minutes stroking my stomach, speaking to my child of how he would punish its mother for her indiscretions. Sometimes he grasped my swollen breast, squeezing till I cried out. Occasionally he brought his mouth down on mine, biting my compressed lips before thrusting me aside, laughing at my squirming revulsion and threatening to bring me to my hands and knees so he might pleasure himself as he would with a man.

Each night, I waited until his breathing steadied rhythmically before I allowed myself to weep, my breasts aching from his hand, my stomach pitching with disgust, until just before dawn, sleep would finally claim me.

My hollow cheeks and purple-rimmed eyes evidenced my nightly torment and Maria suggested I sleep each afternoon, but I refused, preferring to maintain a vigil at the library window. But each evening, as the sun dipped behind the trees in the park, counted another day without Patrick's return, another night with Hamish.

Simon tactfully advised Hamish that it would not benefit the child should we continued to share a bed, but Hamish merely sneered at him, saying, "You can't keep a man from his wife, you know. It's not legal."

Meanwhile, the household tiptoed about, fearful lest Hamish decided to throw me in a coach and drive to Scotland, regardless of the consequences.

Then, one afternoon, five nights after Hamish's arrival, Simon found me, asleep in the chair in the library.

He gently touched me awake, "Zan …?"

I stirred groggily and blinked up at him.

"Wake up, Zan. He's home."

CHAPTER 35

I stood by the glowing hearth in Maeve's room and waited impatiently. Simon had wisely deemed it safer that Patrick and I be reunited in private, and so I remained, counting the long minutes until the footfalls in the hall drew closer and I could hear Maeve's bright lilting notes coupled with Patrick's soft timbre.

And then the door swung open and he was on the threshold, travel-stained and weary. He made to step towards me and paused, his eyes slipping to my belly. He drew in his breath.

A less-guarded man might have reacted demonstratively. My Patrick, reserved and quietly passionate, wordlessly closed the distance between us and pulled me into his arms.

When at last he took his mouth from mine, he placed his hand on my swollen abdomen and splayed his fingers over the curve of his child. "You've made me so happy," he whispered and his voice was husky with emotion.

Maeve continued to stand by the door. Now she cleared her throat indelicately.

"I hate to be a wet blanket, but you two can greet one another later. There are more pressing issues to consider."

As if on cue, we stiffened like posts at the sound of someone approaching but when Simon poked his head around Maeve, she and I exhaled with relief.

He slid into the room and shut the door firmly behind him.

"Pat, Hamish is demanding to see you."

"Very well. Where is he?"

I clung to him fearfully, "Pat, he —"

"I expect he means to kill me." He laid a calming hand on my hair, "Don't fret, it will be alright."

I glanced at Simon who nodded his agreement. "Now Pat's here, we can sort this whole mess out."

"But … he has a pistol. I'm certain he means to use it."

Pat snorted derisively, "I've faced better adversaries than him."

I twisted a handful of skirt. "Please don't underestimate him, he's terribly angry — Simon, tell him!"

"Zan's right. I expect he's angry enough to do something stupid."

"Ah yes, but I'm angry too." My lover extricated himself from my arms and approached Simon, "Shall we? I've a mind to set him to rights."

"Your smell alone ought to terrify him," my brother said cheerfully, as the two men exited. "You reek like a sweaty horse."

Behind them, Maeve and I exchanged bewildered and frightened glances.

❧

"You are my *wife*!" Hamish roared, slamming his fist on the dining table. I sat beside Maeve while Maria was opposite with Simon standing at her back. Patrick, unable to help himself, lounged with measured insolence against the wall, eyeing Hamish disdainfully. If it were possible for a man to burst into flame with the intensity of his anger, my husband would now be a pile of ashes and I a grateful widow.

Rounding abruptly, he turned his beet-red face toward Patrick.

"And you, you philandering swine, you're nothing but a … a … a dog has more dignity … don't think you're the first married woman he's been at Alex – how many bastards has he, eh? Ever asked him? And at court … never a night alone, hiding from duped husbands, cavorting bare-arsed through the bedrooms!"

My husband was breathing erratically and I could see the perspiration on his lip and a blue vein throbbing on his temple. His hands clenched and unclenched at his sides and I couldn't tell if he wore his pistol beneath his coat.

"So, you acknowledge the child is mine," Pat stated, lazily folding his arms. "That's a good start. Now, given that adultery is fair grounds for divorce, no court would fail to grant your freedom."

"Adultery is a crime against God and mankind. I'm within my rights to thrash her if I choose – and call you out."

Patrick's laugh was a derisive bark, and I cringed inwardly at his show of contempt. "If her crime is so appalling, why not divorce her and be done with it? I shall accept the full social ramifications of it – and pay you handsomely for your trouble. Whatever income you expect to receive as a result of this child – I'll double it. It's really very simple for you."

"*There will be no divorce!*" Hamish thundered. His eyes were frenzied and spittle flecked his lips. "I plan to acknowledge that bairn as my own. I'll not be relinquishing it or my wife. They are both mine by rights and by law."

Suddenly Pat pushed away from the wall and I recognised the glint of cruelty in his eye and braced for what would come. "Then allow me to apprise you, you pathetic little deviant. Had you focused your attentions on your wife rather than the tight arses of underage boys we may not have come to this impasse."

Maeve and I, aware of Patrick's verbal capabilities, cringed in unison while Hamish trembled like a volcano about to erupt. Patrick sneered. "Well? Nothing to say? You turn my stomach you marauding pederast."

With a howl of outrage, Hamish launched himself at Patrick, slamming his fist into my lover's mouth with a force that caused Patrick's head to snap.

Maeve and I screamed and clutched at each, other while Simon stepped forwards. Pat held up a staying hand. Wiping the blood from his mouth with the back of his hand, he allowed a small smile of satisfaction to play on his lips, while Hamish shaking and gasping readied himself for Patrick's response.

"So now you've drawn first blood – I'm within my rights to defend myself."

"There's more where that came from, oh mighty warrior," Hamish taunted.

"More of *that*?" Patrick made a derisive noise, "You'll need better if you're planning to do me in!"

Hamish's confidence was high. He made a lunge for Patrick, who easily sidestepped, performing a neat manoeuvre, which saw Hamish trip and land heavily against the wall, the breath knocked out of him.

Patrick leaned menacingly into his face. "I'd call it even now, Hamish. Had enough, or will you take another swing?"

Simon laid his hand on Pat's arm. "Leave it, man." But Patrick sighed and grasped a fistful of Hamish's elegant waistcoat and hauled him unceremoniously upright. Now standing, my husband slapped Pat's hands away and set about righting his clothes.

"You've no idea what you do," Hamish spat through clenched teeth. "Can you imagine the pleasure I shall derive simply knowing I have her? For the first time in your privileged life you're not getting what you want."

Patrick laughed and it was an ominously cheerful sound. It was a warning to most of us, but Hamish would learn that it was not pleasant to be on the receiving end of Pat's gleeful malevolence.

"You filthy creature," my lover said. He took a step towards Hamish, and Maeve grimaced knowingly. "You're unnatural and you know it. Your perversion has ever been your curse – no page-boy was ever safe around you. It was the reason you were rejected at court, the reason you hide yourself away in your clubs where you can indulge your aberrant delights. You disgusted your father, you even disgust yourself, yet you wonder that your wife left you."

"Pat, enough," it was Simon's steadying voice, but Patrick's merciless words had found their target.

"You go too far, Washburn!" Hamish snarled, his voice hoarse and dangerously low. "I've had enough of your self-satisfied rantings – she's my wife, and you'll not have her."

"Oh, you're right, Hamish, I forgot, it is a competition, isn't it. And while we're on the subject of your wife –"

I watched in shocked fascination as Patrick, quick as lightning, balled those long artistic fingers and punched my husband full in the face. Hamish reeled in surprise, his hand flying to his nose, blood oozing between his fingers.

"You bastard!" Hamish shouted. "You broke my nose! You'll pay … you'll regret …"

But my lover dismissed him with a scornful laugh, ducked Hamish's retaliatory attack and struck again. Hamish collapsed bonelessly to the rug.

Turning away, Patrick glared at Simon. With more than a hint of recrimination, he ground out, "That's for his striking Alex, retribution that should have been meted out at the time."

I failed to note Simon's reaction for I'd been watching Hamish's dazed recovery. Now, I stared in horrified disbelief as my husband reached into his coat.

"*Hamish, no!*" I screamed and lunged toward him.

But it was too late.

Hamish had withdrawn his hand to reveal the evilly glinting pistol. Before I could throw myself against his arm, the thing had leapt with a flash of smoke and a deafening explosion. The impact to his back threw Patrick heavily against the wall where a spray of flesh and blood splattered the panelling. Maeve flung herself against her brother, trying vainly to hold him upright, but it was no use and he folded to the floor.

CHAPTER 36

In a rush, my hearing returned and I was aware of my own screams as I clasped Patrick's limp body to my breast. My tears were drenching his face, while blood soaked through his shirt and stained my own clothes.

All was chaos about me. Simon slammed Hamish against the wall with his shoulder, and pinned the hand still gripping the pistol above his head. Maeve was like a demented thing. She launched herself upon Hamish, clawing and tearing, her incredible fury lending her small body the strength to fight around Simon and, when Atchison and two footmen arrived, it took their combined efforts to haul her from Hamish's face where she clung, clawing and raking his skin.

When Hamish dropped the still smoking gun to the rug; Maria, crouching professionally beside Patrick's inert form, eyed it distastefully and placed it on the table.

She turned to me, "Move aside, Alex."

Simon was giving instructions to Atchison to lock Hamish away before turning his attention to Patrick.

"Zan, be quiet!" He attempted to pull me away, but I clung to Patrick with all my hysterical strength.

The blood pumped from him in rhythmic spurts, and Maria, with uncommon aggression shouted, "*Alex – move aside!*" I slumped, rocking back and forth on the floor beside them.

At the time, I was only aware of all the blood and Patrick's lack of consciousness. I was later told that the bullet had entered his shoulder, severing an artery and blasting a hole clean through his scapula. Narrowly missing his lung, it exited his chest and was found embedded in the wall.

Patrick was carried to his room where Simon and Maria worked frantically to stem the bleeding. Maeve and I, refused entry on the grounds that we were too distressed, remained in the parlour, holding each other fearfully, and desperate for news.

After what seemed like hours, Simon emerged, his face grey and drawn, his clothes irretrievably bloodstained.

I ran to him while Maeve poured a glass of brandy. He quaffed the liquor gratefully and clutched the empty glass in his fist. "He has lost a lot of blood –"

"But he will be alright?" Maeve interrupted impatiently.

My brother sighed. "If we can keep the wounds closed and free from infection he should be. But there is a lot of internal damage and he needs rest. Maria has given him a sleeping draught; he must be kept quiet … movement could re-open the wounds."

I let out my breath in a rush, "Oh, thank God!"

"If you wish," Simon said, with a weary, lopsided grin, "or you could thank me. Either way, he's not out of danger yet. If the bleeding begins again …"

I nodded with understanding. "Can I see him?"

"Don't wake him."

❧

Patrick was propped on pillows, his face was pale and bloodless, and his eyes were shadowed in purple. The counterpane was folded to his waist, above which he was naked with a thick bandage binding his right shoulder and part of his torso. The traces of previous wounds showed faintly as pale pink lines and welts on his otherwise smooth chest.

Maeve and I stood beside him with tears coursing silently down our cheeks. "Damn him," she whispered hoarsely. "Why did he have to taunt Hamish so? Why must he always be so cruel?"

"It's his way," I responded, remembering those painful times I'd been subjected to his vicious tongue. "He takes the truth and tortures you with it — he's a talent for it."

"Well this time it was nearly his undoing."

Immediately following the shooting, Hamish had stood immobile and shocked by his own actions. He made no effort to fight off Maeve's frenzied attack, and passively allowed himself to be led away by Simon's butler and footmen who locked him in a guest-room until Simon went to him.

"I told him to return quietly to his home and not importune this family again." It was the day after the incident and Simon, Maria, Maeve and I were gathered in the parlour.

"He would be desperate to know how Patrick fares," Maeve commented.

Simon allowed himself a small smile. "To say he was rather concerned is an understatement. I assured him if Patrick died he would hear of it. Attempting to murder the son of an earl ... the courts would not take it lightly."

"There is the small matter of my adultery," I reminded him.

My brother shrugged. "There is that, but shooting the local farmer who beds your wife in the hay–barn, is vastly different from shooting a peer of the realm. At any rate, I've no doubt Patrick deliberately provoked him. Perhaps he didn't expect to be shot in the back, but he definitely attempted to push Hamish beyond his limits."

"Hamish was wound tight as a bowstring," Maria said. "Small wonder he reacted so violently."

We all nodded, and Simon spoke again. "I don't think he'd ever intended to use that pistol, perhaps he just wanted to threaten with it. Nevertheless, I explained that providing Patrick lives, the authorities would not come to hear of this incident as long as Hamish returns quietly to Scotland and leaves you in peace."

"And what of my divorce? By rights this child should be Patrick's heir."

My brother frowned. "Zan, can you not be grateful? Patrick is alive and you are free. We made a compromise. You will never see Hamish again, but he does not want a divorce. It will go badly with his business associates. He agrees to make no claims on either you or your babe. He requested only that you remain married."

"He shouldn't be allowed to make any requests," Maeve commented petulantly.

"Patrick will be able to recognise the child," Simon said, ignoring her. "You will have your life and children with him. You must be content with that, Zan. If Hamish himself took this matter to the courts – particularly a Scottish court – an enquiry may not see the situation entirely from our point of view."

&

During the following days, Maeve and I sat with Patrick by turns. He slept a lot, and was weak from having lost so much blood. Once while I stared absently into the flickering fire, he awoke for a brief period.

"Alex …?"

I turned to find his eyes like stormy green seas, resting on me. "I'm here."

"Kiss me, love," he whispered. I obliged, touching my lips gently to his before his eyelids fluttered and he slept again.

Simon kept him on the sleeping draught to prevent him

moving about while Maria daily cleaned his wounds and changed the dressing. Within a few weeks he'd started to improve and was eager to be up and about.

One afternoon, as Simon, Maria and I stood about his bed, he asked what exactly had happened. He didn't seem to remember much of the shooting. "You shouldn't have taunted him so. You pushed him too far," I admonished, as he smirked unrepentantly at me. I sighed and passed a hand over my eyes. I was terribly weary.

"Are you alright?" Simon asked.

"Yes, I'm … just tired. He's such a bothersome patient."

"You should rest, Alex," Maria said, and for once I was not inclined to argue. But as I bent to kiss my lover's brow, a sharp cramp gripped my abdomen so that I gasped and stifled a cry. At the same time, a warm liquid broke between my thighs.

Maria, with a knowing look to her husband said, "I shall fetch my bag."

❧

I'd previously spoken with Simon and gently as I could, explained that I would engage a midwife to assist Maria with the birthing. I hoped he would not be offended, but I simply could not countenance the thought of my own brother seeing me that way.

To my immense relief, he had laughed and thrown his arm about me. "Thank heavens for that!"

Maddy was a sprightly and experienced woman. Simon was impressed with her credentials and I offered her a salary and accommodation to ensure her availability when my time came.

It was midnight when my pains truly began. I studied the clock and grew afraid; it was too soon, my baby was coming early. Maddy had been called and she and Maria assured me all was normal. They did their best to calm me, but by the time my travail advanced in earnest, it was after three in the morning and I was becoming panicked. Thoughts of Sylvie, her small frame, unmade to be rent as it were, haunted me. And Jane Carter's terrified face drifted in and out of my mind.

Patrick, moving gingerly, came into the room to soothe me, and it worked — for a while. But when it was time for him to leave, I clung to him so frantically they resolved to keep him away until it was over.

Reflections of Sylvie were perhaps in his mind also, for he was reluctant to leave and Maddy was forced to shove him unceremoniously out of the door.

That pale summer morning on the first of June 1817, the hearty cries of a sturdy baby echoed through the house and I wept with joy and love and sheer exhaustion.

Patrick burst into the room as Maria took our baby aside.

"Now, my lord …" Maddy warned, as he rushed to my bedside. Simon followed and immediately went to his wife to check over the new arrival as Maria held the squirming, slippery bundle for his inspection.

"How are you, my love?" Patrick asked, leaning close and stroking the sweat-drenched hair plastered to my forehead.

I smiled weakly, but happily. "Tired … sore …"

"Thank you," he said in his soft cadence. The emotion was thickening his voice and his emerald eyes were wet. "You've made me the happiest man. Thank you, my darling, *darling* girl." He kissed me lightly on each eyelid, then my lips. "I never believed I could love as I do at this moment."

"Nor I," I said quietly as Maria placed the linen wrapped infant in Patrick's arms.

"You have a son."

∾

The soft breathing of the new life in the crib beside my bed comforted me. I dozed, exhausted by my day's travail. Patrick had been at my shoulder all evening but fatigue, for he was still convalescing, drove him back to his bed. Much later, when he returned, he was freshly shaved and dressed. I smiled wearily and he approached my bed slowly. Kneeling beside me, his hand dipped into his pocket.

"A symbol of my love and my troth, and even if the fates decide we cannot wed, my life will be yours – forever."

Watching my face, he slipped on to my finger a beautiful ring. It was an emerald, the size of a pea, surrounded by diamonds and set into a band of white gold. I drew in my breath and sniffed back my emotion.

"Oh, my love …" I held out my arms and he came into them and before I could control myself I'd begun to cry.

He pulled back in alarm. "What is it?"

"I don't … think Hamish will ever … agree to a divorce."

"Unfortunately I think you're right. The bastard is … Shit, I love you, Alex, with all my heart, yet I've caused you so much grief over the years. Even recently, because it's true: I did antagonise Hamish in the hope he'd do something stupid. I overestimated his bravery – I expected an honest fight … never dreamed he'd shoot me in the back, bloody coward! It's my own fault."

"Don't Pat," I said quickly. "This whole mess is the responsibility of one person alone and it is not you, or me, or even Hamish. It is Anne. Without her interference he may well have been open to negotiation. He at least would not have known I was pregnant."

"Hmm, never have you spoken a truer word, and if that bitch ever has the temerity to cross my path … I'm not one for striking women, but I don't think I'd be able to stay my hand."

I chuckled then. "No need, I've already done it."

"You struck her?"

I nodded.

"Whew," he whistled. "Clearly I'd do well to stay on the right side of your temper. I'm still haunted by the wallop you meted out that afternoon in Devon."

"That was with good reason." We were both smiling now.

"You're right, of course," he said. "I'd been particularly brutal with you that day – taunting you about Hamish. But then, I also had good reason."

"Oh really?"

He gave me a sly sidelong glance and smirked sheepishly. "Remember that morning you'd found me in the old shed in some state of … er …"

"Intoxication? Undress?" I offered helpfully.

He shrugged, "You were quite angry when you discovered Kat Wheeler's headscarf in the straw next to me and jumped to … well, a reasonable conclusion."

I arched my eyebrows.

"The truth is … you'd looked so beautiful at Sylvie's wedding, you stoked my desire, and combine that with too much drink … Kat and I were in the shed and I … went to … er … you know, and I inadvertently called her *Alex*. So you see, yours wasn't the first clout I'd received that day."

He looked so dejected by his confession that I broke into laughter. When I finally regained my control I looked at him seriously. "So you thought a brawl with me would make it better?"

"It was your fault. She crowned me and left me there to sleep it off."

I shook my head. "How could the fact that you missed out on a romp with the village slattern be my fault?"

"Because you had enticed me all through that wedding ceremony. I hungered for you in the worst possible way but Kat convinced me it was merely lust and promised to distract me."

His face sobered, all playfulness gone. "She would never have succeeded. No one has ever been able to take my mind off you, and it wasn't just because of that first night you and I'd spent together – it was everything; you're so much of me, I'm hollow without you. I didn't believe I could love you so damn much."

He reached out and gently cupped my chin in his hand. "And now you've given me this child. I feel so undeserving."

Tears stung my eyes and I covered his hand with my own.

"I don't care if we're never to marry, Pat, as long as we're together."

At that moment our son awoke and commenced such a bawling that his father was prompted to declare him a songster.

"If only it were in key," I commented above the noise.

CHAPTER 37

As the months passed and there was no sound from Scotland, the occupants of Broughton Hall relaxed into a domestic routine that was as close to perfect as I had ever known. Patrick, fully recovered, had moved into my room and we lived as man and wife with our child, whom we'd named William, sleeping in his crib beside our bed. We planned to spend Christmas here before moving to Waterville Place after the winter snows melted.

One night, towards the end of October, I awoke with a start, my ears cocked for a repeat of the sound that had disturbed me. It came again, a rasping, hoarse breathing, shallow and laboured. Immediately I was out of bed and before the baby's crib, touching him in the dark.

But he slept peacefully. I stood there, listening and confused, and suddenly I knew … Oh God!

"*Patrick!*" I gasped in a loud whisper.

"Hmm?" His voice was thick with sleep.

"Quickly … light the candle." He responded promptly and stood over me, the light pooling where I knelt beside Jemima's basket. "What's wrong with her?" I cried, the tears already welling in my eyes.

My adored dog was sprawled on her side, half in and half out of her basket. Her head lolled on the floor, her eyes were rolled back and she was panting fit to burst. "What is it? What's wrong with her?"

"I don't know." He gently stroked the dog's brow.

My mind was in turmoil. I desperately threw about for something to help her, to ease her laboured breathing.

"Should I wake Simon?" I suggested hopefully. "He helped Equus."

Patrick was listening to the dog's chest. He raised his eyes to me and shook his head sadly. "You could but there's probably nothing to be done. She's quite old – we knew this time would come."

"No! *Oh no* …" I was sobbing freely now. "I can't let her go … I can't …" He didn't speak. He took a blanket from the bed and wrapped me in it, then pulled me into his arms, gently rocking as I tried to accept the unavoidable reality.

"Shh," he whispered. "For her sake."

We huddled on the floor together, with my most faithful companion's head pillowed on my lap and it was all we could do to soothe her and comfort her as her breathing slowed, and her honest life ebbed away.

William stirred in his crib and began the first mewling that heralded his demand for food, yet still I would not move. My son would survive if his meal was delayed, but I could not leave this dog now, not after so many years of loyalty and unconditional love; this dog I'd raised from a pup, whose life I'd rescued when she'd have died as a newborn, who had accompanied me to the wild north, who'd journeyed with me to the south – who'd remained devotedly by my side through all.

I relived so many precious moments and wept with each one. And just before the hall clock chimed three times, my beloved Jemima took a deep breath and released it slowly, slipping quietly away to the eternal place reserved for dogs.

Bowing my head over her inert body, I sobbed till I thought my heart would tear in two.

∿

We buried Jemima later that morning. Patrick prepared a place down by the stone wall at the edge of the orchard where she and I had walked together so often over the years. It was a special place, where as a spritely young dog she'd chased rabbits, and witnessed Patrick and I first confessing our love for each other. Simon and Maria, toddling Dudley, Rosalie and Maeve joined us in our sad ceremony.

Maeve knew a village lad who was capable with a chisel. She commissioned him to carve a simple headstone and it arrived a week later. She and I set it in place early one morning, over the plain little grave site.

It was the closing of a chapter.

CHAPTER 38

Patrick, William and I journeyed to Devon in March the following year. Accompanied by Maeve, our arrival at Waterville was met with tears of joy from Amelia as she waited by the fountain with eighteen-month-old Erin in her arms. Aden slapped Patrick's back, "Sure I'm pleased you're finally returned to your senses, cousin."

"So am I," Pat agreed, placing an arm round my waist.

Aden hugged Maeve happily and introduced his wife. "Last time I saw Aden," Maeve explained, "he was about fourteen, and terrorising the county in company with my brother."

Maeve's similarities to Sylvie were remarked upon, and Amelia's eyes dampened a second time. Patrick had sent word of Sylvie's passing and Quinn's subsequent return home and, by silent mutual consent, we agreed the details of Sylvie's death would be discussed at a later time.

William was presented for inspection and immediately Amelia declared, "Oh Pat, sure he looks just like you."

Maeve harrumphed, "I think he looks like me. Don't you, little fellow, you look just like your Auntie Maeve."

"There is a family resemblance," Aden agreed as we all went into the house and I stood once more in that magnificent atrium, that I thought I'd never see again, and stared around me, in awe, as always.

"You're home, my darling girl," Patrick whispered at my side.

I leaned my head on his shoulder and breathed deeply. I would have turned to kiss him then, but Mrs Bath burst into the room, reflected in a million shards, her voice sibilant with the acoustics. "I didn't believe it when they said the master was home with Lady Elginbury, and they —"

"Mrs Bath," Patrick cheerfully interrupted his housekeeper, "please advise the staff that this lady will henceforth be addressed as Lady Thorncliffe. You may consider her as you would my wife."

The loyal servant smiled happily, "Welcome home, my lady," she said. "I'll call Bea to unpack your things."

The woman left to instruct her staff, and Pat and I mounted the stairs. At the landing, I automatically turned to the left but he pulled my hand.

"Not this time — not any more," he shook his head. "Come."

He led me towards the right wing of the house, the residents' wing, down the hall to the room at the end, and upon reaching the door, he stopped and looked at me and his eyes danced wickedly.

"Should I lift you over the threshold?"

"If you wish, but —" He scooped me into his arms.

"Er … can you open the door?"

I giggled and leaned slightly over to turn the handle, and he pushed the door open with the toe of his boot.

The room was exactly as I remembered from all those years ago; masculine, and cluttered with books, though the windows were open allowing a fresh breeze through. Still holding me, Pat kicked the door closed behind him and carried me with single-minded purpose to the bed.

"What are you up to?" I asked archly, as he deposited me on the blue counterpane.

"Our inability to share a room during our journey has left me somewhat eager, and besides, I've waited years to have you bundled in my own bed. Do you mind? Can I perhaps, interest you ..." he broke off as he crawled over me and touched his lips to my mouth, "in a small interlude ..." my arms curled around his neck and I returned his kiss.

Our breathing became rapid as our need for each other grew, and such was our hunger that we dispensed with the removal of our clothes. He raised the skirt of my travelling costume, and unbuttoned his trousers and there, in full daylight, and fully clothed, we attended one another for the first time, in this most splendid house.

Naturally, as was inevitable, the door unexpectedly opened spilling forth a troop of servants carrying our trunks and boxes. Their reactions ranged from stammered, red-faced apologies, to snickers behind hands. They exited rapidly, leaving Patrick laughing and me with a face flaming with humiliation.

"What's the matter?" Pat asked, wiping tears of mirth from his eyes. "They didn't see anything – we're fully clothed."

"Of course they did, look at yourself – look at me." My dress was up to my navel, my bloomers somewhere on the floor and he was no better with his trousers around his ankles.

He shrugged and rolled off the bed to dress, tossing my bloomers at me. Wriggling around, I put them on and straightened my dress. He was still smiling and I found myself growing annoyed. "What's so funny? Last time those people saw us together we were trying to kill one another. Now they catch us on the bed in a most compromising –"

"Delicious position ..." he corrected. "Can't you see why that's funny? Are your ears burning? We'll be the talk of the kitchens at this very moment."

I tried to look sulky, but the dissatisfied warmth in my loins and the tingling of my lips from his kisses made it impossible. I smiled. "I'm embarrassed, that's all."

"I know. Don't worry, we'll finish this later," he added reading my face. "But you know something else? That afternoon all those years ago, when I gave you a tour of the house and we arrived at this room, I think I realised then that I loved you and wanted you for my wife. I remember …" he added sheepishly, "thinking how much I wanted to carry you to this bed then and there."

"But you didn't. Why not?"

"God, Alex, you know why not. You were so young and innocent. It was all I could do to keep myself from kissing you. It was only the fact that I wanted more than a kiss that restrained me. It was a constant struggle. The more I tried to avoid you, the more I wanted to be with you."

I smiled. "Do you know that for all my innocence, I was so aware of you back then … it was like the air was vibrating when you were near. If you'd touched me, or given me the slightest hint that you were interested, I'd have thrown myself at you."

"Well, now that we're both older and wiser, feel free to throw yourself at me whenever you damn well please. My body is yours — take full advantage of it."

I watched as he opened one of the trunks and took out a clean shirt. Stripping off the creased and damp shirt he was wearing, he turned and grinned. "I intend taking full advantage of yours — what?"

As I watched him change his shirt, a thought had occurred to me with such intensity that I could not put it aside. Now he was staring at me. "What is it?"

"How many have there been … I mean … how many have you … brought to this room? Others like …"

"Kat Wheeler?"

I nodded.

He came over to sit beside me on the bed and took my hand in his. "I'd be lying if I told you I've not had other women in this room, but I've never brought Kat here, she's never even been inside this house."

Slightly appeased, I smiled weakly and he went on, "There'll never be anyone else for me, now we're together. Anyhow, who are you to throw stones, you're the one who's married, remember?" His grin was playful but I didn't need the reminder.

Before I could respond there was a sharp knock at the door. "You two in there," came Aden's cheery voice, "you'd best be bringing yourselves out immediately. Haven't you created a stir among the staff already!"

❧

So we settled rapidly into life at Waterville Place. I reacquainted myself with Briggs and the irrepressible Tess on my morning strolls around the gardens. Occasionally Patrick joined us, but more often than not he let me enjoy the mornings with my two traditional companions.

One morning, he did choose to join me. As we exited the house, he tucked my hand into the crook of his elbow and led me along a different path, behind the stables, beyond an old cottage that housed Jimma and Blackie, the two stable-lads.

As we rounded the boys' cottage and followed a path to the outhouse and woodshed, I spotted Blackie waiting excitedly. "In 'ere milord," he said urgently, pointing into the dim shed, which was stacked to its low roof with chopped wood.

Pat released my arm and stooped to enter the shed. "Be'ind that big pile, milord," Blackie directed.

Half of Pat disappeared behind the stack of wood. The other half remained unmoving for a moment, then he backed out and turned to me with a grin.

"I think you ought to have a look," he said.

I raised my eyebrows, "In there?"

He nodded.

"If a spider jumps on me you're in big trouble," I warned, lifting my hem and stepping forwards.

I moved into the dark and damp-smelling shed to where Pat had been standing and letting my eyes adjust for a second, stared at the space on the floor behind the stack of wood.

"Oh heavens," I breathed as I beheld Tess, her face turned to the string of suckling pups at her teats. At the sound of my voice, she looked up and her tail commenced a thumping welcome. "You're a mama, sweetheart. I'd no idea …"

The pups – there were four of them – looked to be only hours old. There were two brown and tan ones, and two pure blondes like their mother. Their little mewing and sucking sounds warmed my heart as I watched. Eventually, I backed out of the shed and turned to face Patrick and Blackie. "I didn't know she was expecting puppies."

"Old Bruce Decker from down th' road, milady," Blackie explained, "'as this brown an' tan mongrel. Coupla months back Mr Decker comes in 'ere sayin' 'ave we seen 'is dog and we says no, but this mornin' Jimma reckoned 'e 'ears summit when 'e collected th' wood. We come lookin' an' we find Tess 'ere like this. Reckon Mr Decker's dog's bin 'ere fer certain."

Now Patrick spoke, "Blackie and Jimma are trusted to look after them. After that they can sell them to local farmers. Obviously there's a few weeks before they'll be old enough, but you've first pick now. If you'd like one, make your choice, and Blackie'll make sure it is yours."

Too overwhelmed with emotion to speak, I stood dumbly and stared.

"Would you like one?" Pat asked.

I nodded and sniffed back the threatening tears. "Yes, I'd like that very much." I turned to Blackie. "I'd prefer a girl, do you know which ones are girls?"

"No milady, Tess weren't lettin' us near 'er to look."

"She trusts you," Pat urged. "Go back in and see which one you'd like."

I wiped my eyes and returned to the shed. Standing there, watching the nurturing scene common between mother and child, no matter what the species, my heart cried with new grief for my lost Jemima. *I'm not replacing you, my beloved girl for you're irreplaceable,* I assured her silently.

I watched all the pups in turn and identified the one that was the smallest and weakest. It may not fare so well as a working dog. It was one of the brown and tans but it had three blonde paws and one brown one.

Crouching low and speaking soothing words to Tess, I reached for the tiny, squirming bundle. Tess looked concerned but did not react so I backed out of the shed and reverently presented the pup to Patrick.

"I'd like this one if it's a girl," I said.

"Shall I do the honours?"

"Yes, please."

Gently, he took the pup from my hands and with no regard for its dignity, held it up and inspected its nether regions. "Well," he said, "what are you going to name her?"

He returned the puppy into my hands and I held her close to my face. Breathing the sweet milky scent of new life, I whispered. "I dub thee ..." thought for a moment, "Bellus," and ceremoniously pressed a kiss to the top of her tiny head.

"Latin for beautiful," Pat said smiling. "Bellus, it is. Best get her back to her mother. Take a good look Blackie, and make sure you keep this one aside."

I returned Bellus to Tess, and arm in arm, Pat and I made our way back to the house.

ೲ

"Excuse me, milady." I started slightly; absorbed as I was in writing a letter to Julia, I hadn't heard Mrs Bath approach.

"What is it?"

"If you please, milady, a messenger arrived from Sir Simon. He's wantin' ter speak wi' 'is lordship and no other."

Patrick was somewhere on the estate with the tenant farmers discussing the haymaking due to begin in a month's time. "Did you tell him the master is out?"

"Yes, milady, but 'e insists 'e speak only wi' … *his lordship.*"

I sighed and dropped my pen into its jar. "Very well. Could you send a boy into the fields and …" I hesitated. *His lordship?* Simon knew better than to address Patrick as … suddenly my stomach lurched and I felt the blood drain from my face.

Turning to Mrs Bath I saw my fears confirmed. "Please … send someone immediately …" Mrs Bath bobbed quickly and left to do my bidding.

The messenger had brought a letter from Simon announcing the tragic news that Gerrard Washburn, Earl of Thorncliffe, had awoken one morning complaining of pains in his chest. His valet left him momentarily to fetch a tonic for dyspepsia but on his return had found the earl deceased in his bed.

Patrick allowed the letter to fall on to his desk and sat, for a very long time, with his head in his hands.

Simon, Maria and Meg brought the late earl's remains to Devon for laying to rest in the family crypt beside Waterville's chapel. We held a small private funeral, just the six of us consoling one another in our grief: Simon, Maria, Maeve, Meg, Patrick and me. Noticeably absent were Mother and Anne – although no one had supposed they would come anyway.

The following week, the will was read and, as expected, Patrick at only twenty-seven years of age, inherited a considerable fortune and numerous titles – the earldom being only one of them.

Sizeable amounts were left to Maeve and Meg, while a lesser, though not insubstantial sum was left to Simon.

Other than instructing the late earl's lawyers to establish a trust account to benefit Gerrard's existing and future grandchildren, Patrick refused to discuss the loss of his father.

While Maeve grieved openly, Pat threw himself into a frenzy of activity, joining his tenants in haymaking with a determination that left him physically exhausted at the end of each day.

I remembered how after Sylvie's death he had stayed on at Broughton Hall, without explanation, and long after everyone had expected him to leave. Now, I recognised that same desire for company coupled with his determination to ignore his grief.

It was the same stubbornness that had enabled him cut me out of his life so effectively after I'd married Hamish. Back then, with nothing else to distract him, he had turned to brandy and women.

Things were marginally different now. Each morning he left the house at dawn, not returning until sunset when he wearily walked in from the fields and I met him on the porch. And regardless that he was dusty and sweaty, and smelled of earth and hay, he opened his arms and I went into them.

The sky grew dark while we stood wordlessly wrapped together, giving and receiving comfort, and secure in our love for each other.

It was how we had always belonged.

CHAPTER 39

1820

"Great heavens above, it is hot," the ancient Dowager Duchess of Chasseby announced, fanning herself with her handkerchief.

"It would not be so bad if you'd stop reminding us Dragon-lady, Patrick grumbled good-naturedly. We were sprawled on pillows in the summer-house by the lake at Waterville Place. All the doors and windows were thrown open to catch the inadequate afternoon breeze.

I was in the fifth month of my second pregnancy and finding the heat quite oppressive. "She's right Pat," I said, my eyes shifting to where William, one month past his third birthday was red-faced and irritable with the heat.

He followed my glance, "I think I'll put him in the water to cool him down. What about you? Are you alright?"

"A bit uncomfortable, but that's to be expected." I looked to where Maeve lay on a day bed with Nicholas, the latest in her string of handsome lovers, whose head rested on her middle. We'd grown accustomed to Maeve's unconventional lifestyle. Pat said we all made quite a team, since he and I were unmarried but living as though we were. His sister had made it patently clear that she'd no intention of being *shackled*, as she put it, preferring her freedom, and her lovers.

Years ago, Maeve had told me the story of Claudio, her one great love, lost to her through an accident during one of their archaeological expeditions. Since that time, she'd had enumerable lovers, but none she'd truly ever given her heart to – much to the despair of the men in question, for Pat's sister was vivacious, pretty and intelligent. The men fell in love with her spirit and her *joie de vivre* – they could not help themselves. And despite her assurances that she was not of a marrying mind, she received their proposals with grace, and declined gently.

Over the years there had been several unfortunates who simply did not understand her desire to remain unwed, and who'd made it their business to convert the little elf. Patrick had consoled more than one broken heart over a bottle of brandy.

She sighed languidly and stretched in a manner reminiscent of a sleek cat and looking towards her brother said, "Perhaps we should all have a swim. You'll join us won't you, Alex?"

I nodded without hesitation; swimming had become a daily pleasure for me during these summer months – since I'd learned how. "What about your grace, did you bring your costume?"

"She doesn't need one," Pat quipped, "The duchess loves to swim in the nick, don't you old girl."

"Mind your manners, Thorncliffe," the older lady snapped with mock annoyance. "I rue the day Aden took Amelia and the children back to Ireland. You've been obnoxious ever since."

"He was obnoxious before," Maeve said, "but in Aden's absence it is more obvious."

Footsteps sounded on the decking outside and a maid discreetly poked her head through the open French doors. Her face was flushed with the heat and the exertion of trotting down from the house in the hot summer sun. She held out the skirt of her servant's dress and ducked a quick curtsy to Patrick.

"What is it, Bea?"

"A lady, my lord, up at the house to see you. She would not say her name – are you at home, my lord?"

"A lady? What does she look like?"

"Well," Bea frowned, "like royalty, my lord. She's very beautiful and dressed like a real lady of the court – jewels and all – she's short and has dark hair and … I cannot think what else, but she talks real snooty, sorry my lord."

During Bea's description, Pat's gaze strayed to me. "I wonder …" he mused.

Maeve sat up abruptly, spilling Nicholas' head on to the pillows. "Surely not. She would not dare … would she?"

I shook my head uncertainly, but deep within some intuitive place in my heart I knew, and a cold clamminess broke beneath my summer gown.

"Would you excuse us, your grace?" Pat said. "If this is whom we suspect, we could be some time." He got to his feet and offered me his hand.

"High time I took my leave, in any case," the duchess said. "Bestir yourself Mr Schenker, and I shall give you a ride home."

Nicholas groaned and reluctantly stood. Pat spoke to Bea, "Please show the lady into the parlour, offer her lemonade, and tell her we shall be with her presently."

Bea bobbed her acknowledgement and turned to leave, "Oh, and call for the duchess's carriage, if you would," Patrick added to which the maid bobbed again.

Pat, carrying William in his arms, Maeve and I, entered the house by the back porch.

Bea waited in the hallway as we entered. "The lady's in the parlour my lord, like you asked."

"Thank you Bea," Patrick responded. "Please take William up to the nursery," he said dropping our son on his chubby legs. "Go upstairs with Bea, Will, there's a boy."

Maeve took my arm and the two of us hung back slightly, allowing Patrick to lead the way. At the parlour door, he threw an encouraging smile at us, before turning the handle and stepping purposefully into the room.

Anne was seated on the settee. As we entered she placed her lemonade on a side table and slowly rose to her feet.

My sister had blossomed over the past years into a devastatingly beautiful creature. Her complexion was smooth and slightly tinged with a natural pinkness at her cheeks. Her dark eyes, sensually hooded, were fringed with long lashes, and her lips were full and stained as though she'd been eating overripe raspberries.

She stood before me in an expensive gown of pink silk, trimmed with white lace at bodice and elbow, slashed at the front with a white underskirt. Garnets bobbed in her ears and glittered at her throat. Her rich chestnut hair was swept into the latest style and left to tumble gracefully over one shoulder.

I paused beside Maeve, feeling completely dowdy and inferior, but my sister made no move to acknowledge our presence. Fully aware of her charms, her eyes for Patrick alone, she swept a courtly curtsy, providing an unhampered view down the bodice of her gown.

"Some things never change," Maeve hissed for my ears alone.

While bowed, Anne raised her lovely eyes to Pat's. "Greetings, my Lord Thorncliffe," she spoke in a low, seductive voice. "Which title, I am given to understand, you have inherited since the demise of our dear father."

"An occasion of bereavement, and one of which I have no desire to be reminded," he said curtly and waved an impatient hand at her. "Get up Anne, for Christ's sake, and stop playing the courtesan with me. Just tell me what you want, so I can get on with the task of throwing you out on your simpering arse."

I was struck by Patrick's composure as I realised the last time he'd seen my sister was when she'd come to Waterville to beg him to marry her – so many years ago. He'd thrown her out on that occasion too.

Anne seemed unsurprised by his disdain. With a little shrug, she got to her feet and returned to her couch, sparing a second's glance to where Maeve and I sat stiffly together on a settee opposite.

"And make it quick, we've no wish to have a pleasant afternoon ruined by your presence," Maeve added.

"I came to pay a friendly visit," Anne responded looking stung. "After so many years I thought –"

"Horse shit!" Pat declared. "You've never done anything without an ulterior motive so get to the point."

"Very well," she said. "I've come to plead your assistance in …" she sighed and glanced once more in my direction, "… in a rather delicate matter."

"Which is?"

"My husband has left me." Here, she paused, as much to let her words sink in, as to arrange her face into an artfully sad expression designed to pluck at our sympathy.

"Woke up to you at last did he?" Maeve sneered.

"Left me for an ugly old crow with buckets of money," she responded, ignoring the barb.

"More strength to his arm," Maeve remarked which provoked an icy stare from my sister.

"I see *you* haven't changed," Anne said, "dried-up old spinster." She threw an assessing glance my way and her eyes sifted over me, groomed brows twitching slightly at the sight of my protruding belly. "Still dealing with that troublesome hair, Alex," she observed, "and still producing Washburn bastards."

I remained stoically silent and imitated Patrick's bland expression.

"You need a good slap across the teeth," my lover observed, "and I'm having great difficulty staying my hand. The longer you're here, the weaker grows my restraint. Get on with it."

He remained standing before her as though to intimidate but

she appeared undaunted and I knew a grudging admiration for her.

"There's no call to threaten my person."

"Shut up!" Pat snapped viciously. "Get to the bloody point or get out. What do you want?"

Anne glared mutinously at Maeve and me for a further moment before turning her face sweetly to Patrick. "Dear brother," she began, smoothly ignoring Maeve's derisive snort, "I come to beg your forgiveness for my youthful foibles, and your help – in that order, for I'd been planning –"

"You're not worthy of the first and not deserving of the second," Pat interrupted. "Was that all you came to say?"

Anne's face adopted a wounded expression. "Oh Patrick, I don't blame you for being annoyed with me, please let me explain –"

"Was that all?" Patrick repeated.

"But –"

"I think that's all she has to say," Pat dismissed her and moved to the bell-pull. "I'll advise Bea you're leaving."

"Wait!" Anne cried and our heads all snapped in her direction. A new firmness set her lovely face in hard lines. Her plump lips were taut and her brows ran together. When she spoke, her voice was low and contrite. "Please, don't throw me out – I'm desperate, you see."

Pat's stony expression gave nothing away but when he looked at me, I easily read his silent query. I shrugged, "We could hear her out, I suppose."

Maeve snorted again. "Who heard Pat out when this bitch lied about him? Not even you, Alex."

"Please," Anne repeated. "I've no one else to turn to."

Pat let his breath out in a rush. "Very well," he said. He flopped into a winged chair and eyed my sister cautiously. "Let's hear it – and I don't want the flowery version."

"I need money …"

"Figured," Maeve interjected.

"A lot of it," she cast her eyes to her hands where they lay in her lap, and I was reminded of a previous time she'd employed that same gesture – when she'd admitted, tearfully, that Patrick had fathered her child. Doubt needled me – I couldn't help it – and even as she looked up, her great hazel eyes glazed with unshed tears, I mistrusted her.

Her sad gaze settled on Pat and drawing a shaky breath she continued. "When George left me, we were living at court. Pat … you understand, it is so expensive there … what with clothes and jewels, and the constant round of parties and balls to attend and … well … we are in considerable debt. George left me … us, me and Domenica, my daughter – they are going to …" she didn't continue for a moment, but pulled a fine lawn handkerchief from her sleeve and dabbed delicately at her eyes.

"Don't fall for this Pat," Maeve warned, "you've no idea what she's capable of … you should've seen her in Italy whenever –"

"You shut up!" Anne hissed viciously, "I'm not even here to see you." She turned her wet face toward Patrick. "They'll throw me in debtors' prison if I don't come up with the money we owe."

"They don't throw sisters of earls into prison," Pat said dryly.

"But I have no home and there's the question of where Domencia will live … we have nothing, Pat, *nothing*."

"You're not my responsibility, Anne," Pat's voice was gentler now and I squirmed inside. He wasn't relenting, surely? After everything, all the trouble and pain she'd caused us. "Have you spoken to Simon?"

"Simon does not have the sort of money I need. I owe thousands and thousands."

"What about the estate my father bought you and George? You could sell it."

"And that's the other part of the story. We did sell it, but he took the money with him when he absconded. I didn't know until I went to the goldsmith. It's all gone – every last penny."

"You ought to speak to Simon," Patrick repeated.

"I can't," she whined. "I've told you, it's a terrible lot of money, you're the only one I know with that sort of money. Oh Patrick, I know I've done wrong in the past, but I'd do anything to make up for it! You must believe me – I've no one else to turn to."

"Oh you're so apologetic," I said acidly, "perhaps if you'd been contrite a few years ago, or even told the truth in the first instance, we'd be more charitable now."

"Well, I'm contrite now," she said. "And besides, Alex I've been through so much … so much more than you could know. I'd say we're even."

"Oh you would, would you? Added to everything else, I don't forget you went running to Hamish when you found out I was pregnant. Do you know he almost killed Patrick!" I was trembling with anger and Maeve rested her hand gently on my shoulder.

Anne stared at her lap for a moment before speaking again. "I do know, and not a day goes by when I don't regret what I did."

Silence reigned while the mantelpiece clock ticked away the seconds. I stared at Patrick's face but he was giving nothing away.

Finally, he spoke. "Anne, I can't help you."

Tears rolled down Anne's pretty pink cheeks and she raised her eyes, imploring him, "Please, I'm begging you. I don't know what else I can do."

"You could sell your jewels," I said helpfully.

"Or you could sell your body," Maeve suggested, "oh, but I forgot; you've been doing that for years."

"Maeve," Pat warned his sister though his eyes rested on Anne. "The answer's no, Anne. Sorry as I am for your plight and that of your daughter –"

"Don't feed me that rubbish, you're not sorry at all," Anne remarked and her mouth twisted bitterly making her look ugly. "If you were sorry, you'd help me."

My beloved raised a careless shoulder, "You're right, I'm not sorry. Now, the most I can offer you is a meal and a bed for the night. After that you'll —"

"Don't bother," Anne snarled, "and you can take that smug look off your face, Maeve, before I wipe it off for you."

"You —" Maeve began.

"Maeve," Patrick rose, indicating the discussion was over, "please go find Bea and let her know Anne is leaving." Maeve swept from the room and her brother turned to my sister. "Take your daughter to Simon. He won't see her destitute and he'll do all he can to take care of you. He is, after all, your brother. I am not. Speaking for Alex and myself, we cannot help you, Anne. Had things been different perhaps … but they are not."

"I can't believe you'd turn your back on me like this," Anne said and the distress in her voice was genuine.

"I can't believe it either," Patrick said, bemused. "But then, I'm in uncharted territory. You see, in all my experiences during the war, everything evil I've witnessed, the greed, the self-serving cruelty, I've never met one to equal you and what you did to your own sister."

Even I baulked at that. I kept my face neutral but couldn't help but admire my sister as she drew a deep breath and rose with great dignity.

Maeve returned, followed closely by Bea who handed Anne her hat and gloves. Anne turned, with chin out — so like our mother. "You've no idea what you've just done," she spat. "You'll live to regret this, my *Lord Thorncliffe*." Her eyes ran over me and she laughed scornfully. "You've no idea how much."

❧

A week later, the social pages of all the major newspapers from Glasgow to Land's End ran a scandalous and very detailed story about the Earl of Thorncliffe, one of the country's most eligible bachelors, living quietly in Devon with Lady Alexandra

Glendenning, estranged wife of the Seventh Viscount Elginbury, the couple expecting their second illegitimate child.

Disapproving tongues clacked from one end of the country to the other, particularly when an anonymous blonde woman from Astor, claiming to be a former close friend of the earl, came forward to allege that the Lady Elginbury was in fact the earl's stepsister, further fuelling the gossips' malicious pleasure.

"No prizes for guessing who the anonymous blonde from Astor is," Maeve said, slanting an accusing eye at her brother. She did, however, believe the whole thing a storm in a tea cup that would quickly blow over when the next London scandal was unearthed.

I wished I could share her stalwart attitude. I was appalled upon reading the articles, and completely mortified when the local ladies with whom I'd struck up a friendship over recent years, sent messages to say they regretted their inability to attend this tea, or that afternoon party.

Invitations to their houses ceased abruptly as well. Patrick laughed it off saying he was quite happy not being bombarded with invitations to dine and dance. "It's the tattlers and spite merchants who enjoy those things anyway," he said.

Only the duchess remained stoutly behind us. She ignored the stories that were raging through our social set like a wildfire, and continued to invite us to her gatherings. At first, when people discovered we were on the guest list, numbers to the duchess's functions waned but the worthy woman accepted the fact philosophically, assuring us, with a glint in her devilish eye, that she was far too important for her invitations to be rejected for long.

As usual, she was right, and as time passed, people began to drift back and my life rebalanced once more.

CHAPTER 40

Christmas 1825

I leaned in and kissed the brow of the sleeping child, and pressing a hand to the small of my back, I straightened. After my two pregnancies, large and heavy babies both, my back was quite stiff and hadn't really recovered after their births. Doctor James had explained that I was too slight, my back muscles not strong enough, and had recommended I take some form of exercise daily to strengthen them. It was an interesting idea, unconventional, and seemed to contradict the advice of his peers, who advocated rest. But having nothing to lose, I'd followed his suggestion and had been experiencing some lessening of the symptoms.

Tonight, I felt a return of the pain after spending much of the day assisting Mrs Bath to sort the kitchen supplies; counting and listing bottled fruits and vegetables, smoked meats, sugar, flour and dairy items to ensure our winter stores would last. Waterville was a wealthy estate and would certainly see out the cold and unproductive winter months in more comfort than many others. Accordingly, my inventory had identified many items we had in such supply that we could share them among our tenants to increase their winter stores.

I stood, massaging the sore spot on my back, looking down

at my daughter. Lucy, named for our dear friend the duchess, was small for her five years, with a cloud of pale curls and an elfin face that echoed faintly of her Aunt Sylvie, gone these nine years now.

Her other aunt, Maeve, for whom she also bore no small resemblance, adored the child's free spirit and love of nature, encouraging all my daughter's childish explorations of the forest, eagerly sharing stories of adventure and excitement, and nurturing her young respect for all things wild and untamed. The mysteriously dwindling supplies of bread and grains from the storeroom bore witness to the early morning forays of child and adult, bundled against the winter cold, into the woods to feed the animals and birds.

"But Mama," Lucy had said only this morning, when cornered with a large cob-loaf hidden beneath her cloak, "Aunt Maeve says the animals need help in the winter because there is no grass for them to eat."

I smiled now, remembering how that same morning, Monsieur Chartrain had complained bitterly that a plate of butter had disappeared. Lucy, eyes wide and innocent, had firmly denied any knowledge of the theft, but her aunt had shamelessly confessed the crime stating that the woodland creatures needed a little fat on their bread this time of year to keep them warm as they were growing thin.

In the warm glow of my candle, the child so loved slept peacefully in the knowledge that her forest friends would not be denied their daily rations.

Her brother William, now eight years old and quite the little man, scoffed at his sister's exploits with his rather strange aunt, but nevertheless offered his breakfast leftovers each morning.

Taking a deep breath, I turned to leave the small girl to her dreams, and beheld her father, leaning casually against the door frame, arms folded, smiling gently.

As I approached, he pushed away to allow me passage, and

closed the door softly after us. We stood in the corridor outside Lucy's room and opposite William's.

"They're both asleep," I said quietly.

"Are they missing their nurse?" he asked as we walked to the head of the stairs and began our descent.

Jenna, cousin to one of the Waterville maids, had been engaged shortly after Lucy's birth to care for the children. Her ailing mother had required Jenna's assistance and I'd given her a few weeks' leave to return home. It was the first time Jenna had been away from my children and I had originally worried that they would miss her. I needn't have, for William informed me with childish seriousness that he was too old for a nurse anyway, and Lucy's days were certainly full to brimming with activities planned by her doting aunt.

"They don't seem to," I said as we entered the parlour. We took our places side-by-side on the settee before a cheerful fire and a contentedly snoring Bellus, curled in her basket. "Do you think though," I went on, "that Maeve encourages Lucy too much? I mean, our daughter is becoming quite the little hoyden. Yesterday she asked me if she could have an old pair of William's breeches because her petticoats were hampering her activities."

Patrick smiled lazily, emerald eyes glittering with amusement.

"What?" I demanded.

"Why are you surprised that your daughter is growing so untamed? I have very clear recollections of a skinny, brown and quite hoydenish child trailing after her brother many years ago – dressed in a cast-off pair of breeches, I might add. And you, my darling girl, did not have the wild influence of Maeve to encourage you."

I snuggled happily against him and breathed his wonderful scent. "I was not so bad."

"You were quite shocking – the despair of your mother, and I loved you despite your prickly personality and unladylike pursuits."

"Or because of them?" I suggested. He laughed lightly and I added with a smug smile, "And you love me still."

"I've always loved you."

Absently, I twisted the betrothal ring he'd given me so many years ago now, and which had never been paired with a wedding band to validate our union.

I'd never achieved that divorce from my husband, but we lived quietly and discreetly, and I was happy with my one true love, our children, friends and servants. Once it had been the star by which I charted my course. But life and circumstance had taught me that true contentment comes in many forms.

My lover shifted and reached into the pocket of his trousers, extracting a crumpled letter. "Here. Read this."

His face had grown serious and I sat up, eyeing him curiously and unfolded the single page. It had a very important looking crest on the top and appeared to be from some legal offices in Glasgow.

As I read, my hand became unsteady and my eyes blurred. I looked up. "He's dead?" I asked in disbelief.

Pat nodded.

My mind was having difficulty accepting the information, but it was there, addressed in very formal terms to The Right Honourable. The Earl of Thorncliffe, from Master Owen MacCleish, Business Lawyer, advising in impersonal legal terms, the unfortunate demise of his client, The Right Honourable. The Seventh Viscount Elginbury.

I folded the page carefully along its creases and placed it on my lap – I would finish reading it later – and stared into the fire. The bright flames licked and sighed, cracking and sparking against the logs in the grate. My husband was dead. I could not grieve for him, and I would feel no guilt for leaving him in order to live with, and bear the children of, another man; for we should never have been married – our families had wronged us both. Yet, Hamish had struggled to be all that was expected of him, and had failed completely, finally succumbing to the same wasting illness as his father before him.

The letter stated that Hamish's estate had run into tremendous debt and that in a final act of defiance, my husband had instructed Master MacCleish to contact the Earl of Thorncliffe. He was to advise Lord Thorncliffe that the crumbling castle on the banks of the Clyde as well as its associated debts, would now become the responsibility of his client's legal wife – me.

Although I had no idea as to the amount of debt Hamish had managed to accrue, I knew it would be considerable. But since Patrick appeared rather blithe about it all, I decided to worry about it later.

For now, Patrick's arms encircled me and we relaxed together, both with our own thoughts. And that night we made love slowly and gently, giving and receiving of each other that delighted passion and spiritual nurturing our coming together had always brought. And afterwards, he pressed his lips to my ear and breathed, "My darling girl, will you marry me?"

Secure in the knowledge and surety of our love for each other, we had endured the worst that scandalised Devonshire could dole out, and had been living with a measure of social acceptance for several years now. Therefore, we would enjoy a quiet event – engaging a calligrapher to prepare invitations for only close friends and family.

Wrapped lovingly in Patrick's arms, I drifted to sleep with images of the glorious emerald-green silk I would have my wedding gown made in – a pledge to myself that over the years I had come to believe would never be fulfilled.

14 March 1871

You have found the diary, as I knew you would. Are you a relative? I know not. But I have spoken with you in my dreams and I have seen you sometimes in my waking hours. You walk these halls, your lovely auburn hair swinging with your step. I know not if you are aware of me, for somewhere deep inside I know that you do not exist in my time. And for this reason I entrust this to you.

Allow me to introduce myself. I was born Margaret Maria Washburn on the seventeenth of February 1809. This book was placed into my care and I was entrusted with a sacred duty – a duty I carry out this night.

This is a fascinating, sometimes painful, sometimes joyous story. But it's not my story.

So many years ago they pledged to love *openly and honestly*. And so it was that the open and honest marriage of Alexandra Broughton and Patrick Washburn became a matter of public record. By the time of Alex's husband's death, when they were free to wed, I was sixteen-years-old and living at Broughton Hall with a contingent of household staff, including Cook, who'd served the Broughton family longer than even she could remember.

A year earlier, my half-brother, Sir Simon, and his wife, Maria, had relocated their four children and niece Domenica – who had been living with them for some years – to Maria's native Spain.

Naturally, I was invited to join them but opted to remain at Broughton Hall for I'd only recently completed my studies at Dame Margaret's Exclusive School for Young Ladies in Leeds, and was enjoying a new found freedom. This included being an active participant in a thriving social set, and I considered myself quite the modern young woman, perhaps after the style of my half-sister, Maeve, who had deliberately chosen a rebellious and rather scandalous life of uninhibited spinsterhood.

Alex and Patrick sealed their union in the chapel at Waterville Place. Alex wept as Patrick slid the gold band on to her finger and I have to admit that I shed a tear too. She was radiant in an exquisite emerald gown, overlayed by a transparent veil of gold gauze that floated behind like some gossamer cloud as she walked.

Patrick was tall and handsome in black trousers, shiny black boots, crisp white shirt, a black waistcoat shot through with gold threads, and a coat of green brocade. He wore no neckcloth.

They were gloriously happy, and as they took their vows and gazed at one another, the world fell away, and my heart swelled with the enchantment of their almost preternatural love.

It was a quiet affair, their wedding, attended only by family and a handful of close friends. The Dowager Duchess of Chasseby, as I recall, arrived leaning heavily on an attendant's arm, for she'd had some kind of heart episode in the preceding months. Simon and Maria returned from Spain, Alex's friend Julia travelled from Yorkshire with her husband Deon Morehead, her two daughters and stepson, and Patrick's cousin Aden and his wife Amelia, came from Ireland.

Noticeably absent was Alex and Simon's sister – also my half-sister – Anne. The last we'd heard she'd taken ship to America with a wealthy young man in possession of a land grant. The mother we all share arrived in great ceremony, her dried-up companion beside her.

The Dowager Countess of Thorncliffe spent the greater part of the day exchanging hard glares across the room with the Dowager Duchess of Chasseby.

The new Countess of Thorncliffe delivered the couple's third child the following year, another boy, named Gerrard for the father Patrick shared with me.

Alex and Patrick lived gently and happily at Waterville. They visited Aden and Amelia in Ireland several times, and spent nearly a full year in Italy. They saw their children grow to adulthood, marry, and have families of their own. In fact, as I write this, I am reminded that I must send my apologies for my inability to attend the wedding of Matilda, their eldest granddaughter.

Unfortunately though, my health now fails me. I have lived my life here at Broughton Hall as I chose. I have filled my days in celebration of good times and in the company of good friends. I married, and during that brief folly, moved away from my beloved home, but shortly returned to my senses – and to Broughton Hall – and have remained here since.

Yet these days I rattle about the rooms of this lovely old house and hope that its future inhabitants will care for it, and live in it as contentedly as I have and those who came before me.

This diary, the story of Alex's life, came into my possession last year when I was summoned to Waterville. It was a terribly gruelling return journey at my age, but the tone of Alex's request seemed to suggest no argument of mine would be acceptable.

In any case, I did privately enjoy the visit to that magnificent mansion.

Alex and Patrick received me warmly and invited me to relax and refresh myself after my journey, before we gathered to share our news. We supped informally that evening, and afterwards, Patrick and Alex sat unconventionally side-by-side on a settee in the parlour, he with his arm draped casually over her shoulder, while her hand rested on his thigh. And it seemed to me that after so many years together, they were as much in love as I had known them to be when I was a child.

Oh yes, my memory is not so faded that I don't recall the longing looks that passed between them, the touches and secret kisses they had shared when I was still wearing frilly pantaloons and short dresses.

After reading this diary, as you are about to, I now understand the intensity of feeling between them, an elemental force as irresistible and enduring as the tides that crash on the beach.

In his late seventies, Patrick is still tall and straight, and those magnetic, impossibly green eyes are as bright as ever.

Alex's untamed brown curls are threaded with grey, but she who'd always been overshadowed by the stunning looks of her brother and sister, has become a dignified and most handsome woman.

We sipped hot chocolate before the fire and shared reminiscences until falling into companionable silence.

It was then that Patrick suggested I might like to remain at Waterville Place indefinitely, to which Alex added that she was uneasy over my solitary existence. Touched by their concern for my welfare, I politely declined, assuring them that I am, in fact, quite comfortable with my own company and am surrounded by attendants who are equally concerned for my welfare.

The day before I was to return to Yorkshire, Alex spoke to me privately, both of us knowing we would be likely never to see one another again.

She showed me a scuffed, red-leather bound journal and explained that Patrick had given it to her for Christmas, the very first Christmas he'd spent at Broughton Hall. She invited me to read it, explaining that she had documented her life with Patrick and assured me that she had neither secrets nor regrets.

Every experience, failure and success was a marker on the road that had led her into the arms of the man she had always loved, and the subsequent years she had lived surrounded by love and happiness.

Finally, her voice a thin thread, she leaned close to my ear, and I know I made no mistake in comprehension when she said,

"Meggie, please take this journal home to Broughton Hall." Pressing the well-loved book into my hands she added, "It's for the *lady* … You know of whom I speak. Keep it safe for her. Let her find it … somewhere …"

A MESSAGE FROM KAREN

Thank you for reading *Inviolate*.

For other stories in the Broughton Hall series, visit my website to find out more: www.karenturner.com.au

If you enjoyed reading *Inviolate*, I would be very grateful if you could post a quick review on Goodreads or Amazon so that others can discover and enjoy *Inviolate* for themselves.

Karen.

ACKNOWLEDGEMENTS

Writers are solitary creatures. The activity of writing a book is insular at best, and I have enjoyed a most pleasurable journey into the past while those around me have endured my grumpiness, my inattentiveness and my reclusion.

Nevertheless, producing a book is a collaborative effort, which, I imagine, is why we call this an acknowledgements page when under other circumstances it would be called apologies. This brings me directly to my wonderful husband Stuart Turner.

Not only is Stuart my sanity, my researcher and my tech guru, he is also my moderator – stopping me from eating chocolate when I would keep going, making coffee exactly when I need it most and always being there regardless of how moody, obnoxious or stressed I am. Dear, you are my best friend and the nicest person I've ever met, and nothing I've achieved would have happened without you. Thank you.

Then there's my editor Jane Woodhead. Now, Jane, your calm and quiet exterior belies the whip-cracker you really are! You kept me on track and made me accountable and if I had a few wins along the way, you made me earn them. Thanks for everything – we did it again … just as we planned!

To Tamara, my lovely publicist, I can only say a massive thank you; you achieved things I could never have!

Of course, I have to mention Panda and Katie my two pussycat companions. Lost, as I frequently was, in the 19th century, I might have been oblivious to the passing of hours – but you weren't! Thanks, I think, for your irritatingly persistent attention-seeking demands that kept me grounded in the present.

To Paul Higgs and the team at Palmer Higgs: Paul, you have always had so much more faith in me than I will ever have. Thanks for that! You and your crew have been with me for the entire journey, our final destination remains over the horizon.

To those of my family and friends who have encouraged and supported me along the way, a great big thank you.

And finally, to everyone who took a chance on an unknown writer and bought *Torn* – if not for you this book would definitely not exist. More than anyone, *Inviolate* is for you …

Other books by Karen Turner

ALL THAT & EVERYTHING

Ever wondered what life looks like from a cat's perspective?
What about the funny side of daily train commuting?
Are things really what they seem in the mirror?

From Regency London to the Australian bush, *All That & Everything*
is an enchanting collection of award winning short stories.

Karen combines a selection of her late father's sketches with
these carefully chosen stories to offer something for everyone.

Other books by Karen Turner

TORN

1808

When 14 year old Alexandra meets Patrick, her handsome and notorious step-brother, she is confused and resentful as he shakes the foundations of everything she has ever known. Driving a wedge between Alex and her brother Simon, he tears apart the fabric of her quiet world. Yet she is intrigued by the enigmatic Patrick and finds herself increasingly drawn to him.

These are the years between childhood and womanhood, during which Alex begins to realise that her growing affection for Patrick owes nothing to sibling fondness.

But these are turbulent times for England and Patrick and Simon, answering the call of adventure, join the fight against Napoleon with devastating consequences.

In a family ravaged by war and deceit, Alex finds herself betrayed in the worst possible way.

This is the story of one woman's passionate struggle for love and hope against all the constraints of her time.

Other books by Karen Turner

COUNTERPOINT

1808

When Alexandra first meets Patrick, her handsome and enigmatic stepbrother, he tears apart the fabric of her quiet world...

So begins the epic love story that had fans of *Torn* gripping their seats. But there's another side to the story, a darker side: Patrick's side.

Welcome to a world of lust, decadence and violence.

Counterpoint is a retelling of *Torn*, told in Patrick's own words, and by those closest to him.

Just as *Torn* ushers readers into the very proper parlours of Regency England, where young ladies live within the bounds of the social restraints of the time, *Counterpoint* thrusts readers onto a rollicking ride through a clandestine world of wealth, privilege and dark passions.

In glittering ballrooms, sordid London backstreets and bloodied battlefields, Patrick Washburn comes of age in a time of licentiousness, when profligate young men, seasoned by war, live life for the moment, with no restraint and no regrets.

Other books by Karen Turner

STORMBIRD

1941

Stormbird returns readers to the once beautiful rural home, Broughton Hall, the setting of Karen's previous books, *Torn* and *Inviolate*.

It's now 1941, England is at war and Broughton Hall has fallen into disrepair. New owner, war-widowed young mother, Jessica is struggling to raise her two children and run a small dairy.

When she encounters a wounded German fighter pilot hiding in her barn, she commits to helping him.

At first, the barriers of ignorance and prejudice separate them. Yet in a world where danger lurks behind every door, an unlikely friendship becomes a story of love, loyalty and understanding.